CW01500559

BOOKS BY JOHN CORWIN

Books by John Corwin

Want more? Never miss an update by joining my email list and following me on social media!

Join my Facebook group at https://www.facebook.com/groups/overworldconclave

Join my email list: www.johncorwin.net

Fan page: https://www.facebook.com/johncorwinauthor

PSYCHOLOGICAL THRILLERS

The Family Business

AMOS CARVER THRILLERS

Dead Before Dawn

Dead List

Dead and Buried

Dead Man Walking

Dead By The Dozen

Dead Run

Dead Weather Days

Dead to Rights

Dead but not Forgotten

CHRONICLES OF CAIN

To Kill a Unicorn

Enter Oblivion

Throne of Lies

At The Forest of Madness

The Dead Never Die

Shadow of Cthulhu

Cabal of Chaos

Monster Squad

DEAD BUT NOT FORGOTTEN

JOHN CORWIN

OVERWORLD PUBLISHING

DEAD BUT NOT FORGOTTEN

When Carver finds out Liana Cardoso is missing, presumed dead, he'll stop at nothing to find out what happened to her, and he'll avenge her by any means necessary.

Carver and Liana started out on opposite sides. She was NSA, he was trying to stop an assassin from hunting down Paola and killing her. After Carver saved Liana from Enigma, they laid low in the mountains of western North Carolina for a while and then the NSA welcomed Liana back in from the cold.

But someone in the upper echelons of power sold a list of undercover agents to an information broker. The organization Liana had infiltrated on her first mission back to the NSA presumably saw her name on the list.

And now she's probably dead.

Carver goes to Washington DC, his least favorite place in the country because it's filled with some of the worst vermin in the world—politicians. He's going to find out who sold the list, who bought the list, and he's going to kill anyone who had anything to do with Liana's fate.

She might be dead. But she'll never be forgotten.

.

CHAPTER 1

Carver stalked the woman.

It was day sixty-three of getting to know her and others that she worked with. He hadn't taken any shortcuts. He'd done it by the book. In this case, the book disregarded all known legal standards and allowed doing what needed to be done no matter what the means.

It was the same handbook Carver followed in Scion. The same handbook he'd adhered to whenever someone messed with him. That didn't mean there were no rules. There were definite best practices when it came to stalking someone and mapping out their daily routines.

Carver hadn't expected to do this. He'd expected to return to the beach and get back to enjoying life. Liana had made her choices. She'd wanted to return to the NSA. They'd seemingly welcomed her back with open arms despite failing her primary objective of capturing Carver.

If only they knew the truth. If only they knew Liana and Carver had lived together in a cabin by a lake in western North Carolina for a while. Carver had been content, but not happy. Liana had been mostly miserable. A contact within the agency told her that they thought she'd been killed in action. He said they were happy to discover she was alive and that she could return and resume her duties.

Except that wasn't the case. Not even close. She'd returned to work, and they'd immediately used her to find Carver. Except this time, they hadn't simply wanted to capture Carver, they wanted to recruit him.

At least that was what Barry had told Carver. That might be the truth. It might be a lie. It really didn't matter.

What mattered was that Liana was apparently being held captive. She was being used as bait to draw out Carver. He hadn't planned on letting himself be lured out of hiding, but here he was stalking Deputy Director Rachel Evans of the NSA.

She was the highest-ranking civilian at the NSA. The chief operating officer who reported directly to POTUS. Keeping tabs on her was hard. Real hard. She worked irregular hours and often didn't drive herself wherever she was going.

But Rachel Evans had a weakness. A chink in the armor. An irregularity in her schedule. And Carver had taken full advantage of it. Sometimes she left the office without an escort or driver and took her personal vehicle on a drive across town.

Sometimes she did this several times a week. Sometimes just once or twice. Sometimes she even did it on the weekends, leaving her husband and kids at home while she went to a secret meeting.

As usual, Evans was driving her black Range Rover. Carver was on a black motorcycle. He wore dark jeans, a black leather jacket, and a full-faced helmet to hide his face.

The motorcycle was registered to a man in Maryland. The very same man Carver had purchased it from through a social media marketplace. It had been a cash deal with minimum paperwork and no ID check.

The man had sold it because his eyesight was getting worse with age, and he felt unsafe on the road. That allowed Carver to buy the vehicle from someone who wouldn't be able to give a good physical description of him.

The bike was an Indian Scout, a nimble cruiser with decent comfort for long hauls. He'd had the noisy exhaust replaced with something much quieter and he'd installed switches so the lights could be disabled.

A motorcycle could fit in places cars couldn't. It was easy to conceal. Most importantly, it was much easier to navigate through heavy traffic than by car. He would have lost his quarry on multiple occasions without it.

In this case, Carver didn't even have to follow Evans to know where she was going, but he followed her anyway just in case she deviated from the norm. She drove for about thirty minutes to a condominium complex. She parked on the street in a no-parking zone. She slid an *Official Duty* permit on her dashboard to avoid parking tickets, got out of her car, and pulled on a hoodie.

She pulled the hoodie over her head and slid on a facemask. The condo was surrounded by a tall red brick wall covered in well-manicured vines. There was an ornate iron gate to the right of the vehicle gate. It was a posh place. The condos sold for over a million each, and the HOA fees were off the chart.

Cameras watched every entrance. Evans' mask and hoodie were probably enough to conceal her identity, but she looked at the ground and tapped the keycard against the reader to the right of the gate to open it. She pushed through and went inside.

Carver drove straight up to the vehicle gate. He tapped a keycard, and the gate slowly rolled to the side. Once it was fully open, the arm gate lifted. He drove inside and to the parking deck. He found a parking spot and pushed down the kickstand. He took off his helmet and left it on the bike.

He went to the elevator and used his keycard to get inside. He pushed the button for the lobby and for floor thirty-three. The doors closed and the elevator went up one floor then stopped. The doors opened. Evans was in the elevator lobby. She stepped in and reached over to press the button for the thirty-third floor then stopped when she saw it was already lit.

Carver leaned against the back wall and pretended to look at his phone. The elevator doors closed, and it rapidly rose to floor thirty-three. It stopped and the doors opened. Evans went to the left. Carver followed her since it was the only way out of the elevator lobby.

She went left again. Carver went right. He walked slowly for fifteen paces and turned around. Evans had already turned the corner ahead. By the time he reached the corner, she'd be in unit 3302.

Carver reached the corner and looked around it to be certain. The hallway was empty. Each unit was basically the same shape and size depending on the floor. This floor had ten units. The top four floors had half that number.

The units on this floor were about 1500 square feet. They were midsized relative to the other units in this building. Carver knew all this because he'd examined the building blueprints. He'd looked through publicly available real estate files and found out who owned which units. He'd discovered that a full thirty percent of the units in the building were rental units.

The unit Evans had entered was a rental unit owned by Prestige Real Estate, LLC. Prestige was owned by Standard Holdings, LLC, which was in turn owned by Masters Group Limited, which was in turn owned by a long chain of other shell companies.

Unit 3301 was next door to unit 3302. It was owned by James Parham, a wealthy businessman who regularly did business in Washington D.C. and used this condo when he was in town. When he wasn't using it, he rented it.

Carver rented unit 3301 using his own shell company, Breacher Enterprises. He'd incorporated the LLC in Delaware since all they required was a post office box and had very friendly corporate laws.

He'd been renting unit 3301 for two months straight at the very reasonable rate of seven hundred dollars a day. The usual rate was fifteen hundred a night with a three-day minimum stay, but he'd negotiated a heavy discount for an extended stay.

Carver tapped his keycard to open the door to his unit. He went inside and turned on the laptop that was sitting on the marble countertop. He turned it on and watched the live feed from the cameras in the neighboring unit.

Evans and a young man were already undressed and frolicking on the red leather couch in the den. The young man was Paul Callahan, the junior senator from New York. He'd been appointed to the post after his predecessor retired due to health issues.

Callahan and Evans had attended Harvard nearly a decade apart. Evans was eleven years his senior, but clearly that was no issue to either of them. They'd met because Callahan had been appointed to the Senate Intelligence Committee despite being the newest member of the Senate. That was because his predecessor had considerable pull in Washington. His predecessor was also his father.

Callahan and Evans had started meeting outside of committee meetings. They'd become romantically involved seven months ago and met once or twice a week in unit 3302 which was owned by a major defense contractor.

All of this information had been relatively easy to uncover once Carver established a small network of his own people, namely congressional interns who were always eager to dish gossip with each other.

Interns were the low-hanging fruit of Washington D.C. They were the people with all the scuttlebutt a person could hope for. They were usually young, extremely ambitious, and loved to party hard during their time off.

Once Carver had discovered the affair, he'd found out where Evans and Callahan met, studied their patterns, and broken into the place to install cameras. He'd discovered that the place was already wired from floor to ceiling with hidden cameras. Apparently, the defense contractor had offered them his place for the meetups so he could get inside information.

Carver piggybacked on the condo's wireless internet and linked into the existing cameras for his own purposes. He didn't always follow Evans here, but he always reviewed the camera footage to see what the couple discussed once they were done with their physical activities.

To their credit, they rarely discussed business and when they did, it was always in generalities. Callahan had big plans. He wanted to reform the intelligence community from the ground up. He wanted to eliminate government overreach and implement new strategies that relied more heavily on human intelligence rather than electronic surveillance.

Evans didn't agree with him on that part, but that didn't get in the way of them having a good time. She knew it was only a matter of time until the Washington machine turned Callahan into yet another cog in the machine, just like his father.

Carver had been watching parts of that machine for over two months now. There were a lot of moving parts, but he'd focused on the ones most important to his cause. He'd narrowed down the most important players but had failed to find Liana.

The longer he waited to act, the less likely it seemed that Liana would remain alive, if she hadn't already been disposed of. The only thing he felt somewhat certain about at this point was that Evans had no direct role in Liana's fate. But she might be able to find out for sure what had happened.

Today was the day she would become Carver's primary asset.

Evans and Callahan finally finished their fun. He showered and left first. She showered and left about fifteen minutes after him. Carver stepped into the hallway at the same time she did. Evans did a double take when she saw him.

It was evident that she recognized him, but didn't quite know where from despite having seen him just an hour ago in the elevator. She might be the highest-ranking civilian in the NSA but that didn't mean she was a spy.

"Hi," Carver said.

She reached for her purse. Carver twisted her arm behind her and shoved her into his condo. He shut the door behind him with his foot. She took a deep breath to scream. He put a hand over her mouth. "Please don't do that."

She tried to, anyway. He jammed his finger into the base of her throat, and she started coughing. He pushed her onto the couch and set her purse on the countertop. Evans held her throat and kept coughing.

"I imagine you're wondering why I've called you here today." Carver pulled the compact Glock from Evans' purse. He pulled the suppressor from the inside purse pocket and snapped it on. "Give me a few moments and I'll explain."

Evans trembled. She spoke in a raspy voice. "Who are you?"

Carver gave her bottled water. "Sorry about the throat, but I couldn't have you screaming."

She took the water. Unscrewed the lid and sipped it. Her arm tensed.

"Don't throw it." Carver dragged a barstool over from the kitchen and sat down. "I take it you don't recognize me."

"You were in the elevator."

"Yes, but I mean besides that."

"I have no idea who you are."

"Then hopefully that means I'm talking to the right person."

Her forehead pinched. "The right person for what?"

"Liana Cardoso."

She stiffened. Realization lit her eyes. "You're Carver, aren't you?"

It was interesting that she knew who he was in connection with Liana. "You're definitely the right person to talk to."

Evans' face went from confusion to understanding. "That explains a lot. How long have you been following me?"

"Long enough." Carver didn't want to get into specifics. "Are you aware that the apartment you and Callahan meet in is bugged? That everything is being recorded?"

She gasped. "What?"

"You didn't even think of checking for bugs in a condo owned by a defense contractor?"

"I thought it was Paul's condo!" Her eyes widened and she sank into the couch. "I'm finished. They're going to use this against me."

"I wiped the cloud servers of past recordings and prevented new ones from uploading." Carver tapped his laptop. "Although I have kept copies for myself."

Her eyes narrowed. "You want help finding Liana, right?"

"Finding her?" Carver frowned. "No, I want her freed from wherever you're holding her. I want her record purged of any wrongdoing the NSA has accused her of, and I want her fully reinstated. Otherwise, I'm going to do more than just talk to you."

Evans held up her hands defensively. "You don't understand. We haven't done anything to her. She returned to work and was put on assignment by the previous administrator, Latonya Pierre. After the election, I was appointed deputy director. We began an immediate review of everything the previous administration had been doing. We opened the dossiers of all active field agents so we could get up to speed on operations." She licked her lips. "The previous administration had made a list of all undercover operatives across agencies, so that made it easier to get a handle on things."

Carver wasn't surprised. The switching of administrations almost always caused chaos. "You looked at Liana's dossier. Is she undercover?"

"Yes. She was investigating an extremist faction. Her reports were coming in regularly until shortly before the new administration came onboard. She and nearly thirty other field agents all went dark at the same time. We have been unable to reach any of them."

Carver's chest tightened. That wasn't even close to what he'd been told by a supposed colleague of Liana's. He'd been told she was being held by the NSA so Carver would cooperate with them.

"That sort of thing doesn't happen unless someone leaks vital information." Carver worked his jaw back and forth. "Someone sold them out."

"Yes. We think a staffer from my predecessor's office sold the agent list. We haven't been able to figure out who, but we think they were selling information for years and decided to cash out with one final payday."

"A big payday if they sold the identities of undercover agents." Carver hated to admit it, but Liana was almost certainly dead if this was true. "I want proof this is true. I was given a completely different story by someone else."

She leaned forward. "By whom?"

Carver removed the silencer from the Glock and put it and the gun into her purse. "Barry Aust."

She shook her head. "I don't recognize the name."

"How about the name Esther Childs?"

She frowned. "That name rings a bell, but I can't specifically place it."

"Then I suggest you familiarize yourself with those people. I would also like Liana's dossier and everything about her mission."

"She's almost certainly dead."

"What about the other burned agents?"

"Seven are verified dead. Eleven managed to bug out before they were burned. We haven't heard anything from the rest."

"Get a small army, go to their last known location, and find them."

"It's not that easy." She sighed. "Field agents have wide latitude. We don't always know where they are. Liana's last communique said she was headed to Minneapolis to follow some leads. We already sent two rescue squads to that location and found nothing."

Carver knew from experience that she was right. Liana got burned so some Judas could get his thirty silver coins. She was probably dead and buried. Gone forever. And it made him angry.

Angry enough to find and punish the people responsible.

CHAPTER 2

Carver didn't like lost causes.

But in this case, he was willing to make an exception. In this case, he was willing to go above and beyond.

He pulled a beer from the fridge. "You want one?"

Evans watched him closely. "She meant a lot to you."

"She's a friend. I owe it to her to find out what happened."

Evans nodded. "I'll take that beer."

Carver handed her a dark stout. It was the only kind of beer he kept around. "This Judas of yours probably sold the information to a middleman."

Evans nodded. "Yes, but we don't know who. The FBI is investigating, but you have to understand how chaotic things are right now. We don't even have an FBI director yet and minions of the old administration still control vital agencies."

Carver sat back down on the stool. "I need to know I can count on you. I need to know that you're not going to turn me in the moment you leave here."

Evans sipped her beer. "There's no way in hell I'd do that. Did you know that the NSA had me on a watch list? That they listed me as an extremist?" She laughed. "Me, a married mother of four, an extremist!"

"Being a married mother of four doesn't mean you're clean." Carver raised an eyebrow. "You're having an affair with a senator from across the aisle."

"Okay, you're right. I'm not clean or even particularly good. But I do love this country, and I want it to be better. I want justice for our agents. I want to find out what happened to them and who's responsible." She leaned forward. "And you're our best chance at getting that justice."

Carver believed her but he wasn't taking any chances. He was going to keep a real close eye on things until he knew for certain. "This entire thing is going to be under the table. Nothing official. I want a new identity, and I don't want my name to ever cross your lips with anyone else at the agency. Got it?"

"I got it." She stood and held out her hand. "Deal?"

Carver shook it. "Deal."

She pulled up a bar stool and sat across from him. "Tell me about Barry and Esther."

Carver told her about his encounter with Barry at Myrtle Beach. How he claimed to be a friend of Liana's and baited him into going to Bickham, Illinois. How the entire thing was supposed to help the NSA capture Thomas Jericho, one of Carver's former squad mates.

"Jericho is near the top of our most wanted." Evans blew out a breath. "That operation didn't go well at all."

"I left Barry with Jericho."

Her mouth dropped open. "You did what?"

"It's okay. Jericho didn't kill him because I saw him back at the agency about a week after I started my operation." Carver figured Jericho had made Barry an asset before releasing him.

She ran a hand down her face. "Can you tell me the whole story? I feel like context would help."

Carver gave her a ten-minute summary. Told her about his fight with Jericho and his decision to let him live. He didn't go into details about the other events in Bickham. Those weren't important for her to know.

Evans gulped down her entire beer and started on another by the time the ten minutes were over.

"Starting to regret your decision to help me?" Carver said.

"I just need a little liquid courage." Evans glanced at the laptop. "I suppose you're going to hold onto that footage to ensure I cooperate."

"Naturally." Carver shrugged. "I don't trust spooks."

"I'm not a spook." She shook her head. "Okay, so who's Esther Childs?"

"Operations manager for Barry's division."

"Sorry, I should know all of this, but there are a lot of moving parts."

"It's okay. I'll fill you in." Carver finished his beer and got another. "Esther Amy Childs, daughter of Ben and Carrie Childs of Litchfield, Connecticut. Graduated Yale with a law degree, became a prosecutor in Hartford then moved over to Boston. She was tapped as a staff lawyer for the DOJ and moved to D.C. before transitioning over to the NSA."

"I'm not even going to ask how you know all of that."

"It's a matter of public record." Carver shrugged. "It sounds impressive when I spit it out, but it didn't take long to find that information."

"Okay. That's her bio, but what about her work with the NSA?"

"I don't know much about her internal work, but I know that she has two golden retrievers, she likes to jog, and she lives in Georgetown. She doesn't date, but she likes to go to seedy dive bars, get drunk, and hook up with random men she meets."

Evans looked like she wanted to say something judgmental but couldn't say anything because of her own shortcomings. "Um, interesting. Anything else?"

"She's ambitious. She's the one who came up with the plan to use me to capture Jericho. She also planned to recruit me."

"Well, A plus for effort at least."

"I swept her apartment for bugs and found none, so I put in a few of my own to see if I could catch her doing anything naughty." Carver shook his head. "If she does, she doesn't do it at home."

"Did you follow her?"

"Off and on for the past couple of months, yes. But I'm just one man and I have several people of interest to keep tabs on."

"You followed me here and watched me have sex."

"Only a couple of times. I mostly watched recordings but only to see if you and Callahan talked shop before or after sex."

"No, never." She shook her head. "I enjoy our time together, but I don't trust anyone in Washington."

"That's a good policy to have."

Evans bit her lower lip. "Who else have you been watching?"

"No one important." Carver checked his watch. "It's time for you to go." He handed her a burner phone. "My number is in here. Use this to reach me. No official channels of communication."

"Understood." She finished off her second beer. "Am I meeting you here?"

"Only if we need to. Otherwise, we'll keep it digital. I do want all of Liana's files on paper though unless the NSA is no longer tracking digital transmissions."

"I'm authorized to do what I want with our files. I can get you clean, untraceable digital copies."

Carver locked her gaze with his. "You realize that I can detect if a digital copy has a tracker on it, right?"

"Yes." She licked her lips nervously. "It's not hard to do."

He nodded. "Okay, digital is fine as long as you can do it without raising suspicions."

"Due to the undercover agent list leak and subsequent investigations, there are a lot of digital copies floating around. It won't be a problem."

"In that case, get me copies of all the open and closed case files regarding the burned agents. There might be something useful in them."

She nodded. "Anything else?"

"I'll link you to a secure upload site once you're ready."

"You could give me the link now."

He shook his head. "The link expires ten minutes after I generate it and revolves to another secure site. That way it keeps you from tracing the VPN connections."

"I wouldn't do that."

"Just because we're collaborating doesn't mean I trust you."

She nodded. "Fair enough."

Carver showed her to the door. "Don't forget your hoodie and mask."

"Oh yeah, thanks." She covered her head and pulled up the mask. "Talk to you soon, I guess."

"Yep." Carver watched her go. Once she was gone around the corner, he went the opposite way to the service elevator and took it down to the parking deck. He put on his leather jacket, helmet, and gloves and drove out of the garage.

He drove through the gate and parked in a shopping center across the street. He watched the condo for an hour to see if NSA agents raided it. No one came. Either Evans was smart enough to know he wouldn't hang around or she really wanted to help him. Most likely, though, she didn't want the footage of her affair with Callahan to leak if she double-crossed Carver.

It also sounded like she needed all the help she could get. When a new administration took power, employees from the previous administration were typically purged and replaced. At the ninth hour, someone from the old administration had sold out the agency either for a payday or to sabotage the incoming administration.

Evans had a big problem on her hands. She needed to fix it at any cost, even if it meant a temporary alliance with someone like Carver. The videos of her and Callahan were added insurance. If she tried to screw him, the videos would be released into the wild and her career would be finished.

Carver had considered slipping a bug onto her person, but he didn't have anything that could slip past the detectors at NSA headquarters. She probably wouldn't be able to take the burner phone into the office with her either.

She might also suspect there was a tracker on the burner phone. Maybe even spyware. In that case, she would be right. He could track the phone even when it was off and he could watch the screen in real time. It was doubtful she'd do anything with it except hide it somewhere until she was ready to send him a message.

There wasn't much to do now except wait and he didn't plan to wait around on an empty stomach. He drove northwest to a steakhouse he'd passed by several times but never tried. He ordered a thick ribeye and beer and passed the time reviewing surveillance footage he'd gathered.

Several unread text messages were also waiting in his inbox. One was from a congressional intern he'd met at a bar. He'd cultivated a relationship with her and used her to network with other interns. That was how he'd discovered the affair between Callahan and Evans.

She wanted to meet him for drinks later. He told her that his boss was making him work late and that he probably couldn't make it. She responded with an angel emoji and told him what she wanted to do to him after drinks.

It was a very tempting offer, but if Evans got him the information he wanted tonight, he wouldn't have the time to meet. If she didn't get him the information by tonight, then he'd probably take her up on the offer.

Building relationships was time-consuming and difficult even under the best of circumstances. Interns at the federal level worked hard and played harder. That made it a little easier for Carver to get the information he needed.

Carver replied to the other text messages noncommittally. He couldn't make plans until he knew how soon Evans would get him the files. There wasn't much else he could do until then. For the time being, he was in a holding pattern.

He finished eating, polished off the beer, and paid the tab. Another text arrived on his phone. This time it wasn't from an intern. It was from an information broker's proxy. Carver had put out feelers to several such brokers. He'd paid a lot of money for information that hadn't panned out.

This guy was supposed to be one of the best, but this was the first time he'd made contact in four weeks. The timing was interesting, just an hour after Carver sank his hooks into the deputy director of the NSA. Maybe him reaching out now wasn't connected to that. Maybe it was. There was only one way to find out.

He read the text.

Ready to meet?

Carver typed back, *Yes.*

The response was almost immediate. *Meet at these coordinates in one hour.*

Carver typed back, *Okay.* They'd only spoken via text before. This would be the first meeting.

He went outside into the cold. The middle of January wasn't the best time to ride a motorcycle, but the leather helped mitigate the wind chill factor. There was still snow on the ground, but the streets were nice and clean.

It took forty minutes to cross town and reach the meeting spot, a gravel parking lot next to the Capital Crescent Trail. He parked next to a pickup truck at the far end and took up position to watch for the informant's arrival.

The hour mark ticked past. Another fifteen minutes went by. A 1987 Buick Century pulled into the lot and parked near the entrance. The driver put a green sticker on the inside of the window. That was their way of letting him know it was safe to approach.

Carver gave it another couple of minutes just to make sure. He walked down the sidewalk past the car, scanning the environs for any sign of danger. It looked like he was in the clear, so he opened the passenger side door and sat down.

The driver was middle-aged and lean. His head was clean shaven, and it looked like he took good care of himself. He was almost certainly former military. He shook hands with Carver. "You can call me Randy."

"Okay."

"You contacted us some time ago regarding general information about various high-level government agencies."

"Yep."

"I have information you might want."

Carver nodded. "I'm listening."

"Two grand up front."

"And if the information isn't what I'm looking for?"

Randy shrugged. "Cost of doing business."

Carver forked over the money. "I'm listening."

"An interagency task force between the NSA, CIA, DHS, and the FBI just kicked off this morning. They have not gone public with this yet because the new administration hasn't figured out how to spin it."

"What's the task force about?"

"A foreign agent somehow received classified information. I'll give you details for another five grand."

"Is this about the burned NSA agents?"

Randy paused before answering. "Maybe."

Carver wasn't into playing games, so he gave Randy another five thousand. "Keep going."

"NSA agents were burned, yes. Undercover agents from other agencies were also burned by this information. There is speculation it was done on purpose by the outgoing administration so they could sabotage their successor."

"Seems counterproductive to destroy your human intelligence apparatus just to spite the new guy."

Randy shrugged. "I've seen worse."

"Is that why you're in this business? You got burned?"

"What makes you say that?"

"Let me guess. You did multiple tours, probably with the Army if I had to guess. You planned on retiring, but something happened to earn you an early discharge without full benefits. Someone saw your potential and hired you."

"I got my twenty and retired. Full benefits. It was my brother that got screwed. Kind of like you." Randy watched him carefully. "We know about you."

"I'm not surprised." Carver had expected that the information broker would check out anyone he did business with. "Why did you contact me just today and not weeks ago when I requested a meeting?"

"Because we don't do business with unvetted individuals."

"Yeah? And who does the vetting?"

"We have a team that looks into any potential clients." Randy opened his door. "Let's go for a walk. I don't like being a sitting duck." He got out of the car.

Carver got out of the other side. He wasn't sure about this Randy guy. Something felt off. Taking a wait and see attitude wasn't something he could afford to do, so he got straight to the point. "I'm looking for information about a specific individual."

"Specific information comes with a higher price."

"I know."

Randy opened the rear door and grabbed a black jacket from the back seat. He put it on but not before Carver noticed the bulge under his shirt. Randy was packing but that didn't mean anything. Someone in his line of business would be stupid not to carry a weapon. He walked toward the trail that led from the parking lot and into the forest.

Carver walked alongside him. "What made you decide to reach out to me today?"

"You're a hard man to research, Mr. Carver." Randy gave him an all-knowing look. "We only just got enough information to feel comfortable reaching out to you."

"Really? Seems like a high-powered information broker like your boss would be able to find out about me in less than four weeks." Carver kept his head on a swivel as the path entered the woods. There weren't many people out and about on this cold, gray day.

"It looks like your records were purged. We were only able to find basic information on you."

"Really? And you still felt comfortable contacting me?"

"You're something of an enigma. My boss was curious to know more."

"Let's get back to the matter at hand." Carver stopped walking. Not because he wanted to talk, but because his instincts were telling him that something was off. "I want specific information."

"If you have the money, I can find out for you."

"First, you'll need to prove that you're worth it. Give me a hint that you know what I'm looking for."

Randy grinned. "You want to know about a specific agent. Liana Cardoso."

"Yep. Do you already have information about her or are you just wasting my time?"

"I have information for you. But there's more to it than that." He gestured ahead. "Let's keep walking and discuss options."

A wide strip of forest separated them from the gravel parking lot they'd just left because the trail ran parallel to it. The forest was about a mile deep on the right side before it reached a highway. The trees and bushes were barren at this time of year, so Carver could see the parking lot from his position.

A group of four people rounded the bend ahead. Three men, one woman. They were talking and laughing. The woman was walking a dog, a large brown poodle mix. Carver didn't know much about dogs, but he knew that this type of dog didn't jibe with the woman.

The woman wore dark clothing as did her companions. They all wore black knit caps and bulky black jackets. Their vibe was anything but just a group of friends out enjoying a walk. Carver glanced back and saw a single man coming down the path behind them.

This was a trap.

CHAPTER 3

Carver kept walking like nothing was wrong.

He looked at the parking lot on the other side of the trees. It was about fifty yards away. The halfway point was just a little bit behind them. The group with the dog would reach them just as they walked past the end of the parking lot where his motorcycle was parked.

He picked up the pace a little bit and shivered. "It's cold. Can we hurry this up and make a deal?"

Randy adjusted his pace. "A big tough guy like you can't handle a little cold?"

"I prefer the beach." Carver figured they'd be even with the end of the parking lot just a few seconds before they crossed paths with the oncoming group. Carver felt certain that the moment they reached the other group, there would be a whole lot of guns in his face.

He was going to have to cut this short, but first he wanted to confirm that he was right. "Are your friends part of the deal?"

Randy frowned. "What are you talking about?"

Carver nodded at the group with the dog. "Your friends and the one coming up behind us."

Randy reached inside his jacket. Carver gripped his wrist but not before Randy grabbed the gun he was hiding in there. It was a Sig P365. A compact handgun that fit snugly into the jacket's inside pocket.

Carver squeezed Randy's wrist hard enough to make it crack. The other man shouted in pain and dropped the handgun. The group of supposed hikers started running toward them. The woman released the dog's leash and drew a gun. The man coming from behind started running too.

Carver slammed his knee into Randy's midriff and shoved him to the side. He ran through the woods and toward the parking lot. Hopefully there was no one hiding behind the cars or this was going to be a real short trip.

He angled toward his motorcycle. The oncoming group angled toward him through the woods. That was their first mistake. Their second mistake was running full blast through wooded terrain. The leaves were thick and heavy on the ground, and they covered obstacles like rocks and tree roots.

Carver was using short strides to make his way through the trees. It took a little longer, but it kept him from tripping. The woman and one of the men had already tripped and their other companions were well behind them. Barring any major pitfalls, Carver was going to reach the bike a few seconds before them.

The problem was that they'd be well within handgun range. He'd backed the motorcycle into space, but they could put a bullet between his shoulder blades if they wanted to. They hadn't fired their guns yet, so maybe they weren't trying to kill him. They might want him alive for interrogation.

Carver adjusted the angle of his run toward the truck he'd parked next to. That would make it less obvious that he was going for the motorcycle. He reached the truck and ran around behind it. He heard the pursuers shouting that they'd lost sight of him.

He paused behind the truck to pull the keys from his pocket. He dashed to the bike and snatched the helmet off the gas tank. He twisted the key. Pressed the push button start. The bike growled to life. He squeezed the helmet between his knees, so it didn't fall off and gunned the bike.

He ducked in case they opened fire, but the gunshots never came. There were no other hikers nearby and the closest houses were across the highway. They had plenty of opportunity to take him out if they wanted to. Apparently, that wasn't their game plan.

The bike ate up a quarter of a mile fast. He pulled to the side of the road and strapped on the helmet. Safety first. He got back on the road and kept to the speed limit. He saw a pair of black SUVs coming up fast. They must have parked them along the road near the parking lot.

Carver took a hard right into a neighborhood. He pulled into an empty driveway and followed it around behind the house. He turned off the engine and watched the road. The SUVs zipped past a few seconds later.

He wanted to follow them, but the motorcycle would stick out since there weren't many on the road in such cold weather. Following the SUVs would probably be a waste of time anyway. He doubled back the way he'd come and drove to the gravel parking lot. Randy's old Buick was still there. He'd probably jumped into one of the SUVs with the others.

Carver waited and watched for a couple of minutes before driving across the road and parking next to the Buick. He put the kickstand down and walked to the path. He looked up and down it. No one was there. That meant Randy and his crew were all in the SUVs. The Buick was a burner car, but they'd be back for it.

Carver opened one of the saddlebags on the back of the bike. He pulled out a small metal box. The transmitter inside was small, but the battery was about the size of two nine-volt batteries placed side-by-side. He reached under the car and magnetically attached it inside a small hollow.

He took out his phone and checked the signal from the tracker. It transmitted a cellular signal. As long as it was near a cell tower, he'd be able to track it. He zipped up the saddle bag, put on his helmet, and drove away.

This time he went across the Potomac and into Virginia. The houses near the river were big and expensive. They were mostly owned by politicians who didn't want to live in D.C. proper and preferred single-family homes that were large enough to accommodate three families each.

The houses were off the road and secluded. Many of them were also empty because the same politicians who owned them ended up getting apartments closer to the Capitol, so they didn't have to deal with traffic.

Carver had found a home that looked neglected and looked up the owner in public records. It was owned by an LLC that eventually traced back to the husband of a Congresswoman. The husband was a stock trader that had made millions since his wife went into Congress. They'd apparently purchased this home fifteen years prior and hardly used it.

That made it a perfect place for Carver to set up shop. He'd stayed in the condo some nights, but preferred the house off Chain Bridge Road because it was surrounded by woods, was up on a rise, and had a pretty nice view of the Potomac from the back yard.

It also had a large, detached garage where he kept the burner cars he'd purchased during his time in the area. Having a couple of extra untraceable cars was always a good thing and especially now that the motorcycle was burned.

He drove up the long driveway and opened the garage door with a remote. He drove into the garage, closed the door, and parked the motorcycle so it was facing the door. The detached garage was much more than just a place to store cars. It was also a carriage house with a complete mother-in-law suite upstairs. There were two bedrooms, two bathrooms, and a kitchen.

Carver preferred staying here as opposed to the condo because the escape routes were more accessible. He also had picked up an electric offroad motorcycle for quick and quiet getaways. It was basically a glorified mountain bike, but it could reach up to a hundred miles per hour and the battery was good for two hundred miles.

He'd also put silent alarms and triggers around the main residence to alert him if and when anyone decided to pay an unexpected visit to the house. In the two months he'd been here he hadn't seen any cleaning or lawn maintenance crews. That didn't mean that there weren't any who came out every few months to make sure the place wasn't falling apart.

Carver had a 2013 Honda Odyssey minivan parked in one bay, a 2017 Dodge Challenger in the next, and a black Chevy Suburban in the next complete with a police light kit in the grill. These things were a dime a dozen in the DC area because the federal government bought them in bulk for the various law enforcement agencies.

He went upstairs to the suite and opened the laptop on the kitchen table. He reviewed the camera footage and was happy to see that he was the only one who tripped the motion sensors since the last time he'd checked.

He deleted the footage. It was barely seventeen hundred hours, but it was already dark outside. He checked his text messages and found a new one from Randy.

We just wanted to talk.

Carver considered what to say and typed it out. *Who wants to talk to me? Your boss or another client?*

You know I can't tell you that.

Carver checked the tracker on the burner car. It had moved across town and was parked at an apartment complex. *You can tell me now, or I'll come for you and make you tell me.*

There was a long pause. Probably because Randy knew Carver could do it. He was probably looking outside his window to see if Carver was standing there. Randy finally answered. *Another client asked for information on anyone else inquiring about individuals on the undercover agent list. Liana Cardoso is on the list. When we told them about your connection to her they offered big money to bring you in for a conversation.*

Carver thought it over. *How did you know that I'm looking for Liana Cardoso?*

One of our informants at the NSA told us.

Carver had a feeling he knew who it was. *Barry Aust?*

Randy didn't reply for several minutes, but he finally coughed it up. *Yes. And before you ask who the client is, we don't know. They operated through an anonymity broker.*

Who is the broker? There was another long pause. Carver sent another text. *I can come to your apartment and ask in person.*

That got a quick response. *Look, I didn't want to do this. I told them you were someone we didn't want to mess with at any price. They told me to do it or resign.*

You should have resigned.

If I tell you, will you promise to leave me alone?

Carver considered it. Having an informant with an information broker might come in handy. *I'll put it towards your debt. I don't take kindly to being set up.*

Randy was probably pacing around nervously by now. Probably realizing he didn't have many options. *The broker is a middleman named Steve Glover. We don't know who he works for, but we suspect it's one of the top-tier information brokers on K Street. All I can say for sure is that someone's real interested in talking to you.*

Carver could understand that. *If you find out exactly who it is, then your debt will be forgiven. Otherwise...*

Randy replied quickly. *I'll find out something. I just need time.*

Carver didn't reply. There was no need to. He had other matters to attend to. He looked at his other text messages.

There was no message from Rachel Evans yet and another message from Abby Jacobs, one of Senator Callahan's interns. She wanted to know if Carver was still working late and if he could come over afterward.

Abby knew Carver as Chad, a party animal who didn't care about politics. Despite that, Chad would listen to Abby talk about her day whenever she wanted. She liked talking to him because she said he was a black hole. She could tell him anything and not have to worry about him repeating it to anyone else.

Abby was the one who'd told Chad about Evans and Callahan's affair after they'd been drinking and dancing all night. She'd seen texts between Callahan and Evans that made it clear they were hooking up. She'd been dying to tell someone and Chad ended up being the first person she told.

She had a wide circle of friends that Carver had also befriended. All of them worked for senators. All of them had information they were dying to share after a few drinks or some party drugs.

Carver had cast a wide net and out of all of them, Abby had been the only one to provide actionable intel. That was par for the course when it came to intelligence gathering. That wasn't to say the others hadn't given him useful information, but the affair between Callahan and Evans had now given him his first real asset.

He stared at the text from Abby. He didn't have anything else scheduled tonight, and Abby was a good-looking woman with a wild side in the bedroom. It would be good for him to blow off some steam because things were going to get real busy once Evans sent him the agent dossiers.

Carver texted her back. *What time is good for you?*

She replied moments later. *Ugh we're working overtime, so probably not until after nine PM. Are you going out tonight?*

Carver replied in his Chad persona. *Dude I'm hurting so bad from last night. Probably not. I'd be happy just hanging with you.*

Aw, me too! You better not be falling in love. I don't have time for that. She added a laughing emoji after it.

Nah I know babe but it's fun right? Carver assiduously avoided using any advanced punctuation because Chad was definitely not smart enough to know where to put commas.

Abby replied with a black heart emoji. *Ok. Text you when I'm going home. I have a new bottle of Wild Turkey if you decide to drink.*

Thanks babe ur the best. I wish ur boss wasn't being an asshat.

She sent a string of laughing emojis. *He's been acting real weird today. He left early. Probably to visit his special friend. You'd think emptying his balls would calm him down, but he was just as antsy this afternoon. Now he's meeting with his damage control team.*

Carver sent an eggplant emoji. *Yeah, bro needs to take a chill pill.*

She sent back laughing crying emojis. *He's got too much going on. Like he's trying to prove that he's as good as his dad. Oh well. I'm looking forward to seeing you.* She sent a kissing emoji.

Carver knew better than to ask too much about Callahan. It sounded like something had certainly rattled Callahan's cage if he was talking to his damage control people. Had Evans spoken to him? Told him about the recordings?

Asking her over text wasn't ideal. It would be better to pay her a personal visit, maybe later after he left Abby's place. Evans had a home in Virginia. That was where her husband and kids lived. She usually went home on the weekends and stayed in an apartment in D.C. during the week.

She might have changed her routine after the meeting with Carver. She might have decided that staying in the apartment wasn't safe anymore. Despite that, the odds were good she hadn't changed a thing. It was strange how people would still stick to routine even if they felt like they were in danger.

He would just have to wait and see.

Carver went to bed and got three hours of sleep. He woke up and checked his texts. Abby had texted him that she was on her way home a little over an hour ago. She'd texted again when he hadn't replied.

He texted her back. *Sorry babe I fell asleep. I'll shower and head over.* He hopped in the shower and put on his clubby Chad clothes, skintight jeans, a tight T-shirt, and dress shoes. He'd let his hair grow out a little longer to shed his military aura. It was long enough so he could use hair product in it to give him that extra party-boy look.

Abby had replied while he was in the shower. *All good. I'll be ready for you when you arrive. Just come straight into the bedroom.*

You got it babe. Carver finished getting ready. He went downstairs to the garage and cranked up the Dodge Challenger. This was definitely a Chad car. He opened the garage door and pulled onto the driveway, slowing to make sure the garage door closed behind him.

It took him twenty minutes to reach Abby's rowhouse in Georgetown. It took another five minutes to find a parking space. Most interns couldn't afford to live in a place like this, but Abby's parents were rich and were generous donors to Callahan's campaign. Working for him was considered prestigious and it would look good on her resume. At least, that was what she'd told Carver.

The red brick rowhouse was over a hundred years old. Abby's parents had bought it for 2.5 million right before she started her intern work. Two million didn't buy much in this part of town. The place wasn't even two thousand square feet.

Carver got out of the car and walked down the street. He turned the corner and took the service road behind the rowhouses. After they'd seen each other a few times, she'd started leaving the back door unlocked when she knew he was coming over.

He turned the doorknob and went inside. Pop music was playing loudly upstairs. Carver didn't care for it, but his Chad persona loved it. That was probably why she played it every time he came over.

He walked through the kitchen and alongside the stairs. He rounded the balustrade and walked up the carpeted staircase. There were two rooms at the top. He went to the left door where the music was coming from and opened it.

The first thing he noticed was that Abby was naked on the bed. The next thing he noticed was the man sliding a needle into her arm. The man was masked. Abby was drooling like she'd already been drugged with something. One thing was clear.

This man was killing her.

CHAPTER 4

Carver and the man stared at each other for a split second before acting.

The masked man reached inside his jacket and turned toward Carver. Carver lunged forward. He slammed his shoulder into the man, knocking a gun from his grasp before he could bring it to bear.

The man stumbled back into a bookshelf before catching himself. Carver put himself between the man and his prey. The syringe in Abby's arm was still full. The plunger hadn't been depressed. He slid the needle from her arm and tossed the syringe aside.

The masked man pulled a knife and lunged. Carver batted his arm away. The man feinted then ran for the door. Carver thrust out a foot. The man stumbled but didn't trip. He ran into the hallway.

Carver ran after him. The man's shoe caught on the carpet at the top of the stairs, and he tumbled down them. Carver drew his Sig and aimed it at the man. "Try to run and I'll shoot your leg."

The man put up his hands. He looked shocked, like the last thing he expected was to see a gun in Carver's hand. "What the hell?"

"Why are you trying to kill Abby?" Carver watched the man closely.

The man looked from the gun to Carver's face. "Who the hell are you?"

"I think you know who I am."

"Apparently not." The man narrowed his eyes. "You're not who we thought you were."

"What did you give Abby?"

He hesitated then seemed to think giving Carver that information didn't matter. "I sprayed her with a microdose of fentanyl to make her compliant."

"Who do you work for?"

"No one in particular. When politicians have a problem, they call us."

Carver grunted. "You kept saying 'we' and 'us' which tells me you're not working alone."

"Nice deduction, genius. No, I don't work alone." He turned his head and winced. "I think I pulled a muscle."

"So, you're a fixer."

"Yeah."

"Who hired you?"

"I'm not saying."

Carver studied the man. He was probably an inch under six feet. A little round in the midsection. He was the kind of guy who relied on surprise and chemicals to get the job done. He was probably still carrying a sprayer loaded with fentanyl. That made him very dangerous.

Getting up close and personal to torture the answers out of him wasn't the answer. Well, at least not unless Carver could be sure he wasn't going to get sprayed with liquid fentanyl. That stuff could put an elephant on its ass in seconds.

"Where is the spray bottle with the fentanyl?"

He worked his jaw back and forth. "In my jacket pocket."

"Pull it out and show it to me."

The man pulled it out slowly. It was a small bottle about as large as a pinky finger with a small atomizer at the top. It was half full. That was more than enough to kill an adult human or put them in a coma.

"How much did you dose Abby with?"

"One spray." He shrugged. "Didn't take much."

Carver nodded. "Toss the bottle away from you."

The man paused, probably realizing that this was his last line of defense since his gun and knife were upstairs. He tossed it anyway because he had no choice in the matter.

"Okay. Stand up."

The man stood.

"Raise your hands."

The man raised his hands. He winced in pain. "I definitely pulled a muscle."

"Do you know who I am?"

"I thought I did. Chad Mullens, trust fund baby who likes to party."

Carver nodded. "That's me."

"No. It's definitely not you." His eyes narrowed. "Ah, I get it. You're undercover, aren't you?"

"What makes you think that?"

"It's obvious. The new administration is plugging all the holes." He grinned. "Hey, we could be on the same side."

"Doubtful." Carver drew his concealed knife. "But let's have a conversation and see." He stalked down the stairs toward the man.

The man abruptly bolted. Carver didn't want to shoot because he didn't have a suppressor on the pistol. Getting the neighbors riled up was the last thing he wanted. This needed to be handled nice and quiet.

He threw the knife. It planted itself in the man's left buttock. The man howled in pain and crashed face first onto the floor. So much for nice and quiet. Carver yanked the knife from the man's ass and wiped it off on the man's pants. He booted the man in the ribs then rolled him over with a foot.

The man grabbed his injured buttock, gasping in pain. Blood pooled beneath him. "You're an idiot! Do you have any idea what kind of people I work for?"

"If you'd answer my questions then I'd know." Carver stared calmly at him. "Who hired you?"

The man scowled but didn't answer.

Carver whirled the knife in his hand. He knelt next to the man. Pressed the tip into the man's neck. "I can cut you to pieces until you answer."

"I don't know!" The man shivered violently. "I swear to God I don't know. They hire us through an anonymous third party."

"Where's your phone?"

"In my front pocket. But it doesn't have anything on it. It's a burner and they use an encrypted messaging app. Everything gets deleted an hour after it's read."

"Show me anyway."

Eyes watering in pain, the man dug a small flip phone from his pocket. He was telling the truth. It had nothing on it. Well, almost nothing. There was a text from someone else.

Jiminez doesn't know where Chad lives. He never went to his place. Said he only saw him out at the bar. He's taken care of. I'm headed to the other girl's place now.

Carver showed the man the message. "Where is he going?"

The man hesitated. Carver pushed the knife tip harder into his neck.

"Stop!" The man grimaced in pain. "Sharon Reese."

It took a moment for Carver to remember who that was. He'd spoken to her a few times, but she'd never provided any useful information. She'd introduced Carver to Abby. That was it. "How many people are on your list tonight?"

"Five."

"Name them."

The man didn't hesitate this time. "Hector Jiminez, Sharon Reese, Abby Smith, Tara Hernandez, Kyle Svensk."

"Jiminez is dead?"

The man gulped. Nodded.

"Who else?"

"Svensk."

"Your friend took out Jiminez and you took out Svensk?"

"Yeah."

"Your friend is going to get Reese, so that means your next stop is Hernandez?"

"Yeah."

"What's Reese's address?"

"I don't know. They didn't send it to me."

"Okay." Carver saw the fentanyl bottle a few feet away. He picked it up and unscrewed the lid. He gripped the man by the throat and squeezed. The man gasped. Carver poured the fentanyl into his mouth and clamped his jaw shut.

The man struggled and flailed but only for a few seconds. That was all the time it took for the fentanyl to kick in. His eyes became glassy, and his pulse slowed to nothing. Carver frisked him. There were no car keys and no wallet.

Carver ran upstairs. Abby was moaning. Her eyelids fluttered like she was trying to wake from a bad dream.

He gently slapped her face. She groaned and drooled. It looked like she'd be okay, but she wasn't coming down from this high anytime soon. He found her phone on the nightstand and unlocked it using her face. He went through the contacts and found Sharon Reese listed.

He called her. She answered on the first ring. "Abby! You coming out tonight?"

"Hey this is Chad on Abby's phone."

She went silent for a moment. "Why are you calling me from Abby's phone?"

"This is going to sound crazy, but someone hired a fixer to kill Abby."

"What?" she shouted.

"Abby is okay. But someone else is coming for you."

"For me? Why? What did we do?"

Carver didn't know, but he figured it had something to do with Callahan's affair with Evans. He didn't have time to play guessing games over the phone. Not when someone was on the way to kill her. "Just a wild guess, but I think someone doesn't want rumors about Callahan's affair getting out."

"What? You've got to be kidding me. All the interns know Callahan is stepping out on his wife. This kind of crap happens all the time in D.C." She was breathing heavily. "Oh, God. I think I hear something scraping on my door. I think someone is trying to break in!"

"Where do you live?" Carver said.

She started sobbing. "I'm right down the road from Abby. Eight twenty-one Rock Place. It's a gated apartment complex."

"Unit?"

"Eight twenty-one."

"Do you have a chair or something you can jam under the door handle?"

"Yes, I think so."

"Do you know how to do it properly?"

"Yes, my dad showed me how to do it. He said I should do it whenever I stay in a hotel."

"Do it now. Hurry." Carver felt Abby's pulse. It was slow and steady. She'd be okay, but he didn't want to leave her alone. He slung her over a shoulder and hurried downstairs. The fixer was still just as dead as before, but his bowels had released, and it stank to high heaven.

He ran outside and buckled Abby into the passenger seat of the Challenger. He heard Sharon saying something on the phone and put it back to his ear. "What did you say?"

"It's done," she whispered. "Someone is definitely out there. I'm afraid to look through the peephole because that's how they get you, right? They shoot you through the eye when you look."

Carver had only done that to someone once in his life and only because he didn't need anyone inside the house alive. But it was best for her not to risk it. "Don't look. Is there any other way out of your apartment?"

"No, it's on the eighth floor. There's a balcony but no fire escape."

Carver started the car. "Hang on." He plugged Sharon's address into the phone. It was a ten-minute drive. He wheeled the car around and gunned it when he hit the road. "I'm on the way."

"Please hurry."

"Are the balconies far apart?"

"You mean my from my neighbor?" She laughed. "You want me to go outside and jump to my neighbor's balcony?"

"I want to know if it's possible. Go check now." Carver dodged around a slower car and turned right at the next intersection. He took a left two blocks down. It was a straight drive from there.

"It's like four or five feet away," Sharon whispered. "And I'm deathly afraid of heights so I'd probably die just trying it."

"Are your neighbors home? Can you see any lights?"

"No lights."

"Okay, do you have a hammer or something similar?"

"Yes. My dad gave me a toolbox." There was a loud bang. She gasped. "They're trying to break through the door!"

"Does it have a metal frame?"

"No, it's just a cheap apartment door! My dad complained about how cheap everything was for the price when I moved in."

"Grab your hammer. Go to the bedroom and brace the door with a chair if you have another one."

"I don't!"

"Then lock it and do what I say." A car pulled out in front of Carver. He slammed the brakes to avoid ramming it.

"I'm in my room with my hammer."

"Bash a hole in the drywall."

"Do what?"

"Hammer a hole in the drywall. Pull out the insulation if you see any." He heard pounding.

"I made a hole. I see gray wooly stuff inside."

Carver veered around the car in front of him and dodged through traffic. "Yank on the drywall until the hole is big enough to crawl through and pull out the gray stuff."

She started pounding on the wall again. He heard her grunting and pounding for another thirty seconds. She screamed.

"What is it?" Carver saw the apartment complex. He saw a car waiting for the gate to open and pulled up right behind it.

"I think he broke through the door. I hear him cursing and pulling on the chair."

"Okay, just concentrate and do what I say. Smash through the drywall on the other side of the insulation, then crawl through the hole into the next apartment. Run out of their front door and to the elevator. I'm almost there."

He heard more pounding and grunting. The gate arm lifted. The car pulled through. Carver tailgated it inside. He veered around the car. The driver honked repeatedly. He pulled into the parking deck and saw the elevator lobby. He screeched to a halt in front of it.

"I did it!" Sharon said. "I—" she screamed.

The driver of the other car gunned his car and stopped right behind Carver. He got out of the car and ran up to the driver's side of the Challenger. He pounded on the window. "Hey, asshole, what the hell is your problem?"

Carver shoved open the door and sent the man stumbling back. He stood and towered over the other man. The man looked up at him and gulped. The elevator lobby required a key, so he grabbed the man by his shirt and yanked him close. "Give me your key now."

"Please, I'm sorry. I didn't realize—"

"The key!"

The man handed him a key fob. Carver used it on the lobby door. He ran inside and punched the elevator button. He listened to the sound on the phone. He heard Sharon begging for her life. Heard a man shouting at her. The first fixer seemed pretty good at his job. The second guy was messy. Real messy.

The elevator finally opened. The angry driver seemed to notice Abby for the first time. His eyes went wide and he looked from Carver to her.

"She overdosed and I'm getting her friend," Carver said as he stepped into the elevator. He punched the button for the eighth floor. The elevator rose at a leisurely pace. It finally reached the eighth floor and stopped. The doors opened. Carver checked the sign in front of the elevator and ran in the direction of room 821.

He rushed past the low eight hundreds and turned the corner. He saw the broken door to 821 hanging slightly ajar at the far end of the hall. He sprinted the final distance. Stopped outside the door. He gently pushed it open and looked through the crack to assess the situation inside.

It was strange that no one else had come into the hallway to investigate the sound of someone battering down a door. Then again, that was human nature. Some people didn't want to get involved in other people's problems. It was possible the thick sound insulation between the walls blocked most of the sound too.

A guy with a buzz cut and glasses was inside. He was tall and thin. Not a lot of visible muscle. He had Sharon on her knees in front of him and a gun muzzle pressed to her forehead. He was calling her all kinds of names, clearly angry at having to break down the door.

"I was going to give you an easy death, you idiot." He crouched in front of her. "Now you're going to make me happy while I choke you."

"Please, no." Sharon sobbed.

Carver pushed the door open a little wider so he could fit through it. The cheap fake wood was broken where the latch had been. It was a hollow core door. The kind that were only rated for inside use and not as a front door even inside an apartment building.

The inside was carpeted. That was good. Real good. Carver walked slowly on the carpet. He hoped Sharon didn't see him because she was going to look straight at him and make the man turn around to see what she was looking at. Thankfully, she was too busy looking at the floor to notice him and the man was too busy unbuckling his belt for some fun.

The man set his gun down on the counter next to him so he could get his pants down faster. Carver drew his knife and came up behind him. He gripped the man by the neck and slid the knife right under his manhood.

"Hi."

The man froze and whimpered. "What the hell?"

"Who hired you?"

The man trembled and squealed faintly.

"Answer the question or we're making sausage."

"No, please!" He gasped. "I—I just work with Edgar. He's the one who handles the jobs."

"Edgar is the guy you texted about coming here?"

"Yeah." He shivered. "Oh, shit, is he—"

"Yeah. He's dead." Carver reached in with his other hand and took Andy's cell phone. It was a cheap burner phone like Edgar's. It didn't require a code to unlock but it also had the encrypted messaging app.

Sobbing uncontrollably, Sharon backed away from the man on all fours. She looked up at him, her fear turning into anger and loathing. She roared in anger and punched the man in the crotch. Carver pulled the knife away at the last instant, so she didn't cut her fingers or sever the man's genitals.

The man howled in pain and went down on his knees. Sharon stood and kicked him in the face and chest. She cried out in pain when her foot struck his head the wrong way. She hopped around on one foot whimpering.

Carver put the knife to the man's throat. "What's your name?"

"Andy."

"How did you kill your first target?"

"I gutted him."

"You like this sort of work, don't you, Andy?"

"Look, it's just business, okay? These stupid brats probably have it coming."

"Maybe, but not from you." Carver wasn't sure what to do with Andy. The man had no useful information, and he was a menace to society. He yanked him upright. Took him outside to the balcony.

"What the hell are you doing, man?"

"You don't know who hired you or why?"

"No, man. We just get targets and do our thing." He backed up to the railing, hands raised. "It's just business, I swear! Nothing personal!"

"It's personal as hell you sick piece of shit!" Sharon stood just inside. "You wanted to choke me to death while you raped me! That's about as personal as it gets!"

"Yeah, because you made a lot of problems for me! You got me all riled up!" Andy laughed it off. "Come on, I can give you money to forget about all this. How's ten grand cash?"

"I'll tell you what." Carver looked at the neighboring balcony. It was a good six feet away. "If you can make that jump, I'll let you go."

"Jump?" Andy looked confused. Clearly, he wasn't the brightest bulb in the box. "What jump?"

"Jump to the neighboring balcony and you can go."

Andy looked at the next balcony over. He laughed. "I can make that easy."

Carver looked over the side. The balcony overlooked the service street behind the apartment building. There was no danger of Andy falling on anyone.

Andy rubbed his hands together. "You telling the truth? I make the jump and I can go?"

Carver nodded. "Yep."

"Are you kidding me?" Sharon gasped. "Kill that asshole!"

Andy climbed over the railing and stood on the narrow ledge outside. He gauged the distance and bent his knees. "I can make this no problem."

Carver punched him in the back of the head. Andy lost his grip and fell screaming. Sharon screamed the instant he fell. She ran to the side and watched him scream all eight stories to the ground.

She gave Carver a horrified look. "You lied."

"No, I didn't. I just didn't tell him I was going to punch him to make the jump more challenging."

Sharon went weak in the knees and slumped against Carver. "Oh my God. I can't believe all this just happened." She backed away and looked up at Carver. "I don't even remember your name."

"It's Chad."

"Oh yeah, that's right."

Carver looked at Andy's body far below. It looked like his investigation had stirred up the hornet's nest, and he was still no closer to finding out where Liana was or if she was still alive. Not only that, but now four people had died because of him.

One thing was certain. They probably wouldn't be the last.

CHAPTER 5

Carver coached Sharon for the police.

"This guy broke in, tried to rape you. You fought on the balcony, and he fell over the side, okay?"

"No one is going to believe I pushed that man over the balcony."

"Tell them you bit his penis or something."

She laughed and covered her mouth. "How about I kneed him in the balls, and he fell?"

"Yeah, that works. Look, these people mean business. I don't know if they'll come for you again."

"I think I'm going to leave Washington. I hate it here." She threw up her hands. "It's just a stupid internship for God's sake!"

"That might be for the best." Carver walked to the front door. "Abby is pretty drugged up. You sure you can handle that story too?"

She nodded. "Yeah. Maybe I should just tell them that these guys were trying to kill us. That they're hitmen and were sent after us for political reasons."

"That's a good idea, actually. You can tell them that your friend, Chad helped and then ran off to parts unknown. Don't give them an accurate description if you can, although the hallway cameras probably recorded me."

"The cameras in this place have been broken for ages. My neighbor found that out after someone broke into her place and took her jewelry."

"Good to know." Carver figured plenty of other cameras had seen him, but maybe he'd get lucky.

"You're definitely not the same guy I met at the bar. That guy was a real party animal and borderline stupid."

"Let's just say I'm trying to help a friend and unfortunately, someone thought you were involved." He handed her Abby's phone. "I'll bring Abby up and leave this in your capable hands."

"Okay, thanks." She sank onto her couch and buried her face in her hands.

Carver took the elevator down and saw the cops were already there. Apparently, the angry guy from the car had called them. The cop was checking Abby. Carver pressed his back to the side and hit the button to go back to the eighth floor again. He returned to Sharon's apartment.

"Cops are already here. I suggest you go downstairs and explain what happened. Abby is in my car."

Sharon looked confused. "You're just going to leave your car?"

"Yeah. It's not registered to me. In fact, it's registered to a dead hitman in Chicago, so that might raise some eyebrows."

She blinked rapidly. "Who in the hell are you?"

"Just your friendly neighborhood Chad." Carver left her apartment. There were four elevator lobbies on each floor, so he went to one on the opposite side of the building from where his car was parked and took it down.

Tonight had been a debacle but it had proven something. Someone knew he was poking around, and they didn't like it at all. The question was, did they know about Liana or was this primarily about Callahan's affair with Evans?

He needed to avoid further complications and get the info he needed. Because tonight had been way too messy and way too public. In the past, he probably would have avoided any confrontation and let the fixers do their work, none the wiser that he was onto them.

All five of those interns would have died just so Carver could keep his cover intact. Obviously, he wasn't the same Carver from all those years ago. He'd developed something of a conscience and that was okay. He had Paola to blame for that.

His conscience was the reason he was looking for Liana. She was an actual friend that he'd grown to like even if she was a horrible roommate. If something had happened to her, there was going to be hell to pay.

Carver exited the elevator in the parking deck. He walked past rows of cars and turned the corner. He saw his car, the cop, and Sharon. Sharon was talking to the cop and waving excitedly toward the elevator. She was probably telling him about Andy.

The cop got on his radio and started talking. The angry guy who'd called the cop suddenly looked like he regretted it immensely because now he was getting sucked into something much larger.

"Good luck, buddy." Carver stared longingly at the Dodge Challenger one last time before turning and leaving. He'd enjoyed driving that car from Chicago to Washington. It wasn't very practical, but it was fun to drive. Being Chad had been interesting too. A part of him was going to miss it.

The cops would run the plates. They'd discover the car belonged to a mobster named Tony in Chicago. That would raise all kinds of questions. They would probably find very few answers and the investigation would go nowhere.

Carver exited the parking deck on the back side. He followed the service street around to a shopping center that was built into the bottom floor of the apartment complex. That was apparently the new thing to do these days.

A notification for a text message was on his phone. He checked it and saw Rachel Evans had sent it about twenty minutes ago. She wanted the link to the secure upload. He logged into the site, generated a temporary link, and sent it to her.

He sat down on a bench and watched the cars go by. Three cop cars and an ambulance arrived moments later. This place was about to get very busy. He decided to get a taxi and take it back to the general location of the house. He could walk from there.

His phone buzzed. Evans had texted him again. *Files uploading.*

He replied in the affirmative and hailed a taxi. The taxi driver took him to a house just down the road from his house. He paid cash, got out, and waited for the taxi's taillights to vanish into the dark, then crossed the road and walked the quarter mile to the long driveway.

Once back in the carriage house, he took a shower to clean off all the blood and grime from the night's activities. He went to his laptop and logged into the VPN. He then used remote control software to login to a remote terminal at a public library in Bethesda, Maryland.

He used the remote terminal to connect to the secure upload site and downloaded the files Evans had posted. The remote terminal was a laptop that was connected to the library wireless and plugged into the electricity. It was tucked away into a dark corner in the stacks so no one would find it.

Carver ran a deep scan of the files to make sure there weren't any viruses that would track his IP location. He didn't see anything, but he still didn't want to download the files to the computer here.

He opened the case files for Liana first and went through them. The records were complete. Nothing was redacted, which was a pleasant surprise. Carver had expected Evans to give him something with a lot of blacked out references.

There were multiple case files, including one about Liana's operation in Morganville, Georgia and their attempts to capture Carver. The end of the file was marked as incomplete and agent MIA, possibly KIA.

The next case file was about Liana and her long disappearance. There were multiple interviews, and an email sent from Liana to someone named Tasha Sloane at the agency, asking if she could come back in from the cold.

Tasha had replied and said that they'd considered her killed in action and that they were happy to know she was still alive and well, provided there was a good explanation for it. Liana replied with a lengthy email detailing how the dark ops team assigned to assist her had tried to kill her.

She said she had to go on the run and into hiding until the heat had died down. She didn't know why the dark ops team had tried to kill her or why they continued to pursue her but wanted to investigate them if she was allowed to resume her duties.

Tasha forwarded her email to the director, but the email had ended up going to Esther Childs. Childs authorized Liana's return with the stipulation that she give a full and truthful account of her missing time.

There was a long statement from Liana which included everything that had happened except this time it included Carver. She didn't mention him by name, referring to him as Ralph instead. Carver didn't like that alias, but at least she'd kept her word not to mention him by name.

Esther Childs apparently already knew about Carver and his real name but she didn't reprimand Liana for trying to protect him. Liana was reinstated and given backpay for the time she'd been in hiding.

Liana resolved four cases she was given and then was asked if she was ready to take another field assignment. Liana said she was, so they gave her a high priority case to investigate a right-wing group that was allegedly infiltrating and sabotaging left-wing protests.

There were multiple videos of masked people in crowds of protestors. In most of the videos, they were looting, starting fires, and damaging or destroying buildings. Afterward, they melted back into the crowd and vanished.

Liana started going to protests and rallies. Political unrest and wars were fueling a wave of large protests, so there were plenty to choose from. In one report, she stated that she'd found a potential recruiter for the group and would try to become a member.

The next report said she became part of a larger group called the Humanitarian Liberation Front or HLF. She suspected this group was controlled by a core of people who instigated the violence and destruction.

Her final report said that the group was organized into multiple layers, each one closer to the center of command and that she had been invited to join one of those groups because she showed relentless devotion to the cause.

That report was days before the undercover agent list leaked. Liana's cover had been blown, and she had likely been discovered. Extremist organizations didn't make a habit of keeping undercover agents alive. They usually killed them in short order.

Liana was most likely dead. Carver's fists clenched. He hated to think of her like that, but she'd known the risks of being a field agent. Hell, he'd almost killed her the first time they met. He'd certainly wanted to kill her a few times after being cooped up with her in that mountain cabin for months. She was the kind of person who hated sitting still. She wanted to always be doing something. To feel like she was making a difference, that she was making the world a better place.

Carver had just wanted to kick back and enjoy life. Instead, he'd had to listen to her talk nonstop about what she wanted to do next in life. It had been annoying, but he'd gradually come to admire her perseverance. She never gave up. She kept pushing ahead no matter what forces were arrayed against her.

And for that, Carver would move heaven and earth to avenge her death. And now he had a good place to start. Finding a way into this extremist group would be a challenge, but he could do it. It was just a matter of attending the next big protest.

Carver skimmed through files from other undercover agents. There were two other agents who'd been investigating HLF but from financial angles. They'd both been undercover and both had vanished.

The first was Juliet Bianchi. She was an Italian-born cyber-security expert who had come to the U.S. when she was twenty because she wanted to work for the CIA. She'd instead gone to work for the NSA and quickly earned her field agent status.

The next was Andrew Mackey, a former Marine grunt-turned cop, turned FBI agent who transitioned to the NSA as a specialist and field operator. He was the kind of guy usually assigned to tactical operations but had gone undercover posing as Juliet's boyfriend.

They were both missing, presumed KIA just like Liana. They probably never even saw the end coming. It was a little surprising that a guy like Mackey wouldn't have sensed something was wrong before they killed him.

Carver had been undercover more times than he could count. He'd had his cover blown a few times thanks to bad intel. Those times had taught him valuable lessons. They'd taught him to look for the telltale signs that something was about to go horribly wrong.

Sometimes it was a change in demeanor, the way the others in the group interacted with him that gave it away. Other times, a sudden change in routine made it obvious that something was amiss.

Carver had once infiltrated a group of Russians who were killing their own people in occupied Ukraine. Many had parents with mixed nationalities, one Russian, the other Ukrainian. When Russia invaded Crimea, they'd taken the side of Ukraine.

Some had been Russian infantry. Some had been spetsnaz, Russian special forces. Scion had been assigned to infiltrate them and destroy them from the inside. It had been one of Carver's toughest assignments because they were a very xenophobic group, highly suspicious of anyone from outside their two countries.

Carver had gone undercover as Alexey Nazarov, the son of a Ukrainian father and Russian mother who'd been killed during the invasion of Crimea. Alexey had spent his formative years in a boarding school in the United States before returning to defend his homeland.

At least, that was the story. Alexey had been a real person who'd died during the invasion, but he'd never gone to the US. Scion had ascertained that the identity was foolproof and would help Carver fit in much more quickly, so they changed a few things about the story and planted fake information to make it look real.

It had taken a month of attending protests and helping resistance groups before he'd been noticed. At first, he was shunned because of his broken Russian and Ukrainian but had gradually been welcomed into a cell of the resistance.

His group was called Fatherland Defense. They were comprised mostly of civilians who were training to become soldiers. They were just cannon fodder, thrown at the Russian occupiers as diversions so the core group could do its work unnoticed.

The primary group was Motherland's Exiles. Carver's goal had been to work his way up the ranks until he was noticed and recruited by the Exiles. Unfortunately, things hadn't worked out. Mainly because Scion's information about Alexey's family had been missing one crucial element.

Alexey had a stepbrother, Volodimir, that the intel had missed. That brother was a lieutenant in Motherland's Exiles. Due to the way the cells operated, no one in Carver's cell knew about the stepbrother, and the stepbrother didn't know that someone was masquerading around as Alexey.

That had changed when Carver's cell met with Volodimir's group to get anti-tank weapons for an upcoming offensive. Carver hadn't been there, but he imagined that the name Alexey Nazarov had come up in conversation. Maybe they were thinking about finally promoting him to Motherland's Exiles and recommended him to Volodimir. Maybe someone found it interesting that Volodimir shared the same last name as Alexey.

Volodimir had probably been curious about the man with the same name as his dead stepbrother. He'd asked who Alexey's parents were and found out that they, too, had the same names as his dead stepparents.

Then someone had shown Volodimir a picture of Carver or possibly described him and told him that his Russian and Ukrainian language skills were very poor because he'd gone to school in the United States.

Volodimir had then told them that Alexey had never been to the US. That his Russian and Ukrainian language skills were perfect. That this person claiming to be Alexey was an impostor. There was no way to know for sure that was how things had happened, but Carver felt confident it was something like that.

Carver had noticed the change in the demeanor of the men when they returned from the weapons exchange. They'd invited him to go hunting with them that evening, which was strange. These men were a tight-knit group of childhood friends, and they'd never invited Carver to go hunting with them before.

They also usually did their hunting in the morning because hunting by daylight was a lot easier than hunting at dusk. It also hadn't helped that they were absolutely horrible at acting and Carver had been able to tell something was off the moment he saw them looking at him.

Long story short, it had been obvious that something was terribly wrong, and that Carver's cover was no longer intact. So, he'd agreed to go hunting. He figured it would be easier to deal with four men than to deal with the hundred men living in the camp.

They seemed very smug when he eagerly accepted their invitation. They looked even smugger when they turned their weapons on him in the middle of the forest later that day. They asked who he worked for and threatened to torture him if he didn't answer their questions.

What they didn't know was that he'd removed the firing pins on their weapons. When he pulled his own rifle, they tried to shoot him. The four men died with confused looks on their faces. They died thinking they had the upper hand, and that Carver would die like a dog.

A similar series of events probably happened to Liana, Juliet, and Mackey. But instead of recognizing the warning signs, they'd missed them.

And now they were dead.

CHAPTER 6

Carver needed to infiltrate the same group Liana had.

To do that, he'd need to attend some protests. Thankfully, Liana had a complete roadmap to finding and attending protests in her notes. There were several websites listing upcoming protests. One of the sites was funded by a political action group. People could sign up on the site and get paid forty bucks an hour to attend a protest.

Anyone wanting to earn money simply needed to download an app that tracked their location and made sure they stayed within a specified protest zone. The app told them when and where to move and notified them when the protest was over. Once it was done, they entered their bank account information and were paid.

It was pretty slick. It didn't require social security numbers, government identification, or anything else. It did, however, use facial recognition to ensure that one person wasn't running the app on multiple devices so they could cheat the system.

Carver wasn't interested in getting paid. He studied the list of upcoming protests and zeroed in on one in Los Angeles. That was Liana's last known location. It stood to reason that she'd infiltrated the group and was working her way up the ladder only to have the ladder snatched out from beneath her.

He read through Liana's notes one more time to make sure he hadn't missed anything. There had been very little follow up from the NSA. Too much had happened too fast for them to check on each and every agent exposed in the breach.

No one had confirmed her last known location. No one had traced her footsteps or verified anything in her notes. That left it all for Carver to do. It was nothing new for him. He'd gone looking for missing agents many times. He'd found them alive very few times. That was just the nature of the business.

He texted Evans. Let her know what he was planning. He also told her to keep everything to herself. If there was a leak in her agency, he didn't want to be the next victim. Carver could probably infiltrate the organization without her help, but it would be stupid of him to not utilize her resources.

There were other tangents that also needed exploring. Whoever had ordered the killing of Abby, Sharon, and the other interns might be connected to the undercover agent breach, or they might be trying to protect someone or something else that had nothing to do with it.

Carver took out the burner phones he'd taken from the fixers, Edgar and Andy. If there had been any texts on Andy's phone, they'd already self-deleted. The text Carver had read on the other guy's phone was gone too.

The encrypted messaging app didn't store phone numbers. It stored usernames. It looked like the usernames for the fixers were randomly generated eight-digit strings. Carver identified which one was Andy's and which was Edgar's. There was a third username that probably belonged to whoever hired them.

The person who hired them was just an anonymous middleman working for an anonymous client. The client might not even be the person at the top of the ladder. They might just be someone proactively looking out for their boss.

Carver was tired, but he decided it was best to follow what few leads he had and see if they went anywhere. He brewed a pot of coffee and poured it into a thermos. He used the bathroom, packed some snacks, and got into the Honda Odyssey. It was the best car for going out incognito.

He drove back to Abby's place and parked down the street. Edgar hadn't had car keys or a wallet on his person. That was smart. It meant he'd left everything in his car which meant his car was parked somewhere nearby and it was probably unlocked.

If not for Carver showing up, Abby would have died of a heroin overdose. Her death would have been marked as yet another Washington intern dying because she partied too hard. It would have also been swept under the rug by politicians to avoid a public scandal.

Edgar had proven himself competent, but he hadn't been ready for unexpected surprises. That indicated he was also confident. Maybe a little overconfident. He also had a list of people to kill, so he'd probably been in a rush. It was also freezing cold outside.

That meant he would have parked somewhere nearby so he didn't have to walk far in the cold, and he could reach the target and get back in a hurry. Killing Abby was about a ten-minute procedure if everything went smoothly. Thanks to Carver, it hadn't gone smoothly, not even a little bit.

Edgar looked like the kind of guy who wasn't too concerned about appearances. He probably drove something reliable and something that would blend in with everything else. The only question was whether it was a burner car or his personal vehicle.

Carver parked a block down and on the same side of the road as Abby's place. He pulled up his hoodie and put on his facemask. He walked down the driver's sides of the cars parked on the street, pulling handles as he went. He was halfway down the block when the door of a silver Kia clicked open.

He slid inside with all the confidence of the person who owned the car and closed the door. He found a wallet and key fob in the center console. The wallet belonged to Edgar Johnson of 810 Cherry Blossom Court. The paperwork in the glove compartment was registered in his name.

There was a garage door opener on the driver's side visor. Next to the rearview mirror were two adhesive transponders. One was for E-Z Pass toll roads in the DC area. The other was for a parking deck over on K Street.

Now that was interesting. K Street was known primarily as the home to lobbying organizations. There were, of course, many other businesses on the street, but Carver was willing to bet this parking deck was next to a lobbying or legal firm.

Carver put Edgar's home address into his GPS. It was a fifteen-minute drive from there. He searched for the name of the parking deck and plugged the address into the GPS. It was sandwiched between two large firms, Taylor & Barnes and Foundation for Immigrant Justice which went by FIJ.

According to their website, Taylor & Barnes was a one-stop shop for any company looking to influence lawmakers. FIJ was primarily a network of immigration lawyers who lobbied for various immigration causes and also provided legal assistance to immigrants.

There was nothing about either organization that automatically connected them to Liana's case. There was also nothing in Edgar's wallet or in the car that linked him to either organization. It was possible he was a freelancer who worked for multiple lobbying firms and chose the parking deck as a centralized location when he had business there.

Trying to track down Edgar's business associates might be a complete dead end that had nothing to do with Liana, but Carver couldn't afford to ignore the lead. He drove to Edgar's house first. It was a nice single-story brick ranch with a two-car garage and a manicured front lawn.

The neighborhood was solidly middle class with houses that had probably been built in the sixties or seventies. The yards were large and spacious in this old neighborhood and the houses were built well off the street.

Carver didn't know if Edgar had a significant other. The garage door was closed, so he couldn't see if another car was parked inside. He parked on the street and used the garage door opener.

The door opened and the garage light came on to reveal a bright red Porsche 911 convertible inside. It almost certainly didn't belong to a wife. It was the exact kind of car a man in a midlife crisis would buy, especially if he had the money to spend.

Carver waited for a minute to see if any lights came on inside the house. Sixty seconds ticked past, and the house remained dark. It looked like Edgar lived alone, so he drove up the driveway and parked in the garage. He closed the door with the remote and got out once it was all the way down.

He knocked on the door leading into the house and listened for a dog barking or any other sounds. All remained quiet, so he used Edgar's house key to open the door. He went inside to the kitchen and turned on the light.

The sink was full of dirty dishes, and the trashcan was nearly overflowing. The floor didn't look too bad, which indicated the place was cleaned sometimes. Maybe he used a cleaning service.

The den was adjacent to the kitchen. There was a futon couch against the window and a big-screen television on the opposite wall. The one end table had a dirty plate and half-empty glass of dark liquid in it.

Carver was about to check out the other rooms when he noticed a visitor's pass on the kitchen floor next to the trash can. He picked it up with a gloved hand and read it. It was for Plum and Associates. According to the maps app it was close to the parking deck Edgar frequented.

Carver dumped the trash on the floor and used a broom to separate it. He found several more visitor passes for Plum and Associates, all consecutively dated for the past week. Edgar had been there not only multiple times during the week, but multiple times during the same day.

He'd also been to Taylor & Barnes, and the Association of Bankers, Investors, and Hedge Fund Managers, ABIH, on the same day not long after visiting Plum and Associates. Edgar was apparently a very busy man.

But it was the last visitor pass that really caught Carver's attention. It wasn't a full visitor pass, but the stub receipt from the form Edgar had filled out to get the pass. The pass was for the Congressional offices on Capitol Hill and the specific destination was Senator Paul Callahan's office.

There was nothing else of significance in the trash. Carver took pictures of the visitors passes but left everything on the floor. If there was a cleaning service, they'd assume Edgar knocked over the trash can and was too lazy to pick it up.

The pass for Callahan's office was about as close to a smoking gun as it could get. If not for the multiple other visitors passes, Carver would feel certain that Callahan or someone in his office hired Edgar to prevent news of his affair with Evans from getting out.

It looked like Edgar had lied about being anonymously hired. In fact, it looked like the man routinely visited lobbyists because he was a well-known fixer. A guy who could nip things in the bud before they got serious. Maybe he also sabotaged the competition.

Carver was certainly no expert on Washington politics. He was looking at this from his own perspective, that of someone who'd played fixer for the US government but as a black ops agent. Edgar was much the same but in the civilian world and he wasn't acting on behalf of the government, but on behalf of individuals or companies.

Maybe that was the wrong way to look at it. Maybe Rachel Evans could give him additional perspective, or maybe she was the wrong person to ask. If he told her that Callahan or someone on his staff might have hired a fixer to kill interns, what would she do?

It seemed likely that bringing this up to her now would only create problems he didn't want to deal with right now. He needed Evans' full and undivided attention. He needed her relationship with Callahan to remain status quo, not devolve into a government investigation.

Carver went through the rest of the house. He found a weapons safe that required a combination. He found a handgun on Edgar's nightstand next to his bed. He found a stash of cash in a shoebox in the closet.

He searched Edgar's small home office with a push-button phone on an old wooden desk, a dinged-up metal filing cabinet, and a few other odds and ends one might find in an office from twenty years ago. Carver went through the filing cabinet. It was full of old bills, signed documents, and other paperwork a person accumulated over the years.

There was a small metal filing box wedged between the filing cabinet and a bookshelf. Carver pulled it out, expecting to find another hidden weapon, but instead it had an accordion file organizer inside.

There were folders inside, each one neatly labeled with names that meant nothing to Carver. He glanced at the tabs and pulled a sheet of paper from one of the folders. There was a name, phone number, and address typed on it. It was similar to an old-school Rolodex. The names and addresses probably belonged to Edgar's clients.

There were too many to go through and nothing jumped out at him about any of the names, so he closed the box and stuck it back where he'd found it.

He didn't find anything else tying Edgar to Callahan or to anyone else for that matter. There were no pictures on the walls, no posters, no collectibles, nothing. There wasn't even a laptop or a smartphone in the house.

It looked like Edgar lived for his job and the Porsche in the garage. Truth be told, he probably loved his work, especially when it came to killing nosy interns. It was also clear that he'd become complacent about covering his tracks. At the very least, he should have shredded all these visitors passes rather than casually dumping them in his own personal garbage can.

Edgar's burner phone vibrated. A text had arrived via the encrypted app. Carver opened the app and read the message. It was from whoever had hired him for tonight's job.

Status?

Carver didn't think it would lead anywhere, but he decided to shoot his shot anyway. *Just finished.*

The answer came seconds later. *Good. Meet in one hour for payment?*

Carver replied. *Yes.*

This might work out better than expected. If the person who hired Edgar was really being careful, a dead drop was much better than meeting in person even if the payment method was a bag full of cash. All he needed was the location.

The other person replied a moment later. *See you at the usual spot.*

Carver sighed. Of course it couldn't be that easy. He had no idea what the usual spot was, and he hadn't seen anything in Edgar's garbage that would give him a clue. What might have been a solid lead was just another dead end.

He turned off the lights in the house. The Porsche keys hung from a pegboard next to the door. He considered taking it for a joyride but figured that would be a bad idea. He got into the Kia, opened the garage door, and backed down the driveway.

He closed the garage door with the remote and headed back to Abby's. He'd leave Edgar's car where he'd found it and recover his minivan. He was about halfway there when something occurred to him.

Edgar did have a usual spot. A spot that he apparently frequented nearly every day of the week. Maybe it wasn't the same spot that the person who hired him was talking about in the text, but maybe it was. Carver's gut told him it felt right.

And he was going to find out.

CHAPTER 7

Carver changed course.

He plugged a new address into the GPS and headed that way. It was a twenty-minute drive. His arrival time would be fifteen minutes early for the meeting. That was perfect. It would give him time to get set up, provided he could figure out exactly where at the address he was supposed to meet.

The address in question was the parking deck Edgar frequented. The transponder on the windshield would let the car in and presumably charge his account directly. Or it might be a free pass. It really didn't matter. What mattered was that this place might be the usual spot.

Carver slowed as he neared the address. The area was still somewhat busy despite the late hour. There were still lots of lights on in the nearby buildings. Lobbyists probably stayed up late dreaming up new ways to bribe public officials, or something like that. He didn't know much about the industry and really didn't want to.

He took out his monocular and studied the area around the parking deck. He looked for anyone who might be standing outside and watching the place. He looked for anyone sitting in a car and watching the place. He looked at the surrounding buildings. Someone might be watching from one of the windows.

There were a lot of places someone could watch from. Too many for him to cover all of them, but he could try. He checked the time. Ten minutes to go until the meeting. He drove to the parking deck. There were two entrances, one for passholders, and one for the plebs who had to pay the daily rates.

The entrances were guarded by metal rollup doors. He drove to the passholder entrance. The rollup door shot up quickly. He drove through and the rollup door dropped back into place the instant his bumper was through. It would be nearly impossible for anyone to tailgate the car in front of them.

The lower levels were blocked off by thick bars to prevent anyone from getting inside on foot. The ground-level doors were also secured. The pass card in Edgar's wallet was the only way in and out via the pedestrian routes.

Carver drove up all eight levels. There were still plenty of cars parked inside. The parking spaces doubled in size from level four up. There were Bentleys, Rolls Royces, Lamborghinis and all kinds of rich person cars. There were ordinary vehicles too, but they were in the minority.

The big parking spaces were exclusively reserved for executives. Some had the executives' names on them, but most didn't. It looked like low-level office staff parked on the bottom levels and the people running the firms parked higher up.

It was surprising to find a large parking space reserved for Edgar Johnson on the seventh floor. There was a sky bridge on that level connecting it to the buildings on either side of the parking deck and to the building directly behind it.

The connected buildings were Taylor & Barnes, Foundation for Immigrant Justice, and ABIH. Edgar had frequented T&B and ABIH, according to his visitor passes. They'd probably hired him for fixer work.

Carver stopped and studied the area. He didn't see anyone standing around or sitting inside of a vehicle. He felt reasonably certain that this was the regular meeting spot, especially if the client worked in one of these buildings.

There didn't seem to be any cameras in the parking deck. That wasn't surprising. The secure doors kept the riffraff out and the high rollers didn't want all the comings and goings recorded. There were probably a lot of secret deals made in this place.

Carver parked the car in Edgar's slot. He exited the car and concealed himself in a dark corner near the skybridge entrance. This particular entrance led to T&B. Maybe that was no coincidence.

The rendezvous time came and went. No one emerged from the skybridge. No one drove or walked past the area. No one came to meet. Apparently, this wasn't the meeting place.

A new text message appeared on Edgar's burner phone moments later. *Where are you?*

Carver thought fast and typed something back. *Came to the parking deck and my tire was flat.*

A minute ticked past before a response came. *That's a fifteen minute walk from here. Meet halfway at K and 19th behind the Nordstrom.*

Carver looked at the maps app and found the intersection. Behind the Nordstrom apparently referred to the service alley running between the buildings, but he texted back just to make sure. *In the alley?*

Yeah.

Carver didn't like that at all, but he agreed to it. *On the way.*

He got back into Edgar's car and wound his way back down the parking deck ramps. He got back onto the road and drove to the area. There were metal construction plates all over 19th. It looked like they'd torn up the street for underground utilities and never gotten around to patching the road properly.

Carver saw the entrance to the alley. There was a parking deck just to the right of it. He pulled into the parking deck, took a ticket, and found a parking spot. The place was mostly empty since many of the nearby stores were closed for the night.

There was a pedestrian exit leading directly into alley. It didn't lock, so he went outside and surveyed his surroundings. There was lighting in the alley but it was barely adequate. That was good. It gave Carver plenty of places to hide. He ducked into a dark corner and waited.

Seconds later, a black SUV whipped into the alley. It screeched to a halt beneath one of the streetlamps. Two men hopped out. One wore a heavy overcoat over a suit and carried a duffel bag. The other wore dark jeans and a black jacket.

The one in the suit set down the duffel bag and remained under the light. The one wearing jeans hustled into the shadows. The SUV screeched away. The man in the suit folded his arms and looked around furtively. He looked nervous.

Carver put his monocular into night vision mode and found the other guy hiding just a few feet away. He held a handgun with a suppressor attached to the end. It looked like Edgar was being set up. But why?

Edgar was a fixer. He did dirty jobs for money and didn't ask questions. Why were they planning to fix the fixer? It didn't make sense. Not even a little bit. But Carver was willing to play along.

The man with the gun wasn't far from Carver's position and there were plenty of shadows covering his approach. He didn't have a suppressor for his Sig, and he didn't want to outright kill the guy just yet either.

It was also possible that the man with the money brought the other guy along for protection. Maybe he was just a bodyguard. Maybe he wasn't there to kill Edgar with a silenced pistol. If they shot him, they'd have to clean up the mess or at least frame it as a mugging gone wrong.

It was better to be safe than dead.

Carver quietly made his way around the area. There were two entrances to the alley, one from 19th and the other from L Street. The man with the money looked from one entrance to the other.

"Stop fidgeting," the man with the gun said. "Don't look nervous or you'll tip him off."

"Why are we doing this again?" the man with the money said. "He does good work, and he doesn't ask questions."

"I don't know. I just follow instructions. Now shut it and wait."

Well, that answered one question. Carver came up behind the man with the gun. He could see him clear as day through the monocular. The man was leaning against the wall. He wasn't hiding behind anything because the darkness completely concealed him from anyone without night vision.

Carver took a moment to decide how to handle this. The movies made it look like a blow to the back of the head would knock out anyone for a conveniently long period of time. While it did work, it required hitting someone hard enough to cause a concussion which often resulted in permanent brain damage.

It didn't sound like the guy with the gun knew why they planned to kill Edgar. The other guy didn't know either, but all Carver needed was one of them. The gunman held his pistol down to the side. His finger wasn't near the trigger. That was good. Real good.

Carver could choke the guy out, but the man would struggle, and he'd probably have time to get his finger on the trigger and fire off panic shots. Breaking someone's neck was also something the movies exaggerated. It was hard work snapping a spine unless the person was small and had bad bones.

This guy was in good shape. He had a thick neck. Choking and neck breaking weren't options. He wished he hadn't used up all of Edgar's fentanyl spray. That would put anyone down real quick.

He was going to have to resort to Option B. Carver drew his Sig. It was a heavy hunk of metal. The ambient city noises were more than enough to cover his footsteps, so he crept right up behind the guy. He reversed his grip on the Sig, holding the barrel with his right hand.

Carver lined up his aim. He swung the gun hard, aiming right for the base of the guy's skull. It struck hard enough to make a cracking sound. The guy went down like a rag doll. The bagman spun around and peered into the darkness.

"What the hell was that?"

"Nothing," Carver hissed.

"Jesus, it sounded like you hit something!"

"I did." Carver picked up the suppressed handgun. It was a Smith and Wesson M&P 9mm. It felt a little front heavy with the suppressor, but it was nothing that would affect his aim. He walked out of the shadows and pointed the gun at the man. "Hi."

The man in the suit gasped and backed away. He tripped over the duffel bag behind him and went down hard on his rear end. "Who in the hell are you?"

Carver crouched next to him. "I'm Edgar's associate and I don't take too kindly to you trying to set me up."

"It wasn't my idea, I promise! I don't know why they did it. Edgar has always done good work for us!"

"I believe you, but that's not going to save you from a whole lot of pain if you don't answer all my questions." He unzipped the duffel bag. It was full of newspapers. "This is very disappointing. How much was supposed to be in here?"

"A hundred grand." The man gulped.

"What's your name?"

"Steve."

Carver stood. "Get up, Steve. Let's talk."

Steve turned over on all fours and slowly pushed himself up. He was a short, thin guy but he moved like he weighed three hundred pounds in his heavy overcoat. He turned to look at Carver, eyes full of fear. "You're going to kill me, aren't you?"

"Not planning on it." Carver checked the vitals on the man he'd conked. He was alive but bleeding from the back of the head. He'd probably be out for a while. "Your friend is still alive. I can keep him that way if you talk."

Steve shivered and glanced down the alleyway.

"Expecting your ride to show up soon?"

"I have to text the driver when it's over, but he might come back to check if I take too long."

"Let's get to it then." Carver tucked his Sig away and held onto the M&P. "Why did you hire Edgar to kill all those people?"

"I don't know. I'm just a middleman." Steve glanced at the unconscious gunman. "I'm a deal broker. People contact me anonymously and I connect them with other people. I got the order and passed it on to Edgar. I pulled a visitor pass for him so he could see the targets at work."

"So that's why he went to Senator Callahan's office?"

"Yeah." He frowned. "You're not really an associate of Edgar's are you?"

Carver ignored the question. "It didn't raise any eyebrows when an order to kill five people came across your desk?"

"Look, I get lots of orders regarding interns. Sometimes their boss sleeps with them and they threaten blackmail. Sometimes they see or hear sensitive information, and they need to be discredited." Steve suddenly sounded a lot more confident. "Edgar took out three people with a fake car accident once. This is DC. The seat of the federal government. Things get crazy."

"So, five people is no big deal."

"Sure, it's a big deal, but only if you make it one." He sighed. "I have no idea why they were targeted. One of them probably saw something they shouldn't have and talked about it with their friends. Maybe one of them was selling information and the client narrowed it down to five possible perpetrators."

Carver knew it was because of him. He'd asked a lot of questions. Finding out about Callahan's affair with Evans was probably a bigger deal than Sharon made it sound. It almost certainly wasn't linked with Liana and the people she was after.

But he asked Steve about it anyway. "Are you familiar with HLF, the Humanitarian Liberation Front?"

Steve frowned. "Never heard of it."

"How about Liana Cardoso?"

He shook his head. "No. Who is she?"

"Do you have any idea who you work for?"

"No." Steve shook his head vehemently. "I'm just a middleman."

"Did the same client ask for Edgar's elimination?"

"Yeah. They wanted him erased probably because he figured out why they wanted those interns killed."

"Are you a one-man operation?"

"No. I work for a small firm."

"Name?"

"Plum and Associates."

A puzzle piece snapped into place. Unfortunately, it belonged to a puzzle unrelated to Liana. "What kind of business is it?"

"We're lobbyists."

Carver waited for him to continue, but he didn't. "You're obviously a lot more than lobbyists if you're hiring fixers and killing them."

Steve sighed. "Primarily, we're information brokers. We connect people to other people and find information people want."

Now that was interesting. If they were information brokers, then surely, they knew about the undercover agent list. Carver grabbed the new thread of information and pulled. "Do you know anything about a list of undercover agents being exposed?"

Steve hesitated. "Not directly."

"What do you mean by that?" Carver said.

"There were rumors about a list for sale. A lot of our clients wanted it. I heard a rumor that one of our people on the seventh floor made a deal."

This was getting interesting. "Is the seventh floor an important one?"

"It's the one that deals with international clients. Those of us on the fifth deal only domestically."

That made sense. Carver needed specifics though. "How many people work on that floor?"

"Maybe thirty, but only four of them are brokers. The rest are just support." Steve shook his head. "I don't know if the rumor about the list is true."

"I need a name," Carver said.

Steve shook his head again. "I don't know for sure. It would just be a guess."

Carver stepped closer to him. "Then guess real hard."

"If I had to guess, it would be Lash Dalton." Steve stepped back. "Management calls him their rockstar. They say he has access to a lot of insiders, even within the new administration."

That was a useful puzzle piece. Maybe Plum and Associates was part of the puzzle he needed to solve.

"Look, can you talk to Edgar? Smooth this out for us?" Steve trembled violently. "I'm just doing my job, you know?"

"I can't," Carver said.

Steve's eyes flared. "Why not?"

"Edgar is already dead."

Steve's eyes widened. "What?"

"Yeah, and most of the interns survived."

Steve's eyes went even wider. "Why are you telling me this?"

"Do you think your client will put out another hit on them?"

"I have no idea!" Steve shivered. "What happened? Who are you?"

"How much money did your firm receive for this?"

Steve couldn't stop shaking. "My God, they're going to kill me for this."

The irony was almost laughable, but Carver had seen this kind of irony too many times to laugh about it. He decided that maybe sending a message to this anonymous client would be the best way to ensure the safety of Abby and the others.

"Steve, I can promise you that they're not going to kill you."

Steve blinked. "You don't know what you're talking about. Sure, mistakes sometimes get made, but not like this. They're going to be pissed."

"Sure, they'll be angry, but they'll get over it. Especially if they understand my message."

Steve frowned. "What message?"

Carver shot him in the forehead. Steve fell over backwards, his body spread eagled on the pavement. "That message."

Carver dragged the gunman out of the shadows and rolled him onto his back, so he was next to Steve. He shot him in the forehead too.

Thanks to Steve, he now had a breadcrumb to follow. He might be one step closer to finding out what happened to Liana. Maybe this breadcrumb would lead to another and another. One thing was certain.

He wasn't done with DC just yet.

CHAPTER 8

Carver walked around the dead men.

He still had the gunman's M&P. It was a decent piece with a nice suppressor, but it would be best to leave it here so he could stage the scene for maximum confusion. He was wearing gloves, so the gun didn't need to be wiped down. He put the gun in the hand of the would-be hitman. He opened the duffel bag with the newspaper in it and spilled some of it onto the ground.

He frisked both men. Neither had wallets or any ID on them. Steve only had a burner phone with the encrypted app. Carver was impressed by how careful they were. It was probably company policy to leave all personal belongings at the office when going to a meeting.

Carver put the phone in Steve's hand for no real reason except to raise more questions. He looked over the staged scene one more time and decided it was going to give investigators a big headache. He melted back into the shadows and went into the parking garage. He stayed there and waited. A little less than ten minutes passed before the SUV that had dropped off Steve and his pal returned. It screeched to a halt next to the men.

The driver got out and stared in horror at the bodies. He suddenly flinched as if realizing the killer could still be nearby. In a panic, he jumped into the SUV and sped away. He was probably going back to Plum and Associates.

They would get the message. They might even think Edgar did it, at least for a little while. Once they found out Edgar had died by drug overdose and his pal, Andy, had taken a flying leap off a building, they might decide to leave Sharon, Abby, and the surviving interns alone.

In fact, if Sharon and Abby told the police about the hitmen and linked them to the two interns Andy and Edgar had killed, then that might create an even bigger scandal. Carver had given Abby's phone to Sharon, but he'd memorized her number.

He texted her from Edgar's burner phone. Told her that Plum and Associates had arranged the hits for an anonymous client. Told her he'd taken care of one middleman but that didn't mean more wouldn't come for her. Then he tossed the burner phone behind a pickup truck.

He'd been through a lot tonight. He'd saved three lives, taken four lives, and asked a lot of questions. And now he was maybe a little bit closer to finding out who was behind blowing Liana's cover. Maybe that person could tell him who'd purchased the list and that would lead him to the real culprits.

First, he had to find Lash Dalton.

Lash was a strange name. It sounded like the name a modern parent would give their child so they could be different. And that was a good thing, because unusual names made it easier to find a person.

Carver opened the social media app on his phone. He logged in with a fake account and searched for Lash Dalton. He found Dalton Lash, Duston Lash, and a lot of other similar names. He found only one Lash Dalton and it was a woman who lived in Florida.

He tried other social media apps and had even less success. It looked like Dalton kept a low profile. That made sense. If Steve and his buddy hadn't even carried wallets or personal cell phones, then it stood to reason that company policy also required keeping a very low profile on social media. Maybe even no profile at all.

They might even purge all social media accounts for their brokers if they were that careful. It was difficult to completely erase a digital footprint, but not impossible, especially if you had the money and the connections to do it.

Carver went to the Plum and Associates website. They had no company directory. They didn't even have a phone number listed. It looked like someone had made a main page in a website designer and just left it at that. There was no mission statement, no address, nothing.

Apparently, if you wanted to do business with P&A you had to know about them already. In most cases, information brokering was illegal or at least frowned upon. Only in Washington DC could it be a legitimate business model instead of a ticket to prison.

Thankfully, Carver knew where to find them because their building was listed in the maps app. It was late, but there was a good chance someone was still in the building. After all, Steve and his friend had been working late before Carver gave them a permanent vacation.

Maybe he could get into the building and pay the seventh floor a visit. Maybe Dalton had paper files on his desk. It seemed doubtful that he'd store that information on a computer unless the entire system was air-gapped, meaning no connection physical or wireless to the internet or other outside network.

Plum and Associates was about a fifteen-minute walk. Carver opted to drive. He would park in Edgar's favorite parking deck since it was just a short walk to the building from there. In fact, P&A was right next door to Taylor & Barnes.

That gave him an idea. He drove to the top of the parking deck. The edges at the top were four feet tall with wire cables to prevent someone from accidentally falling or driving over the side. He parked right above where the sky bridge exited the parking deck and went to Taylor & Barnes, intersecting with their seventh floor.

The Taylor building was eight stories tall. He looked at the Plum building. It was seven stories tall. A plan began to form. It required equipment and a lot of luck, but it might work. It might also fail spectacularly.

Carver climbed over the railing and looked down at the roof of the sky bridge. He could hang from the side of the parking deck and drop four feet down to the roof. He could cross the top of the sky bridge to the Taylor building.

Using a rope and grappling hook, he could climb to the roof. There was just a narrow alley between the Taylor building and the Plum building. Depending on the layout of the roof on the Plum building, he could secure a line and cross over. Then he could use the roof access door to go straight to the seventh floor.

He had rope and a grappling hook back at the carriage house. If there was one thing he'd learned from Joe Donnely, it was to always have a grappling hook in your inventory. You never knew when it was going to come in handy.

Carver opened the maps app and switched to satellite view. There was a picture of the roof of the Plum building, but it was too blurry for details. He ran a search on overhead views of the city and finally found a high-resolution picture of K-Street.

He pinch-zoomed on the image and located Plum and Associates. The roof had the usual utilities like air conditioners, air stacks for plumbing, and even solar panels. Probably so they could qualify for green tax credits.

There was also a roof access door. He couldn't tell much about it due to the overhead angle of the shot. He searched for other images but couldn't find anything with the door in it. That was fine because he could look at it in person.

It was nearly one in the morning. The lights in most of the buildings were out. It looked like people on K-Street actually did sleep. By the time he returned with his equipment, this area should be nice and empty.

Carver figured he could keep driving Edgar's silver Kia for the time being especially since it had the transponder for this parking deck. He drove it back to the carriage house and packed a duffel bag with all the equipment he knew he needed and some that he might need.

Like Edgar, he had his own spray bottles filled with liquid fentanyl. It was a real handy drug if you needed to incapacitate someone. His bottles weren't as small as Edgar's but they'd do the trick all the same. He wished he had scopolamine. It was much better and marginally less deadly than fentanyl. Unfortunately, it wasn't as widely available in the US as it was in Colombia.

He put the duffel bag into the back seat of the Kia and drove it to the parking deck. He parked at the top and got out of the car. He studied the neighboring building with his monocular. If there were cameras on the Taylor & Barnes building, they were on the ground floor, not the seventh.

The windows were dark on most of the upper floor windows aside from one where a man was pacing back and forth in his office. He looked like he was having a bad night. At least it wasn't as bad as Steve's.

Carver climbed over the railing and lowered himself to the skybridge roof. He hurried across to the Taylor building and set the bag down. He pulled out the grappling hook. It was compressed into an arrow shape. He pressed a lever and the hooks sprang out. He backed away and gauged the distance.

If he threw it too short, it would strike the window, bounce off and fall. It might fall on him or it might fall to the street. He anchored the rope to a vent pipe on the skybridge so if he missed and it fell, it wouldn't fall very far.

Carver let the hook dangle with about four feet of slack. He rocked the hook back and forth at the end of the rope, building the momentum until he could spin the hook. He timed the release and let it fly. The hook soared up and over the edge.

He felt pleased with himself. Tossing a grappling hook took practice. Even a short throw was harder to make than it looked. Despite not using a grappling hook for a while, he hadn't lost his touch. Joe would be proud.

Carver pulled gently on the rope until he felt the hook grab the edge of the roof above. He pulled hard to ensure it was firmly anchored. The lip of the roof was about fifteen feet above him. If the hook lost its grip and he fell, he'd land on the skybridge. He'd probably survive, but it wouldn't feel great.

If he landed wrong, he could break bones or rupture a vital organ. That was just a risk you had to accept when using a grappling hook. Sometimes they didn't hold. Sometimes you fell. Hopefully this wasn't one of those times.

He slung his duffel bag over his back and pulled on the rope until it was taut. He put his rubber-soled shoes on the window and walked up the side. It was easier than muscling himself up hand-over-hand.

He reached the lip of the roof and grabbed it. The duffel bag was heavy—too heavy to sling it up and over with one arm. Thankfully, Carver had kept in shape. He pulled himself up and slung a leg up and over the lip. Rolling onto the roof was easy after that.

The grappling hook had dug into the tar paper at the lip of the roof with two prongs. There had been no danger of it losing its grip. He pulled up the rope and compressed the hook then put it into the duffel bag.

If things worked out right, he'd leave the Plum building via the elevator and a back door. If things didn't work out, he'd be coming back this way. That wasn't ideal because it was hard to get a grappling hook to release when you were at the bottom of the rope. It meant he'd have to leave it.

People would notice it. People would ask questions. Security might be increased. Cameras might be installed above the sky bridge. It probably wouldn't affect Carver that much, but it felt sloppy. He hated leaving a mess. He didn't want to leave any traces of his coming or going. Call it professional pride.

Carver crossed the roof. He got right up to the edge and looked down at the roof of the Plum building. He studied the rooftop door with his monocular. It looked like a standard steel door with a wide latch protection plate on it. Nothing he couldn't handle.

The distance between the buildings was about twenty feet. The roof of the Plum building was about fifteen feet lower than the roof of the Taylor building. Even with a running start, that was still too far for him to jump. Even if it was just ten feet, he still wouldn't attempt a jump because the likelihood of breaking a leg on landing was far too high.

He examined the roof of the Plum building and found a large red pipe that looked promising. It was red because it was for the emergency sprinkler system. It emerged from the roof on one side and ran horizontally along the surface for about twenty feet before going back into the roof. It was just a few feet past the roof's edge, putting it well within range of the grappling hook.

In the movies they often had a grappling hook gun that could shoot a line with so much force that it would impale the side of the building and allow the line to be pulled taut for a zipline. In reality, you needed a much more powerful gun to shoot a line that far and that hard.

Carver did it the old-fashioned way. He pulled out the grappling hook, decompressed it, and anchored the rope to a pipe. That way he wouldn't lose it if he missed. He whirled the hook by the end of the rope and tossed it.

He didn't give it much arc since it needed to essentially fall onto the other roof. The hook sailed out and down. It landed just shy of the red pipe. That was no good. It might hook into the edge of the opposing roof, but the angle was wrong and wouldn't allow it to grip.

Carver pulled the line back. The hook caught on the edge of the other roof. He had to walk to the left so he could pull it sideways to make the prongs lose their grip. At last, the hook swung off the other roof. It smacked hard into a window below and bounced off it.

He quickly reeled it in. It was doubtful anyone heard it at this hour but there was no sense in taking chances. He tossed the hook again and this time overshot the red pipe. He pulled slowly and ensured two prongs hooked onto the pipe. Now to pull it tight and secure it on this end.

There was a tall air conditioner unit with a steel ladder bolted to the side a few feet to his left. Carver wrapped the rope high on the ladder, so the line was above his head. He tied it tight and realized as an afterthought that if he didn't come back this way, he'd have to leave the line here since there was no way to untie the knot from the other side.

He could unhook the grappling hook from this side if he pulled it sideways until it reached the end of the pipe. But then he couldn't unhook it once he climbed down the side of the building. Not unless he exited through the Taylor building instead of the Plum building.

He was probably overthinking things. If he found what he was looking for then he didn't want to leave behind any traces because then the people he was after might be on full alert. Even if he didn't find what he was looking for, it was best to be like a ghost, in and out with no one knowing that he was ever there.

"Just do it," Carver told himself. He couldn't expect to leave everything flawlessly clean behind him, especially when he was working alone and making do with what he had. He hung from the line to test it. Bounced up and down. It felt solid.

He hooked a pulley on the line. It wasn't motorized, but it had a handbrake on it so he could use it to climb back up the zipline if need be. He zipped up the duffel bag and slung it over his back again. He walked to the edge of the roof and looked down.

This was the moment of truth. If the line didn't hold here, he wouldn't survive the fall. He would also make a big mess on the pavement below. That would give the street cleaners something to talk about.

Carver hooked his harness onto the pulley and engaged the handbrake. He hung from the line then eased off the brake and slowly slid across the void. He reached the other side without incident and unhooked the pulley from the line and the harness from the pulley.

He put the gear into the duffel bag and pulled out a flat crowbar and slim jim. He went to the door and tested the doorknob just in case it was unlocked. It wasn't. He pulled on the doorknob. There was a little bit of play in the latch, maybe an eighth of an inch. That was all he needed.

He slid the slim jim in from the top above the latch protection plate while using the crowbar to hold the plate as far off the jamb as possible. It was just enough for him to spring the latch. He pulled open the door and went down the stairs to another metal door. It was locked but from this side. Carver unlocked it and walked through.

He was in.

CHAPTER 9

Carver checked the hallway for cameras.

There weren't any, probably for the same reason there weren't any in the parking garage. A company like Plum and Associates dealt in extreme secrecy. They didn't want any recordings of the activities in their building. Less evidence equaled more security in their line of business.

The roof access door was at the end of a short, narrow hallway. He went down to the end and looked around the corner. A wider hallway led past executive offices. He knew they were executive offices because of all the big windows and nameplates.

He checked the nameplates and walked past the offices to an elevator lobby. The next intersection offered a choice of going left or right. He checked out both directions. One led to a large executive lounge complete with pool table, a full bar, and a nice view of the city. There was also an emergency stairwell tucked into the back corner.

The hallway on the other side led to a locker room with a gym, a sauna and steam room, and a room with two hot tubs. It was quite a setup. There was a shower room, a bathroom, and another emergency stairwell. That would probably be the way out of the building.

The elevator dinged. Carver hurried to the corner and looked around it. He saw a security guard exit the elevator lobby and walk in the opposite direction. The man walked casually while looking at his cell phone. He was obviously just making the rounds.

Carver looked for a place to hide and chose the gym. He watched the guard walk to the end of the hall, turn around, and come back his way. He went into the gym and ducked behind a stair machine. The guard walked into the room a moment later, flicked on the lights for a second, then turned them off and left.

Carver emerged from his hiding spot and went to the gym doorway. He saw the guard going toward the executive lounge in the other hallway. The man flicked on the lights in the lounge and turned them off just a couple of seconds later. He came back to the main hallway and went to the executive offices on the other side.

About five minutes later he passed back by on his way to the elevator lobby. Carver watched him go then listened for the elevator doors to close. Once they did, he went around the corner and watched to see which floor the elevator went to next.

It went one floor down. That meant the guard started on the top and worked his way down. He'd stepped off the elevator right at the top of the hour. Maybe he made the rounds hourly. That was useful information.

Carver went down the main hallway to the other executive offices. Dalton's was the last one on the left. The CEO's office was at the very end, and a nameplate for Robert "Robby" Sanchez was on the office across from Dalton's. Carver couldn't help but wonder why the nameplate didn't just have Robby on it if that was his preferred name.

He went to Dalton's office door and tested the doorknob. It was locked. The slim jim popped the latch easily enough and he went inside. There was a laptop on the desk. He turned it on. It booted to a login screen.

The network icon showed offline. He clicked on it with the mousepad and a password prompt appeared. Apparently, you couldn't even connect to the wireless automatically. If they were adhering to the kind of security protocol he thought they were, then only a hardwired network connection would allow internet access.

The laptop required a password. Biometrics were disabled. That was smart too. Fingerprints and face ID could be defeated by dragging a person physically to the computer. Getting a password required interrogation.

He turned off the computer and opened the desk drawers. The filing drawers required keys. He jimmied them open. There wasn't anything interesting in either of them. He looked around the office. It looked slightly smaller on the inside than the outside.

Carver went into the hallway and looked into the neighboring office. It also looked smaller than it should be. He went back into Dalton's office. The back wall was one big window. The right wall was normal drywall. The left wall was covered with vertical slats of stained wood. The lines between the slats were perfect for hiding the outlines of a doorway.

He pushed on the panels until one clicked and a magnetic latch released. He opened it and found a large closet on the other side. Inside the closet there were several metal cabinets. They weren't quite safes, and they weren't quite filing cabinets, but something in between. Carver had seen plenty like them in places all over the world.

These kinds of cabinets were used to keep things like hard drives, USB sticks, paper files, and anything else you didn't want to keep on a computer. They weren't something you could pick up at a big box store. These were made of thick steel and had heavy-duty locks.

Carver had anticipated something like this, but it was going to be messy. These weren't full-blown safes. They used latches like ordinary cabinets, but the latches were made of thicker, heavier steel than standard ones.

A thermite torch would cut right through the latches, but it would probably set off the fire alarm. Same for an acetylene torch. He'd brought along a battery-powered cutting tool but that was a last resort.

First, he'd try it the hard but quiet way. He closed the closet door from the outside to see how much light leaked through the cracks in the wood paneling. The fit was so seamless that no light leaked through. That was good. It meant he didn't have to use a headlamp to do the tricky part.

He went into the closet and closed the door. He studied the lock on the first cabinet. It was a normal pin-tumbler lock. There was nothing too special about it. He opened the duffel bag and pulled out a small bag. He emptied the contents onto the floor, a small metal snap gun and a tension tool.

He attached a thin rod called a needle to the end of the snap gun and pulled the trigger. The needle popped up slightly. When inserted into the lock, the needle would pop up against the bottom pins. The kinetic energy would drive the bottom pins against the top pins causing them to clear the chamber.

Once the chamber was clear, the lock would move freely with the tension tool. The snap gun could be set to various levels increasing the force. Too much force could potentially damage the lock and jam it.

He set the tension to about medium. In his tests, that usually worked fine. He inserted the tension tool and put a little pressure on it. He inserted the snap gun needle and pulled the trigger. It clicked, popping up the pins. He pulled it repeatedly. The pins cleared the chamber after a few tries, freeing the cylinder and allowing him to twist open the lock.

He opened the cabinet and looked inside. It was full of hard drives, paper folders, old computers, and more. There was probably a treasure trove of information inside if you knew exactly where to look. Carver had no idea where to look. None at all.

Everything was labeled, but the labels seemed to be encoded because they didn't make any sense. One hard drive was labeled *HD-20110911NK0112*. HD stood for hard drive. The middle number was the date, September 11, 2011. The last part was probably an index or codex number that described what was on the hard drive.

The index or codex was the key to this mess, but he might not need it. All he needed to do was look for something with a more recent date. He looked through everything and concluded nothing in the cabinet was recent. It went back to 2008. The most recent item was from 2014.

He opened the second cabinet. The most recent item was from 2018. He skipped the third cabinet and went straight to the fourth. The most recent items were inside it. He found a hard drive with dates from a few months ago. He found paper files with the same general date range.

Carver skimmed through the paper files. They weren't just paper files, they were full-blown classified documents. It was usually easy to spot classified folders because they had big red letters on the cover declaring their classification level.

Not these. These were kept inside normal folders to hide the classification warnings. Maybe so if someone unauthorized happened to see inside the cabinet they'd just think these were normal folders.

Some of the information regarded military activities in foreign countries. One detailed an airstrike in Yemen. Another was about secret activities in Ukraine. It was a treasure trove of information to the right people.

Carver wasn't the right person. He wanted one document in particular. He kept searching for it and found it bundled with a solid-state hard drive that was imprinted with DHS labels—Department of Homeland Security.

The paper files were printouts of the contents of the drive. Apparently, DHS had records on undercover agents from all the various three-letter organizations, including the IRS's treasury and secret service agents. The list didn't just cover undercover agents, it detailed thousands of operations as well.

This thing was the Rosetta Stone to the entire national security apparatus.

There was a reason DHS had access to all of those records. It all went back to the Patriot Act and other legislation passed in the aftermath of 9-11. The legislation opened communications between all the three-letter agencies. It required them to share information.

It didn't always work. The agencies fought each other more than they cooperated. And the infighting within agencies was even worse than the interagency fights. It was a wonder any of it worked.

DHS had become the central hub of the massive apparatus. DHS agents with a high enough clearance could access all other agency files. Which meant this list of undercover agents from multiple agencies couldn't have been pulled by just anyone. Only people with top-level clearance could have done it.

That included a very small circle of people from the director of DHS up to POTUS. That didn't necessarily mean that someone within the top echelons of government had sold the list. The list could have been stolen by any staffer with access to administrative offices.

Anyone who dealt with this level of information trading would be certain to cover their asses just in case the seller decided to sell them out. Scion had bought and sold information to such brokers using a middleman to keep their own people from being recorded or photographed doing it.

The brokers always had people hiding near dead drops and other meeting spots so they could spot the sellers. They would record them, follow them home, and get to know everything about them. One reason for that was establishing trust. Knowing where a person lived and who they associated with went a long way towards establishing that trust.

And if that failed, you could always let them know that you knew where they lived. Let them know that their survival and the survival of their loved ones depended on them being extremely trustworthy.

Plum and Associates was no different. Carver opened a folder right next to the one with the undercover agents list. This one had photographs of various people doing various illegal things. One was a woman dropping a packet into a large planter outside of Sapori de Italia, an Italian restaurant.

Another showed a man exchanging a briefcase for a paper bag, presumably full of money. The man was presumably a middleman hired by the broker, Lash Dalton, to carry out the transaction as a buffer for him and his employer.

There were several more pictures of the same man. On the back of each photograph was a record of the transaction. One transaction involved a list of upcoming executive orders that could sway the stock market or affect the futures indexes. Another was a list of attendees for a presidential ball. Another detailed upcoming clandestine meetings between the President and big donors.

There were many such transactions, most of them quite minor but still highly lucrative because someone was willing to hand over big money for insider information. All of the information traded was inside the folders next to the one with the list of undercover agents.

Carver finally found the record of the agent list transaction. The first transaction was when Plum and Associates purchased it from the sellers. This time the middleman didn't receive a bag of money. This time he handed over a USB drive with five million dollars of cryptocurrency on it.

There were two people in the picture with the middleman, a man and a woman. Their names were Peter Harris, a staffer to the former director of national intelligence and Kim Robinson, a staffer to the director of DHS. They were the ones who'd sold out hundreds of US agents for money and probably to sabotage the incoming administration.

There were video recordings of the initial meetings with them. Dalton himself had vetted the pair and interviewed them inside what looked like a high-end restaurant. The place was empty, probably rented out so they could eat and talk without anyone else present.

The recording had been made with a high-resolution camera, but the high angle and distance suggested it had been a hidden camera. Despite its location the sound was crystal clear, probably due to a hidden mic in the breadbasket or flower vase in the middle of the table.

Dalton was a tall guy with a head of thick black hair. He filled out his expensive suit with an athletic physique. Peter, on the other hand, was a short fat man with glasses and a double chin. Kim was taller than and rounder than him. She had a shock of green hair, a nose ring, and a sleeve of tattoos on her right arm.

Dalton started by introducing himself and then quickly moved on to the business at hand. "What made you decide to get into this business?"

"The system," Kim said. "It needs to be broken and burned to the ground. I figured we could break it and make money at the same time."

Peter nodded in agreement. "Yeah." He laughed uncomfortably. "Might as well do what the big boys do."

"And women," Kim said. "Don't bring your patriarchal prejudices into this, Peter."

"Yeah, sorry." Peter looked down and went silent.

"Anyway." Kim shrugged and rolled her eyes as if she hated dealing with Peter. "So, we doing this or what?"

"Absolutely," Dalton spoke with a golden voice. A voice that belonged on the radio. "I just need to know who I'm getting into bed with."

Kim smiled. "Only the best."

"Good." Dalton's tone changed from friendly to deadly serious. "I just need to make sure you understand a few things. I am just a broker. A middleman. I work for very powerful people who do not take kindly to being misled or betrayed. If you sell them bad information or lie, then the consequences can be very dire."

Peter tugged at his shirt collar. "Um, what kind of consequences?"

Kim elbowed him. "What do you think? They'll kill you."

"I thought so." Peter nodded.

Dalton turned to him. "Peter, are you being forced into this? I can't go into business with someone who's not a hundred percent in. You need to tell me right now and we can go our separate ways, no harm, no foul."

"Are you kidding me?" Kim said. "Peter's the one who came to me with the idea."

Dalton looked at her. "Kim, can you step outside for a moment? I need to talk to Peter alone."

A pair of beefy men in black suits stepped up behind Kim. One of them gestured for her to leave.

She barked a laugh. "God, no need to get stupid on me. Yeah, I'll step outside." She left with the two men.

Dalton resumed talking. "Peter, be honest with me."

Peter's demeanor changed considerably after Kim left. "She's right, I came up with the idea. If I'm being honest, we want to destroy the system from within. We want capitalism to die a horrible death." He pounded a fist on the table as if to underscore it. "Kim is just a little overbearing, you know? She bosses me around."

"I understand completely," Dalton said. "I'd like to help you make your dreams come true, Peter. I just had to make sure you're completely in because once we get started, there's no going back."

"Yes, yes, and yes," Peter said.

"I take it you both have a strong disdain for the government?"

"Oh, I've always hated the government," Peter said. "When I went to college, they really opened my eyes about the horrors our country commits around the world. We need to stop it."

"So, that's what got you into government? To destroy it from within?"

"Absolutely. My parents are the kind of people who thrive off corruption."

Dalton nodded. "Your father owns a very successful import business, right?"

"Yes. I told them I don't want their dirty money once I graduated from Yale."

"Did they help you get your current position?" Dalton asked.

"They're personal friends with a lot of government officials, so yeah, that helped. Kim comes from a similar background. She has rich parents who thrive off the backs of the poor. When we met, I just knew that we could make a difference from the inside."

Dalton motioned to someone off camera. The men brought Kim back in.

"Well?" She dropped heavily into her seat and elbowed Peter. "Did you screw it up?"

"On the contrary," Dalton said. "I think this is the beginning of a beautiful relationship."

"Hell yeah." Kim grabbed a hunk of bread from the breadbasket and stuffed it into her mouth. "Can we eat now? I'm starving."

"One more thing," Dalton said. "This agreement is exclusive. By accepting this money and signing our NDA, you agree that you will not sell the same information to anyone else. And if you become aware of someone else selling similar information, you will report them to us."

"Seems strict," Kim said. "A lot of people would pay big bucks for this."

"That's why our agreement is very generous." Dalton shrugged. "Thirty million is far above market value, especially considering you don't have an extensive list of prospective buyers like we do."

"Yeah, but you're going to make ten times that." Kim pursed her lips. "What if we want more, or maybe a cut of the action?"

"We will pay the flat fee that was agreed upon initially."

"And if we want more?"

Dalton smiled coldly. "As I said, we have extensive contacts with very powerful organizations and people. We could give them your information directly and let you deal with them. But there's no guarantee they'll pay for the information."

Peter gulped. "They'd kidnap and torture us for it?"

"Okay, fine!" Kim held up her hands in surrender. "We'll sign and we'll be happy with the money."

"Good." Dalton slid over a sheet of paper. "Both of you sign on the dotted line. This will assign me and Plum and Associates as your agents of record."

Kim signed and slid the paper over to Peter. He signed it with a smile on his face. Those two might not know who bought the list or who was directly responsible for Liana's fate, but he'd be sure to circle back to them.

Carver skimmed through the rest of the video. After Kim and Peter left, Dalton turned to the camera and stated an assessment of the pair. "I submit to the board that we've found two more useful idiots that I think will be great additions to our information providers." The video ended.

And just like that, Carver knew where he was going next.

CHAPTER 10

Carver sorted through the other classified files.

Dalton had purchased the information from Kim and Peter, but nothing told him who Dalton had sold the agent list to after that. Maybe multiple entities had purchased it. Something like that would be valuable to a lot of people and organizations.

It was one thing for Plum and Associates to sell non-classified material. It was something else entirely to sell information that directly betrayed people who were just doing their jobs and national secrets. Maybe Carver didn't always agree with what federal agents were doing but selling them out like this was the same as putting a gun to their heads and pulling the trigger.

Dalton, Kim, and Peter had all pulled the trigger. They'd all contributed to killing undercover agents. They'd all killed Liana. And they were all going to have to pay for that. The question was, how did he want them to pay?

He could leak these videos and the evidence. Let law enforcement handle it. Let the agencies handle it. Surely the intelligence agencies knew about Plum and Associates, but it was possible they didn't or that their employees were complicit in the sale of information.

That approach would be the easiest, but it didn't feel right. Plus, Carver needed to know who purchased the list so he could track down the organization Liana had infiltrated. Attending a protest without knowing who or what he was looking for would be pointless. He needed specifics.

Besides, there was extensive corruption in government agencies. They might fight among themselves, but they also banded together to protect themselves in the face of a scandal. The system had an autoimmune system that fought back viciously when the host was in danger.

That was why he preferred his one-man operation. It was easier to circumvent the immune response and put a knife directly into the heart both literally and figuratively. One thing Peter said was correct. The system was broken.

Carver pulled another duffel bag from inside his gear bag. He unfolded it and stuffed it with classified documents, USB drives, and most importantly, the recording with Dalton, Kim and Peter.

There were lots of other files. So much blackmail material that it looked like Plum and Associates had the most important people in Congress under their thumbs. As an information brokerage, they understood one major principle of politics: *information is power.*

And it was a good way to make money.

Carver looked for anything that would indicate why they'd hired Edgar to kill him and the interns but found nothing in Dalton's cabinets. Maybe Dalton had nothing to do with it. Maybe it was limited to something Steve had been working on. It would be nice to have find closure in that regard, but it wasn't his top priority.

He could come back and clean up those loose ends once he dealt with Liana's killers. Dalton dealt in valuable information that could be used for all kinds of nefarious purposes. Now Carver had valuable information about Dalton. Information that could be used for his own nefarious purposes such as blackmail.

The next step was putting it into action.

There were various ways of doing that. Carver could find out where Dalton lived and do it there. He could snatch him off the streets and take him somewhere for interrogation. Or he could play it the same way Dalton probably did, by sending the target a manila envelope with a sample of blackmail material and negotiate from there.

Carver locked up the cabinets. He left his duffel bags inside the closet and closed it. He wanted to look around the building before he left. He had a gut feeling that although Plum and Associates outsourced certain things to people like Edgar, they probably handled certain things in house.

For example, spying or monitoring people required robust surveillance methods. Outsourcing that would get expensive real fast. It was much more efficient for a company like this to have their own surveillance department. Unfortunately, there wasn't a company directory to tell him where that might be.

He left the office and went to the emergency stairwell. He went down a level and quietly eased open the door. The floor was carpeted so he couldn't exactly listen for footsteps. He figured the guard had probably finished his rounds by now if the perfunctory march around the seventh floor had been any indication.

Carver had his fentanyl spray ready just in case.

He went down the hallway to the junction. There were several smaller offices here. Most belonged to executive assistants and other support staff. There was a workroom with copiers and other supplies in it. There was a small break room with a microwave, sink, and refrigerator. There was nothing of interest on the floor.

The fifth floor had slightly larger offices. One of them belonged to Steve. There was another break room, slightly larger than the one on the sixth floor, and there was a small executive lounge just to make the brokers on the floor feel moderately appreciated.

Steve's office didn't have a hidden closet or secure cabinets full of classified documents. Apparently, the boys on the seventh floor were the only ones trusted with keeping that kind of information.

Carver searched the remaining floors. A huge room on the second floor looked as if it had once housed a call center but the cubicles were all empty. AI and modern phone systems had nearly eliminated the need for hundreds of warm bodies in chairs.

He moved more carefully when he reached the first floor. The stairwell door on that level locked, presumably to prevent anyone from entering the building on the ground level and taking the stairs. He used a wad of paper to block the latch before exiting.

There were a lot of sparkling clean executive offices on the first floor. Lots of nameplates and titles. There was a company directory and map for the first floor. It listed twenty registered lobbyists and their specialties. Apparently, this floor was just a front for the upper levels. It was designed to make the entire company look like a legitimate lobbying organization.

They probably did have legitimate customers. They probably made good money. But they were mainly here to make the rest of the company look like something it wasn't. They were smart. The way they ran things, they had a good chance of never getting caught.

They were so far above the law that they couldn't even see it below the clouds anymore. No one could touch them. No one dared try. Anyone powerful enough to do anything about it was being blackmailed to play along.

But Plum and Associates had made a mistake. They'd sold information that affected someone Carver liked. Carver had almost nothing to lose and couldn't be blackmailed or coerced. They'd attracted the attention of an individual who had no problem doing whatever needed to be done to do right by a friend. Even if it meant burning everything to the ground.

Carver found the security station and lobby right where he expected it to be in the front of the building. There was just one guard there and like the rest of the building, there were no cameras.

He scouted the back of the first floor and found a service entrance leading into a parking deck directly behind the building. That would be his way out.

There was no sign of a department with surveillance equipment. It looked like his presumptions had been wrong. Maybe they did outsource their surveillance needs. He went back to the stairwell and started the hike back to the seventh floor. He was halfway between the third and fourth floors when something occurred to him.

He went back down to the second floor and walked down the hallway to the large but empty call center. Subterfuge was this company's bread and butter. They hid top secret documents in the last place someone would expect right inside their executive offices. They hid an entire information brokerage behind a lobbying façade.

Maybe they hid a surveillance department behind a supposedly abandoned call center. Carver went to the front of the large room. It took up approximately half of the entire floor. There were management offices with windows overlooking the street in front of the building. The rest of the space was covered with cubicles.

He went into the hallway. There were bathrooms and a large break room next to each other. The hallway was on the outer edge of the floor which was different from the design on the other floors. Carver could see the side of the Taylor & Associates building through the windows.

Another hallway bisected the call center. The elevator lobby was in the center of the hallway. Walking down this hallway led to another corridor on the other outer edge of the building. The neighboring building was visible through the windows.

There were more cubicles in another abandoned call center that mirrored the one on the front of the building. But there was one major difference with this room. There were no windows and the room was probably half the size of the other one.

There were cubicles on the back wall. The back walls of the cubicles were much taller than the rest of the prefabricated barriers. These were eight feet tall and covered the entire wall. Carver didn't know much about cubicles, but that seemed suspicious to him.

He went into the first cubicle on the left side and pushed on the back wall. It felt firm. He did the same in the next few cubicles. The one on the right-hand side clicked when he pushed on it. It popped out far enough for him to grasp the edge. He pulled on it and it swung open like a door.

It was dark in the room on the other side of the door. Carver found a light switch and turned it on. LED lights blinked on, bathing the space in cool white light. There were shelves full of everything from parabolic microphones to old-school VHS cameras. There were tables loaded with equipment that Carver didn't recognize. There were old VCRs, reel-to-reel tapes, DVD recorders and more.

If he had to hazard a guess, it looked like a lot of the equipment was designed to convert analog tapes and other recordings into digital for easier storage. Some of the equipment was probably designed to clean up damaged hard drives, tapes, and other media so they could recover what was on it.

There were high-resolution scanners and other equipment designed to convert paper records into digital archives. This room was essentially a one-stop shop for duplicating, repairing, and recording valuable documents.

There were desktop computers attached to server racks on the other side of the room and all of them were in use. One was scanning and repairing a damaged hard drive. Another one was using AI algorithms to restore a heavily damaged photo. It looked like they all fed into the server rack.

There were rows of network attached storage devices. These things were beyond being measured in terabytes. There were ten storage devices, each one labeled as a hundred terabytes. That meant they had a petabyte worth of storage onsite. This was probably the most expensive room in the entire building.

Carver went to one of the running computers and opened the file system. There was a local drive and several network drives listed. Each network drive was about a hundred terabytes. They were only labeled with an alpha numeric string.

He tried to open a network drive and was prompted for a password. He tried to browse to the internet and received a 404 error. These computers were only connected to the local network inside this room. They probably weren't even connected to the local area network in the rest of the building. It was air-gapped, hidden, and protected. And these servers probably had secrets on them going back decades. It was probably the cold archive for everything they didn't want to keep in the executive cabinets up top.

There seemed to be no long-term storage for paper files in the room, though there were old banker's boxes filled with files that looked like they were in a queue to be digitally converted and archived.

It was a pretty slick operation. This place probably housed as many secrets as the servers in the NSA building. The amount of money Plum and Associates made was probably astronomical. Trying to find anything in all that data would be as difficult as finding a specific piece of hay in a haystack if you didn't know what you were doing.

Then again, they were clearly using AI, so it was possible they had a highly advanced indexing system that allowed searching by multiple methods. It was a fascinating setup, but ultimately unimportant to the matter at hand.

Carver got back to his entire reason for finding this room. He went to the shelves with the surveillance equipment to see what they had on hand. He was ecstatic to find a leech. It was a top-tier leech, the kind that had backdoor access to most mobile devices via wireless and could download the contents of most computer hard drives if it was plugged into a USB port.

This was the kind of leech the NSA and CIA used, or very close to it. One of their so-called providers had probably supplied it to them. There were other leeches on the same shelf. Two were identical to the one in his hand. The others were older models, some of which he'd used during his time in Scion.

He wanted to take all the top-tier leeches, but he settled for the one in his hand and a slightly older one. They would immediately notice if all the leeches were missing. If it was just one, they might think it got lost in the mess.

Both leeches were the same size as an old-school USB thumb drive. They were three inches long and both were equipped with adapters, each one plugged into the next one like nesting dolls. Unplugging them all revealed a USB-A, mini variants, micro variants and USB-C with a cap over it.

They had tiny LED touchscreens and a thumb stick to navigate the menus. They had a USB female port at the end so they could be hooked up to a larger hard drive or a monitor. They were tiny technological marvels that Carver could have used on many occasions. Now he had two of his own, provided he got out of the building nice and clean.

There were equipment bags on a rack. He took one and loaded it with other useful equipment. He had to be careful not to load it down too much or he wasn't going to be able to walk.

There was a lot that he wanted but couldn't take unless he returned with a pickup truck and a rolling cart to haul it all away. Even if there was just one guard in the building, he wasn't going to risk getting greedy.

He took mostly devices that money couldn't buy, mainly because only the government was supposed to have access to them. They had auto-lockpickers, alarm disablers, camera blockers, micro cameras, and everything a spy could want. It was better than money.

Once he'd thoroughly sorted through everything and packed what he could, Carver left the room and headed back to the stairs. He returned to the seventh floor and made sure the guard wasn't sauntering around before returning to Dalton's office.

He left his surveillance bag in the closet and then went to the roof access door. Leaving behind signs of his visit really stuck in his craw. He didn't want anyone to know how he got in. In fact, he didn't want them to even know someone had broken in. He wanted them to be completely mystified. If he left a grappling hook and rope lying around, that wasn't going to be the case.

Carver went to the roof and studied the situation. After some thought, he realized what he needed to do. He untied the grappling hook from the rope and let the rope fall back across the road where it hung limply against the Taylor & Barnes building.

He went back to Dalton's office and got his three bags. He slung the rope bag over his back one way, slung the bag with the files and recordings over the other way. He carried the smaller bag of surveillance equipment in his hand.

He made sure the cabinets were all closed and locked tight then left the closet and closed it. He crept down the hallway to ensure the guard wasn't lurking around and took the stairs to the first floor.

He exited through the service exit and double-checked for cameras. Like the rest of the building, there were none. Maybe they'd reconsider their stance once they realized what was missing from Dalton's safe.

Carver looked up and down the street before leaving the parking deck. When it was clear, he jogged across the road behind the Taylor and Barnes building. He kept to the shadows and made it back to the parking deck.

This was the next challenge, but he was ready for it. The bottom level of the deck was fortified with bars and concrete so no one could simply climb over the ledge and into the deck. The second level was the same, but the third level only had the wire cables running laterally to prevent someone from falling over the side.

The bars actually made things easier. He grasped the bars and pulled himself onto the first level. He jumped up and caught the lip of the next level. It was a little tricky thanks to the extra weight he was carrying, but still nothing too difficult.

He pulled himself up and balanced on the ledge. If he fell, he'd land on the hard-packed dirt below. He'd probably be okay, but the odds of twisting an ankle or breaking something were still pretty high, so he'd have to make sure he didn't miss the ledge above.

Carver steadied himself and jumped. He caught the ledge with his fingertips. He shifted his hand and got a better grip. He muscled himself up, grabbed the wire cables, and used them to pull himself up to the ledge.

He slipped over the top of them. The bags shifted and the gear inside conked him on the head. He gave himself a moment to recover, then walked up the stairwell to the top deck. He dumped everything except the grappling hook and rope into the Kia's trunk.

He was tired, but he was determined to do this right. Just like a professional tradesman, he wanted to make a job look perfect. At least like any tradesman with a little bit of pride in his work.

Joe had always told him to do things as nice and neat as possible. And if it wasn't possible, then do it as messy as possible. That advice had never made much sense to Carver, but Joe liked to say it a lot, so he just nodded and went along with it. Now he kind of understood. If you couldn't make it neat, make sure the enemy damn well knew for certain that you'd been there.

Carver went to the edge of the roof and lowered himself the five feet to the sky bridge. He hurried across then tossed the grappling hook to the roof of the Taylor & Barnes building. He walked up the side of the building and pulled himself onto the roof.

He went to the ladder where he'd tied off the rope that had spanned the distance between the Taylor building and the Plum building. He untied it, looped it up, and dropped it down on the skybridge.

The drop from the roof to the skybridge was about fifteen feet. He could dangle over the side and cut the fall distance by about half. A controlled fall from that height wouldn't hurt or damage anything.

He also had another option. The rope he'd tied to the grappling hook this time was stiffer. He could push up on it and the grappling hook might come loose. He might be able to coax it over the edge after a little while.

Carver wasn't going to do that. He unhooked the grappling hook and dropped it onto the skybridge. He climbed over the side and dangled from his fingertips. He dropped and bent his knees to absorb the shock. There was virtually no shock from the seven-foot drop.

He compressed the grappling hook and coiled the rope, then picked up the coil of rope he'd picked up from the roof. Now there was no rope, no grappling hook, nothing suggesting that some lunatic had ziplined from the Taylor & Barnes building to the Plum and Associates building.

Carver went back across the top of the skybridge to the parking deck. He tossed the rope and grappling hook up and over the ledge, then climbed up after it. Now he had everything. Now the job was so nice and neat that Dalton was going to be scratching his head hard enough to make it bleed.

But the more Carver thought about it, the more he realized that he couldn't give the enemy time to realize what had happened. He had to act now.

The night was still young and there was a lot more to do.

CHAPTER 11

Carver had no choice but to find Lash Dalton tonight.

Come later this morning people would be waking up to the news of a double homicide behind Nordstrom and the news of two dead hitmen and two dead Senate interns. Certain people were going to get nervous. They were going to be on guard.

Especially people at Plum and Associates, and even more especially Dalton. Which meant Carver had to get to Dalton before the morning news did. This was going to be an all-nighter. Unless, of course, the SUV driver had run straight to his bosses to tell them what happened to Steve and his gunman.

That was the primary unknown variable. Had Dalton already been notified? Was he already up and alert? Was he already making calls to other company executives to tell them that Edgar had presumably killed two of their men?

It was highly unlikely that they would find out Edgar was dead until sometime later in the morning. That meant they'd be on guard against Edgar, not Carver. Even if Dalton knew about Steve, it didn't mean he could prepare for what was coming his way.

He'd better have his own private army if he thought he could hide from Carver.

The first major challenge was figuring out where Dalton lived. There were probably employee records at Plum and Associates, but Carver hadn't considered visiting the human resources office while he was there. It was a major oversight on his part.

Without Dalton's contact information, there was no way to make him come to Carver. There was another possibility, however. That filing box in Edgar's home office had contact information in it. Possibly contact information for Edgar's clients.

Maybe Edgar kept information on people he worked for just in case he got caught and needed someone to pull strings for him. Maybe he kept blackmail material in case he needed to get out of a hairy situation, i.e. being killed by his clients.

Carver closed his eyes and envisioned the names he'd seen on the folder tabs. He remembered seeing Steve on one of the tabs. He didn't remember seeing Lash Dalton on any of them, but he might just have missed it.

He guided the car down the parking garage ramps, left the building, and aimed the car back toward Edgar's house. It took fifteen minutes to get there. He slowly approached the house just in case Edgar had late night visitors.

It was possible Edgar had a girlfriend or someone else who knew about his fixer business. They might have tried to reach him to make sure everything had gone smoothly. When he hadn't answered, they might have driven to his house to physically check on him.

Someone with less friendly intentions might have also gone to Edgar's house. Maybe someone from Plum and Associates, or maybe even a kill squad to finish the job Steve hadn't.

There were plenty of hypotheticals to consider. Too many to think of them all. Carver took his time observing the house from a distance and scanning the area with his monocular before deciding no one was inside and he could proceed.

He parked Edgar's car in the garage and went inside as boldly as before. He went straight for the filing box in the office and brought it back to the car without looking in it. He backed up and drove a short distance down the street, closing the garage door on the way out.

It was possible Edgar didn't keep all his information in this small box. He might have more files hidden inside the house, but Carver didn't feel safe sitting inside. If Dalton thought Edgar killed Steve and the gunman, he might send more men to Edgar's house to finish the job or bring him in. In fact, it seemed a near certainty.

He pulled out the entire accordion file organizer and set the metal box aside. Something rattled in the bottom. He looked inside and found a small round key. It was the kind of key used for a barrel lock. The kind commonly used to lock rollup doors in storage facilities.

There was a folded slip of notebook paper in the bottom too. Carver unfolded it and found a handwritten note in blue ink. He read it.

Gary, I assume that you are reading this because I missed my weekly check-in. You did as I instructed and got this filing box from my house or from one of the duplicate dead drops I told you about. Inside the folders you will find the names and addresses of people I worked for in the past.

Those papers also have index numbers on them linking them to banker's boxes filled with all kinds of information about things I have done for those people. If I am missing or found dead, it is highly likely that one of these people killed me to protect sensitive information.

I have warned them time and time again that killing me would release all the dirt I have on them. Gary, it is up to you to ensure this happens. You will go to Safety Storage at 135 Booker St. unit 007. You will open the banker's boxes and find everything already packaged for mailing and ready to go to various news organizations.

There is money in one of the boxes so you can pay for all of this to ship right away. I know there are a lot of packages, but it's vital you do this and pay cash. Make sure you do not give your ID or any personal information. You must remain anonymous.

You can go to Harun Fast Ship and safely ship everything from there. Just tell Harun that you're friends with Edgar and he will make sure there are no recordings of you shipping these packages.

I understand if you're afraid of doing this but knowing how you've always wanted to burn the government to the ground, I think you'll enjoy the fireworks once all this gets out.

Thanks, Gary.

-Edgar

It was nice seeing Edgar had a backup plan. A plan that his friend Gary would probably carry out once Edgar missed his weekly check-in. And since there were duplicate dead drops, Gary didn't need this specific filing box or key.

There was a small typewritten note at the bottom of the letter.

IMPORTANT REMINDER! Enter through the garage door with the key I gave you. Entering through any other door will activate the alarm system.

YOU DO NOT WANT THE ALARM TO SOUND!

To deactivate enter 0566 on keypad within 30 seconds.

That explained why the alarm system hadn't triggered when Carver went inside. The garage entrance was the way Edgar would normally enter the house. It was also the only entrance guarded by both a heavy garage door and a heavy entry door, making it the hardest route for an intruder to use.

What was unclear was why he would include the instructions on a handwritten note that Gary would only find once he'd recovered one of the boxes. Maybe it was just a reminder in case Gary retrieved a box from another location and considered entering Edgar's house.

Carver put the key and note back in the box and looked through the names on the tabs. He found the one he was looking for right in the D section—Lash Dalton. His phone number and multiple addresses were listed. It looked like Dalton owned multiple properties in the area.

Edgar had marked two of the properties with dashes, probably indicating those were the primary places where Dalton laid down to rest at night. One was in Georgetown, and the other was a house on the Potomac in Maryland about an hour and a half northeast of DC.

It was the middle of the work week. A new administration was in town. In other words, there was a lot happening in DC which meant Dalton would almost certainly want to stay as close to the Capitol as possible.

The Georgetown residence seemed the most likely place to find Dalton, so that was where Carver would start. He tucked everything back into the filing box. It seemed best to return to the carriage house. He would drop off his gear and collect the minivan. Edgar's silver Kia was probably known to Dalton, so it was best to take the vehicle off the board.

A black SUV with its headlights off zipped past Carver. It slowed in front of Edgar's house and turned into the driveway. Four men piled out, all of them dressed in black body armor, and with MP5SD submachine guns. The SD version had a suppressor built into the barrel. It was a great weapon for close quarters combat.

Steve and his pal had been amateurs. These guys were the real deal. Since Carver had closed the garage door, they couldn't see inside. They didn't know if Edgar's Kia was on the other side of the door. It was such a common car that they hadn't even looked twice at the Kia parked on the side of the road.

Maybe these guys weren't pros. If Carver had been on their kill squad he would have noticed a car identical to the target's car if it was in the vicinity of the target's house. That was because the target might have parked away from the house and approached from the backyard or another angle besides the street.

It could also be that these men were in a big hurry to do the job because their boss was antsy about having Edgar on the loose after he'd escaped an ambush and killed the two men sent to kill him. Dalton or whoever ordered Edgar's death probably thought he was going to be next on Edgar's list.

The men went to the front door and stacked up two by two on either side. One of them stepped in front of the door, raised his foot, and slammed it down flat on the door. The door didn't budge in the slightest. The kicker hopped around in pain.

The door was solid oak in a steel frame. The garage door and the back door were the same. Edgar had fortified his doors because he was the kind of guy who played it safe. He had not, however, done the same with the windows. At least not from what Carver had seen.

One of the men used the butt of his rifle to smash out a window on the front of the house. It took him a moment to clear out the triple panes of tempered glass. Anyone inside the house would have had plenty of time to escape or shoot back.

Carver decided he'd prematurely pegged these guys as pros. They had pro weaponry and a can-do attitude, but this was like watching the four stooges in action. They were just lucky Edgar hadn't been inside, or they'd have been cut to pieces by now.

They piled through the window, heedless of any danger that might be lurking inside. A red light started blinking inside the house. That was probably the alarm system warning them that it would sound the alarm in thirty seconds. Carver rolled down the Kia's window. He heard the faint beeping of the alarm system counting its way down to zero.

Edgar's note to Gary had been very explicit in all CAPS that sounding the alarm was a very bad idea. Most domestic alarm systems called the cops when they went off. Carver had a feeling that Edgar's alarm would play judge, jury, and executioner for any home intruders.

The beeping grew louder and faster. There was a muzzle flash, and the blinking light went off. Apparently one of the gunmen shot the alarm console. One of the men dashed through the broken window. Carver got a good closeup of his panic-stricken face through the monocular.

There was a loud crack. A deep boom. The house flew apart. Debris flew in all directions. The man who'd jumped through the window rode the shockwave, a rag doll spinning like a frisbee until he smacked into a large pine tree in the front yard.

"So that's why Gary doesn't want the alarm going off." Carver grunted in approval.

The explosion hadn't been from C4 or gunpowder. It looked more like a gas explosion. Edgar had probably rigged a tank of natural gas or propane in the basement to open all the valves and flood the space within seconds of the alarm going off.

When the alarm triggered, all it took was a spark to demolish the house and anyone inside of it. It was also a good way to make it look like an accident. Most investigators would take a good long look at the tank in the basement and conclude it was a tragic accident.

The rest of the house was on fire, reducing everything and everyone inside to ashes. Maybe Edgar was more of a pro than Carver gave him credit for. One thing was certain—the heat was about to get a whole lot hotter once Dalton found out his second attempt at killing Edgar had ended with four dead men.

This really piqued Carver's interest. What secret was so worth guarding that a handful of interns and the fixer had to be killed? This couldn't just be about Callahan's affair, could it? In this day and age most politicians could easily survive an extramarital affair scandal. There had to be something more to it.

It didn't seem likely that this was linked to the undercover agent list if Callahan was involved, but then again, anything was possible.

Whatever it was didn't matter right now. Carver was sticking to the mission—finding the people who killed Liana and holding them accountable. Dalton was one of the people involved in the undercover agent leak. He'd facilitated its sale, so he might as well have pulled the trigger.

Carver plugged the address to Dalton's Georgetown residence into the GPS. It was a fifteen-minute drive. He took one last look at Edgar's burning house and shifted the Kia into drive. He exited navigation and routed himself toward home base, the carriage house.

He reached it fifteen minutes later and parked Edgar's car inside. He moved his infiltration gear over to the minivan along with the surveillance equipment he'd stolen from Plum and Associates. He considered leaving the files he'd taken from Dalton's office but decided to take them along in case he needed to show the man proof that he had them.

The GPS showed eighteen minutes to Dalton's Georgetown residence. Carver checked the time. The city would be waking up before much longer. He needed to get this done before the new day dawned and the news reported the mayhem of the night.

He sped down the driveway and gunned the minivan onto George Washington Memorial Parkway heading south. He crossed the Francis Scott Key Bridge across the Potomac and it dumped him right into Georgetown.

The GPS led him down narrow streets between narrow rowhouses that probably cost two to three million each. Maybe more. A lot more. A lot of rich politicians and lobbyists probably owned these as second or third homes and only because of the proximity to the federal government.

Dalton's house was on the east side of Georgetown not far from Oak Hill Cemetery. The rowhouses looked a little bigger than the ones on the west side of the neighborhood, probably because this area had older buildings constructed when there was more land.

Although the neighborhood was full of rowhouses, Dalton's place stood alone on a half-acre of land on a hill between 28th Street Northwest and 29th Street Northwest. The driveway was guarded by a black iron gate and the house was surrounded by a tall iron fence.

A steep stone stairway led up to another black iron gate with no visible lock. It probably had a magnetic lock that required a keycard or possibly a biometric ID like fingerprint or face. There was a steep slope leading up to the iron fence except where the fence connected with the driveway gate.

The slope rose for about fifty feet before flattening out where the builders had evenly graded the lot so the house could be built. The slope and positioning of the fence made it a tricky place to infiltrate.

There were also cameras watching the road in both directions near the gate, and another one on a pole looking down at the gate. There were poles spaced evenly along the perimeter and each one hosted a camera looking down at the area right around the fence. Dalton wasn't playing games when it came to security.

This place was going to be a challenge to infiltrate and Carver was running out of time.

CHAPTER 12

Carver didn't drive anywhere near Dalton's property once he saw the cameras.

The minivan was excellent camouflage, but he wasn't ready to expose it just yet. Instead, he parked with a clear line of sight on the driveway and thought about how to crack this particular nut.

A car drove past the front of the house. The camera on the poles near the gate turned to follow the car as it passed. It was probably triggered by motion sensors and automatically followed whatever activated it until it passed out of view. The camera rotated back to dead center once the car was out of range.

The other cameras didn't move. It looked like all the other cameras were stationary except for the ones on the pole near the gate. The ones on the poles near the fence were about ten feet above sidewalk level.

The house itself towered over the fence by twenty feet. It was three stories tall with a contemporary design. That was surprising because historic neighborhoods usually had old houses that couldn't simply be torn down on a whim due to government restrictions.

A person like Dalton probably blackmailed someone so he could raze the existing house and throw up the monstrosity that currently sat there. The house consisted mostly of large windows with thick black panes that probably doubled as support beams.

The top was flat with an open trellis roof. It was a design Carver had seen often in Mediterranean cities, and it looked way out of place in Georgetown. It would certainly make infiltration easier but only if Carver could get past the cameras around the perimeter.

Thankfully, Plum and Associates had provided him with a solution. Among the useful items he'd taken was an auto lockpicker, an alarm disabler, and best of all, a miniaturized signal jammer. It could scramble cell phones, landlines, and internet connections within about a fifty foot radius. Beyond that, it was unreliable due to the transmitter strength.

It should theoretically also jam the signal from the cameras whether they were wireless or hardwired. Carver had used such devices plenty of times during his time with Scion. They could be hit or miss, but were mostly hit.

One time a jammer hadn't worked but Carver got lucky because the guy who was supposed to be watching the cameras was asleep. The other two times it hadn't worked, guards had shot at him and missed.

Dalton might have bodyguards. He might even have one watching the camera feed locally, but in this day and age, most of the people watching the cameras were doing so from a company that provided such a service. They used motion detection and AI to increase successful detection.

Then again, these cameras might not be monitored at all. Normal homeowners didn't sit around watching their camera feeds day in and day out. They recorded the footage and reviewed it after the fact.

If the cameras were actively monitored, hopefully it was being done by a computer and not AI. Humans were less likely to ring alarm bells if the camera feed went down for a few seconds. AI or automated algorithms were designed to trigger the alarm if certain conditions were met.

The cameras were the only source of motion detection that Carver could see. There were even more cameras on the house itself as well. Without the signal jammer, infiltration would be quite literally an uphill battle.

Carver had grown accustomed to not relying on gadgets to get things done. While they often provided nice shortcuts through difficult obstacles, they also had their downsides. One downside was that they didn't always work or that using them caused side effects that alerted the target. The biggest downside was becoming overly reliant on technology to solve an issue.

He wasn't too proud to use a gadget, but it was still a good idea to look for alternatives just in case there was something he was missing. Even the most secure perimeters had cracks that could be exploited.

There were no lights on in the house. That was promising. It might mean that Dalton hadn't been alerted by the driver that Steve was dead and that things had gone horribly wrong. It could mean that he was snoozing peacefully in his bed with his phone set to silent.

But a person like Dalton probably wouldn't sleep with the phone set to *Do Not Disturb*. A person who'd just facilitated multiple hits including one on his own favorite fixer probably wouldn't sleep peacefully at night until he'd found out that the mission was a success.

It wasn't just that there weren't any lights on inside the house, but there were also none on outside the house. If there were armed guards on the premises, there would usually be some outside lights on so they could keep watch.

It could be that the guards relied on the camera's infrared and night vision rather than physically patrolling the perimeter. Maybe the guards themselves wore all black and patrolled with night vision goggles. Carver hadn't seen anyone patrolling so far.

The other option was that Dalton wasn't at this address. He might be at the house outside of town. Maybe he thought that was a better place to wait out the fallout from tonight's carnage. Dalton's other house had a river on the western perimeter, a long driveway, and a tall iron fence like the one around this house. Carver had seen it on the satellite view in the GPS.

It was a good place to hunker down if a person didn't want to be too close to the action. But it was also far enough away that a person couldn't respond to any emergencies, at least not in person.

There were too many hypotheticals to consider, and not enough hours of darkness left to worry about them. Carver was just going to have to go in and make sure no one was home. He just had to figure out how to do it without raising the alarm.

The cameras on the poles around the perimeter were angled down to look at the sidewalk and the fence. They probably angled them specifically to not capture movement in the road because cars would constantly trigger the motion detectors.

Carver got out of the minivan and walked closer to the house. He remained on the sidewalk across the road out of view of the cameras. There were very few streetlamps, so he was able to keep to the shadows during his stroll.

He walked the perimeter using the monocular to examine every inch of the place. It took time, but it was better than bum rushing the house and getting taken out the moment he scaled the fence. It was also worth it because he found a crack in the defenses on the south side.

There were a lot of cameras, each one angled to maximize their field of view but also to avoid capturing every single car that passed through the neighborhood. Because the cameras were on tall poles, they attracted the interest of birds.

Most of the cameras were stained with bird crap. Some poor soul had to keep cleaning it off, probably by climbing a ladder and wiping it because there was no way a water hose would reach all the way down to the fence.

One of the cameras was absolutely covered with a thick layer of bird droppings because there was a bird's nest in the tree branch right above it. It was probably getting crapped on day and night, too often for someone to keep it clean.

It was the perfect place for Carver to breach the perimeter without using the signal jammer. He studied the area and made sure there were no other cameras covering the approach. It looked like he was in the clear. Now all he had to do was clear the next hurdle, the fence.

The fence was at the top of a steep slope. It was ten feet tall and topped with security spikes. The iron bars were about as thick as an index finger and spaced widely enough to climb without too much trouble. The spikes at the top curved down to dissuade anyone from doing that. There was also a spike going straight up at the top and another spike curving down on the other side.

Thankfully, these weren't barbed spikes or razor spikes. Those kinds were extremely hard to bypass unless you had the right equipment. Carver hurried across the road. He climbed the slope. It was just steep enough to be an inconvenience and not a barrier.

When he reached the top, he tapped a voltage testing pen against it to make sure it wasn't electrified. The pen didn't beep, meaning he wouldn't have fifty thousand volts running through his body if he touched it.

He gripped one of the bars. He wanted to make sure it was actual iron and not aluminum. It felt like commercial grade wrought iron with a slightly rough surface that made it ideal for climbing.

The bars were spaced just far enough apart to fit his hand through. There were about four bars per foot. They were too large for a bolt cutter to handle. He'd need a cutting tool or a torch. He had a thermite wand that could cut through a single bar in a few seconds, but he'd have to cut a minimum of three bars at the top and bottom to fit through.

That would require six thermite cartridges. They would make a lot of light for about ten seconds each time. On the other hand, they were nearly silent and fast. It would probably be worth it to cut himself a hole because he could get in and out much faster than scaling the fence.

Carver heard the hum of an engine and crouched in the shadows. A car passed by on the adjacent street. He waited until the sound faded in the distance then crossed the street and went back to the minivan.

He packed what he would need in a backpack and went back to the chosen breaching point. He climbed the slope and crouched next to the fence. The area was dark, but it was about to light up bright as day, so he made sure no one was out walking their dog in the middle of the night before beginning.

The streets were empty and silent. Carver pushed a thermite charge into the wand and pressed the tip against the iron bar. He clicked the igniter. Bright flames shot from the tip. The superheated thermite melted through the bar in seconds.

It was still burning so he pressed it against the base of the next bar. It cut through that one just before burning out. He ejected the cartridge and put another one in. That one cut through the bottom of the third bar and cut it again about halfway up.

The third bar fell free. He repeated the process on the first two bars and soon had a convenient hole. He went through the hole and stood on level ground. There was a slight slope leading to the house, but nothing like the fifteen-degree grade outside the fence.

He slid on his night vision goggles and turned them on. He was in the back yard now. There was a large saltwater pool, a gazebo with a large stainless-steel grill, and lots of outdoor furniture. There was a huge television mounted on one wall and a fire pit in the center of a sectional couch.

It was a good place to study the next hurdles in front of him, namely getting past the cameras on the house. There were two sets of French doors on the back of the house and cameras over both of them. There were cameras on the corners of the house as well.

Carver eyeballed the cameras and imagined their cone of vision. They were about ten feet high and angled to capture most of the back yard. It didn't look like they could see the pool and there were no cameras in the pool area.

The French doors were made of wrought iron and had latch protectors. Depending on how tightly the doors shut, he could probably jimmy one of them open. The automatic lock picker might also do the trick.

Another option was to approach the house from a blind angle and use the grappling hook on the rooftop trellis. It would require a very high toss. If he missed, he might hit the side of the house or break a window and raise the alarm.

Carver decided on the high-tech approach. He unzipped the backpack and found the signal jammer. Theoretically, it should jam the signal before the camera saw him. He turned it on and covered his face with a mask just in case.

He jogged across the yard to the French doors on the right. There were no visual cues that the camera was being jammed but at this range the jammer should definitely be working. He slid the tips of the automatic lock picker into the keyhole and pressed the trigger.

It worked a lot like the snap gun by popping the pins up and out of the chamber while turning the door lock. It took about the same amount of time as the manual snap gun before the lock opened.

There was probably an alarm system on the door. The signal jammer wouldn't do anything to stop it from triggering because the door sensors would trip the moment the door opened. It was also impossible to know if there were sensors since they'd be at the top of the door.

If there was an alarm system, it would start to beep the moment he opened the door. He would have thirty seconds to reach the alarm panel and disarm it with the disabler he'd procured from Plum and Associates.

It was harder than it sounded because he'd have to pop the alarm panel off the wall, unplug the wire harness from the back, and plug it into the disabler. He'd done it dozens of times before, but finding the panel would require precious time.

The French doors were mostly glass in an iron frame, giving him a clear view into an open den and kitchen area. There was no sign of guards or dogs. If he encountered either, he'd use fentanyl spray before resorting to lethal means.

They might be guarding a guy who contracted with hitmen, but that didn't mean they were killers themselves. If it came down to survival, he'd do whatever he had to do. Killing out of convenience was just lazy.

He pushed open the door and braced for the beep of the alarm. There was no beeping. He looked above the door and didn't see any sensors. He also didn't see any motion detectors or cameras inside the house.

Maybe Dalton thought he had plenty of external layers of protection that he didn't need an alarm system. Whatever the reason, Carver was glad he didn't have to worry about yet another layer of security.

He walked across the kitchen and den area. It was wide open for the most part and no one was there. He walked upstairs to the second floor. There was a large game room and several guest bedrooms. He cleared them all and didn't find anyone. It was starting to look like no one was home.

The third floor had an indoor hot tub and a swimming pool that went out to a glass balcony overlooking the neighborhood. A pair of French doors presumably led into a master suite. Carver tested a door handle. It was locked.

That was a good sign. There was nothing protecting the latch, so Carver jimmied it open in a flash. He opened the door and saw a man sprawled out on a bed the size of four king beds pushed together.

The room took up about half of the third floor. Two other doors presumably led to a bathroom and walk in closet. Another pair of French doors led to a balcony and another set of stairs led to the rooftop.

Carver didn't care about any of those, but he played it safe and cleared the bathroom and the closet. Once he was certain no one else was present, he studied the man in the bed. The face was a match to the picture in Edgar's file. This was Dalton.

And he was about to have a rude awakening.

CHAPTER 13

Carver had to crawl onto the massive bed to reach the target.

He grabbed Dalton by his silk pajamas and yanked him out of bed. The man was barely awake by the time he hit the floor. He stumbled around in the dark, grasping blindly and trying to get to his feet, but it looked like his legs weren't cooperating.

Carver calmly walked to the light switch and raised his night vision goggles. He flicked on the switch. Dalton grimaced and covered his eyes. He fumbled for the nightstand drawer. Carver shoved him back on the bed and put the muzzle of his Sig on Dalton's forehead.

"Wake up sleepyhead."

Dalton rubbed his eyes. His mouth fell open. "You're that Chad guy!"

"Yeah. I didn't like that you tried to have me killed."

Dalton shivered then seemed to take control of his emotions. "Okay before you pull that trigger, I just want you to know that I'm not the one who ordered the hits."

"I know. You're just the middleman. The facilitator." Carver opened the nightstand and pulled out a gold-plated Desert Eagle. He wrinkled his nose. "What were you going to do with this thing? Break an arm when you pulled the trigger?"

"I-I know how to shoot it. I've done it at the firing range."

"Good for you." Carver holstered his weapon. He popped the magazine out of the large handgun and cleared the chamber. He tossed the gun across the room and threw the magazine and bullet in the other direction.

"I'm sorry, okay?" Dalton tried to firm up his voice. "I just process orders. I do what I'm told."

"No, you're more than that. You're a high-level information broker who sold out federal agents for a quick buck." Carver shoved everything off the nightstand. The lamp, Dalton's wallet, and other odds and ends clattered on the marble floor. He sat on the edge and stared at Dalton.

Dalton worked his jaw back and forth. "I don't know what you're—"

"I broke into your office and your secret closet," Carver said. "I have the files in my car."

Dalton's mouth dropped open. "Who the hell are you?"

"Normally I wouldn't care about this whole mess." Carver sighed. "The problem is, one of those agents was a friend of mine and now she's most likely dead thanks to you."

"I didn't kill anyone!" Dalton tried to stand but Carver shoved him back down hard. "I didn't even want to sell the information, but my boss paid a lot of money for it and insisted we sell it."

"Selling out your own people for a quick buck is bad for business." Carver pursed his lips. "Is your boss Mr. Plum?"

"Martin Plum, yes, that's him." Dalton spoke rapidly as if mildly relieved that he could pin the crime on someone else. "I told him it was a bad idea, but he gave me no choice!"

"I've seen the video of you recruiting Kim and Peter." Carver smiled smugly and said nothing to let that sink in.

Dalton paled. "Yes but—"

"Let's back up a second." Carver picked up Dalton's wallet from the floor and started going through it. "Who hired you to kill me and the interns?"

"It was an anonymous request paid for in crypto." Dalton cleared his throat uneasily. "Surely you understand that anonymity is something we have built into the system."

"Tell me how the system works."

"In this case it was a physical meetup in a parking deck."

"The one next to Taylor & Barnes?"

Dalton's brow furrowed. "Yeah. The client representative wore a mask to conceal his identity and used a voice disguiser."

"Sounds pretty elaborate. Why not use an encrypted messaging app with VPN tunnels?"

"Because those systems can still be hacked."

Carver had seen Jericho hack several such systems, so he knew it took a lot of time depending on how many VPN tunnels were used. "What's to prevent someone from following the guy?"

"Business ethics," Dalton said with a straight face. "We don't want to know who we're dealing with."

"Makes it easier on the conscience?"

"We need to air-gap our deals, so to speak. Anonymity gives every client peace of mind."

"How many clients purchased the agent list?"

"At least five."

"Even clients from enemy states were allowed to purchase it?"

"Yeah." Dalton's voice sounded dry. "Not my decision. Martin insisted."

"How much per pop?"

"The entire list was a hundred million. Specific lists were ten million each except for the CIA and DEA lists. Those are twenty-five million each."

"Because foreign countries wouldn't care so much about FBI, ATF, and NSA agents."

"Yeah." Dalton swallowed hard. "I can't help you much more than that, but like I said. Martin is the one you want, not me."

"And like I said, I saw the video of you recruiting Kim and Peter."

Dalton licked his lips. "Only at Martin's insistence."

"You're selling him out just like he sold out our agents."

"I just want you to focus on the right target, you know?"

"Yeah." Carver thought it over. "Is he staying in his Georgetown home tonight?"

Dalton blinked rapidly. "How do you know so much?"

"Your buddy, Edgar, had a lot of dirt on your company." Carver shrugged. "That's how I found you. Now, answer the question."

"He's in town."

"What kind of security does he have? Similar to yours?"

"He has two bodyguards who live on premises. No cameras though. He doesn't want records of the people who come visit his home."

Carver nudged him. "Elaborate."

"Lots of politicians from both parties. Important officials from other countries, and all kinds of businesspeople."

Carver picked up Dalton's phone off the floor. There were several missed calls from Martin. "Looks like your boss tried to call you tonight but your phone is on silent."

Dalton gulped. "I always put my phone on silent at night or it would wake me up constantly. I have international clients who call at odd hours."

Carver turned the phone to Dalton so his face would unlock it. He scrolled through the texts. There was nothing but normal text messages from what Carver could tell. A guy like Dalton wouldn't keep anything incriminating on his personal phone. At least not in the vanilla messaging app.

He found Encode, a popular messaging app used by people who valued their privacy. It could be set to delete messages after they were read or at any time intervals after that. He turned the phone to Dalton. "Unlock the app."

Dalton punched in a long code. "I have it set to automatically delete after twenty-four hours."

There were a handful of messages in the inbox. There was nothing about killing interns or anything sinister at all. At least not on the surface. One conversation was with a contact named Sally's Flowers.

Carver read them.

Sally's Flowers: Order received, sir! Your girlfriend and her friends will be very surprised.

Lash Dalton: Thank you. Payment submitted.

Sally's Flowers: Payment received! Delivery confirmation will be sent upon completion sometime tonight.

There were updates from earlier.

Sally's Flowers: First delivery completed.

Sally's Flowers: Second delivery completed.

Carver knew what they meant, especially since there were no other updates after that. The first two deliveries referred to the interns killed by Edgar and his friend.

He exited the app and went to voicemail. There were ten missed calls from Martin Plum but no text messages either in the normal app or Encode. There were two voicemails. Carver opened the first one.

"Lash, call me. We need to talk about a business deal that went south. Call me as soon as you get this." Martin spoke in a rich baritone that normally probably sounded like a radio host. But tonight, the voice was extremely nervous and urgent. Steve's driver must have reached Martin.

There were other missed calls all around the time the driver had seen Steve and the gunman's bodies. When he couldn't reach Dalton, he'd called Martin.

Carver opened the second voicemail sent about fifteen minutes prior. Martin spoke again this time in an angry voice. "Damn it, Lash, you need to answer your phone! I'm coming over right now."

Dalton's eyes went big. "What the hell happened?"

Carver grinned. "Take a guess."

Dalton gulped.

"How do you open the gate?" Carver said.

"What are you going to do?" Dalton said. "You know that I didn't have anything to do with this, right?"

"Yeah, of course. Don't worry, Martin's going to pay."

Dalton sighed in relief. "Thanks, man. Just tell me what to do."

"Open the gate when he arrives. Welcome him inside."

"Sure, you got it. And then can I go?"

Carver shook his head. "You'll need to stay put until I'm done. I don't want to worry about the cops."

"I would never call the cops." That was probably true. He would be far more likely to call in another kill squad.

"Stay on the bed until I tell you to get up." Carver turned up the volume on the phone.

Dalton nodded and sat on the bed.

Carver dimmed the lights and looked through the window at the driveway below. An Aston Martin whipped in front of the gate. Dalton's phone buzzed. A notification asked if he wanted to open the gate. Carver tapped the screen, and the gate slid open.

Once it was open, The Aston Martin sprinted down the driveway and screeched to a stop outside the garage. It was interesting that a man named Martin bought a car named Aston Martin. Or maybe it was just coincidence. Carver didn't plan to ask which it was.

"Okay, let's go greet your friend downstairs." Carver nodded toward the stairs.

Dalton walked down just ahead of Carver. They went to the first floor as the doorbell began ringing rapidly. Martin was apparently in a real tizzy over tonight's events. That was good.

Carver stood behind the door because the open floor design didn't give him anywhere else to hide. He nodded at Dalton. "Let him in. Don't say anything about me being here." He patted his gun. "Just FYI, I'm a real good shot and I have night vision goggles."

Dalton gulped. "I promise I won't do anything, okay?"

"I know."

Dalton opened the door. Martin stormed in past him. "Damn it, Lash, of all the nights I needed you to answer your damned phone!"

Dalton played innocent and left the door open so Carver could stay behind it. "Martin, what's wrong?"

"Everything!" Martin took deep breaths. "We've had screwups before, but not like this."

"I have updates from Edgar. Two deliveries complete."

Martin laughed hollowly. "Yeah, well he didn't finish the job and then he apparently killed Steve and Nick at the meetup."

Dalton gasped. He sounded genuinely shocked probably because he was. "Edgar killed Nick? How in the hell is that possible? That guy was special forces, right?"

"Exactly!" Martin blew out a breath. "Edgar didn't meet at the usual spot. He said he had a flat tire, so Steve agreed to meet behind the Nordstrom. You know the one."

"Yeah," Dalton said.

"Alex hustled them over there and dropped them off so Nick could put a knot on things. When he didn't hear from them for fifteen minutes, he went back over there and found them both dead."

Dalton whistled. "You think Edgar knew?"

"He had to know something," Martin said. "He probably got the drop on them."

Carver hadn't told Dalton that he'd killed Steve and Nick, but he had told him that he'd killed Edgar. It looked like Dalton was starting to put together the missing pieces. Starting to realize Carver was the one who killed their men.

"So, what do we do about it?" Dalton said.

Martin groaned. "It gets worse."

"How could it get worse?"

"I called in Pedro."

"Are you serious?" Dalton sounded genuinely surprised. "They cost a million a pop!"

"I had no choice. Nick was our main guy, you know? We didn't have anyone else available."

"I told you it was a mistake to ace Edgar. He does good work, and he keeps his mouth shut."

"The client insisted that all loose ends be tied up."

"Hold on," Dalton said. "You said things got worse. How?"

"Edgar had his house rigged. They went in and the alarm triggered a gas explosion somehow. I don't know the details, but the cops are all over the place now. There's nothing left but ashes and several heavily armed corpses. Cops are going to know it was a kill squad."

Martin kept whining and complaining about how bad things were, but he didn't say anything useful. Carver finally came out from behind the door.

Martin jumped a foot back and shouted in alarm. "Who the hell are you?"

Carver aimed the Sig at him. "I'm Santa Claus."

Martin's face paled. He looked from Carver to Dalton. "What the hell are you up to, Dalton?"

Dalton raised his hands in surrender. "Nothing, Martin. This man woke me up and put a gun in my face. Then you came over and he told me to play along."

"Son of a bitch!" Martin's face turned red. He was a slim, short man with a small paunch. Probably in his mid-sixties. He looked like the kind of guy that had worked his way to the top but had been there so long that he'd grown comfortable and forgotten where he came from.

"Let's sit down." Carver motioned them into the kitchen. There were some tall iron stools next to the bar. There was a nice set of cutlery in a wooden block. He moved the knives over to the other counter so they wouldn't be a temptation.

He pulled out stools for the two men and patted one of them. "Sit."

Dalton and Martin sat.

Martin's red face began to cool back to pale as he realized all the anger in the world wasn't going to solve things. "Who are you and what do you want?"

Carver pulled out another stool and sat facing them. "Who's the client that wanted the interns dead?"

"I don't know. They're anonymous."

"That's what Dalton said. But here's the problem with that." Carver laid the Sig on the counter next to him. "You're information brokers. You keep dirt on everyone. I got inside Dalton's closet and looked in all his cabinets."

Martin gasped. "What? How did you get inside?"

"Not important. What's important is that I also saw your hidden server room. I saw your cold storage unit. I saw the discarded documents that had already been digitally preserved." Carver watched the men carefully. They were both fiddling nervously with their fingers because he was getting close to something.

Dalton spoke. "What does—"

"Don't talk," Martin said. "I will deal with this."

Carver raised an eyebrow. "So, deal with it. Tell me who the client is. I know you have some idea as to who all your clients are because there's no way in hell you'd risk being busted by an undercover agent."

Martin cleared his throat nervously. "And if I tell you what will you do?"

"Probably nothing right now because it's not my primary focus."

"It's not? Then what is?"

"Let's stick to the matter at hand," Carver said. "Tell me who's behind it and then we'll move on to what I really want to know."

Martin's eyes narrowed. "I remember your face from the dossier. You're Chad."

Carver didn't say anything. He stared at the man and let him keep talking.

Martin seemed to realize Carver wasn't going to respond and continued. "It came to our client's attention that some rich trust fund kid was getting awfully close to interns and staffers who worked very sensitive jobs. It was revealed that this kid was actually a foreign agent working for the SVR."

Carver frowned. "The Russian Foreign Intelligence Service?"

"Yes." Martin seemed very sure of his information. "This individual recruited several other interns to help him plant information that would make it appear as if several US senators and representatives were trading top secret information with Russia."

Carver was confused. "To what ends?"

"Once those congresspeople were voted out, they would be replaced with people sympathetic to Russia." Martin shrugged. "That's the information I was given."

It made little to no sense. "And I'm the supposed recruiter?"

"Yes." Martin raised an eyebrow. "Is it true?"

It wasn't true. Not even close. But it was possible that Carver had been mistaken for someone else who really was a Russian agent. Either way, he wasn't answering Martin's question.

Dalton frowned as if this was the first he'd heard of it. "This guy is a Russian agent? Why didn't you tell me any of this?"

"Because it had nothing to do with you," Martin said.

Carver reached over to the counter and rested a hand on the Sig. "So, who's the client?"

"The client used a proxy to preserve anonymity." Martin sighed like he had bad news. "Our team followed the client proxy after the initial meeting. The proxy, one William Scott, is a professional liaison with no direct link to any particular client, but they watched him leave a yellow rubber duck on top of a trash can."

"Smart," Carver said. "No digital transmissions. No physical meetups."

"Yes. It was a signal that the request had been accepted." Martin blew out a breath. "All the client or his representative had to do was see the signal and leave."

In other words, they had no idea who had ordered the hit on Carver and the interns. At least it confirmed that it had nothing to do with the affair between Evans and Callahan, nor did it have anything to do with the undercover agent list.

But maybe it did. Carver certainly wasn't a Russian agent. Either he'd been mistaken for someone else, or someone had tried to frame him as an SVR agent. In other words, someone was running a psyop in an attempt to kill Carver.

Someone with a lot of power.

CHAPTER 14

Carver was used to being a target.

Maybe Enigma had found out he was in town and wanted him dead. Maybe he'd been close to finding out about the undercover agent list and killing Carver and the interns was a desperate attempt to stop it.

He would find out who and why one day and have a word with them, but today was not that day.

He made sure he had the facts straight. "So, a professional liaison met your people and arranged for the death of five people including yours truly, and the death of Edgar and his partner all to stop a Russian plot against the US government?"

Martin blinked rapidly. "Yes."

"And the rubber ducky on a trashcan was the end of your investigation?"

Martin looked nervously at Dalton. "Our investigation team is excellent. We have cameras and other devices set up around the city to track the anonymous people who contract with us. We watched and followed William Scott for twenty-four hours before initiating the contract and found nothing."

Carver moved his hand away from the Sig. "Understood."

Martin seemed relieved. "I'm glad you do." He clasped his hands together. "So, now that we have satisfied your curiosity, what is it you really want?"

"It's about Skia," Dalton said.

Martin raised both eyebrows. "Skia?" Understanding dawned on his face. "Who are you really?"

"What is Skia?" Carver said.

"It's our internal code name for a set of documents," Martin said. "It means shadow in Greek."

Carver grunted. "That's what you call the undercover agent list?"

Martin nodded. "Yes."

"I need a list of the people who bought those documents. I also want to know who sold them to you."

Martin got the same look on his face a car salesman gets when he's about to make a deal. "What's in it for me?"

Carver patted his gun. "This doesn't make it clear enough for you?"

The other man stiffened as if trying to keep his resolve. "Killing me won't solve anything. You have questions and I have answers. Let's keep this nice and simple. Let's make a deal so we all walk away happy."

"Let me lay things out for you nice and simple." Carver stared him dead in the eyes. "Someone sold you a list of undercover agents. You sold that list to multiple clients. A lot of agents got burned. One of them was a friend of mine and odds are she's dead."

Dalton gulped and opened his mouth to speak, but Carver held up a hand to stop him.

"In my quest to find out what I want to know, I have so far had to put down Edgar and his buddy and your employees Steve and what was his name? Nick?"

Dalton nodded uneasily.

Martin flinched. "You killed Edgar?" He went still as if seeing events in a new light thanks to this information. "You wanted to meet with Steve to question him, but didn't know the meetup spot, so you got him to come to you. That's how you got the drop on Nick."

"More or less," Carver said.

"Who are you?" Martin's hands trembled. "Are you an undercover agent?"

"I was with a dark ops unit called Scion."

Martin's mouth dropped open. "Oh, shit."

Dalton looked confused. "What does that mean?"

Martin recovered and answered. "He was in a unit that was more off the books than black ops. I found out about it too late to profit from the information, unfortunately."

"So, are you undercover or not?" Dalton asked.

"I'm retired." Carver tilted his head slightly as if studying Martin. It was a psychological ploy Rhodes had taught him. To make the other person feel like prey. "Sometimes I come out of retirement when someone pisses me off. This is one of those occasions."

Martin held up his hands. "Our team made a list of buyers but it's on the server. We need to go to the building to get it."

"I think you already know who they are." Carver stood and drew a short knife. "I think with a little persuasion I can get that information from you."

"No! Please!" Martin tried to get off the stool and fell onto the floor. "It's been months since we sold the list, and I only remember a couple of the clients."

"Who?"

"We sold the list to officials in the UAE, Iran, Russia, and a man named Walter Simmons."

Carver slid the knife back into its sheath. "Who is Walter Simmons?"

Dalton answered. "He's an old-school billionaire. Made his money in stocks decades ago."

Carver stared at Martin who was still on the floor. "Get up and sit down."

Martin climbed to his feet. He set the stool upright and sat down. "I swear on my mother's grave that I don't remember the rest."

Carver looked at Dalton. "I thought there were only five clients. He just listed four and claims he can't remember them all."

Dalton held up his hands defensively. "I told you that I was only aware of five."

"There are dozens," Martin said. "Too many to remember. Not all of them cared about being anonymous."

Carver stared him down. "I don't suppose you have that list on your phone?"

Martin shook his head. "No, but I can give you everything at the office. The keys to the kingdom. But first, I need assurances."

"That I won't kill you?"

He nodded. "Yes."

Carver made a show of thinking it over. He worked his jaw back and forth. Went silent for a moment and looked up and to the right as if thinking real hard about it. After a while, he finally nodded. "I think we can make an arrangement."

Martin sagged with relief. "Good. I will give you this information and then we can all go our separate ways. You can get your revenge and do whatever you want after that."

"Agreed." Carver stood and extended a hand.

Martin stood and shook his hand. He managed a smile. "Then it's settled?"

Carver extended his hand to Dalton.

Dalton shook it enthusiastically. "I'll give you whatever you want, man."

"It's settled," Carver said. He holstered his gun. "As long as I get what I want."

"I promise you will." Martin looked toward the door. "Shall we?"

The door was still wide open, and Martin's Aston Martin was visible in the driveway. "That's a coupe. We need something bigger."

"We can take my car," Dalton said.

"Okay." Carver closed the front door. "Lead the way."

"Uh, can I put on some clothes?" Dalton tugged on his silk pajamas.

"Yeah." Carver motioned them upstairs. "Let's go."

They followed Dalton up to his bedroom and into the massive walk-in closet. Suits hung from a rack on one wall. Jeans and casual wear were on another wall. One wall was entirely covered in a huge shoe collection.

Dalton put on jeans, a T-shirt, a jacket, and black sneakers. "Much better."

Carver watched him carefully the entire time. A closet was a good place to hide weapons. If there were weapons inside, Dalton was apparently too scared to make a play for one. That was good.

Carver motioned toward the stairs. "Let's go."

Dalton led them downstairs and outside. He followed a covered walkway toward a large circular driveway in front of a detached four-car garage. Five cars were stuffed into the garage, a McClaren, a Lamborghini Aventador, a couple of foreign cars that Carver didn't recognize, and a Lamborghini SUV.

Carver looked at the two cars he didn't recognize. "What are these?"

"Chinese electric supercars." Dalton grinned. "You can't even buy them in the US, so I imported them myself and got a special dispensation to be able to drive them."

"Must have cost a pretty penny," Carver said.

"Like you wouldn't believe, not to mention all the bribes just to get them through customs."

Dalton opened a metal box and pulled a set of keys from inside. "Let's take the Urus." He walked toward the Lamborghini SUV.

Carver motioned Martin into the front passenger seat and climbed into the back. There wasn't a lot of leg room, so he made Martin slide his seat all the way forward until even Martin's short legs were uncomfortably cramped.

Dalton looked at Carver in the rearview mirror and licked his lips nervously. "Here we go." He started the car. The powerful engine roared to life. The garage door opened, and he backed them out of the garage.

Carver buckled in not because he was safety conscious, but just in case Dalton decided to get cute and crash the car on purpose. Dalton drove nice and steady all the way to the office. He drove to the gated entrance behind the Plum and Associates building and used a remote to open the gate.

The driveway sloped down into an underground garage. It looked large enough to park a hundred cars or so inside but was divided up into spaces reserved for a select few executives. Dalton parked in the one reserved for Martin Plum because it was closest to the entrance.

They got out of the car and Dalton buzzed them in with a security badge. They entered the basement level just below the first floor. There was a single executive elevator that allowed them to bypass the main elevators. That was good because Carver didn't want to deal with the security guard.

Dalton hit the up button. The elevator arrived quickly. He licked his lips nervously like he was contemplating something but pressed the button for the second floor. If he'd been smart, he would have pressed the button for a different floor to make sure Carver actually knew the correct floor for the hidden data room.

They got off and Dalton led them straight to the concealed door to the data center. Apparently, he believed what Carver had told them and wasn't about to test him. It seemed they planned to comply with everything because they wanted to survive.

Once inside the room, Dalton looked at Martin. "I don't have the clearance to pull up the clients." He turned to Carver. "Martin has full access to everything. Mine is limited to only my projects."

Martin bit his lower lip and narrowed his eyes at Dalton. Then he went to a laptop and minimized a scan job the laptop was working on. He clicked on the network drive and entered a password. A long list of folders appeared. They were labeled by year, date, month, and a name.

He scrolled down to the current year and clicked on a folder with the name *Skia* at the end. He opened it and opened a file named *info*. The sellers, Janet Hutch and Peter Kaminsky, were listed at the top. Below that was a much longer list of buyers and their affiliations.

They were divided up by domestic and foreign buyers. Foreign buyers with domestic interests were broken out just above the purely foreign buyers. The domestic list was short and comprised of individual's names.

He clicked on Walter Simmons and pulled up a dossier. The man had a lot of interests and assets. He had a hundred-million dollar yacht and dozens of multi-million-dollar estates all over the world. He spent most of his time at his Seattle, Washington estate and spent a lot of money on environmental lobbying.

Carver clicked the back arrow and went to the next person in the list, Tad Bedford. Bedford made his money on tech. He'd created a PC texting app in the late nineties and sold it for a hundred million just before the big tech crash of the early 2000s. He'd leveraged that to make other internet ventures and diversified his portfolio greatly since then.

He outright owned several large firms that weren't publicly traded, including multiple security and private military companies. He also owned several weapons manufacturing facilities around the world. The man had enough firepower at his disposal to overthrow a small country.

The man had more red flags than a bullfighting convention, so Carver put him at the top of the list. He turned to Martin. "Can you put all of this on a portable drive for me? I don't plan on sitting here for the rest of the night."

"Yes, of course." Martin nodded toward the shelves in the back. The very same shelves that Carver had raided earlier. "I'll need to get one."

"Let's go." Carver escorted him to a shelf. Martin grabbed a small box and a laptop. They went back to the laptop that was connected to the server. Martin plugged the box into the laptop and started the data transfer.

While that was processing, Carver went to the next name in the list. It was another billionaire, this one an American born citizen who spent most of his time in Italy. It didn't look like he'd been to the States in three years according to the dossier. He also had only purchased the ATF and DEA lists. Maybe he made money on drug smuggling.

Inside the dossiers were summaries of the methods by which Martin's team had spied on the individuals and confirmed they were indeed the buyers. They had not been able to discern why the domestic buyers wanted the lists.

The foreign buyers with domestic interests were easy to understand. Most of them were linked to drug trafficking. They'd purchased mostly the CIA and DEA undercover agents lists. They wouldn't have anything to do with Liana.

The foreign buyers almost all purchased the CIA list and nothing else. That narrowed it down to two domestic buyers and one foreign buyer. The foreign buyer who'd purchased all the lists was a billionaire linked to dozens of political organizations.

Many of those organizations had affiliates that operated within the United States. It would take some time to go through all the data thoroughly, so Carver just skimmed while he waited for the download to complete.

He went back to the main directory and looked at the names. One stood out in particular. He opened the folder.

"That doesn't have anything to do with what you want," Martin said.

Carver looked at the files inside. There were high-level computer passcodes for various government agencies inside. There were records of billions of dollars in disbursements to various organizations.

He turned to Martin. "You sold usernames and passwords for government systems to the highest bidders?"

"Yes, but we were sold that information by government employees."

"You really will buy and sell anything, won't you?"

"It's a living."

Carver perused the long list of folders. He searched for his name, for references to Scion and members of his former unit. He got a hit on Jericho, but none on his name. Jericho's dossier was empty aside from a blurry photo and a promise of big money if anyone could get more information.

He searched for Enigma.

Martin's eyes widened. "How do you know about them?"

"We've had a few run-ins." Carver looked at the two results that appeared. "You don't have much on them, do you?"

"No." Martin shook his head vehemently. "We were warned to leave them alone by some very powerful people, so we took their advice."

"Good advice." Carver glanced at the files in the results, but they were several years old. That told him one thing. Enigma had been around for a while.

The data transfer finished. Carver checked the portable hard drive to make sure everything was there. All the lists and supporting files were there, including gigabytes worth of pictures and videos taken by Plum's team when they were cracking their clients' anonymity.

It was impressive, actually. Then again, the company was in the information gathering business and they spent tens of millions of dollars gathering it. It looked like they actively recruited information gatherers of their own and accepted walk-ins like Janet and Peter, the people who'd sold the agent list.

Information was power, especially in DC. There were probably many companies like Plum and Associates. Many of them would have sold the agents list without hesitation. Many might not have done it because they didn't want people to die.

Carver went back to a folder he'd discovered earlier, this one labeled Callahan-Evans. It was all the information Plum had on the affair between the senator and the deputy director of the NSA.

There were a lot of files about staffers and interns in the mix, including an incomplete file about a party boy named Chad. There were no pictures in Chad's file, mainly because Carver had been very careful about allowing any pictures when he was with the staffers.

He copied the file to his hard drive and deleted it permanently from the Plum servers. "Are there backups?"

Martin nodded. "Yes, we have a duplicate data center in the basement that encrypts and makes incremental backups."

"Incremental? As in it only records recent changes?"

Martin nodded. "Yes. There's far too much data for a full backup every night."

"Show me. I want this file completely gone."

Martin pulled up the backup and opened the backup folder. He pressed the delete button. A message appeared.

Warning-this will permanently delete this folder. Proceed?

He clicked *Yes.* The file was gone.

Martin looked nervous. "Does that conclude our business?"

"Yeah." Carver stuffed the hard drive into his backpack.

He had the data he needed. Now he just needed to see if he could put together enough puzzle pieces to find out where Liana had been when her cover had been blown.

And find out who to punish for her death.

CHAPTER 15

Carver had what he needed.

It had been a long night, but finally he could get out of here and rest. There were just a few things to tidy up first.

"I got you this laptop to use with that hard drive." Martin held up the laptop he'd taken from the shelf.

"It's in a standard file format already," Carver said. "I can use any laptop with it."

"Yes, I just thought you might need one to make things easier." Martin held it out to him. "Might as well take it."

Carver booted up the laptop. He plugged in the hard drive. The files came up. He ensured the hard drive wasn't encrypted or password protected. "Looks good."

"See? I told you I'd give you whatever you wanted. We won't call the police for obvious reasons, so you can completely trust that we'll do absolutely nothing to get in your way."

"Thanks." Carver glanced at the laptop settings and saw that the location tracking was enabled for the laptop. He closed the lid and put it in his backpack. "I'll be on my way then. Mind if I borrow the Lamborghini, Dalton?"

Dalton handed him the keys. "Absolutely not. Go crazy, man." He shivered like a man who'd just been given reprieve from a death sentence.

"I'm going to secure you to something before I leave," Carver said. "Better safe than sorry."

"As I said, we won't call the authorities." Martin sighed. "But do whatever makes you feel safe."

Carver pulled plastic cuffs from his backpack. He pointed to one of the shelves. They were large metal units that were bolted to the floor so there was no way the men could drag the shelf away from its moorings. He zipped one of Martin's wrists to the frame and did the same to Dalton.

He made sure the cuffs were nice and tight then walked toward the door. "Behave yourselves, okay?"

"Good luck," Martin said. "I hope you find the justice you're looking for."

"Yeah, good luck." Dalton gave him a thumbs up.

Carver left and closed the concealed door behind him. He put an earbud in his ear and sat down on one of the desks in the abandoned call center.

There was a loud sigh of relief. "Holy crap, I didn't think he was going to let us live," Dalton said.

"His mistake." Martin growled. "He has no idea who he's dealing with."

"Yeah, for a former black ops guy, he's a moron." Dalton laughed. "Once I get free from here, I'll put out a bounty. We can track the guy down and have him brought back."

"No need." Martin chuckled. "That laptop I gave him has location tracking enabled on it. The moment he turns it on, he's a dead man."

Carver had taken several small listening devices when he'd been here earlier. He'd turned one on and left it in the room with the men to see if they said anything useful after they thought he'd left.

"I think I can cut the cuff if I can just reach that hard drive bracket," Dalton said.

"I should have put an RFID tag on the laptop." Martin sighed. "That way we could find him whether the laptop is on or not."

"I have a GPS tracker on my Lambo." Dalton laughed. "If I can get free, we can have someone intercept him."

"I'll also send out a warning to our clients that there was a security breach. If we can't take care of him, then one of them can."

"We don't even know his real name," Dalton said. "I know it's definitely not Chad."

"He was searching for a lot of names on our server. I think one of them was his real name. I think it's Jericho."

"Jericho?" Dalton sounded confused. "That's a strange name. Sounds biblical."

"I think it is." Martin sighed long and loud. "I want that man dead so badly I can taste it."

"He won't survive long. Not with the heat we're about to bring down on him."

Carver listened to the men talk for a good thirty minutes. They didn't talk about anything he didn't already know. They mostly talked about how they were going to kill him. He let them fantasize.

It was almost zero five forty. People were waking up and getting ready for work. It was time to get out of here and vanish back to the carriage house for some rest. Carver opened the concealed door to the data center.

Dalton and Martin looked at him in open-mouthed surprise.

Dalton started shaking. "Why are you back?"

"Sorry, I forgot something." Carver walked to the shelving and picked up the microphone. "Silly me, always leaving bugs behind." He pulled out a spray bottle of fentanyl. "Man, you guys really want me dead."

"No, it was just trash talk," Dalton said. "I swear to God—"

Carver sprayed him in the face. Dalton's words slurred and he slumped.

"Please, no!" Martin struggled against the cuff.

"I noticed the laptop had location tracking enabled, by the way." Carver smiled. "Enjoy your nap." He sprayed Martin in the face. Within seconds, Martin was down and out.

Carver grabbed one of the push carts and cleared all the junk off the top. He cut the cuffs off the two men and piled them onto the cart. He put the cut cuffs in his backpack and looked around to make sure everything was in order.

He wanted to upload the server contents to a cloud service, but since the laptops had no internet connection, he couldn't do that. Taking care of Dalton and Martin would have to suffice.

He'd never planned to let them live. They'd killed some innocent young people for no good reason, and they didn't deserve to keep breathing. It was just a shame they hadn't known who'd paid them for the killings.

Carver pushed the cart to the elevator and took it down to the basement level. He pushed it out to the Lamborghini and dumped the sleeping men into the trunk. He pushed the cart back to the elevator and took it back to the data center. He didn't want to leave any questionable traces.

He drove the Lamborghini back to Dalton's place and took the two men up to Dalton's bedroom. He stripped them and put them face down in the indoor hot tub. Their drugged bodies struggled when they couldn't breathe, but ultimately didn't have the strength to overcome the fentanyl.

He made sure they were dead, then he looked through all of Dalton's things. It didn't take him long to find a drug stash in the closet. There were all kinds of party drugs inside. Everything a guy could want to have a good time, including Rohypnol, also known as roofies.

There were also fentanyl pills. They would tie up the scene perfectly, making it look like Dalton and his boss got high to have some fun and ended up drowning instead. It wasn't a perfect staging, but it would do.

Carver looked for anything else of value in the room. There was some spare cash, some expensive watches and fashion accessories, and a lot of old smartphones in a drawer. Nothing useful.

He also looked for a security room or someplace that was recording the camera footage. He'd been careful to avoid all cameras, but the Lamborghini would have been recorded leaving and arriving. He needed to make sure there was nothing incriminating in the footage.

There was a small room on the second floor where air ducts, internet cables, and other utilities were hidden from sight. The hardwired camera feeds came into a router in the room and fed into a laptop and a storage array.

There was no password on the laptop so he was able to access the feeds. The only footage recorded was when Martin's Aston Martin drove up to the front of the house. The driveway camera and the door camera recorded him. He looked restless and agitated.

The next footage was of Dalton's Lamborghini leaving the house. Carver couldn't be seen in the back seat, at least not clearly. Someone with image enhancing software might be able to see his shadow or the outline of a hand.

Carver was much more visible in the next footage when he drove the Lamborghini back into the garage. His face was obscured because the sun visor was down, and he'd kept his face averted from the camera.

The outer perimeter cameras had captured a few clips of people walking on the sidewalks but that had been much earlier than Carver's arrival. He deleted the two clips of the Lamborghini so it would look like Martin arrived and never left. That would tie up everything nicely.

He left the house and went back through the hole he'd made in the fence. He fastened the bars in place with strips of black duct tape so the hole wouldn't be noticeable until someone took a closer look.

He got in the van and drove back to the carriage house. He took a shower and lay down. It was time to sleep.

Carver woke at ten. He could have slept until noon, but four hours of sleep was good enough. He made eggs and bacon to fill up his empty tank. He also made a lot of coffee because this next part was going to require a lot of reading.

The information Rachel Evans had given him said Liana's last known location was Los Angeles and that she'd infiltrated the Human Liberation Front, a supposed terrorist organization working to create chaos on American soil.

Carver hooked the hard drive from Plum and Associates to his laptop. He turned off the wireless just to be safe and opened the files. He went through the list of people and organizations that purchased the agent list.

He searched for HLF and Human Liberation Front and came up with nothing. They might not have directly purchased the list. They might just be a front for some other organization. In fact, it was almost guaranteed.

Liana's reports said the organization was layered like an onion. HLF was closer to the core than wherever she'd started. It must have been close enough to warrant killing her. Some of the people responsible for that were now dead.

But there were a whole lot more who needed killing.

His phone vibrated. Rachel Evans had sent him a text from her burner phone. There were pictures of two news headlines: *Lobbyists Found Dead in Alley* and *Mystery Man Thwarts Two Murders*. Next to the headlines was a question. *Was this you?*

Carver replied. *No.*

He wanted her out of the loop on his actions. It was better for the both of them to keep as much space between them as possible. The flow of information was a one-way street unless he said otherwise.

It looked like Dalton's and Martin's bodies hadn't been discovered yet. It probably wouldn't take long before someone got worried and went to check on them. Hopefully the cops would chalk up their deaths to drug overdose and drowning but it really didn't matter one way or the other.

Evans replied. *I don't believe you.*

He sent a clear message. *Unless you have more information, let's keep this channel clear.* She didn't respond.

Carver looked through all the files. There was the client and seller list, there were dossiers, and there were countless supporting files like images, videos, and sound recordings. Plum's servers had indexed everything to facilitate searching on their system.

Copying the files to an external hard drive had retained the indexing, but he didn't have the software used to run the searches. The software in question was SQL or *Standard Query Language* with a graphical interface.

Jericho had been the expert on that kind of stuff, but Carver had learned a thing or two during his time with the man. He reconnected to the internet and connected to a VPN service to hide his location and IP address.

He went to a website and downloaded a free version of SQL. There were multiple SQL versions and platforms, but they used most of the same commands, which was why it was called *Standard Query Language.*

He installed the SQL software and then found a free app called Digger that created a graphical interface to construct queries, so he didn't have to type them in manually. The program located the indexed files and constructed a new index. Any of the files with text in them would now be searchable.

The images, video, and audio files were another matter. Jericho had been using advanced AI programs with those kinds of files months before Scion was shut down. Back then only the military had access. These days anyone could use AI for the same thing.

He considered asking Evans for access to the NSA's AI cloud, but decided it was best to leave them out of this. Someone else at the agency would certainly wonder who was processing the files through their servers and why.

There were already tons of services that could transcribe video and audio into searchable text. The problem was paying for the service in a way that wasn't traceable. He found one that accepted crypto payments and paid upfront for a hundred processing hours and ten terabytes of storage just in case.

He started the file uploads. The VPN slowed it down a little, but all the files would be uploaded in a few hours. With that started, he began looking through the image files. Having the NSA's face tracking software would be aces, but he didn't want to use them for the same reason he wanted Rachel Evans out of the loop. They couldn't be trusted.

Liana had once given him access to several NSA websites that were used by agents in the field. The websites allowed anonymous usage without a login because only NSA agents would supposedly know their web addresses.

Carver had made a list of the websites, but he hadn't touched them since Liana helped him track down Paola. Using the websites would give him access to a lot of resources but techs at the NSA would see the jobs and could stop them or refer them to administrators.

He was very interested in the social media tracker. It used public data and facial recognition to find people in social media posts. There were so many people taking pictures and videos everywhere and all the time that it was difficult to completely hide unless you lived in the woods.

He avoided the temptation to use the NSA sites and searched civilian sites for an answer. He found a few social media trackers, but they were basic and meant to be used by influencers.

He changed his search parameters and started looking at software designed for large marketing firms. The social media giants sold access to their information, but only if you went through them. None of them offered direct access to the data because it was their bread and butter.

It looked like he was going to have to resort to a black hat on the dark web to find what he needed. Then he stumbled on a site that looked as if it had just been thrown up recently and not fully finished. It linked to a crowdfunding website for software called Yonder. It was designed to crawl the web and gather public information for marketing purposes.

Carver clicked the link and arrived on a site saying the fundraiser had been disabled for violating the site terms. He went back to the main website and found an email address. He crafted a short email and sent it from one of his many secure email addresses. Then he went back to searching.

The first few video files had finished uploading and were already being transcribed. He went to Digger and ran searches for Human Liberation Front, HLF, Los Angeles, and any other pertinent search terms he could think of.

Three names on the list had Los Angeles addresses. Five names had Los Angeles listed in their dossiers for reasons other than living there. He read the context for those mentions and found nothing related to HLF.

Unless something was mentioned in one of the media files, this was a dead end. One of the people or entities on the buyer list was linked to HLF. They were probably linked to a lot of similar organizations and sent the agent list to all of them.

Carver turned to a public search engine and looked for mentions of HLF. He found several, all related to protests in cities across the US. It looked like they moved around a lot. Los Angeles was just one city they'd been in before moving on to Portland and Seattle. They had protests scheduled in Chicago and then Washington over the next week.

They had a website for donations. They had pictures of their people helping the poor, cleaning up neighborhoods, and even rebuilding houses destroyed by natural disasters. There was no way to know if the people in those pictures actually worked for HLF.

Non-governmental agencies, or NGOs funded by USAID had created tons of fake websites to make it look like the US was doing great deeds in foreign countries while in reality they were destabilizing the local governments either for regime change or so they could swoop in and take control of natural resources.

The HLF website seemed too good to be true, but it was impossible to know without actually investigating the organization itself. Liana's reports told him little to nothing about the HLF because her cover had been compromised shortly after being promoted to that layer of the organization.

There were forms to fill out if a person wanted to volunteer with HLF. Carver filled out a form with the name Sam Pusher. He checked a box that said he was willing to travel to help. He put another check in a box saying he could be available in Chicago and Washington DC.

While he'd been doing that, an email had arrived from Yonder. He opened it and read it.

Thank you for your inquiry. Unfortunately, a court ruled that my software violates fair usage and privacy laws and cannot be used to gather and index information. Big Tech also paid off lawmakers to effectively kill my company. I'm sorry we can't help with your business.
-Jessica

Carver emailed her back and told her to call him. He gave her his burner number. Then he turned to the first transcribed files and ran searches. He came up dry. Jericho made this kind of thing look easy. He knew how and what to look for in a sea of data. He needed someone like that helping him.

Without help, it looked like he was dead in the water.

Chapter 16

Carver kept searching.

He spent an hour trying various search combinations and retried them on the new transcripts as they became available. He was going nowhere fast and getting frustrated. It looked like he'd have to rely mostly on good old-fashioned footwork even if it took him forever.

His phone rang. The number had a California prefix. It was most likely the woman from Yonder calling him. He answered. "Jessica?"

"This is Sam?"

"Yeah. Thanks for calling me."

"Sure, but I don't know what I can do for you. My startup company went belly up and my software is dead."

"Does the software work?"

"It works great, but you can't use it."

"Maybe not for a big marketing campaign. But what if I want to find someone?"

She went silent for a moment. "Why do I feel like this is a trap? Do you work for the government?"

"No."

"Are you lying to me?"

"No." Carver could understand her hesitation. "Can we meet in person?"

"Why?"

"Because I really need your help." Carver let a hint of desperation creep into his voice. "I'm trying to find someone who's missing."

"Oh." She sounded surprised. "Where are you?"

"Washington DC."

"Are you sure you don't work for the government?"

"I promise," Carver said. "Where are you?"

"I lost everything so I'm back to living at my parents' house until I can get back on my feet." She sighed. "It's sad, really."

"Okay, but where is that?"

"Oh, I'm in Austin, Texas."

"If I pay for your flight to DC, will you come meet me?"

"Are you a creep? A serial killer?"

"We'll meet somewhere public, and I'll send you enough money to pay for a return flight."

She blew out a breath. "You're lucky I don't have anything better going on right now or I'd definitely not come."

"Do you have a crypto wallet?"

"Yeah."

"Give me the address."

"Don't you use an app that can transfer US dollars?"

"I prefer it this way," Carver said. "I don't want anyone knowing my business."

"I'm equally creeped out and intrigued." She sighed. "Okay, I'll come meet you and see what's up."

"Thank you."

"I'll email my crypto wallet details. What do you need me to bring?"

"Your software and knowledge." Carver wasn't really sure what else was necessary. "Does it need specialized software?"

"It needs a lot of server space and CPU power. This isn't some light app that you can run on a laptop."

"Is it AI based?"

"No, it's not necessary for what I'm doing." She sighed. "I'd prefer not to talk about this over the phone. I'm a little paranoid."

Carver understood. "Email me your details and I'll send the money. Get the first flight you can and take a rideshare to the address I give you."

"Wouldn't it be better to rent a car?"

"No. If things work out, I'll give you something to drive in the meantime."

"Who are you?"

"I'll let you decide that once we meet."

She blew out a long breath. "I'm equally frightened and intrigued."

"That's a good combination. Thanks for your help." Carver ended the call and sent her the promised information in an email. The balance in his crypto account dipped slightly moments later after she withdrew the money. It looked like she was coming.

She emailed her flight details not long after that. She would arrive early in the evening. Carver stopped searching and started thinking about how he was going to secure the processing power she needed.

The more he thought about it the more he realized he didn't even know what kind of processors she needed. Some processes needed CPUs while others needed GPUs. Crypto mining, for example, was optimal with GPUs or graphics processing units.

GPUs were once primarily for video games and graphical applications but had apparently advanced well beyond standard central processing units or CPUs. Jericho had once schooled him on that kind of thing, but it was far from his specialty. Jessica would just have to tell him what she needed when they met.

He located cloud services that offered space for AI processing and others that offered it for other high-end needs with lots of GPU power. There were no flat pricing options. Everything was charged by processing hours. It was going to get real expensive real fast.

It also lacked anonymity. There were no options to pay with crypto. He would have to use a credit card with a high limit.

He noticed a new email in his inbox. It was outreach from HOI, Human Operations International. He read it.

Sam, we're so glad you reached out to our sister organization HLF. On behalf of all caring people in the world, I want to thank you for volunteering to help our mission to advance human freedom and wellness across the world.

HLF deals with some of our biggest challenges and as such requires a lot of organizational knowledge and training. For that reason, we'd love to welcome you onboard as a member of HOI first so you can get a grass-roots feel for how things work. And if you're up to even greater challenges, then you can be accepted into the elite ranks of HLF.

If you're good with that, please come see us in our regional office located on K-Street. The address is at the bottom.

Thank you!

-Shady Williams

Carver read the name a couple of times before processing it was Shady and not Sadie. Maybe it was a nickname. It didn't much matter. Now he knew where to start if he was going to follow in Liana's footsteps.

He went back through Liana's notes. She'd also joined HOI first, moved from a grunt to a group leader within a month. Her HOI group was strapped to an HLF group during several protests to give the HLF agents camouflage while they firebombed stores, incited looting, and encouraged regular protestors to engage in violence.

Liana wasn't interested in low-level thuggery. She was looking for something else. Something that she didn't explicitly state in her updates. The operational statement only said that she was investigating potential domestic terrorism. Maybe she was looking to link HLF to an international terrorist group so the NSA could move in and sweep them up.

The mission didn't really matter to Carver. What mattered was that HLF operatives had probably killed Liana once they found out she was an undercover agent working for the NSA. The people who'd done that were going to die once he found out who they were.

Carver kept reading through notes and searching through the data from Plum's servers. When he finally came up for air, it was time to go meet Jessica. He drove the minivan to a small dive bar in Potomac West not far from the airport.

He backed into a parking spot with a view of the parking lot entrance and the front door. A silver Altima stopped on the street. A woman got out. The trunk lid popped. She pulled a black carryon suitcase from the back and shut the trunk. The car left.

The woman was five feet, nine inches. She wore a baggy gray sweatsuit that looked right off the rack from a discount store, and a black knit cap pulled down low over her forehead with thick-rimmed glasses just below it. She pulled the suitcase behind her, eyes casting back and forth over the parking lot.

She was obviously nervous. Obviously concerned that the stranger who'd called her here was going to jump her and kidnap her. She patted her side as if reassuring herself that something was there. Probably a concealed handgun.

Carver waited until she was inside then he got out of the van and went in after her. She stood near the bar looking at the dozen or so patrons at the bar and nearby tables. It probably just then occurred to her that she had no idea what Carver looked like.

He came up beside her. Up close he could see Asian features behind the glasses. "Jessica?"

She flinched. Looked up at him. "Holy crap you're big." Her hand touched her side again.

"Got a gun under there?" Carver asked.

She flinched again. "How did you know?"

"Let's get a seat." Carver went to a back corner table well away from the bar. He sat down.

Jessica hadn't moved. She stared at him long and hard before taking a deep breath and coming to join him. She set the suitcase next to the table and sat across from him. "I'm so nervous."

"Did you wear sweatpants and sneakers in case you have to run?"

"Yes."

"Smart." Carver placed his hands on the table. "If you choose to help me, I'll make it worth your while."

"What exactly are you trying to do?"

"A friend of mine went missing. She might be dead already, but I want to use your software to see if she can be located."

"Do you know how many people have contacted me about my software since my startup went belly up?"

"No."

"Zero. You're the first since it all went down months ago." She bit her lower lip. "I'm toxic, okay? I lost investors millions because the gatekeepers with all the power decided that my software infringes on copyright and all kinds of other laws."

"Can't you freely use publicly available information?"

She shook her head. "Just because social media companies make people's private lives public apparently doesn't mean it's freely available for commercial purposes."

"How does it work?"

"It gathers all available public images and videos, and an algorithm indexes the facial patterns. It can then be plugged into all kinds of other software for various uses. It basically takes image searching to the next level." She sighed. "The big companies tried to buy me out, but I wanted my own company, you know? I didn't want to become a cog in a giant corporate machine."

"So, the core intent of the software isn't for facial recognition searches?"

"At first it was, but then I realized it could be used for more accurate image searches, it could discern AI generated images from real pictures, it could detect image alterations, and more." Jessica tapped her fingernails on the table. "Like I said, my algorithms massively improve upon image and video indexing."

"So, if my friend is in any public social media posts, your software can find her?"

"Yes." She leaned forward and looked him in the eyes. "Your request is far too specific for you to be some random kidnapper. At least that's why my intuition tells me."

"I can promise you that you will be safe and well compensated. But you will also have to turn off your cell phone and not use it at all while you're doing this. It's possible that you're on a watch list because of the software you created."

"I was put on notice by the FBI that any unlawful use of my software would result in prosecution." She blew out a breath. "They wiped all my servers and laptops and made me sign an affidavit that all copies of the software were deleted."

"But they weren't."

"Of course not."

A server came over. "Can I get you two something to drink?"

"Sure." Carver ordered a stout beer and Jessica ordered a brand of beer he'd never heard of.

When the server left, Jessica turned back to Carver. "Social media always fascinated me, not because I enjoy using it, but because people trust it with their virtual lives. I became obsessed with learning about every type of social media and what drove people to use it. Then I came up with a lightweight social app that hooked into other social apps and allowed people to cross post to any site they wanted."

"Sounds impressive."

"My dad is a video game designer. I started learning from him at a very young age." She laughed. "Programming is like a native language to me."

The server delivered their beers and set glasses on the table. "Can I get you anything else?"

Carver looked at Jessica. "Want food?"

"Oh, yes, I'm starving!" She ordered a burger and fries.

Carver got the same for himself.

The server took the orders and left.

Carver popped the lid off his beer and drank from the bottle. Jessica's beer came in a can. She poured the amber liquid into her glass and sipped it.

"Okay, so I had a point I was getting to," she said. "I made a lot of experimental apps when I was in high school. My ex-boyfriend stole my source code and took credit for it. He sold it to a mega-corp and got five million dollars for my work."

"Couldn't you prove it was your work?"

"I trusted him with everything." Her gaze went distant. "He knew where I kept everything. He took the source code and erased my originals, so I had nothing. And since I never published most of it to app stores, there was no record of it being mine."

"Didn't he have to pass himself off as an app developer to do all that?"

"He is an app developer. His plan was to skip college and create his own startup company." Jessica stared forlornly at her beer. "His big problem is that he has no creativity. If someone told him what they wanted, he could make it happen, but he wasn't very good at coming up with original ideas or even at improving existing ones."

"If you can't create, then steal."

"Yep." She bared her teeth. "Ironically, he's Chinese."

Carver tilted his head slightly. "American, or straight from China?"

"Second generation Chinese. Overbearing parents, high expectations, emotional damage. All that good stuff."

"You're of Chinese origin too?"

"I'm half Japanese, half Chinese." She shrugged. "Close enough."

"Are his parents proud of him now?"

She laughed half-heartedly. "Yeah. When I told them what he did, they accused me of being jealous and cut off all communications. It was sad, really. I thought they were good people."

"I don't meet many Asians with the name Jessica."

"Yeah, that's the point." She smiled. "My parents wanted me to be a hundred percent American."

The burgers arrived. Jessica took a big bite of hers and spoke with her mouth full. "So, anyway, my whole point with that story is that I don't trust anyone with anything. So I keep multiple copies of my software and hide it. That's how it escaped being destroyed."

"I gathered that." Carver dipped a tater tot in ketchup and ate it. Sometimes he preferred those to fries. "Will you help me?"

Jessica pursed her lips. Nodded. "Sure. I mean, you're big but you get this cute look on your face when you talk about your friend. It's like you really care, you know?"

Carver hadn't realized he'd developed a tell when talking about Liana. "What kind of look do I get?"

"It's like your eyes look a little worried and you press your lips together. Maybe you blame yourself for what happened to her." She shrugged and took another bite of her burger. "It's just a gut feeling."

"Good to know."

She stared at him. "You're one of those guys who doesn't like to show emotion, aren't you? You're like emotionally unavailable and all that?"

"Possibly." Carver sipped his beer. "What kind of hardware do we need?"

She blew out a breath. "That's the hard part. My software doesn't require a lot of space, but the indexes do."

"Terabytes?"

"Minimum. Petabytes preferably." Jessica leaned forward on her elbows. She took off her glasses and set them aside. "My algorithm converts images and videos into matrixes, so they take up much less space but are still programmatically identical for indexing."

"I don't really need to know the nuts and bolts," Carver said. "I just need it to work. What kind of processing power do you need?"

"Depends on how fast you need it to work." She nibbled on a French fry. "An optimal setup would utilize multiple CPUs with sixty-four gigs of dedicated RAM per processor, NVME solid state hard drive arrays, and a GPU maxed out with thirty-two gigs of RAM. It would be best to have multiple machines running in arrays so they could download and convert millions of images in a day."

Carver understood the specs, but he wasn't sure where he was going to find that kind of computing power in a short period of time.

Jessica snapped her fingers. "Oh, and obviously we need a five-gigabit internet connection minimum. Ten gigabits would be optimal."

"Do you have any idea where to get that kind of connection?" Carver said.

"Datacenters have all of that. The problem is, once we start downloading all that data, they'll probably flag our servers for a closer look to see what we're downloading."

"What if we set up under the pretext of being a video service website?"

"Yeah, that could work."

"Okay, I'll need to think this over."

"The reason the requirements are so high is because we're starting from scratch." Jessica looked at the remnants of her burger. "My old servers had two petabytes of indexes and were only adding new information."

"Can we limit downloads geographically?"

Her forehead pinched. "Yeah, we could geofence the downloads with the locational information stored in the media." She dipped her burger in ketchup. "That's their dirty little secret, you know? They say they don't always collect locational data, but they do. The smartphones imprint everything with a timestamp and locational stamp."

"That's why I stick to burner phones," Carver said.

"Depending on how specifically we geofence the downloads, we could get results much faster, if your friend left a digital footprint somewhere." She smiled wanly. "If she did, then we'll find her."

Carver noticed when his lips pressed together. He felt the fleeting sadness that cut through him when he thought about finding Liana.

"You just did it again," Jessica said. "That sad look."

"Yeah." Carver clenched a fist under the table. He was sad, but some people were about to get a whole lot sadder when he tracked them down.

CHAPTER 17

Carver drove them back to the carriage house.

He considered putting a bag over Jessica's head so she couldn't see where they were going, but didn't want to give her any reasons to run. Plus, she'd be able to figure out where they were once she got her hands on a computer. He still didn't know how he was going to find the processing power or the internet speeds that she needed.

At the very least he could put her to work helping him search the material from Plum and Associates. Maybe that would be enough to pinpoint Liana's last known location or at least get close to it.

She looked at his collection of cars when they arrived. "You don't have much taste in vehicles, do you?"

"I like to keep a low profile."

"But you live in a mansion?"

"I live in the carriage house."

"Oh." She shrugged. "How's the rent?"

"Very reasonable." He took her upstairs and took her to the second bedroom. "This is where you're staying."

She looked across the hall at the other bedroom. "You're in there?"

"Yep."

Jessica shivered. "That's a little weird, but I guess I can deal."

"It's a small place. I can sleep downstairs if that makes you more comfortable."

"No." She waved off the objection. "It's fine. If you had bad intentions, I think I would have already found out."

"Meet me in the den when you're settled in." Carver walked down the hallway to the table with the laptop.

She followed him. "I'm good. Show me what you've got."

He motioned for her to sit in front of the laptop and took the chair next to it. "I hooked it up to SQL and indexed the files. I also had the audio and video files transcribed so I could search the text."

"Did you want to search the image files for your friend?"

"Not exactly."

Jessica looked through the folders and frowned. She pulled up Liana's NSA files. "What in the hell is this?"

"There are a few things I haven't told you."

Jessica opened file after file. Her mouth dropped open. "How did you get these files?" She jumped up from her chair. "Are you a spy?"

"No." Carver went to the fridge and got a beer. "You want one?"

"How can you be so calm?" Jessica backed toward the door. "You have top secret files on your laptop! NSA files!"

"Because my friend works for the NSA."

She blinked rapidly. "What? Then why aren't they looking for her?"

"Long story." He motioned toward her chair. "I'll give you a summary."

Jessica hesitated. "I'll have a beer. Maybe shots of something stronger if you have it."

"No hard liquor, sorry." Carver popped the lid off a beer and gave it to her. "I don't have that brand you ordered at the bar."

"It's fine." She sipped the stout. "Hmm, this is actually not bad." She sat down and gave him an angry look. "Now I know why you didn't tell me very much at the bar."

Carver sat across from her. "It all started when I was trying to find another friend, a woman named Paola." He told her how he'd met Liana. How they'd initially been on opposite sides and soon became allies out of necessity.

He told her how they'd ended up becoming roommates in western North Carolina since Liana couldn't go back to work for the NSA and Carver needed to lie low for a while. They'd become friends over the next several months, getting used to each other's company until Liana had a chance to return to the NSA.

"According to Rachel Evans, Liana was welcomed back with open arms. They even put her on undercover assignment to track down an extremist group." Carver finished his beer and went to the fridge for another. "Then someone sold a list of undercover agents to Plum and Associates. They sold it to multiple organizations. Hundreds of agents got burned. Some got out before anything happened, but others weren't so lucky. Many were confirmed either dead or missing, and Liana is one of them."

Jessica's fists clenched. She pounded the table. "This is outrageous! How can the NSA not know where she is? Why haven't they sent in the troops to rescue their own agents?"

"According to Evans, everything is in chaos right now thanks to the leak and they're low on resources." Carver shrugged. "I don't know what's true. I just know that I'm going to find everyone responsible and make them pay."

She gulped her beer and set it down. "So, you think by using facial recognition we can track Liana's last known locations? Maybe get lucky and find social media posts that get us close to the people who probably killed her?"

"Yeah."

"I'm all in, okay? I can't stand corruption or bullies or people who stab you in the back and it sounds like all of those kinds of people are involved in this." Jessica took off her beanie. Black hair spilled down her back. She rubbed her forehead. "We still need serious processing power to make it happen. I don't know what I can do about that."

Telling the story to Jessica had given Carver an idea. "If I can get you access to a computer system, how long will it take you to get your software up and running?"

"I need to copy the files to a server and that's it. If there are multiple servers, I'd need to copy the files to each server and then link them to run in parallel."

"How big are your files?"

"Under a gig. It'd take a couple of minutes to copy from a portable hard drive."

Carver nodded. "Do you have the software with you?"

"No, but I can download it from one of my cold storage units." She tossed her empty beer bottle into the trashcan. "I'd prefer not to have it on my person unless and until we have servers to run it."

"If I get you access to such servers, could you install a backdoor or software to access it remotely?"

"Yeah, that's easy peasy." Jessica pinched the bridge of her nose and yawned. "What do you have in mind?"

Carver got up and went to his backpack. He opened it and pulled out what he'd taken from Dalton's place. Among the items was a security badge. "I know just the place, but the big problem is the internet connection."

She picked up the card. "Plum and Associates? The same place that sold the agent list?"

"Yeah." Carver hadn't told her about his recent activities. She might get nervous if she knew the current body count. "They have servers where they keep files in cold storage. Files on their clients, on information they've sold over the years, and more. I downloaded everything about the people who bought the agent list, but I haven't found anything useful in it."

"They don't have an internet connection?"

He shook his head. "They're air gapped for security."

"The building must have an internet connection. Was there another server room?"

"I didn't see another one."

She pursed her lips. "Did you notice network switches or bundles of ethernet cables anywhere?"

"There were switches mounted at the top of the rack. Everything else was servers and storage."

"Okay, so the servers are networked together." Jessica drummed her fingers on the table. "I'd need to look at it." She looked at Dalton's company badge. "Do I want to know how you got that?"

"Probably not." Carver checked the time. It was just past twenty-two hundred. "Do you want to come check out the servers with me or would you prefer to watch remotely?"

She stared blankly at him. "Is it dangerous?"

"Not if this security badge still works."

"Why wouldn't it work?"

Carver checked the local news on his phone. The stories about Steve and Edgar were still front page. There was nothing about Lash Dalton and Martin Plum. It was possible no one had gone to Dalton's residence to look for them.

Others at the company might think the pair were lying low because of the carnage of the past twenty-four hours. They'd lost Steve, Nick, and an entire kill squad in the space of an evening, not to mention two hired fixers.

Carver thought back to what Plum told Dalton. Nick, the guy who was supposed to kill Edgar first, had been their main guy. They didn't have anyone else. They'd hired Pedro's crew for a million bucks to take out Edgar at home and they'd promptly blown up after setting off the alarm.

With Nick dead, Plum and Associates no longer had a dedicated security crew. A crew that did whatever was needed in times of crisis. Now they just had a vanilla security guard and whatever high-level executives were left.

Those executives were probably waiting for Martin Plum to tell them what to do. They were probably huddled up somewhere doing nothing because no one could contact Martin Plum. Not unless they could talk to ghosts.

Plum seemed like a real hands-on kind of guy. The kind who gave all the orders. Without him barking orders, no one else would know what to do. In other words, Plum and Associates was virtually unguarded.

Jessica walked around the table to look at Carver's phone screen. She gasped and took his phone. Scrolled through the stories. "Wow, that's a lot of dead people." She looked from the phone to Carver and back at the phone.

She dropped the phone and backed up, eyes wide. "When you said you'd make them pay, you didn't mean sending them to jail, did you?"

Carver caught the phone before it hit the floor. "No." He set the phone on the table. "If you want to leave, I understand."

She gulped. "You'd just let me leave or would you shoot me in the back?"

"I won't harm you. You're free to go anytime."

Jessica ran a hand through her hair. She said something in Japanese and shook her head. "I must be crazy because I'm not running."

"Maybe this is preferrable to living at home with two disappointed Asian parents."

A full-throated laugh burst from her mouth. She clapped a hand over her mouth as if surprised by it. She went to the refrigerator and opened it. "You mind if we get some sake? I need something lighter than beer."

"Whatever you want."

Jessica sat down and peered into Carver's eyes. "I should be more afraid of you than I am. I think I'm not because I saw how Liana's disappearance affects you. But that was nothing compared to what I saw in your eyes when you talked about Paola. You must really love her."

Carver didn't like that she could read him like a book. "I've developed some weaknesses since becoming a civilian."

"No, that's not weakness." She reached over and put her hand on his. "That's strength."

"Is it?" He pulled his hand back. "It makes me vulnerable."

"Is life worth living if you're incapable of love or feeling something?"

"Yeah." Carver sighed as he thought about the long-gone days of being a beach bum. "I just want to sit on the beach."

"You and me both." She smiled. "So, what happened with Paola?"

"Long story."

"You had something, and it didn't work out?"

"She wants to be a crusader. I don't."

"Did you and Liana ever have anything?"

"No." He leaned back in his chair. "Nothing meaningful."

"But you slept together."

"Let's get back to the matter at hand." Carver tapped the security badge. "Do you need to be there?"

Jessica nodded. "Yeah. I prefer to see everything with my own two eyes. And if we get into trouble, it looks like you can take care of things."

"You'll be safe with me."

"I'm starting to believe that." She smiled. "I mean, if Liana and Paola trusted you, I think I can."

"Good." Carver stood. "I'll get prepped. Be ready to go in an hour."

She stood and saluted. "Yes, sir."

Carver handed her a burner phone. "Use only that. Never turn on your personal phone unless we're somewhere else."

"So, what were you before all of this? An assassin or something?"

"I just played a lot of Call of Duty."

Jessica stared at him. "You just played video games?"

"That was a joke." Carver didn't smile. "I'm going to get ready."

"Not funny." She narrowed her eyes. "You had to be an assassin."

Carver didn't answer. He grabbed his backpack and went down to the garage. He didn't need the grappling hook or any of that this time since he had a security badge. It seemed unlikely that Dalton's security clearance had been revoked yet even if his body had been found.

That didn't mean it wouldn't be revoked tomorrow. That was why it was imperative to get in tonight and set things up, provided they could overcome the lack of an internet connection. He figured Jessica was the expert on that stuff.

He tossed the backpack in the minivan then tossed in the duffel with the climbing gear on the off chance that he needed the grappling hook. Better safe than sorry. He returned upstairs and found Jessica digging through the information on the laptop.

She glanced up at him. "You didn't build the indexes correctly. You also didn't link Digger's API with the connection tool. I'm waiting for it to clean up the data."

"How long will that take?"

"A couple of hours." She stood and stretched.

"Did you bring any dark clothing?"

She looked down at her gray sweats. "No. I came dressed to run if I needed to."

"Are you a fast runner?"

"Probably not faster than you, but I'm pretty nimble."

"Good."

"My parents wanted me to become a gymnast when I was little. I trained up until I was a teenager but I just wasn't good enough to win competitions, so they switched me over to tennis."

Carver wasn't all that interested in hearing her biography, but he let her talk.

"I was pretty decent at tennis, but not good enough." She sighed. "And then I really disappointed them when I graduated salutatorian because I was a few social club credits behind Amy Ling."

"Sounds rough."

"Do you know how much emotional damage I've accrued over the years?"

"I can't imagine." Carver held up a hand to stop her from continuing. "I just wanted to know if you have dark clothes or if we need to get you some."

Jessica blinked. "Oh, yeah. Sorry, I get off on tangents sometimes. I guess we need to get some."

"I'd suggest yoga pants over baggy sweats."

"Sure. I just love my sweats, you know? I'm not big on tight clothing."

"We can get you black sweats if you want."

"Truth be told, wearing yoga pants or shorts just reminds me of my athletic days. It's like a depression trigger." She seemed to mull it over as if it was the most important decision of her life. "But yeah, let's go with something that won't snag easily if we need to make a quick getaway."

"Okay, let's go." Carver headed to the stairs.

"Give me a minute." Jessica stood and looked around. "I really have to pee all of a sudden. Pre mission jitters I think."

"There's a bathroom in your bedroom."

"Okay. I'll be down in a moment."

Carver went down to the garage and sat in the minivan. Jessica came down a moment later.

"I'm so sorry. I got really nervous."

"It's normal." Carver opened the garage door and drove them to an athletic gear store.

Jessica talked the entire way, mostly about how she'd get nervous before competitions and nearly wet her leotard during her horizontal bars routine. Carver let her talk. He couldn't blame her for being nervous about what they were doing tonight.

Jessica went to the clothing racks in the store and picked out a few pairs of yoga pants and cold-weather shirts. She switched outfits in the changing room and came out. "Is this dark enough?"

Carver was surprised by the difference the clothing made. The baggy sweatpants had hidden a muscular lower body. Her upper body was petite but toned. All those years of gymnastics had stuck with her apparently.

He nodded. "Yeah, it's dark enough."

"Good." She pulled off the tags. "I'll just wear it out of the store."

"Okay."

She smiled. "It reminds me of when my parents would get me new shoes, and I could wear those out of the store. It just doesn't feel the same when you're an adult, you know?"

Carver didn't know. He'd never experienced that with his parents. He nodded toward a coat rack. "Get something warm. You're going to need it."

After she chose a jacket, they went to the front and Carver paid for everything. They went back to the minivan and headed toward K Street. Carver parked around the block from the rear gate. They grabbed their backpacks, got out, and walked the rest of the way.

He observed the parking entrance before approaching it. He didn't see any activity, so he walked up to the gate and used Dalton's card. The card reader flashed red and beeped.

It wasn't working.

CHAPTER 18

Carver tried the card again.

The reader did the same thing. It flashed red and the gate didn't open. It looked like they'd already revoked Dalton's access. They must have found the bodies and kept it quiet so the press didn't catch wind of the scandal.

"Let me see that." Jessica took the card and looked it over. She pulled up a flap to reveal a small chip. "Try it now."

Carver tried it. The reader blinked green and the door rolled up. They walked inside. "What did you do?"

"Some badges use foil to block the chip so they can't be read by a cloning device just by getting close to it." She took the card and closed the foil flap. "This way you have to actually get the card if you want to clone the chip."

"Good to know." Carver didn't remember seeing Martin raise a flap on his badge when he'd opened the garage. Probably because he was sitting in the back seat at the time.

"Why are we walking when we could have just parked down here?"

"Because if someone does show up, I don't want them wondering why a minivan is parked in the executive garage."

Jessica nodded. "Oh, good point."

There were no cars inside the parking deck. That was a good sign that only the security guard was here. The badge opened the back door. He looked inside to make sure the security guard wasn't in the hallway, then went past the executive elevator to the stairwell.

They went to the second floor and into the call center. Jessica looked confused but followed Carver closely without comment. He pushed open the rear wall panel. She gasped softly and followed him inside.

He closed the door and Jessica broke her silence. "Are you kidding me? They have a secret room? This is crazy!"

Carver got straight to business and went to one of the laptops. It looked like most of them had finished the jobs from yesterday and were sitting idle. He opened the file viewer and logged in using Martin's account.

Jessica studied the laptops and the files. She looked at the network properties. "Yeah, no internet." She walked over to the server racks and looked at the switches. She walked behind the racks and examined a piece of plywood on the wall with telecommunications equipment on it.

She tapped a white box. "This is a fiber internet modem." She followed thin fiber optics cable to a network device. From there she followed a network cable over to another device. "Okay, so this is the incoming fiber cable and the firewall."

Jessica touched a telephone terminal block. "This feeds the voice over IP phone system which is really old school. These days a lot of companies just use cell phones. It's probably legacy wiring from the call center. They need a fat pipe for voice and data."

Carver let her keep talking. It seemed like she was one of those people who thought out loud.

She wrapped her hand around a thick bundle of ethernet cables. "These fed the phones that used to be in the room outside." She unplugged a cable from a switch and plugged it into her laptop. "We have internet!"

"Is it fast enough?"

Jessica browsed to a website and ran a speed test. "Five gigabits! We're in business!" She held up a hand for a high five.

Carver didn't leave her hanging. He wanted to keep her excited and happy. "Can you connect the servers?"

"Oh yeah, no problem. I just need a long enough ethernet cable." She looked at the cables running into the ceiling and then at the cables running between switches. They were all too short to reach the servers in the racks.

Carver went to the shelves and found a box full of ethernet cables. He pulled out a couple that looked to be ten feet long. "Do these work?"

"Yes, that's great." She opened the doors on the backs of the racks. "Looks like we have to fill fifteen physical ethernet ports if we want to use all the servers."

Carver counted fifteen cables and gave them to her. She unplugged the phone cables from one of the switches and ran the long cables from the switch ports to the backs of the servers. She went to one of the laptops and studied the applications on the desktop.

Jessica opened an app. "They're using Virtuaware. That's good."

Carver was vaguely familiar with the software. "They're running virtual servers?"

"Yes, but they're only running a couple per physical host. Probably because the processing requirements are off the charts for whatever they're doing." She typed as she spoke, often trailing off before completing a full sentence. Nothing of what she said had anything to do with what she was doing.

"My parents never would let me have a pet." She opened a command prompt window and started typing. "Dad said, Jessica, you don't deserve a pet because you got an A minus in English Lit." She blew out a breath. "They could be real monsters, you know?"

She opened an administrative control panel and stopped talking for a moment as she searched for options among the tabs and checkboxes.

Carver watched over her shoulder. She knew what she was doing and adeptly navigated the menus.

"Oh, baby, that's nice." She bit her lower lip. "Damn, these people know how to excite a girl."

Carver looked at the specs. He understood the RAM and hard drive space just fine. Some of the other stuff was beyond him. "Is it good?"

"It's better than good. Did you know that entire rack on the right is nothing but crypto mining hardware?" She laughed. "It's not being used right now which is crazy because the costs of the GPUs alone have to be well over half a million."

"What's the bottom line?" Carver asked.

"Oh, we're in business." She rubbed her hands together. "God, I just want to take you home to meet my parents." She flinched and looked up at Carver. "I'm talking to the hardware, not you."

"I know." He pulled up a chair and sat down. "Can you control the servers remotely?"

"Yeah. I'll place some remote-control software on this laptop and several virtual servers so I have backup." She opened her backpack and pulled out a device with an antenna on it. She turned it on and looked at the screen. "My cellular hotspot is getting two bars. That's good enough to serve as a failsafe in case someone disconnects the hardwires."

"It's not enough bandwidth though, is it?"

"No, this is only so I can remotely connect if the hardwired connections go down for whatever reason." She walked behind the servers and plugged the hotspot into power then tucked it into a space between the phone equipment. "They shouldn't find that."

Jessica got back to work on the laptop. She opened several windows to the virtual servers and copied her software to each of them. After that, she opened a central console on her laptop and linked them together with a graphical interface.

"I'm just going to start it running and we can geofence or narrow the parameters once I confirm it's going."

Carver just nodded. "Do what you've got to do." He let her do her thing and thought about other things. With the internet connection they could copy Plum's entire secret archive onto cloud storage. But that was of secondary value. He needed Jessica's software to have all the bandwidth it needed.

"We're in business." Jessica showed him a console with graphs and numbers. "I throttled back the bandwidth, so it leaves a gigabit open for the rest of the company. I don't want them to wonder why their connection is so slow."

"Good idea." He watched the bandwidth graph. It was leveled out right around four gigabits. "How long for a searchable index?"

"It'll be searchable right away but there won't be much of an index. I can feed it images to search for along the way so that it can do both at the same time."

"Yeah, whatever will speed it up."

"I already fed it the images from Liana's file. Do you have more?"

Carver shook his head. "I'm not much of a photographer."

"You didn't take any selfies with your friend? Nothing?"

"It's better for me if there aren't any images of me floating around out there."

"Yeah, the whole assassin thing, right?"

Carver put back the box of ethernet cables and looked around to make sure everything looked more or less how they'd found it. "Are we good to go?"

"Yeah." She shook her head sadly. "Man, that must suck to have to be so secretive."

"It's better than dying."

"Is it, though?" She pressed a few keys and closed all the virtual server windows. She hid the software console on the laptop and stood up. "Should we wipe this down to get rid of our fingerprints?"

"Yeah." Carver pulled a spray bottle from his backpack and applied a light mist to the keyboard and other things they'd touched. It would dissolve the finger oils that made fingerprints.

Carver opened the door and stepped into the old phone center. He closed the door when Jessica was through, and they headed for the exit. Male voices echoed from the hallway. It sounded like two men having an urgent conversation. They were getting closer.

Carver pulled Jessica behind a cubicle and put a finger on his lips. She trembled and gripped his hand. He looked around the corner and saw two men enter the call center. The first guy wore rumpled clothes beneath a long overcoat. He looked like he'd just crawled out of bed.

The second guy wore black jeans and a matching T-shirt. He looked keen and alert. Carver had a gut feeling the guy was in security. Maybe he was Nick's protégé because he certainly wasn't the security guard from the first floor. Maybe he was the last man standing for the internal security.

The first guy yawned. "Why would he come here? Do you think he's wiping the servers?"

The security guy shook his head. "Phil, all I know is that Lash's badge unlocked the rear gate and the door in the executive garage."

"But his car isn't there." Phil ran a hand down his face. "What the hell is he up to? Why aren't he and Martin answering their phones?"

"I don't know. With Nick gone, I'm the only guy left."

Phil stopped and turned to the other guy. "Scott, we appreciate you keeping it together. I don't know why Martin and Lash decided to go into hiding without telling us anything, but I'm going to give him an earful when I find him."

"Yeah, you should." Scott chuckled. "All hell's broken loose and nobody knows what to do."

The pair went into the server room. They came back out a moment later. Both looked angry and uncertain.

"Damn it!" Phil pounded his fist on a cubicle wall. "What in the hell are they up to? Why would Lash sneak into the building and leave without telling anyone anything? Maybe he just got something from his office."

"They're up to something. Something big." Scott stared grimly at the other man. "We just have to be patient."

"Did anyone go to Lash's house?" Phil said.

"I've been putting out fires all morning with Karen over in the PR department." Scott leaned against a cubicle. "The press is all over this. They're asking a lot of inconvenient questions. Karen is good, but she's afraid of pissing off the boss, you know?"

"Yeah, I know." Phil rubbed a hand on his chin. "I think Lash is at his Georgetown residence. That place is locked down tighter than a nun's crotch, though. Unless he answers his phone and opens the front gate, I can't get in."

"If I get some free time I'll go check it out," Scott said. "But that won't be until later this evening at the earliest."

"I understand. Do what you got to do. I don't like being in charge."

Scott laughed. "Yeah, I don't blame you. I still can't figure out how Edgar killed Steve and Nick and then somehow got aced by one of his targets. It doesn't make sense."

"I mean the guy blew up his house to kill Pedro and his boys." Phil punched the cubicle again. "We never saw it coming."

"Yeah, he was either so good at his job that he killed our guys, or so bad at his job that his target killed him. Something don't line up."

"Last night was just pure chaos." Phil sighed and walked toward the exit. "I'm starting to think Lash and Martin aren't coming out of hiding until all this blows over. They came to get something from the servers. Probably some blackmail that can buy them protection for the storm that's coming."

"Agreed." Scott followed him. "I say we just dig in our heels and wait until the boss decides to let us in on his plan."

"Yeah, good idea. Probably no chance that Lash is going to stay at a known residence, so don't waste your time going over to his place."

"You're probably right. I'll just hold tight for now."

The pair vanished around the corner, their conversation growing fainter by the second.

Jessica stared at Carver. "They think their boss is coming up with a brilliant plan to save them, but he and the other guy's naked bodies are floating face down in a swimming pool."

"That sums it up," Carver said. "Sounds like they won't be discovered for a while either. Not unless Dalton has a maid."

"Dalton?"

"Lash Dalton."

"Ah, yeah." She stared at him. "You're a real sneaky guy. Tricky too. You've got these people running around like chickens with their heads cut off."

"That's usually the goal," Carver said. "Distract them with chaos while you get your work done."

"How long should we wait before we leave?"

Carver stood. "We can go now. Just have to keep an eye out."

Jessica grinned. "Maybe you should use Dalton's keycard somewhere else to really confuse them."

"No need." Carver went to the hallway and looked around the corner. He didn't hear anyone talking, so he proceeded down the corridor to the rear stairwell. He went to the executive garage exit and opened it. There were no cars inside.

It looked like Phil and Scott had taken off. It was no surprise that the security computers kept a record of keycard usage, but it was surprising that the two men had come running to the office not long after Carver had used Dalton's keycard.

They probably had it flagged so the system would alert them the moment it was used because everyone at the company was looking for Martin Plum and Lash Dalton to give them guidance with the company emergency.

Leaving through the garage didn't require using the keycard so they exited the executive parking garage and walked down the street to the minivan.

"That was exciting." Jessica shivered. "I've never done anything crazy like that."

Carver turned the car around and headed back to home base. He figured that even with a best-case scenario Jessica's software wouldn't have any usable information for several days. He'd use that time to investigate HOI starting with going to their regional office on K-Street tomorrow.

"You don't say much," Jessica said. "I guess this kind of thing is old hat for you."

"I'm just thinking about what to do while we wait for results." He stopped at a red light. "Liana was undercover in an organization called Human Liberation Front. I need to know which branch she was at and who she was associated with. Failing that, I need to know who sent the agent list to HLF so they knew Liana was an agent."

"An image search of the existing information probably isn't going to help but I can cross-reference some search terms and see if there's anything that links one of the buyers to HLF." Jessica tapped a finger on her bottom lip. "Is that a government funded NGO?"

"I think so."

"Okay, that's a start. I'll see what I can find."

Carver took them over the bridge and back to the carriage house. It was late and he was tired. "I'm going to bed."

"I'll stay up for a while. I'm absolutely wired right now." Jessica shivered. "I don't know if it's because I was scared half to death or because I'm excited."

"Probably both." Carver went to the bathroom to shower. He'd just stepped under the water when Jessica pounded on his door.

"Hey, I found something!"

Carver turned off the water and wrapped a towel around his waist. He opened the door.

Jessica's eyes widened. "My, what big muscles you have."

"What did you find?"

"Oh, uh, come with me."

Carver followed her to the den.

Jessica pulled up several images side-by-side on the screen. "My real time search found Liana."

He blinked. "Already?"

"Yeah, the real time search doesn't rely on indexing. It analyzes images while down-loading media."

Carver stared at the pictures. They were from social media posts by several different people. Liana was in the background. She was in the middle of a crowded protest. She was dressed in black.

And she was holding a lit Molotov cocktail.

CHAPTER 19

Carver examined the other photos.

Liana was in the background, one person in the middle of a sea of protesters. She was dressed in normal civilian clothing but holding up large signs in three of the pictures. It was the fourth one that stood out because she was clearly about to firebomb something.

"She's pretty," Jessica said. "Is she Latina?"

Carver sat down next to her. "Can we see the context?"

"Yes." Jessica clicked on the Molotov picture. It had been taken at a large protest in Seattle by one of the protestors. There was a series of images featuring a pair of older women. Most were taken in selfie mode.

The one with Liana had also been taken in selfie mode. The photographer had held her phone high above her head to capture it. She was among a group of people dressed in black and wearing skateboard helmets and masks.

It looked like most of the people in Liana's group were men. Liana was shorter, wearing skintight athletic clothing. There were other similar images, but Liana was masked in them. Apparently, she'd only lowered her mask while prepping the Molotov cocktail.

Carver looked through the same woman's other photos. She and her gray-haired lady friends had attended protests in Portland and San Francisco as well. According to their public posts Minneapolis was their next stop. The other images with Liana mirrored the same journey.

"It's a traveling protest," Carver said. He clicked on an image of protestors boarding dozens of buses. "Probably paid for by HLF."

"That's how we find these people," Jessica said. "Follow the money."

"Or follow the protests." Carver had to find the group Liana had been with. He needed to get into that group to find out what happened to her. He examined the pictures for any clue he could possibly find.

"I've linked the hashtags from the images to other pictures from the protests and I've changed the parameters of one server to index only related images, so we should—" Jessica clicked a link. "Ah, found some more."

There were several more pictures of Liana from different angles, all of them from that same moment, or close to it. In one picture she was cocking back her arm to throw the firebomb. In the next few images her arm was forward as if she'd thrown it.

One protestor had recorded a video of the incident. Liana stood in a small group of about ten people. She was the only female among them, that much was obvious from the shapes. Two men were smaller and more effeminate, but most of them were athletic.

One of the men towered over the others in size and stature. He had to be nearly seven feet tall. He wore black cargo pants and a heavy wool overcoat. A black ski mask covered his head and face.

The video started before the firebombs were lit. The audio was loud. People were chanting in time with drums and clapping hands. The person taking the video was also chanting and cheering. He rotated the recording device to show the huge crowds and then stopped when he saw the group of people in black holding Molotov cocktails.

The big man raised a gloved hand and mimicked flicking a cigarette lighter. Liana doubled over, hands going to her face as if sneezing. She raised her mask and looked up and to her left.

One of the shorter men handed her a brown bottle with a stiff cloth in it. There was probably gasoline or kerosene in the bottle even though the original recipe called for alcohol. The short man raised a hand and mimicked pulling down a mask.

Liana wiped her nose and said something, probably related to the sneeze. Maybe she'd gotten snot in her mask. The other man shrugged and lit the fuse on her firebomb. The big man pointed to a strip of old buildings.

They were the kind of buildings usually found in poor neighborhoods. A grocery store, a barber shop, and a used tire store were all right next to each other. An old black man stood in front of the barber shop waving his arms frantically.

The big man threw his firebomb. The others did the same, Liana included. Cheers rose from the protestors. The person taking the video shouted in approval as well. "Hell yeah! Burn it to the ground! Whoo-hoo!"

The big man turned to face Liana, eyes angry behind the ski mask. He yanked her mask down so hard she stumbled forward. He gripped her shirt and pulled her close. Probably shouted at her for raising her mask.

He released her. Raised a hand and chopped it forward. They melted back into the crowd about as well as they could, though the big man was a good head taller than almost anyone else. He must have slumped his shoulders and hunched over to make himself smaller because even he vanished into the crowd a moment later.

Before long, it was impossible to tell who was in the group of firebombers and who wasn't. The recording ended. Carver read the comments associated with the video. Most were positive, cheering on the destruction. A few people claimed it was domestic terrorism and hoped the instigators were found and prosecuted.

He backed up the video and went through it at half speed. He saw a tattoo on the neck of one of the short men. Saw a dark marking on the wrist of the tall man. The video had been taken from too far away to see clearly.

Carver went through the other images. They were all from the same protest called March for Justice in Seattle.

"Here's more." Jessica opened a fresh batch of pictures. "These are from Portland."

There were more images of Liana with her mask raised. She was with the same group of men, judging from the size and shape of their bodies. Several of the pictures had been taken much closer than the video from Seattle.

The short man with the tattoo on his neck was standing next to Liana. It looked like he stood close to her a lot. He might have a crush. His tattoo seemed to be a series of Asian characters.

Jessica laughed. "Oh my God, that's too funny."

"You can read it?"

"Yeah. It says get a job in Japanese." She giggled. "The tattoo artist probably told him it said something else."

Carver saw the dark mark on the big man's wrist. It was a tattoo. He zoomed in. It looked like a curved black dagger with letters or symbols beneath it. The symbols were too blurry to make out. "Can you sharpen those symbols?"

Jessica pressed her lips together. "They're really pixelated and the image is compressed, but I can try." She ran the image through several filters but the symbols under the dagger didn't resolve into anything readable. "Sorry, that's the best I can do. I can upload to an AI filter, but all it can do is make a guess about what it is."

Carver shook his head. "Doesn't matter. The tattoo is enough to help identify him."

"Yeah, as long as it's in a picture somewhere. I'll add it to the search parameters." Jessica cropped the image and uploaded it.

Carver stared at the group. One of those men probably knew what happened to Liana. One of them probably killed her. He was betting the big guy had done it.

He noticed something else. Liana had briefly raised her mask and looked at something just like in the video from Seattle. She was looking at a bank. No, not a bank. The exterior bank cameras.

He went through another batch of images. She did it several times, each time after the group moved to a new location. She would reveal her face to the nearest cameras, probably so the NSA facial recognition software would pick up on her location.

That was smart. It was important, because it meant the NSA might have passively collected data on her movement after she infiltrated HLF. They might have a whole lot more information than Rachel Evans knew.

He picked up his phone and saw a slew of missed texts, all of them from Evans. She wanted to know if he had anything to do with the chaos of last night. He ignored the question and replied with a request.

Run a facial recognition search for Liana.

Evans responded quickly. *I need to know what in the hell happened last night.*

Carver didn't feel obligated to tell her, but he figured it was best to humor her even if it wasn't with the truth. She was a fed and trusting her with the truth about last night would be a mistake. He sent back another text. *Let's meet at the condo and discuss in one hour.*

She replied after a brief pause. *Okay. I'll look into the facial recognition searches and tell you what I find.*

Carver was a little surprised she hadn't pushed back on the time. Then again, he had enough dirt on her to almost guarantee her cooperation.

"What's that about?" Jessica looked curiously at his phone.

"How much do you want to know?"

"All of it?" She frowned. "Or is that dangerous?"

"You're already in deep, so it probably doesn't matter at this point."

"You really enjoy making ominous statements, don't you?"

Carver stood and stretched. He'd been hunched in front of the computer for too long. "I'm going to meet with someone I'm blackmailing at the NSA."

Her mouth dropped open. "How in the hell did you do that?"

"I was looking for a way into the NSA so I could find out what happened to Liana." He leaned against the wall. "I befriended staffers and interns who worked for important people and found out that the new deputy director was having an affair with a senator from across the aisle."

"That's actually really smart." Jessica tapped on the keyboard. "People forget that good old-fashioned human intelligence is the best way to find the best-kept secrets."

"The affair wasn't much of a secret to the staffers, but they were too loyal to let that info leak, at least to the usual sources." Carver grinned and put on his party persona. "Chad totally fooled them, bro."

Jessica's eyes went wide. "How did you do that? You're so serious and quiet and reserved. You definitely don't look like the kind of guy that could put on a show like that."

"Yeah, bro." Carver grinned goofily and scratched his head. "I've got some dope drugs, no cap. If you wanna party, I'm your man."

She laughed. "Chad is the perfect name for that persona."

"Yeah." Carver reverted back to his normal self. "My parents taught me how to slip into other personas when I was a kid. They used me frequently for ops."

"Your parents used you on operations?" Her mouth dropped open. "Holy crap, that's horrible!"

Carver shrugged. "Sometimes it was fun getting to lie to other adults and trying to trick them. But when I wasn't in pretend mode, as they called it, I had to be quiet and respectful."

"You've got some serious issues." Jessica shook her head sadly. "I sure would hate to get on your bad side."

Carver sat back down. "Let's keep looking. I need to find Liana's last known location."

"I've already got more results. Let me plot the data points." Jessica opened a spreadsheet. "This is an index taken from the metadata of the images." She highlighted one column. "These are dates, and the next column is locational data."

Carver sat back and watched her manipulate the data. She did some programming magic, linked the index to a map, and a few clicks later, dots and lines appeared on the map.

She clicked on the dots in San Diego. Dates and coordinates appeared. "The traveling protests started two months ago in southern California." She traced the lines connecting the dots across the state. "The protests worked their way up through large cities in the Midwest."

She opened a website. "According to this, the next destinations will be Chicago and Washington DC."

"There are multiple dates for each city."

"Yeah." Jessica highlighted some dates. "They stage multiple protests in each city before moving to the next one." She tapped the dates. "Although Chicago only has two protests and Washington DC only has one scheduled. You'd think there would be more once they got to Washington."

Carver leaned forward and studied the dots. "Are these just locations where your image search found Liana?"

"No, these are compiled from the social media accounts of the people who went to all the protests." She clicked a few more buttons and several cells highlighted green. "These are the batches with positive IDs on Liana."

Jessica tapped on the keyboard and images appeared next to the dots on the map. Liana was in all of the images. She clicked on the first set of images, and they spread out on the screen in a grid. There were twenty pictures with Liana in the first batch in San Diego.

There were some obvious differences from the later pictures. Carver looked closer. "She's dressed in black, but no mask. She's also not with that group of people from Seattle."

Jessica bit her lower lip. "She must have first joined the protests back then and worked her way into that group we see her with later." Another mouse click arranged the images of Liana from all the protests in chronological order.

Liana seemed to be marching alone during the San Diego protests. It was during the two weeks of Los Angeles protests that things changed. In the last few batches of images, she started hanging out with a group of masked people.

There was an easily recognizable figure next to her in the last few pictures from the LA protests. It was the short guy with the neck tattoo. In one picture, Liana was smiling brightly at him. In another she held his hand raised above their heads as if celebrating victory.

That was her mark. She'd met him. Seduced him into the friendzone. He was the one with connections to the inner circle.

Jessica wrinkled her nose. "Ew, do you think she slept with that guy to work her way in?"

Carver shook his head. "She didn't need to. Men like that will try to please a woman any way they can because they think eventually the woman will sleep with them. Unfortunately for them, they're permanently locked into the friendzone."

She laughed. "You have it all figured out."

"Not really. I've seen a lot of men get worked the same way in my line of business. It's not like the movies where female agents just jump into bed with a guy. They have to build rapport. Make the man work hard for it so it seems completely real when it finally happens."

"Sounds like most regular relationships."

Carver shrugged. "I wouldn't know. Usually, a good female agent will get what she wants before ever having to sleep with the mark. I've seen marks get strung along for years but they never give up because they think they have a chance."

"That's so sad." Jessica sighed. "I can't do relationships because it's too hard for me to trust anyone after what happened to me."

"That's for the best." Carver checked the time. "I've got to go meet my contact. I know this isn't part of the agreement, but I'd like you to come watch my back."

"That's got to be the most ironic ask ever after what I just said about trust." She laughed. "You have to trust me a lot to ask me to watch your back."

"It's in your best interest to help me out."

"So, you don't trust me."

"I trust you to do a job that you enjoy and that's in your own best interest. There's a big difference between a professional and a romantic relationship."

Jessica frowned. "Yeah, that makes sense, but it's still super twisted."

"It is what it is." Carver stood. "You can stay here and work, or you can come and help me avoid an ambush."

"An ambush?" She jumped to her feet. "You think Evans might betray you?"

"It's in her best interest to get rid of me if she can."

Jessica tapped a finger on her bottom lip. "So, you trust her to do what's right for her."

"Exactly."

"It's so weird how this makes perfect sense to me." She sighed. "I guess even romantic relationships are based on self-interest."

"There are other factors in friendships and romantic relationships that make people ignore their own best interests at times." He was still wrapped in a towel, so he went to his room and changed into dark clothing.

He came out of the bedroom and turned to Jessica. "You coming?"

"Yeah, I'm in." She looked around. "Uh, do I need binoculars or something? Or will you wear a bodycam and a wireless mic?"

Carver hadn't actually considered that. He'd planned on asking her to watch the back of the building to make sure there wasn't a squad of NSA agents waiting to storm inside. He gave it some thought. "What I need is advanced warning if she has people coming for me."

Jessica nodded. "That's not really my area of expertise. Also, it's not like the television shows where people can hack into anything with a few strokes of the keyboard. I'm just a software engineer."

"What if you geofenced the streets around the building and indexed social media images?"

She narrowed her eyes. "Yeah, if enough people in the area are taking pictures and posting them publicly, I could. But if they're posting privately, then I have no access."

"Give it a try."

"Sure, but it'll take a few minutes. How much time do you have?"

"Forty minutes."

"Is it far from here?"

"About fifteen minutes."

Jessica closed the laptop. "I can set the new parameters on the way. Maybe by the time we get there I'll have found something."

"Sounds good." Carver went downstairs to the garage and opened the side door of the minivan. He sifted through the items he'd taken from Plum and Associates and pulled out a communications kit.

Inside were several earbuds and bodycams. They used cellular and other wireless technologies for connectivity, so they could be used at any distance. Carver opened one of his burner laptops and paired a body cam and two earbuds.

The image from the bodycam appeared on the screen. He handed Jessica an earbud and spoke into the other one. "Testing."

She nodded. "It works. So, I'll just sit in the van and watch?"

"Probably. The building is gated and there's no back entrance, so unless she drops agents from a helicopter, they've got to come in the front gate even if they're entering the back door."

"Yeah, we wouldn't want them to back door you." She giggled. "Sorry."

Carver zipped the backpack shut and got into the driver's seat. Jessica closed the side door and got into the passenger seat. He opened the garage door and headed for the condos. He parked on the side street with a clear view of the gates. He doubted that Evans would try anything, but he wasn't taking any chances.

It was better to be safe than dead.

CHAPTER 20

Carver scouted the perimeter of the condominium complex.

He strolled around the tall iron fence looking for anything out of the ordinary while Jessica stayed in the minivan and watched the gate. It was nice having another set of eyes. It was nice having someone technologically proficient even if she wasn't a hacker.

He planted bodycams with a wide field of view in strategic locations on the fence as he walked so they could see the area remotely. He liked having high-tech options instead of relying solely on his own two eyes.

There were no suspicious vehicles parked in the vicinity. The only one that drew his attention was a black SUV with black steel rims. It was government issued but it wasn't federal. It probably belonged to a cop. Once he completed the circuit, he returned to the minivan.

Jessica looked up from her laptop. She'd moved to the third row of seats. "You really are paranoid, aren't you?"

"Just thorough." Carver looked at her screen. The cameras he'd planted were watching all sides of the condo building. He saw Evans' black Range Rover approaching from the north. That was where she usually came from.

Although she seemed to be alone, Carver didn't feel at ease. She might have a small army coming behind her. He watched her pull into a parking spot on the road. She pulled on a ballcap and a mask and got out of her car.

"What now?" Jessica asked.

"Wait here." Carver got out of the minivan and came up behind Evans. "Hi."

She shouted and jumped. "You scared the crap out of me!"

He nodded his head to the side. "Come with me."

"Why aren't we meeting in the condo?"

"It's easier to do it this way. More secure."

"It doesn't feel that way."

He walked for a short distance to a bench. He sat down.

Evans hesitated and sat down next to him. "What in the hell happened last night? Two Senate interns were killed along with two apparent hitmen."

"I saw the news. What makes you think I had anything to do with that?"

"Because the timing is too coincidental. I know you used staffers and interns to find out about the affair. I thought maybe you were cleaning up your sources."

"That's not my style." Carver leaned back and crossed his legs to look casual and relaxed to any passersby. "I traced the agent list to the source and got a buyer list. I'm getting closer to finding the last place Liana was alive."

She pretended to inspect her fingernails and kept her voice calm, also making the conversation look casual from a distance. "You found out and didn't tell me?"

"I just found out last night. I still don't know exactly who first sold the list, but I know who sold it to everyone else." He was lying because he knew exactly who sold the list. Telling her would only trigger an investigation that could potentially get in his way, so he'd hold onto that information for now.

Evans pursed her lips and stared at him. "I'm waiting."

"Did you check to see if there are facial recognition searches for Liana?"

She nodded. "You help me, and I help you."

"That's not how this works." Carver made a show of yawning. "I own you."

Evans groaned. "Yes, you own me, but isn't it better to give me crumbs at the very least?"

"That's all I wanted to hear." Carver waited for a man walking a dog to pass by. "It's all related to the undercover agent list."

"The interns were involved?"

"No, but apparently someone thought they were." He looked around. "Plum and Associates were behind the hits."

"Who the hell are Plum and Associates?"

"A lobbying firm."

Evans raised her eyebrows. "Clearly they're more than that."

"They have different departments. One department ties off loose ends and sells state secrets."

"How do I not know this?" She struggled to keep her face calm. "I work at the NSA for God's sake."

"You're a new political appointee. The old guard isn't friendly to you, so they've kept you out of the loop."

"And they got a lot of agents and now interns killed." She blew out a breath. "Who did they sell the list to?"

Carver hoped Jessica was recording everything. He'd forgotten to explicitly tell her to do that. "At least five entities that I'm aware of, but I'm almost certain there are more. A lot more."

Evans clenched her fists. "Who? Give me a name so I can go after them. It'll help my career and then you'll own me even more."

"If I find out, you'll be the first to know. But it's not my priority." Carver watched a black sedan go by. It was too nice to be government owned. "Liana infiltrated HLF. Somehow HLF got the agent list and probably killed her. I want to know who got the list and who gave the order to kill her."

"Well, it sounds like you're getting closer than I am." She sighed. "I feel like I'm fighting against my own agency."

"Because the loyalists are still playing for the other team." Carver shrugged. "I need you to get me the results of the facial recognition search. I'm also going to give you images of some other people to search. I'll upload everything to a secure site and send you the link."

"Why do I get the feeling that you're keeping me out of the loop on a lot of useful information?"

Carver met her gaze. "Because you can't trust your own agency. Get me what I need and I'll do the work, okay?"

"Fine. I'll get you whatever you need." She sighed. "Is there anything I can do that you can't?"

"Follow the money."

"What money?"

"Investigate Plum and Associates. Find out who paid them recently. Trace it back to the source. That's something I can't do."

"Okay. We can certainly comb through their bank accounts, provided I can get a warrant."

Carver stood. "You're with the NSA, an agency that spies on everyone with or without warrants. Don't make excuses. Just do it."

"I'll do my best." She stood and looked toward the condo.

Carver raised an eyebrow. "Did you arrange to meet Callahan?"

She bit her lower lip and looked down. "I told him I'd be in the area if he wanted to meet. He'll be here in an hour."

That didn't surprise Carver. "Contact me the moment you have those facial recognition search results."

"I will." She hurried across the street and entered the condo complex through the pedestrian gate.

Carver went back to the minivan.

Jessica gave him a disgusted look and rolled her eyes. "That woman is married with kids! This is why I don't do relationships. If your significant other gets bored, they'll just cheat on you."

Carver got in the driver's seat. "Did you record any of that?"

Jessica left the third row and slid into the passenger seat. "Of course."

"Good." Carver drove around the block and picked up the bodycams he'd placed. He put them in the case to charge and headed back toward the carriage house. "We need to find clear face shots of the people with Liana. I need to locate those people and have a word with them."

"By a word, do you mean kill them?"

"No. Not right away."

"If they killed your friend, I guess I'm fine with it." She stared at the traffic ahead. "Seems like people get off too easy these days. If you intentionally murder someone, that should be a life sentence. It's like they don't even lock them up anymore. They just release them back on the streets."

"Depends on where it happens."

"Yeah, you're right." She looked back at her laptop and started sorting through images. "I don't know if these people ever showed their faces. I think we're going to have to start with the little guy who had a crush on your friend."

"We have his face?"

"I have a profile picture of his face. It might be enough." She opened another window and moved the image there. "Okay, it's searching indexed images and a real time search."

"What's the last place the search saw Liana?"

"Minneapolis Minnesota." She shivered. "What a nasty place to go missing."

"Nasty?"

Jessica nodded. "Dude, it's freezing up there!"

"Not always." Carver stopped at a red light. He considered catching a flight up north but decided it wouldn't do much good. Liana's body might be buried in a shallow grave somewhere near Minneapolis. It might be in a field hundreds of miles away. He wouldn't know where to look until he tracked down the people in that group.

"Are we going to Minnesota?"

Carver glanced at her. "We?"

She nodded. "Yeah. I'm enjoying this more than I thought I would. I love mysteries and I've been binging tons of murder documentaries lately because I have nothing else to do. So, I guess you could say I'm an expert."

He barked a laugh. "Well, at least you're not squeamish."

"Oh, I'd probably faint if I saw someone die. But if it's a documentary or a movie it doesn't bother me at all." She paused. "Was that a real laugh?"

Carver nodded.

"Wow, I feel honored that you didn't have to fake it for me."

"You have a strange sense of humor." The laugh had caught him off guard, but what she'd said had also been funny. He didn't know why. Maybe because it had to do with killing.

"Can we get lunch somewhere? I'm hungry."

"Yeah. What do you want?"

"I don't know. I didn't think that far ahead." Jessica consulted her burner phone. "You're treating, right?"

"Yeah."

"Okay. How about tacos?"

"Fine by me."

She selected a place, and Carver followed the GPS instructions. They arrived at a seedy looking restaurant that had nearly a thousand five-star reviews.

"Either the food is amazing, or the reviews were all done by bots." Jessica closed her laptop and tucked it under an arm after she got out of the car.

They went inside. A young Latino gave them chips and salsa. Carver ordered five tacos. Jessica ordered the same. The food arrived moments later, and they emptied their plates in short order.

Jessica sipped a glass of horchata. "Wow, that's really good. I could go for a couple more."

"You eat a lot."

"Because I'm all muscle." She patted her leg. "I burn calories fast."

"You still keep in practice?"

"For gymnastics?" She laughed. "No way. I keep flexible and I work out, but gymnastics is really bad on the joints. So, don't expect me to flip-kick a baddie."

"That's disappointing." Carver signaled the waiter to come over.

"I can still do a back flip, but I don't want to break my foot on someone's face."

"That would be a sight to see."

The waiter arrived. Carver ordered a couple more tacos. The ones with cow tongue and cheek. Jessica ordered the same.

"I can sprint for long distances, and I can walk on my hands." Jessica shrugged. "But that doesn't really help me fight bad guys."

"You don't need to fight anyone. Just keep your head down."

"Oh, I plan to." She smiled. "Okay, so how much of this conversation is for real and how much is you play acting?"

"I'm not acting." Carver shrugged. "You're easy to talk to."

"Was Liana easy to talk to?"

He shook his head. "Not at first. She keeps things to herself because of training but she loosened up over time."

"And you definitely had sex, right?"

Carver raised an eyebrow. "Why are you obsessed with that?"

"I'm just nosy. I want to know everything."

Carver sipped his guanabana juice. He thought about the last time he'd seen Liana.

###

Liana and Carver sat at the end of the dock, their fishing lines sitting in the lake. It was a nice day. Mild weather, calm winds, and quiet. Carver popped open another beer and offered it to Liana.

She was staring at her phone, mouth hanging open.

Carver raised an eyebrow. "What's wrong?"

"I'm back in. I just got that secure message I've been waiting for."

"Your contact at the NSA?"

"Yeah." She closed her eyes and breathed a sigh of relief. "Finally." She jumped up and started dancing around "Finally!"

Carver knew this moment might come. She'd been going stir crazy for a while.

Liana stopped dancing and turned toward the house. "I'm leaving right away. No offense, but I can't stay in this damned lake house another minute. I feel like I'm wasting away."

"I'm happy for you." Carver stood. "I can help you pack."

She turned to him. Put a hand on his chest. "Will you survive without me?"

"Yeah." Carver felt a stab of sadness in his gut. He'd gotten used to having her around. For the first time in a while, he felt like he had a friend. Someone he could trust with the small things. Someone he liked that wasn't Paola.

Liana squeezed his hand. "Hey, I'm a little sad too, big guy. But I know we're both bored out of our minds here. Maybe it's time to get back to living instead of existing in this purgatory."

"Well, once you're back, find out if I'm in the clear to go back to the beach."

She laughed. "Definitely."

"Good." Carver reeled in the lines and packed up the cooler. He handed the rods to Liana and carried the cooler back to the house. He left them on the back porch and followed her into the house.

Liana ran upstairs and packed. It didn't take long because she didn't have much. Neither of them had much more than a handful of things because they'd been laying low and tried not to show their faces in town unless absolutely necessary.

They'd only gone to Asheville once in all the time they'd been here. It had been a nice day, and they'd had a good time. But it was too risky exposing their faces to cameras, especially when the NSA might be looking for them.

She came back down with a duffel bag. "Carver, I'm sorry. I feel guilty rushing off like this."

"It's no problem," he said. "If I could have gone back to the beach before now, I would have left immediately too."

She wrapped her arms around his neck and kissed him. "I kind of dreaded being cooped up here with you if I'm being honest. But it was nice pretending to be something I'm not for a while."

"Yeah."

"You're a good guy. Better than I thought you were." She kissed him long and hard. Pulled back. "Just keep on being you, okay?"

"I will." He walked her outside. They'd purchased an old beater car for cash a while back in case they needed more than just the pickup truck. "Need more guns?"

She laughed and patted the Glock holstered on her waist. "One is enough." She stopped and stared into the forest for a moment. "I hope." She got in the old Buick. It started right up.

Carver stood on the front deck and watched her leave. He was going to miss her and that was saying a lot, because the only other person Carver missed was Paola. But he was also happy that she knew exactly what she wanted to do with her life even if he didn't like who she worked for.

Maybe they'd see each other again someday, but most likely, this was it.

###

Knowing that she was probably dead made the memory sting a little more than usual. It had been her choice to go back to the NSA. She'd died doing what she wanted to do. People always said that like it made death better or happier, but it didn't.

Liana had died doing her dream job, but she'd probably died after being tortured for hours or days. Maybe they'd done worse to her. It almost certainly hadn't been a quick and easy death. About the only positive way to spin death was to hope it was painless.

"Bingo!" Jessica spun her laptop around so Carver could see it. "We found the little guy."

Carver looked at the face on the screen. It seemed to match the profile of the man. The size and shape were certainly the same. The tattoo on the neck confirmed it. An image of Liana smiling and radiant as she packed to leave flashed through his mind.

A low growl rumbled deep inside his throat.

Jessica's eyes widened. "I wouldn't want to be Braden Cutler."

"That's his name?"

"Yeah." Jessica stared at him. "Wow. You're angry."

"A little." Carver took a breath and leaned back. "Where is he?"

"The last photo was taken a day ago in Chicago. The traveling protestors arrived two days ago."

Carver felt the urge to get up and leave right then and there. But he forced himself to remain calm and to eat his last tacos. He finished off his guanabana juice and paid the bill in cash.

"I'm going with you," Jessica said.

"You sure you want to? This is getting way beyond the scope of your original reason for coming."

"Yes." She smiled brightly. "Like I said, I dig real murder mysteries, and I'm totally invested in the story. I want to know what happened to Liana too. And I kind of want to see you kick ass."

"You hardly know me. Hanging out with me might be bad for your health."

"If we're keeping it one hundred, I know it's unhealthy being around you." She shrugged. "But it's fun."

"Okay. Let's go." Carver stood. They were leaving for Chicago immediately.

It was time to introduce himself to Braden Cutler.

CHAPTER 21

Carver packed heavy for Chicago.

He brought along all the gear he'd taken from Plum and Associates and all the clothing he'd accumulated over the past few months. It was the most he'd owned in a while since losing everything else to a landslide in western North Carolina.

He still hadn't replaced the bullpup fifty caliber rifle, but he thought about it almost every day. As long as he didn't need to stop an armored vehicle, his other weapons should suffice. He'd stick to his Sig P365, an MP5SD, and M4 carbine.

Jessica stared in awe at the duffel bag with the guns and ammo. "Wow, you're prepared to fight a war."

"I'm prepared to survive." He zipped up the bag and put it in the minivan.

She looked at the other cars in the garage. "Why are we taking this old minivan? Wouldn't that black Suburban be better?"

"The Suburban looks like an undercover police car. I don't want Braden to associate me with cops."

"I mean, I guess you're right."

"The minivan is virtually incognito and the second row folds down into a bed. I can stretch out and sleep on it if I need to."

"Yeah, I guess you're right." She looked at her burner phone. "I plan to sleep most of the eleven hours it takes to get to Chicago."

"Good idea." Carver went back upstairs. He sprayed surfaces with the oil dissolver and wiped them down just in case the homeowners returned and realized someone had been living in the carriage house.

He left the cars. They couldn't be traced to him, and they'd all been wiped down. They would be a mystery to anyone who found them. Depending on how things went, he might never return here, but it was hard to say for sure.

Jessica folded down the second row into a bed and put pillows and sheets on it. She found a bed tray in the kitchen and set it up for her laptop. She also had an inverter that converted the twelve volts from the cigarette lighter into AC power to keep the laptop battery charged.

Carver looked over her setup. "Are you ready?"

"Yep!" She got into the passenger seat. "I'll keep you company for a while, but then I'm retreating to my private chambers."

He chuckled. "You're...different."

She grinned brightly. "Thank you."

It was late in the afternoon when they got on the road. Traffic was already bad on Interstate 270, and it would be dark before much longer. He almost wished he'd taken the black Chevy Suburban so he could flash the lights and make people get out of his way.

He stopped for supper about two hours north of town at a steakhouse. They ate, used the bathroom, and got back on the road.

"I still haven't gotten any hits on the others in that group." Jessica yawned and stretched. "Braden's public pictures seem mostly political. He also seems to openly advocate for violence and political change at any cost."

"Extremists are like that."

"Yeah, but this is pure brain rot." She angled her screen so Carver could see one of his social media posts. "He talks about protecting the environment in one post and then in the next he advocates for torching oil depots to keep refineries from processing it."

"So, he wants to burn crude oil before it's burned by vehicles?" Carver shrugged. "Makes sense to me."

"Then he's got lots of pics of him protesting for women and protecting women's rights but he's clearly doing it to win favor with the women." She made a face. "Simps are just gross."

"Simps?"

"Yeah, guys who try to please women hoping they'll get laid. Except it just turns off women."

Carver listened to her go on about simps and weak men for a while, then she stopped talking and went silent.

"Sorry. I go off on tangents."

"It's fine," Carver said.

"You don't talk about yourself at all. What did you do before all this? You were definitely in the military, that much is obvious."

"I was in the Navy SEALS." Carver didn't want to talk about Scion or what had happened since then. "I got out and retired to the beach. A few things happened since then."

Jessica laughed. "Yeah, I'd say so if you became friends with an NSA agent."

"Things have been complicated for a while." Carver shrugged. "The less you know the better."

She leaned on the armrest and fluttered her eyelashes. "Now I'm really interested. And we have so much time to kill."

"I thought you were going to retire to your private chambers."

"I mean, yeah, but talking to you is a lot more interesting. I want to know more. You never even told me your real name. At least I don't think you did. Carver doesn't sound like it's real."

"Carver is my real last name." He glanced at her and back to the road. "My first name is Amos."

"Amos Carver." She frowned. "Kind of a weird name. Who names their kid Amos these days?"

"My parents told me I was named after my fraternal grandfather."

"What's your middle name?"

"I'm not saying."

She laughed. "Okay. So, how did you get from the SEALS to meeting Liana? What path did Amos take to get here?"

"Just call me Carver."

"I can see why you prefer to be called by your last name. Amos doesn't feel right. Although you kind of remind me of this guy named Amos Hardy."

"Who's that?"

"He's from this really cool TV series I used to watch." She smiled. "He's a real tough guy who will do anything to protect his friends and will kill anyone without remorse because he grew up on the streets."

"Sounds like a decent sort."

Jessica snorted. "Yeah. Kind of sounds like you."

Carver just nodded. He didn't plan on giving her the roadmap of his life.

She watched him in silence for a moment. "I guess you're not going to tell me anything."

"There's no need to. We don't know each other all that well, and I don't like involving people in my personal business. It can be dangerous for them."

"Oh, blah, blah, blah." She rolled her eyes. "You're so dramatic."

"That's me, the drama queen." Carver checked the GPS and saw they still had seven hours to go. "I'll probably stop in a few hours."

"Can we stop sooner? I have to pee."

Carver nodded. "Just say when."

"I don't have to go bad. I'll let you know." Jessica unbuckled her seatbelt and went to the back. "I'm going to relax until then."

Carver nodded and kept driving. He spent the next few hours giving thought to how he was going to introduce himself to Braden Cutler and get into that inner circle. It seemed almost certain that Braden was a useful fool and not a big player. He was almost certainly in the outer layer of the inner circle.

Inner circles almost always consisted of two to three core people. Even their spouses, kids, and other loved ones weren't part of that core group. He felt certain that the big guy who'd yelled at Liana was part of the real inner circle.

Carver had to impress Braden somehow. Get him on his side immediately. The best way to do that was by saving him from a situation. A guy like that enjoyed seeing cops get hurt. Maybe there was a way to create a situation like that.

It all boiled down to resources. Carver might be able to bring Evans into this. She could probably make something like a fake fight with police happen, but it would require making this an official operation. That was the last thing he wanted.

It was best to hire outsiders for the setup. That should be easy enough. He'd outsourced that kind of thing in places all around the world. Surely, he could find something similar in Chicago. He just had to give it some thought.

He'd been in Chicago right before starting this operation. In fact, the person who'd instigated the events of Bickham and Chicago had set him on this path. That path had intersected Jericho, one of the most dangerous people from his past.

He'd had a chance to kill Jericho but hadn't taken it. It wasn't that he liked him, but killing someone so skilled was a huge waste of talent. That didn't mean Jericho would let him live the next time they crossed paths.

It was best to handle this with the kind of help money could buy. He just had to find the right people for the job. That would require finding someone who knew the lay of the land. He knew exactly one person near Chicago who might be able and willing to help him but contacting that person would be risky.

Jessica had grown awfully quiet. He looked in the rearview mirror and saw that she'd fallen asleep. He kept driving until he pulled off at a truck stop a little after zero one hundred hours. He parked on the backside and got out to go to the bathroom.

"Wait." Jessica jumped out of the sliding door. She closed it and ran past him. "Oh, God, I've got to go so bad!"

Carver used the restroom and got back into the van. The third-row seats didn't have space to fold down and make a bed. The passenger seat, however, folded down flat. Carver got into the passenger seat, leaned it all the way back, and closed his eyes.

Jessica climbed into the van a moment later. "Hey, what are you doing?"

"Going to sleep."

"Here? I thought we'd get a hotel somewhere."

"No need. The van is just as good."

"Yeah, but what about a shower? I like to shower before I go to bed. I like to shower in the morning too. I feel icky and gross otherwise."

"You were sleeping just fine a moment ago." Carver looked over at her. "Just deal with it for now, okay?"

She sighed. "Fine. Believe it or not, I used to love camping. Then I got addicted to my creature comforts and have a really hard time forgoing them."

Carver knew the feeling. Civilian life had made him soft until he was forced to adapt to survive. He closed his eyes again.

"Good night," Jessica said. "Can you roll down the window if you pass gas? I don't want to suck down methane fumes."

Carver turned so he could look at her. "You really think of the most obscure things, don't you?"

"Are you saying you don't fart? Because everyone does, even me. But girls are just better at hiding it."

Carver cracked the front windows. "Now all my methane will go outside."

"Thank you." She sighed happily. "Good night."

Carver closed his eyes. He waited a few moments to make sure Jessica didn't have any other concerns, then did his relaxation routine and fell asleep. He woke up right at zero six hundred feeling nice and rested.

He went to the restroom and relieved himself, then got back on the road while Jessica snoozed. Instead of going into Chicago, he detoured south to Bickham. It was risky going there, but he needed local help and figured the reward could outweigh the risk.

A familiar face was sitting behind the receptionist desk when he went inside. She jumped up and lunged for something behind the desk. Carver put up his hands. "I come in peace."

Alicia already had a Sig P365 aimed at him. She lowered it slightly and stared uncertainly at him for a moment. "Peace?"

He nodded. "I need your help."

She blinked a few times before answering. "Are you crazy?"

"Probably."

Jessica walked inside, yawning and stretching. "Where are we? This doesn't look like Chicago." She noticed Alicia. "Wow, you have the prettiest blonde hair." Then she saw the gun and jumped back. "Whoa, what's that about?"

"Who in the hell is that?" Alicia said.

"No one." Carver gave Jessica a warning look. "I just need some help and then I'll be out of your hair."

"With what?"

"That might take a moment to explain."

Alicia sighed. The gun vanished. "Let's get coffee and talk about it." She nodded to the double doors behind her. "Back here."

Carver hesitated. "You're not leading me into a trap are you?"

"Carver, I personally have no ill will toward you. But I'm loyal to Jericho and he's really pissed about what you did to him." She smiled. "He's also happy that you helped us finish the job we did. That said, he'll probably try to kill you if he sees your face."

"Is he here?"

"No, he took the new recruits out west for training exercises."

"Carver, who is this woman? And who is Jericho? And what are we doing here?" Jessica stared at the long white scar down Alicia's cheek. At the large scar on her neck. "And how did you get those scars?"

Alicia stared at her without answering.

"Let's get that coffee," Carver said.

Alicia nodded. "This way." She took them down the corridor to a pair of locked metal doors. She took them through the doors and into the next room. The room had been full of stuff the last time Carver had been here. Now it was almost empty except for a table, a mini refrigerator, and a coffee maker.

Carver went to the coffee machine and took out the used filter. "Jericho cleaned the place out."

"Yeah, he wasn't about to leave anything here or in Chicago now that you know about it."

"Smart move."

Jessica sat at the table and rested her chin on her hands. "Is anyone going to acknowledge that I'm here and completely confused?"

Alicia laughed. "Expect to always be confused with this guy. I used to think Jericho was the master of chaos until Carver came along."

"Thanks," Carver said. He poured bottled water into the coffee machine reservoir and scooped fresh coffee grounds into the filter. He started the machine and let it run.

"Do we have to wait for the coffee before you start talking?" Alicia said. "Because I might just shoot you instead."

"If you shoot him, I won't tell anyone." Jessica yawned. "But make sure I get paid first."

"Paid to do what?" Alicia said.

Jessica smirked. "Well, it involves sexual favors."

Alicia snorted. "Doubtful."

Carver sat down. The smell of fresh coffee filled the air, making him wish he already had a cup of it in front of him. "This relates to Barry, the NSA agent."

Alicia rolled her eyes. "By the way, thanks for leaving him with us. It's a good thing Jericho was able to make a deal with him, or he'd be buried in a shallow grave somewhere."

"He's back at the agency but chained to a desk at some remote outpost in Alaska." Carver had learned that early on when he'd hoped to utilize Barry as his inside man. "His operation was a big failure, so no one cares what he has to say anymore."

"Well, that's great news." Alicia steepled her fingers. "Tell me everything. And by that, I mean everything. Otherwise, you can go stuff a broomstick up your ass."

Jessica snickered to herself.

Carver got up and poured himself a cup of coffee before the entire pot was done brewing.

"Now the rest of the coffee is going to be weak," Alicia said. "Be considerate for God's sake."

Carver put some half and half and sugar in the coffee. He tested it. It was nice and strong but not bitter. He sat down at the table and told her the plain unvarnished story about what had led him to seek out her help.

He told her that he'd recruited the deputy director of the NSA as an asset and was using her and Jessica to find Liana's last known location and last known associates so he could track down every last person responsible for her death.

Alicia downed a cup of coffee and a donut while he spoke. "You sure she's dead?" Alicia asked after he was done.

"What do you think?

Alicia shrugged. "I agree. I just wanted to make sure you're not holding out hope."

"I want to hold out hope, but it's not realistic."

"Yeah." She got up and poured herself another cup of coffee. "I get why she's a friend even if she's a fed. I also know what it's like to lose someone thanks to their cover being blown by a traitor. I'm still loyal to these United States and anyone who betrays the trust of our soldiers or agents deserves to die."

"What exactly do you do?" Jessica asked.

Alicia smirked. "Maybe Carver will tell you."

"Oh, God, you're as bad as he is." Jessica sighed. She was still working on her first cup of coffee. "I know I'm just a lowly civilian, but I'm here to help. I deserve to know everything."

Alicia stared long and hard at Carver. She pressed her lips into a thin line and sighed. "I'll help you get in. All I want in return is to know that you succeeded."

Carver reached a hand over the table. "Deal."

She shook it. "Deal."

Jessica put her hand on top. "Deal."

Alicia glanced sideways at her. "You've got a strange one on your hands."

"She's good at what she does," Carver said. "Real good."

"Maybe Jericho could use her services." Alicia turned to Jessica. "Your software would be really useful."

"Uh, maybe." Jessica frowned. "I still don't know what you and this Jericho guy do."

"Come back after this is done and we'll talk," Alicia said.

Carver was feeling better about his odds of getting into HLF now. Alicia had the resources to pull off his plan.

It was time to put it into motion.

CHAPTER 22

Carver explained his plan.

It was nothing special. Nothing new. It had been done countless times throughout history. Only the methods varied slightly from case to case. It involved gaining the trust of a gatekeeper so they would open the gate, let the agent in, and vouch for them with the others on the inside.

Alicia leaned back and listened. She offered some ideas of her own. "We did something similar to the Bickham police. Once we had an agreement with them it was easy to manipulate them."

"You did what to the police?" Jessica leaned forward. "I've got to hear this."

"Later," Alicia said. She turned to Carver. "Jericho told me about the German operation. Something like that would work."

Carver frowned. "Did Jericho tell you how badly that plan failed?"

She grinned. "Yes. But in this case, I think it would work."

Carver hadn't thought about Germany in a while. Scion had been assigned to help the German government find and deal with extremists. By helping, they meant they wanted the extremists terminated or vanished.

The plan had gone sideways from the start because the target organization was completely misrepresented by the German government. What was framed as a right-wing terrorist organization turned out to be mostly farmers and blue-collar workers.

Jericho's gambit to infiltrate the group had failed miserably because the people in the organization didn't want to use violence to achieve their goals. They wanted to vote out the party in power.

In the case of HLF, however, the target organization was clearly using violence to achieve political goals. Carver nodded. "Yeah, it'll probably work in this scenario. Can you help me set it up?"

"I'll make some calls and hire personnel, but it won't be cheap. You need to figure out when and where to make it happen."

"Are you going to spell out the plan for me?" Jessica looked from Alicia to Carver. "I can help, you know. I can find out the route the protest will take."

Carver nodded. "It's simple. Our target, Braden Cutler, will get in trouble. I'll save him. He'll owe me. We just need to separate him from the herd."

Jessica pursed her lips. "I know how to do that."

Carver raised an eyebrow. "You'll be putting yourself in harm's way. I don't like that."

"You don't?" She grinned. "How chivalrous."

"Because I need you and your software. I don't know how to operate it."

"Oh." Her grin flattened. "If I can find the guy early before his buddies start blowing things up, I can make this work."

"I like that approach," Alicia said. "I can shadow her to make sure it goes smoothly. She'll lead him to the ambush point, and then you do the rest."

Carver nodded. "Okay." He got up and poured himself another cup of coffee. "Let's do this."

Alicia left the room to make some calls. Carver and Jessica searched for information on the protest route. According to city permits, the protestors would gather at the Art Institute of Chicago near East Monroe Street and then take North Michigan Avenue to Wacker Drive where they would follow the loop around downtown and end up back at the same place it began.

"The police will probably block off streets during the protest." Carver pulled up images from previous protests. "The same way they've done it for years."

Jessica turned her laptop screen toward him. "Whenever violence broke out at past protests, the cops formed a line and pushed back with riot shields. I don't see many instances of cops going into the crowd."

"Because there are ten times more protestors than there are cops. Their strength comes from holding the line."

"Okay, so how are we going to do this?"

"That all depends on you."

"Using my feminine wiles to lure him into a trap?"

"Basically, yeah.

"A tale as old as time." She stared at the laptop screen. "I need a new outfit. I want to go in full revolutionary gear."

"Black clothing is fine."

"Yeah, but I want a full-face gasmask, army boots, and a helmet."

"He needs to see your face."

"I can take off the gasmask. It's not that big of a deal."

Carver watched her expression carefully to see if she was being serious. He couldn't tell. "A helmet is probably a good idea in case things go wrong."

"And body armor too?"

"Sure, if it makes you feel safer."

Jessica tapped a finger on her chin. "Nah, it'll be too bulky for what I have in mind. Can you take me clothes shopping?"

"I'd prefer to stay here and nail down a plan."

"Proper attire is part of any good plan." She smiled and fluttered her eyelids. "Come on, Carver, lighten up a little."

Alicia entered the room and sat down. "I've got five guys, uniforms, and a van we can configure however we like."

"Do I know any of them?" Carver said.

"No. These are former CIA guys who freelance. They're expensive, but you have the funds to pay them, right?"

"How much?" Carver asked.

"Fifty grand."

Jessica whistled. "That's a lot of money."

"Manpower isn't cheap, especially when you need specialists." Alicia shrugged. "Do you have a location for me?"

"We'll find the target where the protestors are gathering. Jessica will engage him in conversation and accompany him during the march." Carver traced a finger along the protest route. "We need to separate the target from the group before they start tossing firebombs so I can become part of that group."

Alicia nodded. "I still need a specific location. They can't exactly drive around if the streets are blocked off."

Jessica tapped a finger on the map. "There's a coffee shop right next to this little side street. I can get him to buy me a cup of coffee and then your men can do their thing."

Carver looked at the area in street view. It was a good spot. "That works for me."

Alicia nodded. "If you can get him there, it's perfect. Just don't be too obvious about it, okay? If he's suspicious it's going to derail everything."

"I'll do my best." Jessica turned to Carver. "Can you take me shopping now?"

"Shopping?" Alicia looked confused. "For what?"

"I need proper clothing to tell the world that I'm an anarchist girl who's ready to set the world on fire." Jessica shrugged. "Just wearing black won't cut it. Not for this crowd."

"I'll take you." Alicia wrote down a number and gave it to Carver. "Call this number and talk to Beck. He'll want half up front. He'll also want to nail down the plan precisely. He's a real stickler for details."

Carver took the paper. "Thanks."

Jessica turned to Carver. "Speaking of half up front, can I get a downpayment? I need some shopping money."

Carver stood. "Yeah, it's in the car."

Alicia went to the door. "I'll meet you out front, Jessica."

Carver walked back through the hallway to the lobby and outside. He grabbed a small stack of bills from inside his money bag and gave it to Jessica.

Her eyes grew large. "Wow, this is a lot of money." She took her backpack purse out of the minivan and stuffed the money inside. "I feel like a gangster now."

Carver put a hand on her shoulder. "This is deadly serious business we're about to get into. I want you to understand the potential danger involved. You're a programmer, not a special agent. You don't have to do this."

"Who else is going to lure this guy into an alleyway? Alicia?" Jessica shook her head. "Those scars on her face would just scare off Braden."

"She got those scars because she put herself in danger." Carver took his hand off her shoulder. "You could end up with scars of your own if you're not careful."

Jessica touched her neck about where the large scar was. "It looks like she got her throat cut."

"Shrapnel, probably."

She frowned. "You don't know for sure?"

"It's not my business to ask."

"How can you stand not knowing?" Jessica bit her lower lip. "I guess it's rude to ask."

A black BMW whipped around the corner, Alicia at the wheel. She rolled down the window. "Get in."

Jessica walked around the front of the car and got in.

Alicia looked at Carver. "You're not a bad sort, you know? I kind of wish Jericho didn't want to kill you. We could use someone like you."

"I don't want a boss, especially not someone like Jericho." Carver shrugged. "Retirement is much better."

"Yeah, if you want to wither away and die." She stared at him silently for a moment. "By the way, you can go into Bickham now if you want. Nobody knows your face and since the entire department got wiped out, no one is looking for you."

"The entire department?" Jessica said. "Are you talking about the cops? Are they all dead?" She gasped. "Did you kill them?"

Alicia ignored her.

"What's the aftermath?" Carver said.

"Silence. I think the NSA was too embarrassed to bring in another agency, so they buried everything."

"Good. I like that burger joint in town."

"Yeah, it's pretty good." Alicia rolled up the window and gunned the BMW out of the driveway. The tires screeched as she rounded the corner.

Carver called Beck.

He answered on the second ring. "Village Flowers, how can I help you?"

"This is Carver. Alicia gave me your number."

"Yeah, you ordered a delivery with a singing telegram."

"Yep. Can we meet to discuss?"

"We'll come to you. We know the address."

"How long?"

"An hour and fifteen minutes. We usually come to the back door."

"Okay, see you then." Carver ended the call. He got into the minivan and headed to downtown Bickham. Hopefully it was as safe as Alicia promised.

He arrived downtown. It looked as busy as the last time he'd been there. He drove past the burger place and saw it had a new name. It was called Retro Burgers now and still had the same fifty's aesthetic to it.

He slowed when he saw the two police cars parked in front of the diner. They weren't just any old police cars. One was a Mustang and the other was a Challenger. The cops who'd once used the vehicles were dead. Davidson, Morales, and Palmer had been their names.

A batch of new cops were probably driving them now. Cops who hopefully were nothing like their predecessors. There was a good chance they were clean, not crooked, but he'd reserve judgement for now.

He parallel parked a couple of cars down from the police cruisers and went into the diner. Two cops sat at the bar. They were both young, both Caucasian. Their uniforms were the same black design like before.

Carver sat at a booth in the back. A young man hurried over to him, a bright smile on his face. "Hello, sir! What I can get you today?"

"Burger, fries, vanilla milkshake."

"Coming right up, sir!" He hurried away.

Carver saw a familiar face working the shift. The slim young woman did a doubletake when she saw him. Her eyes grew huge. She just as quickly looked away and smiled at her current customer. She wrote an order down on her pad and went into the kitchen.

She came over to Carver's table a moment later smiling as if everything was good. "It's you!"

Carver nodded. "Best if you pretend not to know me."

"Things are good now. You were right about Sutton and Archer. He and pretty much the entire police force died in a raid gone bad." She giggled almost hysterically. "It was insane!"

Carver said nothing.

"The mayor really took charge after Commissioner Bo died." She shivered. "Did you know he was found murdered behind the police station? They think it was revenge for that raid on the drug house or something."

"Good to hear."

"And I owe you my life. I would have died of starvation or thirst in Sutton's basement if you hadn't found me."

A cook called out, "Order's up, Jen!"

"I have to go. Are you staying in town now?"

"Just passing through."

"Oh." Her smiled faded a little. "Uh, if you stick around, call me." She wrote a number on her order pad, tore off the sheet and gave it to him. "I could use a good man in my life, you know?"

"You're a little young."

"I'm eighteen. A full-grown adult."

"I've got other plans. Sorry."

"Oh, okay." Her smile vanished. "I just need to get out of this town, you know? The pickings are really slim in these parts."

Someone shouted a little louder, "Jen, order is up!"

"Okay, got to go." Flustered, she turned around and almost hit another server in her hurry to get to the order window.

Carver's food arrived. He took his time eating and watched the cops at the bar until they left. They interacted in a friendly manner with everyone. There was none of the authoritarian bullying he'd seen from Sutton, Archer, and the other members of Bickham's finest.

Jen looked at him from time to time but didn't come talk to him anymore. That was good because he didn't want to have to crush her spirit by repeatedly refusing her. She might technically be an adult, but she was still a kid in all the ways that mattered.

He also studied the plan for the upcoming operation while he ate. It was just a small op, but it was important. Once he was on the inside he could hopefully figure out how things had played out with Liana. How she'd been burned, and who had been responsible for it.

Carver dropped cash on the bill and left. By the time he returned to Hope House, it was almost time for his meeting with Beck. He went to the back room and made a pot of coffee. He filled a to-go mug, dumped some creamer and sugar into it and exited via the side doors.

Those doors led into a large garage bay with rollup doors. There were a pair of old ambulances parked on the other side. They were in much better shape than last time. The tires had been flat and dry rotted last time. Now they looked new, and the thick layer of grime on the paint had been washed off.

He went to the rollup doors and pressed the button to raise one. A black Dodge Ram TRX was just pulling onto the rear drive. The driver waved and drove into the garage. The four doors on the crew cab opened and four men got out.

They varied in size. The driver was an unassuming five feet eight inches or so and slim. The two men from the back seat were taller and more muscular. The front passenger was short and stocky.

All four men had graying hair, crows feet around the eyes, a few wrinkles here and there, and decades of experience gazing at him from their eyes. They were all packing sidearms on their waists. All were dressed in jeans, T-shirts and boots. Anyone with two eyes would peg them as retired military.

They would be mostly right. Retired CIA operators weren't quite the same but close enough depending on the career path they'd chosen to get there.

The driver held out a hand. "I'm Beck."

"Carver." Carver shook his hand. He had a firm but not overbearing handshake.

The front passenger shook his hand. "I'm Johnson."

One of the big men from the back seat spoke. "Boucher."

"We call him Water Boy," Johnson said. "Like Bobby Boucher."

The other men chuckled.

Carver didn't get it, but he laughed as if he did. "I'll just call him Boucher."

The last guy shook his hand. "Jonas."

Carver looked around. "I thought there were five of you."

"Ronnie had to go to his kid's birthday party," Beck said. "We can fill him in later."

"That's fine." Carver took them inside to the break room. "I made coffee."

"Thanks." Beck poured himself a cup.

"Doc says I got to cut caffeine from my diet," Boucher said as he poured himself a cup. "Getting old sucks."

Johnson laughed. "Amen to that."

Beck sat down across from Carver. "You're a young fellow."

Carver ignored the comment. He turned on a tablet and displayed the protest route on the map. He dropped a pin at the ambush point. "This is where the target will be." He explained the operation.

"Quick and simple," Beck said. "Maybe we should practice the choreography."

"Sounds good," Carver said. "It needs to look and feel real."

Jonas grunted. "Oh, we can do that no problem."

"Good." Carver zoomed in on the ambush zone. "We have a female lure, a non-com, so we need to take care."

"She'll be safe," Beck said. "We'll extract her nice and smooth."

"Good." Carver explained the rest of the plan. It would require a lot of trickery and some luck, but if they did it right, it'd look extremely convincing and would withstand scrutiny.

It was going to have to stand up to a lot of scrutiny and doubt because the targets had just discovered one of their own was an undercover agent. They would be running low on trust and high on suspicion and doubt.

This had to go off flawlessly and it had to look real after the fact. Because if it didn't, this would be a one-way ticket to an early grave.

CHAPTER 23

Carver took the men to the garage for practice.

They ran and re-ran the routine until they had it down. They made a list of supplies needed to make it look real. They made a list of things to do to make it pass muster after the fact.

Alicia and Jessica returned a few hours later. Alicia greeted Beck warmly. "Good to see you again."

"Always a pleasure, Alicia." Beck looked at Jessica. "You're our lure?"

"Yep, I'm the bait." Jessia pulled a skateboarding helmet out of a bag. It was black with bright green rubber spikes on the top. "Carver, what do you think?"

Carver took it from her and looked it over. "If anyone tries to hit you on the head, it'll keep you safe."

She groaned. "You're no fun."

"He's certainly all business," Beck said. "But that's good. Our goal is to keep you safe."

"And to get paid, right?" Jessica smirked. "I know how things work."

Beck turned to Carver. "How about another run through with the lure?"

Carver nodded. "Yep."

"Can I put on my new outfit?" Jessica said.

"Save it for tomorrow." Carver put the helmet back in the bag. "Let's get the basics down before a dress rehearsal."

"All right." She held out her hands. "Where do you want me?"

Carver led her to the starting point. There were chalk outlines representing the streets and the alley near the coffee shop. "Alicia, can you be the target?"

"Sure." Alicia stood next to Jessica. "How will you seduce him?"

"Well, the outfit should get his attention first. Then I'll start a conversation."

"How?" Alicia said. "What are you going to say?"

"I haven't really thought that far ahead yet."

"Small talk," Alicia said. "That's how you do it. For example, ugh, it's so cold out here! I wish I'd worn a warmer jacket. Or you could pretend to trip and fall into him, then say something like, God, I'm so sorry! I'm such a klutz."

"Sounds like you've done this before," Jessica said.

"Dozens of times. I learned the hard way that it takes practice to make it look natural."

"But like, do men respond favorably?"

"To me?" Alicia raised an eyebrow. "Or in general?"

"Um, you know because of the—" Jessica touched her own throat and face.

"Because of my scars?" Alicia laughed. "Honey, men dig scars."

"Hell yeah," Jonas said.

Johnson laughed. "Calm your tits, Jonas. You don't want none of her."

"She's a dangerous one," Boucher said.

"I like 'em dangerous." Jonas grinned. "But business before pleasure and all that."

Alicia winked at him. "Good idea." She turned back to Jessica. "Men are men. They respond to women. This guy will be putty in your hands as long as it seems genuine."

Jessica nodded. "I get it. And I'm sorry I asked about your scars."

"They're part of me. I have zero shame about them because I earned them protecting my brothers and sisters in arms." Alicia put a hand on Jessica's shoulder. "I could be the lure, but I think the target will respond a lot more favorably to someone closer to his own age."

Jonas smirked. "Kids his age are scared of cougars."

Everyone laughed.

"I can do this." Jessica steeled herself. "Just let me practice a little bit."

"Okay, try it on me," Alicia said. "Show me what you've got."

Jessica walked a short distance away and took a deep breath. "I need you to pretend like you're protesting or throwing firebombs or whatever it is they do."

Alicia pretended to light a Molotov cocktail and throw it.

Jessica raised a fist and shouted, "Yeah, fight the patriarchy!"

Alicia gave her a disbelieving look. "Really?"

Jessica tripped and fell against Alicia's chest. Alicia caught her with both arms.

Jessica looked up at her with big eyes. "God, I'm so clumsy. Thank you!"

Alicia smiled and stood her upright. "You sure you haven't done this before?"

"No comment." Jessica winked.

Jonas chuckled. "That boy is toast."

Beck clapped his hands together. "Okay, let's run it from the top."

They reset. Alicia continued the role of Braden Cutler. Jessica seduced her and kept to the script. After a few run-throughs everyone felt confident they had it down pat. Carver knew from experience that things could change drastically in the real world, so he came up with some alternative scenarios just in case.

"We should go onsite and make sure everything looks like it should," Carver said. "Walk the actual streets."

"Agreed." Beck checked his phone. "Then we can go for some deep-dish pizza."

Jessica wrinkled her nose. "I never liked that pizza style. It's so greasy and gross."

"Neapolitan is the best," Alicia said. "And I know just the place."

Beck shrugged. "As long as you're buying." He turned to Carver. "Speaking of which, we do need our downpayment."

"Crypto or cash?"

"Either."

"Be right back." Carver went to his money bag and pulled out twenty-five thousand dollars. He went back to the garage and gave Beck the stacks.

"Thank you, sir." Beck rifled through the bills, randomly pulling one from the stack to inspect it. "Sorry, but we have to be careful."

Carver nodded. "I'll pull my car around the front."

Jessica wrinkled her nose. "No offense, but I'd rather ride in Alicia's BMW."

Alicia shook her head. "I'm not taking my personal vehicle to the scene. Too many cameras. Speaking of which, we'll need to mask up. I don't want the cops looking back through footage and seeing us."

"We use a pro-privacy website that tracks all camera locations." Beck pulled up the website on the tablet. There was a map populated with red, blue, and green dots. "Red is government, blue is corporate, and green is private."

"Does it include doorbell cams?" Carver said.

"It has everything that's affixed to a building." Beck zoomed in. "It even has direction and field of vision for most of them."

Alicia studied the map. "In this day and age, it's the phone cameras you have to worry about."

Carver liked knowing where the cameras were, but the map made it obvious that they couldn't avoid them all. "I'll be out front in the minivan."

"I'm riding with Beck," Alicia said. "I'll catch a ride back with you since they live near Chicago."

Carver went to the minivan.

Jessica hurried after him and climbed into the passenger seat. She leaned it back a little and sighed. "On the road again."

"Yep." Carver aimed for Chicago and hit the gas.

Jessica opened her laptop and studied the camera tracking website. "I'll bet the NSA has access to all those cameras. I wish I could backdoor them."

"The NSA doesn't have direct access, and they can't monitor every single camera. Even with computers doing the work, they still need to prioritize."

"But how do they have access? Do they need permission or what?"

"There's a patchwork of different systems even among government agencies, so there's no guarantee they have access." Carver shrugged. "That's why it's best to cover your face the best you can without looking suspicious."

They reached Chicago in about an hour and a half. It was just past seventeen hundred hours and traffic was heavy. Carver found a pay parking lot that took cash and texted Alicia to let her know where it was.

Beck's van pulled in a few moments later and parked across the lot from him. They linked up across the street. Everyone wore ballcaps and face masks. The face masks still passed muster in some big cities, so no one gave them a second look.

They walked a few blocks to the Art Institute of Chicago. The place was bustling. The streets were packed with cars, scooters and probably even more people riding bikes. The sidewalks were packed with people just leaving work and hurrying to get home.

Alicia pointed out a restaurant. "That's the authentic Italian pizza place."

"I'm already hungry," Jonas said.

Evan chuckled. "You're always hungry, man."

They walked the route, went to the coffee shop near the ambush point, and inspected the area to make sure it worked as well in practice as in theory. Carver thought it looked ideal for what they had in mind. Alicia agreed.

"Let's run it through a couple of times." Carver walked back out to the main road. "We'll start here."

They rehearsed a few times. None of the passersby batted an eyelash. They were used to people doing unusual things in the big city. Carver tossed in some random problems as they practiced to ensure the fallback plan looked good as well.

As with most plans, it might not survive the first minute. Braden might do something unexpected or take a different route. He might not leave his group to go with Jessica, or he might just ignore her. But the latter seemed unlikely. Jessica was attractive and athletic. She was way out of Braden's league. The only danger was him being smarter than they gave him credit for.

Considering the company that he kept, that also seemed unlikely. He might be in the inner group, but he was a lemming just following the crowd. Like most protestors in this day and age, he was just bored and doing something that made him feel like a hero.

By the time they finished, the rush hour crowds had diminished significantly, leaving behind the people who called this part of town home. They went to the pizza restaurant and got a large table in the back.

The pizza was on par with the best pizza Carver had ever had. He'd had pizza in Naples, Italy, the origin of Neapolitan pizza. This place obviously stuck to the strict rules of making the dough.

Alicia took another slice of the Italian sausage pizza. "What do you think, Jonas?"

Jonas shrugged. "It's good, but I like my crust thick and crunchy."

Evan laughed. "Jonas doesn't like it unless he can taste the grease squeezing out of the bread."

"I think this is the best pizza I've ever had." Jessica took another bite and sighed. "Yep, it's definitely the best."

Carver looked out the window and imagined the large crowds that would fill the streets tomorrow. It was going to be a busy day. A dangerous day. Hopefully in the end, a successful day.

HLF was going to be highly suspicious of anyone trying to infiltrate its ranks. Even if he won Braden's gratitude and help, he might still end up on the outside. That was okay, though. As long as he had his foot in the door, he had a chance.

Carver footed the bill for the pizza. Jonas had eaten an entire pizza by himself which was impressive considering he was lean and muscular even at his age. Afterwards, Beck and his crew went back to their headquarters and Carver drove Alicia and Jessica back to Hope House.

"You can use the staff rooms," Alicia said. "The doors have locks and the rooms have their own bathrooms."

"Do you live here too?" Jessica asked.

"No, I got a house after our big score." Alicia handed them room keys and left.

Carver got his things from the secure room in the back and found the room number that matched the one on the key. He noticed that the ten staff rooms were all empty. It looked like Eddie no longer lived on the premises.

Eddie was the driver and jack of all trades for Hope House. At least he had been a few months back. Maybe things had changed.

"You're in room 1?" Jessica stopped outside room 10. "Why did she give me the one all the way down the hall from yours?"

"She knows I like my privacy." Carver unlocked his door and went inside. The room was about the size of a one-bedroom apartment. The den and kitchen were one room. The bedroom was to the left and the walkthrough bathroom was connected to the hallway and bedroom. It was a nice setup.

He still felt a little leery staying in a place controlled by Alicia and by extension, Jericho. She could probably be trusted, but he was going to play it safe just in case. He put his Sig on the nightstand next to the bed. He tested the window to make sure it opened, and he could climb out of it.

He put a steel wedge under the door so it would be impossible to open without making a lot of noise and set motions sensors to watch the door and the window. If Alicia decided to betray him, he'd at least have a fighting chance.

There was a knock on the door. "Hey, it's me," Jesscia said. "I got another hit on that Braden guy."

Carver opened the door. "With your software?"

"Yeah." She was holding the laptop. "Can I come into your private chambers, good sir?"

Carver backed up and motioned her in.

"You should joke around more often," Jessica said. "Let out all that stick in the mud energy."

"It would just be an act." Carver sat down at the kitchen table. "What have you got?"

She set the laptop down and opened it. The screen came on. There were some new images of Braden Cutler. They were posts from two different social media sources.

Braden was dressed in black fatigues and wearing a helmet. He held a fist overhead and at the top of the image it said, *RESIST! Join the March for Justice tomorrow! Meet in front of the Art Institute of Chicago and make your voice heard!*

"I know it doesn't really add anything, but I figured you'd want to know."

Carver nodded. "It further confirms that he'll be there."

"I also found something else." She winced. "I don't know if you'll like it."

Apprehension stabbed Carver in the gut. "Show me."

Jessica bit her lower lip and pulled up another window. She played a video. It showed large crowds marching through city streets. Buildings burned in the background. The person recording the video rotated it and focused on a group of people in black clothing.

The people were masked. All except for one. The unmasked person was Braden. He was unmasked because the mask had been torn off by someone he was wrestling with. He and the other men were shoving one of their own into the trunk of an SUV.

The big man yanked off the mask of the struggling individual to reveal the face Carver expected to see. It was Liana. Seconds later, the big man pressed a rag over her face. She went limp. They pushed her into the trunk and closed it.

The big man got into the driver's seat. The others piled in after him. The vehicle drove off down a side street.

"Can you get the license plate?" Carver said.

Jessica shook her head. "No. There was no clear shot. At least not that I've found so far."

"Where was that?"

"Minneapolis. Someone snapped a picture of Braden just a moment before. I geofenced the area and found lots of social media posts with bits and pieces of Braden's group. That's how I found the video." She closed the file and opened another. "This video shows a different angle, but it's too low to see the license plate."

Carver watched the second video. The perspective was lower, probably because the cameraman was short. Only bits and pieces of Liana's struggle were visible through gaps in the crowd.

Carver's fist clenched involuntarily. "I don't suppose your software can track vehicles?"

She frowned. "I mean, it could certainly track vehicles by appearance, but I'd have to build an index."

"And then there'd need to be a publicly available image of the vehicle?"

"Yeah." Jessica ran several internet searches and found a site with 3D images of vehicles. She looked at the video. "That's a Chevy Suburban?"

Carver nodded.

She downloaded a profile file and put it into a directory called *Indexer*. The file vanished a second later. "It's indexed. But I don't have anything in my software to narrow the vehicle down by color. I'd need to code that in and test it."

"This is good enough for now."

Jessica opened a map. The geofenced area was shaded green. She widened it slightly and ran the search. There were multiple hits. She opened the images. The first was a white Suburban. The next one was black, but the driver was clearly female.

She scrolled through the images and finally found one with two women posing together for the picture. Some distance behind them was a black Suburban with a large man behind the wheel. She zoomed in but the background was slightly out of focus.

Jessica highlighted the area and opened a cleanup tool, but it couldn't resolve the blurry part into clarity. "That's about a mile from where she was taken." She kept scrolling through the other images, but there were none of the same Suburban.

"Widen the search area to all of Minneapolis."

Jessica grimaced. "That's going to find a lot of false positives."

"Do it. I'll spend all night looking through the pictures if I have to."

Jessica put her hand on his. "Carver, give me some time to polish the code. I can narrow it down." She sighed. "At this point, I don't think it matters how long that takes me."

Carver worked his jaw back and forth. He felt something churning deep in his stomach. Felt it burning. It was anger. Rage. He thought he'd made peace with Liana's probable death. Clearly, he hadn't.

When it came right down to it, there was no making peace with death. He was still angry about Joe's death. He was still angry about Rhode's death. They were good people who deserved better.

Despite all the training from his parents, Carver didn't always see the world in neutral gray. The emotions they'd tried to squeeze out of him were still there, just buried deep in rocky soil.

Apparently, everything he'd been through since Scion was slowly churning up that hard-packed earth and bringing with it a lot of unwelcome baggage.

And that was fine. Just fine.

He could deal with it. The people responsible for Liana's death, however, would not be able to deal with it. He was going to find them. He was going to transfer the heat from his anger into their bodies. And one thing was dead certain.

Their deaths would not be easy.

CHAPTER 24

Carver buried the anger.

He needed a clear head. Anger clouded logic. It made people do stupid things. He had to make sure he didn't do anything stupid. But he really wanted to know where they took Liana. Because he knew what had happened at the end of that journey.

Liana had breathed her last breath, and they'd buried her.

Carver had ended a lot of lives in various ways. He could think about any one of those times and it didn't bother him. But thinking about Liana's death bothered him a lot. It was strange how knowing a person changed things.

"Carver." Jessica rubbed his hand. "We'll find these guys, okay?"

"I know." Carver pulled his hand away. "Try to find out where that SUV went."

"I'll refine the code so it can search by unique vehicle characteristics." She zoomed in on one of the pictures. "Looks like there's a dent in the rear quarter panel. Something like that differentiates this Suburban from the others."

"Thanks." Carver stood and went to the kitchen. He rummaged through the pantry and found lots of canned food. He opened the fridge. The top two shelves were filled with cans of soft drinks. Among them were a few cans of domestic beer.

He popped one open and tasted it. It was mass produced crap, but sometimes you just made do with what you found. "You want one?"

Jessica grimaced. "Gross. How can you drink that stuff?"

Carver leaned against the wall and looked at her computer.

"You have a way of ignoring questions."

"Not every question deserves an answer."

She laughed. "I guess you're right." She turned back to the laptop and opened a window filled with lines of code. She leaned back and stared at it for a long time before highlighting a section and copying it into a new window.

Jessica manipulated the code for a while. Then she compiled it. While it compiled she downloaded images of various vehicles and indexed them. She ran the images through an analyzer, or at least that was what it looked like to Carver.

A matrix of lines and dots formed over the images, mapping the surface of the vehicles the same way they did facial recognition. Instead of just doing the face or front of the vehicle, the software mapped out all four sides, creating multiple profiles.

The software noted any defects no matter how minor to differentiate one vehicle from others of the same make and model.

After a while, she leaned back and stretched. She worked her neck back and forth, cracking it. "Obviously a license plate is the best way to check a vehicle, but I've got a working prototype."

"Already?"

"I basically just copied existing code and modified it." She stood and walked around the room. She reached over her shoulder and winced. "That's what I get for hunching over for two hours."

"They might have cold heat packs around here somewhere," Carver said. "I can find one."

"Can you just massage it a little?" She lowered the side of her shirt to bare her shoulder. Carver worked at it with his thumb and the heel of his hand.

She hissed. "Not that hard."

He eased up. "Sorry. I don't really give massages."

"I can tell. It felt like you were trying to break bones, not massage muscles."

"Is this better?"

"Yes, much better." She relaxed and sighed. "Well, this isn't working."

"The massage?"

She laughed. "No, not that." She stepped away and raised her shirt to cover her shoulder. "You're just oblivious to my wiles."

"You mean trying to seduce me?"

Jessica turned around. "You knew what I was doing?"

"I suspected. It's a common technique employed by women."

"Ugh. When you say it like that it just makes me feel dirty."

"There's nothing dirty about it. I'm just not in the mood to take the bait." He shrugged. "Sorry."

"Yeah, that just makes me feel worse. Because you're thinking about your friend, and I'm thinking about something else." She slapped her forehead. "God, I'm so stupid when it comes to things like this. And I have the worst taste in men."

"Thanks." Carver sipped his beer. "For what it's worth, I'm interested. I'm just preoccupied."

"I get it." She walked toward him and stumbled, falling against him.

Carver caught her reflexively.

She looked up at him with big eyes. "God, I'm so clumsy. Thank you, sir."

Carver grinned. "That's better."

Jessica stepped back and bowed. "Thank you."

"Braden Cutler doesn't stand a chance."

"I know. But it's his friends I'm worried about." She sat down in front of the laptop. "Okay, the final build is compiled. Let me test it." She pulled up the picture of a black Dodge Challenger. "There's like a million of these on the roads. Let's see if my program can differentiate."

She entered an indexed image and started the search. "This vehicle has no obvious dents or defects, so it's likely I'll get a lot of false positives."

Carver finished off the beer and got another one. There was nothing on the screen to indicate the search was running. No progress bar, no spinning circle, nothing. A few minutes later, an image appeared. Then another and another. Soon there were twenty pictures of the same car.

Jessica compared the pattern matrix to the original. "It's recognizing different wheels, the paint color, and different models of the same car." She pulled up two of the pictures. "But these are different cars. I know that because they're on a car dealership site and the VINs are different."

"But they're both new and otherwise identical?"

"Yes. So, that's success. It's about as good as it can get without knowing the license plate number." She pulled up the Suburban and applied the new pattern matrix to the various pictures. Then she started the search. "If I had access to the footage from traffic cameras, then we could probably find it real fast."

"That's a possibility, but I'm not ready to pull those strings just yet." Carver could call Rachel Evans, but he didn't want her involved if he could find these people himself. Mainly because he wanted to deal with them personally.

"Because you want to kill those people and not give them a chance at due process?"

Carver sipped his beer.

Jessica smiled. "I'll take that as a yes."

The search ran for a long time before producing a single hit. The image that appeared was definitely the same SUV. The big guy was behind the wheel, but he still wasn't in focus. The vehicle had been captured in the background of a photo by tourists taking selfies. The SUV had been stopped at a traffic light.

It was a little south of where the protests had been. Carver plotted the first sighting on the map, then the second and the third. The plot points showed the vehicle heading southeast. They waited but the search didn't produce any other images.

"I'll widen the search area." Jessica expanded the geofence to the southeast, narrowing it into a corridor. "The further away they get from people, the less likely it is that we'll find any images."

"Yeah." Carver dumped the rest of the beer in the sink. "Might as well get some shuteye."

"Okay." Jessica closed her laptop. She stood and stretched. "Yep, time to recharge the old batteries." She cracked her knuckles. "Catch a few z's and all that."

Carver stepped closer to her. He leaned down and kissed her. She responded enthusiastically, reached around and squeezed his butt.

She smiled. "You have a nice ass by the way."

"Thanks." Carver picked her up and tossed her onto the bed.

She laughed. "That was fun." She squirmed out of her clothing and down to her underwear, revealing a toned athletic body. "Show me what you've got."

Carver obliged by removing his clothing.

Jessica clapped. "Very nice."

He slid into bed next to her and pulled her close.

She smiled. "Thanks."

"For what?"

"For making me feel useful. For dragging me out of my depressing life to do something meaningful." She ran a finger down his chest. "I like the way you make me feel even if you're one scary guy sometimes."

Carver didn't want to admit it, but she made him laugh. He liked that. But putting his feelings out there just wasn't something he did easily. So he kissed her and ended the conversation in the best way possible.

They met Alicia for breakfast before heading out to Chicago the next morning. Carver showed her the video of Liana being taken and told her about the search for the SUV.

"No license plate?"

"Only a partial." Jessica showed her the last image the search had found. The first three letters of the front plate were visible. "It's a California plate. This is probably the same vehicle they've been driving around the country."

"Maybe expand the search to include the other cities the protests stopped in." Alicia picked up her coffee mug and took a sip. "If we get the full plate, I have a guy who can run searches."

"Someone you bribe?" Jessica asked.

"No, a veteran who believes in the cause."

Jessica looked confused. "What cause?"

"Better treatment for vets." Alicia set down her mug. "Our primary business is helping reform veteran affairs policy."

"I'm pretty sure there's a lot more to it than that." Jessica cut her pancakes. "Hope House has dozens of locations in the northeast. The company that owns and operates them is a church charity that also operates similar places under other names in other parts of the country."

Alicia raised her eyebrows. "How did you find that out?"

Jessica tapped her temple. "I have my resources."

Alicia laughed and looked at Carver. "I like her."

Jessica grinned. "I like you too."

"We could always use another tech geek in the organization." Alicia studied her reaction. "The pay isn't great at first, but it gets better."

"Is it commensurate for the danger?" Jessica's smile faded. "If you're at all associated with Carver then I know what you're doing isn't exactly kosher or safe."

"Perceptive for a civvy." Alicia nodded. "I like that. And you're right. We don't exactly follow protocol when it comes to achieving our goals. But someone like you wouldn't be a field operator. You'd be behind the scenes."

Jessica turned to Carver. "What do you think?"

Carver paused with a strip of bacon halfway to his mouth. "Once you get in, there's no getting out. No chance of a normal life. Jericho doesn't exactly offer retirement plans."

"Au contraire, mon frère," Alicia said with a passable French accent. "You can leave whenever you like as long as you understand the non-disclosure agreement."

Jessica pressed her lips together. "I'm definitely interested, but I'm also not looking to get into a life of crime."

Alicia laughed. "It's not exactly a life of crime. Think of it as governmental reform without all the red tape."

Jessica looked at Carver again. He ate his bacon without comment.

"No comment?"

"It's your life."

Jessica plunged a fork into her soft fried egg and watched the yolk run out. "Starting my own business didn't go anywhere because the giant corporations paid the government to shut me down. They even updated the Internet Privacy Act to explicitly undermine my business model."

"That's how they work." Alicia shook her head sadly. "The only thing keeping us from sliding into a corporatocracy is that the big companies are also at each other's throats. I can see why your startup company sounded alarm bells with them."

"It was only going to use publicly available data." Jessica stabbed her egg again. "Then I spoke with several social media platforms about deeper integration. They wanted a big chunk of my pie for that kind of access. When I refused, things got ugly."

"They farm personal data all day every day," Alicia said. "It's pay to play."

Carver looked at the mangled egg. "Are you finished? We need to hit the road."

"Yeah." Jessica scraped up the egg yolk with a spoon and ate it. "I'm ready to go."

Carver paid the bill, and they left. They met Beck and crew in a parking lot a few blocks down from the art institute. They didn't have the van. This time they had two black Ford SUVs with black steel rims.

They looked exactly like Ford police interceptors but without all the police markings. Even cops would probably think they were unmarked police cars.

Jonas patted one of the vehicles. "You like them?"

"They look authentic."

"They are authentic." Beck smiled proudly. "We procure them through a small police department so there's no big paper trail."

"Smart." Alicia looked at the gathering crowd down the road. "Gonna be a big turnout today."

"The buses carrying the protestors parked in a government parking lot a few streets over." Beck pointed east. "There were some reporters trying to gain entrance and the CPD threatened to arrest them if they didn't leave."

Jessica frowned. "But that's public property. They can't do that."

"Oh, they can, and they will." Jonas grunted. "They don't want journalists recording all the protestors getting off of buses because they know it'll make it look like this isn't an organic protest."

"Chicago is a big city. They won't have any problems getting a lot of the native population to turn out." Alicia pulled on a black leather jacket and pulled a black beanie over her head to cover her hair. "Let's get into the crowd. We've got to find the target ASAP."

Jessica put on her spiked skateboarder helmet and spiked elbow pads. The spikes were rubber, but they made her look like a futuristic rebel. She'd opted out of the full-faced gasmask because she needed Braden to see her face and expressive eyes.

Carver pulled three protest signs from the back of the minivan. Jessica had come up with the slogans on the signs. He took the one that said, *Eat the Rich!* Jessica took the one with *Death to Fascists!* on it. Alicia took the one that said, *No One is Illegal!*

Jonas chuckled. "Man, you guys are going all in."

A guy Carver didn't recognize walked out of a nearby bagel shop, a box in his hand.

"That's Crocker," Beck said. "He's the one who couldn't make the meeting yesterday."

"Yeah, sorry." Crocker opened the box. "Want a bagel?"

"I'm good." Carver started walking down the street. "We've got to find the target."

"We'll help you," Beck said. "That's why we're wearing civvies right now."

The street was barricaded a short distance from the parking lot. They spread out and walked into the growing crowd. A woman shouted a chant into a megaphone. The crowd repeated the chant to the beat of drums.

A group of kids on electric scooters zipped past them, whooping and shouting, "Burn it down! Burn it down!"

The march didn't begin for another thirty minutes, but the crowd was already getting rowdy. It didn't take long to figure out why. Carver spotted small groups of people in black clothing, helmets, and masks spread throughout the crowd.

They were whipping people into a furor, shouting and screaming chants about overthrowing the government and burning society to the ground. Some people really responded to the message. Others simply followed along. It was typical mob think.

These smaller groups reminded Carver of the group Liana had been in. But the people in the groups seemed extremely emotional. They seemed to believe everything they were saying. These weren't part of the core group. They were the true believers that had been recruited for just this thing.

There was a stage not far ahead. An attractive man and woman stood on the stage waving and smiling. They were dressed in black and holding signs. They stood near microphones, indicating they were probably going to speak at some point before the march started.

Jessica appeared out of the crowd and grabbed Carver's hand. "I found him." She pulled him through the throng and toward the other side. Carver was taller than most people, so he could see over their heads.

He saw another uncommonly tall man wading through the crowd. He caught glimpses of the other men with him. They were all masked so he couldn't see their faces, but he knew who they were. Among them were two shorter, thinner men. One of those men was Braden Cutler.

They'd found the target.

CHAPTER 25

Carver stopped walking and looked at the stage.

He kept Jessica from going any further. "Good job. How did you find them?"

"The tall guy is like a beacon." She nodded toward the stage. "He walked around from the other side, and I knew he'd lead me to Braden."

"How close did you get? Did they see you?"

"I don't know if any of them saw me, but that shouldn't matter, right?"

"It shouldn't." Carver watched the big man out of the corner of his eye. The group had stopped walking and were hyping up the crowd around them. It was like they were trying to manufacture a riot right off the bat.

Carver had seen manufactured riots plenty of times. He'd helped instigate a number of them. All it took was leveraging emotions into action. The angrier people became, the easier they were to manipulate. HLF members were clearly here to cause trouble.

Large crowds were like a force of nature. They could be used to kill and destroy. Unlike forces of nature, they could also be directed at a specific target. HLF was using a tactic familiar to Carver.

In Scion, they called it priming because it was basically like priming a bomb fuse. The objective was to cause as much civil unrest as possible and direct it toward a target, usually a political figure.

It was easier to do in smaller countries because there weren't so many cities and such a long distance to travel in between them. The geography of the US made it much more difficult to pull off unless large crowds were available in the same city as the target.

The protest route made it obvious what the end goal was. They were priming crowds across multiple cities, snowballing the crowd size as they moved along. By the time they reached Washington DC, the number of protestors would have swelled to possibly a hundred thousand people or more.

It was amazing how just a few people could essentially herd thousands of people across vast distances to serve as an army of sorts. An army meant to wreak havoc and destruction.

If the people in Washington were smart, they'd see this coming from a mile away and be prepared.

But it was likely that they considered this just another protest and not an existential threat. Maybe it was just another big, destructive protest that would fizzle out naturally at its terminus. But Carver doubted it. Someone was spending a lot of money to make this happen.

The objective of the protests wasn't Carver's concern. The current administration could either handle it or they couldn't. It was just that simple. All Carver wanted was to make the big man and his bosses pay for what they'd done to Liana.

Everything he'd done for the past few months had led to this moment. Now he could get to the actual people who'd done the deed. He would bleed them for more information and find the people who'd purchased the agent list and ordered Liana's murder.

He just had to make sure everything went right.

Jessica tugged his sleeve. "You look a little distant. Are you worried I can't pull this off?"

"No, I think you're going to do fine." He checked the time. "Fifteen minutes until the march starts. Time for you to go meet your future boyfriend."

"Wish me luck." Jessica turned on her earpiece. It looked just like a standard Bluetooth earphone so it wouldn't arouse suspicions. She pushed into the crowd toward the tall man.

The introduction came moments later. "Oh, God I'm sorry. I'm so clumsy."

"Whoa, you scared me." Braden spoke with a boyish voice. "You've got to be careful moving through a crowd."

"Thank you." Jessica spoke breathlessly. "I came here with a group of friends, but we got separated. I just hope I can find them."

"I'd totally help you, but I have to stick with my friends," Braden said. "Maybe once the march gets going, I can help."

"That would be amazing."

A deeper male voice spoke with a slight Slavic accent. "There's no time for flirting, Cutler."

"Sorry, Dimitri. She just got separated from her friends."

"He was just helping me," Jessica said. "Are you guys working security or something?"

"You could say that," Dimitri replied.

Carver was watching the interaction from his position. He could see the top of Jessica's head over the crowd, but not Braden. Now he had a name for the big guy, but he still couldn't see the man's face because of the mask.

"Well, thanks," Jessica said.

"Yeah, no problem," Braden said. "I really like your helmet. It's so punk."

Dimitri turned away from them and pushed through the crowd to talk to another small group of people in black clothing. Braden took the chance to keep talking to Jessica.

"Sorry about Dimitri. I'll help you find your friends once we start marching."

"Oh, really? That would be amazing!"

Braden cleared his throat uneasily. "Uh, so what brought you to the protest today?"

"I want to end women's suffrage," Jessica said.

"Oh, yeah it's a huge worldwide problem, but especially now with the new administration. They like suffering."

"Oh, they're a huge cause of suffrage," Jessica said. "It's crazy."

"Um, yeah." Braden sounded confused. "Is suffrage a new term?"

"I don't think so. I just really want to end women's suffrage worldwide, you know?"

"Yeah, I'm a hundred percent with you."

"All right!" Jessica raised a hand. Braden high-fived her.

"Someone's got a sense of humor," Alicia said over comms.

Beck chuckled. "Yeah. Sounds like the target is hooked."

"Agreed," Alicia said. "Five minutes to parade start."

The attractive man and woman on the stage started talking.

"Hello, Chicago!" the pair said in unison. "Are you ready for change?"

The crowd roared in approval.

"I can't hear you! Are you ready for change?"

The crowd roared even louder.

The woman took the microphone. "They want to take away your rights. They want to keep you silent. They want to kill marginalized people. And they want to suppress the vote so they can stay in power forever!"

The crowd booed. Signs rose from the throng, shaking vigorously in response.

The man took the microphone. "Those toxic assholes in Washington want to end the US as we know it. They want to erase the middle class and turn us into a slave state. Let me be clear: they want to get rid of us by any means necessary. If we don't end their reign of terror, millions will die."

"Millions!" the woman shouted.

The crowd grew angry, booing and shouting. The people around Carver looked absolutely furious. A pair of women screamed at the top of their lungs as if someone was flaying them alive.

Carver was impressed. These people really knew how to work the crowd. They knew how to stoke the embers of fear into a raging inferno of fury. He wondered what the ultimate plan was once they reached Washington DC.

"Kill them all!" Jessica shouted. "Drown them in a sea of their own blood!"

Braden said something to her, but his words were drowned out by the roar of the crowd.

"It's time to march!" the woman said. "Make your voices heard!"

"And most importantly of all, don't give those monsters in Washington a moment of peace." The man raised a fist. "We are the army of change. We will bring peace to this world by any means!"

A drum beat started. Someone shouted on a megaphone. "Move out people! Time to march!"

The people started moving. Some marched like they were in the military. People cheered and whooped with joy, caught up in the pure emotions of the moment. The person on the megaphone started a chant.

"Give me peace, peace, peace! Peace by any means! All of us together can kill the kings and queens!"

"Not very subtle, is it?" Alicia said.

Carver grunted. "Sounds like most of these people are past the boiling point."

"Yep. It's impressive, actually."

Carver picked up the pace and moved along the outer edge of the crowd so he could get ahead of Jessica and Braden. He was taller than most people, so he slouched to make himself look shorter. Before long he was about a hundred feet or so ahead of the target.

He heard Jessica talking to Braden, but the chanting crowd around her made it impossible to hear what she was saying even over the earbud. The chant died down after a few minutes and he heard bits and pieces of what she was saying.

"One click to target," Alicia said. "Are teams ready?"

"Teams are in position," Beck said. "Awaiting signal."

"In position," Carver said as he rounded the turn toward the coffee shop. There was a small crowd of people on the side street. Carver slouched a little lower to blend in with them better.

The crowd around Jessica became quieter and Carver could hear what she was saying again. "My friends said they wanted coffee from this place nearby. Maybe they'll be there."

"Where is it?" Braden said.

"Here." Jessica was probably pointing to the place on the map. "If they aren't there, I don't know where they could be."

"I'd totally come with you to look, but Dimitri might get pissed."

"Oh, I was going to treat you to a coffee for being so nice to me," Jessica said.

Braden was hooked. "Oh, well I'm sure I could sneak away for a moment."

"Awesome!" Jessica giggled. "So, is your name Cutler?"

Braden laughed. "No, that's my last name. You can call me Braden."

"I'm Francine."

"Francine?" Braden sounded confused. "You don't, uh, look like a Francine."

"Because I'm Asian?"

"Oh, no, I would never judge you by your looks. I just imagine Francine as some older woman."

Jessica laughed. "Aw, I know you would never do that. Francine is a really common name in Asia."

"Huh?" Braden sounded like his brain hit a speed bump and nearly wrecked.

"Yep, it's true."

"Man, I never would have guessed."

"Here's the turn." Jessica giggled. "Let's sneak away before Dimitri looks."

Carver saw Jessica round the corner, towing Braden with her hand. Once they cleared the crowd she released his hand and high-fived him. Braden was completely enamored with her. They started walking toward the coffee shop.

Carver trailed along behind them, slouching to fit in better. There were enough people walking in their direction that he didn't stand out.

Two police SUVs roared toward the coffee shop. They screeched to a stop, blocking off the road. Four cops jumped out of the SUVs, two from each vehicle. They raised batons and riot shields and charged toward the people walking toward the coffee shop.

"Holy crap!" Braden said. "They're coming right at us!"

"Get down on the ground!" the cops shouted. "Down on the ground!"

People scattered and ran, shouting in alarm.

Jessica fell to the ground and cried out in pain. "My ankle!"

The cops grabbed anyone they could. One of them got Braden. He whipped back his police baton and beat Braden on the back of his legs. Braden cried out in pain and went down. Another cop started beating Jessica. She screamed.

Carver rushed toward them. He slammed a fist into the first cop's gut. The cop grunted and doubled over. Carver slammed his knee into the cop's face. The cop went down hard. Carver grabbed the cop beating Braden and slammed him into the building wall. He punched him in the kidneys and the cop went down.

Another cop drew a gun. Carver grabbed his wrist and snapped it hard. The cop screamed in pain. Carver caught the gun as it fell from his hand. He pistol whipped the cop and knocked him out.

He pointed the gun at the last cop. "Drop your weapon, you fascist asshole."

The cop dropped the gun and raised his hands.

"Beg for your life, you piece of garbage."

"Please don't kill me. Please!"

Carver tensed as if he was really going to pull the trigger. Then the cop got up and ran away. Carver helped Braden up. "Hey, man, you okay? They were beating the crap out of you."

Braden looked woozy. "God, they really hit me hard."

"We've got to get out of here." Carver pulled him by the elbow and got them back into the sea of protestors. "They're lucky I didn't waste them. Damned pigs deserve to die."

"I hate them!" Braden said. He flinched and looked around. "Where's Francine?"

"Who?"

"The woman I was with."

"Another group of cops came and took her, man." Carver shook his head. "They stuffed her and a lot of other people into a van."

"No!" Braden stopped ran to the edge of the crowd.

Carver caught his elbow. "What the hell are you doing? They're going to snatch you too."

Carver saw a tall man in black working his way through the crowd toward them. A mask hid his face, but his eyes were angry.

Braden saw him too. "Oh, crap."

"Where the hell did you go?" Dimitri said.

"The cops came." Braden looked confused. "They attacked us. Tried to arrest us. Then this guy beat the hell out of them, and we ran."

"He did what?" Dimitri looked Carver up and down. "Who are you?"

"Nobody." Carver walked away.

Dimitri grabbed him by the arm. "I asked you a question, boy. Who the hell are you?"

Carver glared at his hand. "Let go of me. I don't want to fight a brother in arms, but I don't like being touched."

Dimitri was much taller up close. He was a full head taller than Carver and bigger in every way that mattered. He pulled Carver closer and towered over him. "Answer me."

Carver stiffened. "The name's Sam and I hate fascists. I also hate people who grab me, so unless you want to lose a hand, you'd better let go."

Dimitri chuckled. "Well, Cutler, looks like a guardian angel saved your bacon." He released Carver. "So, Sam, do you want to fight fascism with us today?"

"Of course." Carver rubbed his arm where Dimitri had gripped it. It actually hurt a little. This guy's grip was no joke. "What do you want me to do?"

"Just hang out with us. Do what I say." Dimitri patted his shoulder. "I want to see how you perform under pressure."

"I perform just fine under pressure." Carver clenched his fists. "I was a Marine."

"Yeah, we'll see." Dimitri tweaked Braden's ear. Braden cried out in pain and tried to free himself from Dimitri's grip. Dimitri shoved him roughly to the side. "If it wasn't for daddy's money, this kid wouldn't even be here."

"I'm a fighter!" Braden backed away. "And if you keep talking to me that way, I'll take my money somewhere else."

Dimitri motioned to the rest of the group. "Let's go. We're way off schedule."

"Way off schedule for what?" Carver said. "It's a protest march."

Dimitri put an arm around Carver's shoulders and started walking, forcing Carver to walk with him. "You were in the Marines, so you either developed a respect for authority or a hatred for it. I'm guessing since you just beat up a bunch of cops that you don't like authority."

"I don't like bullies," Carver said. "The authoritarian regime is trying to bully the populace into submission."

"Like I said, you don't like authority." Dimitri tapped his temple. "You can't fool me."

Carver stared into the man's eyes, trying to figure out if he really thought he was an expert on human psychology or if he was just toying with him. He didn't like the man's arm around his shoulder or how close he was, but he was playing the part of Sam, a vet with PTSD and a grudge.

Thankfully, Sam also didn't like strange men wrapping arms around his shoulder, so he could act naturally uncomfortable with it.

Dimitri had a light eastern European accent. It was hard to say which country, but it was definitely Slavic. He used American idioms easily which meant he'd been in the States since he was a kid.

His comfort being this close to another man was definitely an eastern European thing. While American men preferred to keep their distance from each other, Slavic men were comfortable being close like this.

Carver played along with him. "Fine, I don't like authority. I also don't like bullies."

"You like freedom. Absolute freedom. Anarchy."

"I like absolute personal freedom." Carver shrugged. "If that's anarchy, then so be it."

"Good." Dimitri removed his arm and patted him on the back. "Good. Let's free the people."

Carver cracked his knuckles. "I'm ready."

"We'll find out soon enough," Dimitri said. "I'm taking you to one of our other groups. You may not like authority, but if you follow their orders, you will be paving the way for ultimate freedom. Do you understand?"

"Yeah." Carver didn't want to have to work his way up through the outer layers. He'd hoped he could skip all that and get right to the core. But it looked like even beating up cops wasn't going to do that.

He had to stay in Dimitri's group no matter what or this was over.

CHAPTER 26

Carver had a couple of more cards up his sleeve.

He scratched the back of his neck.

"You need a phase two?" Alicia said over comms.

"Yeah."

Dimitri nodded. "You're in?"

"I've been in way before I ever met you." Carver stopped walking. "I don't need a group to do it, okay?"

"You'll be far more effective helping us than just being on your own," Dimitri said. "We could use more men like you, but you have to prove yourself. If you can do that, then nothing can stop our movement."

Carver put a hand on his chin and pretended to think about it real hard. "I'll be honest with you. I want to beat the hell out of fascists. I also want to get what I'm owed. If you can promise me that, then I'm in."

"I can promise you that and much more," Dimitri said. "But prove yourself first. If that's too much, then leave right now, because we don't want dead weight."

"I've never been dead weight in my life!" Carver said. "Never!"

Dimitr grinned. "Good. Good."

"Phase two is in position," Beck said. "End of the block right at the alleyway."

"Okay," Carver said. "Let's go."

"Yes!" Dimitri clapped him hard on the back. "Let's go."

They started walking again. As they neared the alley ahead, a woman started shouting, "Leave her alone! Leave her alone!"

Carver ran to the alley. A pair of cops were dragging a man and a woman toward a police van. Carver rushed them.

"Stop or we'll shoot!" One of the cops tried to draw a weapon. The cops were wearing helmets with visors, so he punched the cop in the stomach and grabbed his weapon.

The other cop went for his weapon. Carver threw the gun at the second cop. He rushed him and slammed him with his shoulder. The breath exploded from the other cop. He flew backwards into a dumpster with a hollow metallic ring.

The two people the cops had been dragging got up and ran. Carver pounded the second cop while he was down. He calmly walked to the first one and kicked him hard in the ribs. Both cops went still.

"Holy shit!" Dimitri bellowed with laughter. He pulled a knife and grinned. "My turn for fun."

Three more cops rounded the corner, guns drawn.

"Maybe not." Dimitri turned and ran down the alley. Carver and the rest of the group ran with him.

They melted back into the crowd and crossed the street, Dimitri laughing the entire way.

"Did they buy it?" Alicia said over comms.

Carver coughed three times to indicate he was unsure.

"I told you he's crazy." Braden laughed. "He's not afraid of anything."

One of the other men spoke. "I think he killed those cops."

"He broke a lot of ribs, that's for sure." Dimitri clapped Carver on the back. "I like you. You're a man who does what he says with no fear. Maybe you should stick with us today. Tell me a little more about yourself."

Carver coughed once for yes. "Fine. What do you want me to do?"

"Confirmed," Alicia said.

"Man, I'm glad I wore the body armor," Beck said. "You didn't hold back on your kicks."

Carver had barely kicked him, but even a light kick to the ribs hurt.

Dimitri checked the map app on his phone. "We went right past a target, but I'm not going back. The cops will be all over this place soon."

One of the men patted his bulging backpack. "So, what do we do with the extra?"

Dimitri looked behind them. "I don't see much activity, but it won't take long for the cops to come looking for the guy who beat the hell out of them."

"We have orders," the man said. "But you're the leader."

"Okay, let's backtrack." Dimitri turned to Carver. "Keep your mask on at all times. Do what I say, no questions asked. Got it?"

Carver nodded. "Got it."

"Okay, let's go." Dimitri led them against the flow of the march. They went about a block to a small neighborhood grocery store.

The man with the bulging backpack handed out glass bottles filled with liquid as they walked. He nodded at Carver. "Am I giving him one?"

"Yeah," Dimitri said. "I assume you know what to do, Sam?"

Carver took the bottle. He unscrewed the plastic cap. Pulled out the cloth that was stuffed inside. He sniffed it. "Kerosene? You're not playing around, are you?"

"No, we're not." Dimitri took out a lighter. "Light them up, boys."

The man with the backpack lit Carver's firebomb. Dimitri threw his at the grocery store. Carver threw his right after. The other men threw theirs at the cars parked in the parking lot. Within seconds, the entire place was ablaze.

People ran shouting and screaming from the building. A car's gas tank ignited with a loud whoosh. Some of the marching protestors stopped and watched with delighted smiles on their faces. Others ran as if the entire place might blow up.

"Okay, move out." Dimitri led them back into the protestors. "Next target is four blocks ahead on the right."

The firebombing had started something. People stopped marching and started breaking the windows on the bank next door to the grocery store. Others charged into a fast-food restaurant, ripping out cash registers and running away with them.

The single act of violence had triggered an even more violent reaction from the other protestors. It was simple psychological manipulation. There were elements of the crowd that wanted to do this, but they needed a little nudge.

By firebombing the grocery store, Dimitri had emboldened others to let loose with their worst desires. Individually, people were usually good. But people in a crowd could be dangerous and violent, prone to being emotionally manipulated.

Some marchers kept going. Some stopped to record the looting. Others cheered on the looters but didn't take part themselves. Carver imagined that when the marches first started on the west coast, they weren't nearly so violent.

But as Dimitri and the other gangs started trouble, the temperature of the marches slowly increased, building toward a crescendo. By the time the protests left Chicago, the protestors would be primed for the grand finale in Washington DC. They would be so desensitized to the violence that they would fully support it.

They reached the next target moments later, a small convenience store with gas pumps. The owners, an elderly Asian couple, were outside trying to keep protestors out of their store. They were pleading in broken English. Begging the crowd to spare the business they spent their adult lives growing and maintaining.

There was no sympathy to be found. Looters smashed windows. They ransacked the shelves and refrigerators, taking everything they could get their hands on. A young boy grabbed the cash register and ran from the store, holding it over his head like a trophy.

The crowd roared in approval. People recorded everything with their phones, some even livestreaming the event to their social media. They celebrated the destruction of the convenience store.

Dimitri led his crew through the crowd. They lit their firebombs and threw them at the store. Several struck gas pumps. Protestors shouted in alarm and scattered. The owners gave up trying to save their store and fled.

The store burned but the gas pumps remained unaffected. No one had been pumping gas, and the safety valves prevented the pumps from catching ablaze as easily as the movies made it seem.

That didn't matter. Dimitri and gang had accomplished their task. They went to the next target, a liquor store. The place was already burnt to the ground. Apparently, other rioters had already hit it. They melted back into the crowd and slowly made their way to the next target.

The march had devolved into a series of riots. It was like watching a horde of locusts descend on a place and leave behind nothing but wrack and ruin. No business was spared whether it was a large department store or a small boutique.

Nearly a hundred thousand protestors were rampaging unchecked through the city and Dimitri was grinning like a madman.

The man with the backpack full of Molotov cocktails laughed as he watched the pandemonium. "Man, that didn't take long."

"I told you it wouldn't." Dimitri clapped his hands. "Let's keep going. No rest for the wicked." They hurried across the road.

The cops came out of nowhere. An armored transport burst from the mouth of an alley. Protestors scattered to avoid being run over. The back doors opened, and a squad of police in riot gear ran out, shields and batons at the ready.

This was not part of Carver's plan. Apparently, the real police were starting to respond to the violence. Another two trucks emerged from the alleys across the street and disgorged more riot police. They were going to be trapped and arrested. Carver needed to make sure Dimitri and gang stayed out of jail.

He rushed straight at the cops getting out of the truck ahead. They were still spreading out, not even in formation yet, and they were getting knocked around by the huge crowd. Carver plowed through them.

A cop pulled a rifle and fired a shot. The shot missed Carver but struck a protestor. The man screamed but there was no blood. The cops were using rubber bullets. Carver gripped the cop's wrist and flipped him on the ground. He turned the cop's rifle on him and fired three times.

He fired on the other cops. The cops cried out in pain as the rubber bullets found soft flesh unprotected by body armor. Protestors shouted in fear at the sound of the gunshots, scattering and knocking cops over in their haste to get out of there.

It was absolute chaos.

"Into the truck!" Carver shouted. "Now!"

Dimitri looked uncertainly at the fallen cops and collected himself. "Into the truck!"

Everyone piled into the police truck. Braden was the last one in. He struggled to close the rear doors. The other short guy helped him. Carver hopped in the driver's seat and gunned it out of there.

Protestors screamed and scattered, clearing the road ahead. He took several turns until they were well away from the scene of the crime and stopped the vehicle. "Everyone out!"

The group piled out.

"Holy crap, did you see that?" The guy with the backpack whistled. "That pig was going to shoot us, and then Sam pulled an Uno reverse on his sorry ass."

The others laughed.

"Sick moves, man." One of them punched Carver in the arm.

Dimitri looked around furtively. "Let's keep moving. They probably have a GPS tracker on this vehicle." He nodded at Carver. "Good job with the pigs. I love hearing them squeal."

Carver nodded. "Music to my ears."

Dimitri led them down back alleys until they rejoined the march and found safety in the crowd. Sirens wailed in the distance. A helicopter swept overhead. The shooting of all those cops was going to escalate things even if it had been with rubber bullets.

It hadn't been part of Carver's plan, but it was going to be effective.

Dimitri put an arm around Carver's shoulders again. "You didn't hesitate at all. You're a natural born killer."

Apparently, he hadn't realized that the rifle was loaded with rubber bullets. Carver didn't correct him. "Like I said, I don't like bullies."

"He wasted those cops." The other guy who was similar in build to Braden raised a fist. "That was awesome!"

"Listen to Gage talk." The guy with the backpack snorted. "As if he has the balls to hurt anyone, much less a cop."

"Shut it, Dex!" Gage balled his fists. "How about I hurt you right now?"

Dex squared up on him. He stood a full head taller than the little guy. "Go for it. I'll even give you the first shot."

Dimitri sighed. "Gage, you're a little guy with a big mouth. How about you keep it shut?"

"Maybe Dex should keep his shut! I'm just happy to see some cops get what they deserve." Gage backed away from Dex. "We should kill more of them. Send a message."

"Shooting cops isn't the answer," Carvers said. "I only did it out of necessity. As much as I hate them, I don't want to create martyrs out of cops. We need to make the people see them as the bad guys, not heroes or saviors."

Gage threw up his hands. "How can they not already see them as the bad guys?"

"Some do, but not enough." Carver made a fist. "Make the people angry at the cops. Fill them with rage. Then they'll tear the system apart for us."

"Exactly." Dimitri clapped Carver on the back. "You get it, man. At first I thought you were just some typical anarchist but you actually understand what we're doing here."

"Same thing the US has been doing in other countries for years." Carver shrugged. "Destroying the system from the inside."

"That's all wrong." Gage shook his head. "We need to get the crowd to help us. We arm the crowd, take down the cops, problem solved. Sam's an uneducated idiot. He doesn't know anything about real revolutions. I have a master's in history. I did my thesis on Che Guevara, Lenin, and other great revolutionaries. I know what I'm talking about."

Dex burst into laughter. "Our boy's got a master's degree in history!" he said in a mocking tone.

One of the other men doubled over laughing. "Dude, you're not even a pint-sized Che Guevara. You can't even see over the crowd."

"Why are you laughing, bitch?" Gage shoved him. "You think you're tough, Manny?" Manny laughed harder.

Gage roared in frustration. "Keep it up and I'll show you size doesn't matter."

"That's not what she said!" Dex burst into more laughter.

Dimitri grabbed Gage by the arm. "How many times do I have to tell you to keep your mouth shut? Every damned time we have an operation, you decide to go off the political deep end." He shoved him away.

Gage nearly fell over backwards. He was short, skinny, and probably would have folded from a single punch. That drew a fresh round of laughter from the group.

"I'm the one who hooked you up with all our people!" Gage shouted. "I'm the one who let you into our organization!"

Dimitri studied the live news feeds on his phone. He checked the time. "The cops can't hold back the crowd, and the governor is refusing to call in the national guard."

"As expected," Dex said. "The politicians don't want to look like dictators, so they just let us run all over them."

"Yep." Dimitri flipped through different video feeds. "We're in the clear. Time to move to the primary target."

Dex nodded. "Let's go, boss."

Carver kept quiet. He'd impressed Dimitri but he didn't want to overplay his hand. The next few minutes would tell him if all of this had been worth it.

Dimitri turned to Carver and studied him. "You got any questions?"

"About what?" Carver looked around. "I'm just along for the ride."

Dex laughed. "Along for the ride? Man, you're the one giving us the ride."

Manny clapped Dex on the back. "In a police truck, no less."

Dimitri turned to Dex. "What do you think?"

Dex gave him a thumbs up. Manny did the same.

"He's one of us," Braden said, giving a thumbs up.

Dex rolled his eyes. "As if your opinion matters."

Braden flipped him off. "Does my money matter?"

Gage folded his arms and grunted sullenly.

Dimitri turned to the other man who'd remained quiet for the most part. "Rashid?"

The man with the black and white keffiyeh on his head nodded. "I like him." He spoke with a Middle-Eastern accent.

"Okay, Sam, you're in." Dimitri put a hand around his shoulder again. "Congratulations!"

Carver played the part of a western man and nodded uncomfortably.

Dimitri laughed. "American men and their fragile masculinity. They can hardly stand the embrace of another man."

"Hey, I don't blame him," Dex said. "I don't like it when you hug me either. It hurts!"

Dimitri laughed harder.

"It's the weakness of westerners," Rashid said. "They form no masculine bonds, and it makes them weak."

"You're right, my friend." Dimitri cracked his knuckles. "Okay, let's go. Time to put the finishing touches on this march." He started walking.

The others followed him. It looked like the gambit had paid off.

Alicia spoke over comms. "What's going on, Carver? Is everything okay?"

Carver coughed once for yes.

He was in.

CHAPTER 27

Carver didn't know where they were going.

He didn't know what Dimitri had planned to put the finishing touches on the march. This was just day one of a three-day march before the protests moved to Washington DC. The protests were going to move through other parts of Chicago, presumably wreaking havoc as they went.

The cops had retreated. There were about twelve thousand cops in Chicago. Carver knew because he'd looked it up during the planning phase. Not every single cop was a beat cop. Some were detectives or support personnel. That left less than ten thousand street cops.

The protestors numbered nearly a hundred thousand. In the first marches in San Diego, the number had been twenty thousand. The snowball effect of the increasingly violent and emotional protests had reached critical mass. Not even ten thousand cops could contain it.

Looting and vandalism were completely out of control. Every store along the path had already been broken into and cleared out by the time Carver and the others passed them. Dimitri kept a brisk pace because he didn't want to be too far behind the violent edges of the storm.

He wanted to use the looters to his advantage. But what was his big finale? What else could he possibly have planned for this march since it was already spreading chaos across the city?

They hurried along a back alley, paralleling the marching crowd and jogging to get ahead of it and catch up with the looters. After a couple of blocks, Dimitri cut down a side street and they rejoined the protestors.

Drums started beating again. Someone with a bullhorn started a chant and the crowd repeated it.

Eat the rich and feed the poor! That is what we're fighting for!

There was a sea of flags in the crowd, most of them representing Mexico, Palestine, or Ukraine. The only United States flags were flown upside down or defaced. A swastika had been painted over the stars and bars on one flag. Another had a large black X across it.

Gage raised a fist and chanted as they moved through the sea of bodies. He was really into it. The others ignored the crowd and kept moving. The street was so packed that it was difficult to move laterally through the bodies, so they had to work their way across diagonally.

It seemed like the crowd was even larger than before, but it was hard to tell from the ground. Carver was itching to get out of the crowd and up to a high point so he could get a bird's eye view.

"I lost you," Alicia said over comms. "The street is packed."

Carver raised a fist and extended a peace sign.

Alicia spotted the signal. "I see you now."

"We have eyes in the sky now," Beck said. "Our drone is tracking you."

Carver looked up and around but didn't see the drone. It was probably just a small speck somewhere high above them.

"This crowd is amazing!" Gage shouted. He pumped a fist and danced through the crowd. "It's time for a revolution!"

Dimitri kept pushing through the crowd. He was easy to follow because he towered over almost everyone. People got out of his way when they saw him coming.

Braden noticed Carver watching Dimitri. "He's scary, isn't he?"

Carver shrugged. "He's big. Doesn't mean he's scary."

"Once you get to know him, you'll understand." Braden looked at a scantily clad girl longingly. He turned back to Carver. "Man, I hope Francine is okay."

Carver didn't respond. He kept walking. Kept following Dimitri. He had no idea where they were going. Dimitri slowed and looked at his phone. He looked around and seemed to find what he was looking for.

Dex turned to Carver. "Sam, just follow our lead, okay? And don't do anything stupid."

"What are we doing?" Carver said.

Rashid gripped Carver's shoulder tight. "Just follow us and stay close."

Dimitri stood next to Carver. "This is your test, Sam. You pass it and you get to help the cause."

"A test?" Carver looked confused. "Did you already forget that I shot some cops?"

"No, but this is different." Dimitri gripped the back of Carver's neck. "Do you doubt I could break your neck like a chicken?"

Carver doubted he could, but he might be wrong. He stiffened. "No."

"Just follow our lead and don't even think of leaving us."

"Okay." Carver gripped Dimitri's wrist and squeezed. It was hard enough to cause most men to cry in pain, but Dimitri just laughed.

"I like your spirit, Sam." Dimitri released Carver's neck. "Target is right ahead."

Dex pulled the welding goggles down off his helmet and put them over his eyes. He pulled a rubber respirator from the side pocket on the cargo pants and put it on. The others did the same with goggles and respirators.

Rashid handed Carver a pair of goggles and a small rubber respirator. "Good thing I brought an extra one."

Carver put them on without question. He had a feeling they were about to deploy tear gas, but why? That would only disrupt the march, not help it.

Dex pulled out a small metal cylinder. Carver identified it almost immediately. It wasn't tear gas. It was a smoke grenade. Rashid, Manny, and Dimitri all had one. They pulled the pins and dropped them on the ground.

Multicolored smoke filled the air. The crowd seemed to think it was part of the march and started cheering. The smoke was thick and not particularly healthy to breathe. Despite that, marchers plowed right into it.

The goggles and respirator kept Carver's eyes and lungs clear. He followed Dimitri and the others into the crowd. There was a scuffle. Some shouting. The nearby marchers were rubbing their eyes and coughing. They began to scatter.

Carver kept close to the others, so he didn't lose them in the thick clouds of smoke. They emerged into clear air in an alley. They had someone with them, a chubby man with a bag over his head.

They slammed the man against the brick wall.

"Just do it," Dex said. "I don't want to waste time."

"No." Dimitri turned to Carver. "This is it, Sam." He pulled a revolver from his backpack.

It was a Smith and Wesson 357 magnum with a five-inch barrel. Carver didn't know the exact model, but he knew for damned sure it was about to be used in a homicide, and he was going to be the trigger man.

Dimitri opened the cylinder and slid a single bullet into a chamber. He flicked his wrist to close it and rotated the cylinder, so the bullet was under the hammer. He handed the revolver to Carver. "You have one bullet. Put it in this man's head."

Carver frowned. "Who is that?"

"No questions. Just do it."

The man struggled and tried to scream, but his cries were muffled. He probably had a rag stuffed in his mouth beneath the bag. The man wore a coat and gloves so Carver didn't know anything about his appearance except his large belly and medium stature.

This was it, the fork in the road. If Carver wanted to keep working his way up the chain to find out who killed Liana, he had to end the life of a stranger. If he hadn't been with this group today, this stranger would have been killed by Dimitri or one of his people. Now it was being used as a loyalty test.

Dex and Rashid held Glock 19s down by their sides. They weren't pointing them at Carver, but the intent was clear. If he tried to shoot anyone except this man, they'd shoot him.

Alicia spoke. "What the hell is going on, Carver?"

"We don't have eyes on you," Beck said. "The drone lost you in the smoke."

Carver figured it was good that the drone couldn't see this. This man was dead one way or the other and Carver had no intention of blowing his mission after putting so much work into it. He put the gun to the man's head and pulled the trigger. The revolver boomed. The man's head whipped back and struck the alley wall.

Carver wiped off the gun handle with his shirt and handed Dimitri the gun. "There you go."

Dimitri grinned wide and clapped Carver hard on the back. "Look at those eyes, boys. Nothing at all behind them."

Rashid nodded. "The dead eyes of a killer."

"Aw, sounds like you're in love." Dex whipped out a long strap. "Now, get to work before someone comes over here."

"Carver, what the hell happened?" Alicia said. "Was that a gunshot? I can't hear what the others are saying to you."

Gage and Braden pulled spray paint cans from their backpack and sprayed swastikas on the alley wall while Dex and Rashid strapped the dead man to a trash can next to the wall. They unzipped the man's coat and cut his shirt open with a knife, revealing black skin.

Gage unrolled a large piece of paper and taped it to the man's chest. It said, *Keep protesting and we'll keep killing you.* There were racial slurs filling the last part of the sign.

Dimitri tugged the bag off the man's head. There was a rag stuffed in the man's mouth and a bullet entry wound in his forehead where Carver had shot him.

"Who is this guy?" Carver said.

Dex set something on the ground placing it halfway under a nearby dumpster. It was a wallet flipped open to an ID. It was no ordinary ID. It was an FBI badge. They weren't just staging a hate crime, they were pinning it on an FBI agent.

Carver couldn't see the name on the badge. He bent down as if to pick up the shell casing from the gun. "Are we leaving this?"

"Don't touch anything." Dimitri tossed the revolver into another dumpster.

Carver got a look at the name on the badge, Phillip Morgan. The pic was of a middle-aged white man with a balding head.

"Okay, move out!" Dimitri said. The group ran down the alley and cut north on the next street. They pulled off their goggles and masks and started high fiving.

"This is going to be lit," Dex said. "I can't wait to see what happens next."

It didn't take a genius to figure out why they'd done what they'd done. They wanted to stoke racial hatred and anger. They wanted the staged hate crime to blow up these protests just days before they were supposed to go to Washington DC.

Dimitri turned to Carver. "That was city councilman Kaden Roberts."

"We would've settled for just about any of the city council members, but he was the easiest target," Dex said.

Carver nodded. "Staging a hate crime and pinning it on the FBI so the protestors start targeting law enforcement. Smart. Real smart."

"Yeah, you get it," Dex said. "Sacrifices have to be made."

"How'd you get an FBI agent's badge?" Carver said. "Who's Phillip Morgan?"

"I'm looking into it," Alicia said. "Did they kill someone?"

Carver coughed once.

Jessica spoke from nearby. "They did what? Is Carver okay?"

"He's fine," Alicia said. "Someone else isn't, though."

Dimitri tapped out a message on his phone. He waited for a reply. Nodded. "We're done for the day." He turned to Carver. "I hope you didn't have other plans today, Sam."

"We're just leaving the protest?" Carver looked disappointed. "I was just starting to have fun."

Dex belly laughed. "Man, this guy is cold. I love it."

Braden looked confused. "So, you weren't trying to help me or that girl. You just wanted to beat up some cops."

Carver shrugged. "I mean, yeah. But if I ended up helping you, too, then it's all good, right?"

"Aw, Braden's feelings are hurt." Manny rubbed his eyes like he was crying. "You're so soft, it's pathetic."

"That's what relying on daddy's money does to a man," Dex said. "Make you weak."

Braden balled up his fists. "Keep it up and I'll take my money elsewhere!"

Dimitri gripped the back of his neck. "You know that's not an option, boy. Besides, you stick with us, and you have a better chance of finally becoming a real man."

Carver wasn't too sure of that. They'd probably kill Braden or get him killed well before he ever became a so-called real man.

Gage stopped walking. "I'm not leaving until the protest is over."

Dimitri stared dully at him. "Keep your mouth shut about everything. No bragging. Nothing. You got it?"

"I won't breathe a word." Gage mimicked zipping his lips. "Unlike you, I actually believe in the cause."

"Yeah?" Dex smirked. "Which one?"

"Whichever one gets him laid," Manny said with a laugh. "Our little femboy, Gage, is almost as bad as little Braden here."

Gage flipped them off with both hands. "Go fuck yourselves." He turned and walked back toward the march.

Dimitri looked at his phone. "Let's go." He headed away from the march. They eventually reached a windowless van parked on the side of the road. Dex opened the sliding side door and motioned for Carver to get in.

"Ladies first."

Carver got in and sat on the bench seat. Dex and Manny sat next to him. Braden sat on the third row by himself. Dimitri and Rashid took the front seats. Dimitri drove them south to a large property surrounded by a chain link fence.

A faded sign said something about a factory. There were old red-brick buildings. A tall smokestack with gaping holes in the side. There were several outbuildings and old vehicles left to rust and rot. It had been a factory once, but not for a long, long time.

The chain link fence was topped by razor wire and the North Branch Chicago River formed the eastern border. Dimitri used his phone to open the gate and drove through. He used his phone again to open a rollup door on one of the old buildings.

The place looked abandoned on the outside, but the inside looked freshly renovated. The concrete floor had been painted and sealed recently, and the walls also had a fresh coat of white paint.

There were several vehicles parked near the right wall, including high-topped vans, SUVs, and several nondescript sedans. It was a full-blown base of operations.

It was real interesting how much stuff they had here. If this crew was moving with the protests and they'd only be in Chicago a few days, why did they have a full getup like this? Either they had a lot of money, or another organization owned this place and was letting them use it.

Carver suspected both things were true. The parent organization of HLF owned this place. They probably owned a lot of places like this across the country. Dimitri and gang were using it for a couple of days and would use similar facilities in DC.

This place might offer a few clues as to who was funding HLF. Clues that would help Carver find who ordered Dimitri to get rid of Liana.

Dimitri parked next to a black SUV. He got out and walked across the open space. There was a table with a laptop, a big monitor, and keyboard on it. There was a rollaway cart with a giant hundred-inch television on it. Carver knew the size because there was still a sticker on the upper right-hand corner with the specs.

There was a walled-off area to the left. The walls didn't even come close to reaching the ceiling of the building. They'd apparently been built to partition off a kitchen space, complete with refrigerator, microwave, and range.

In the area where the cars were parked there was a repair bay with hydraulic lift, engine hoist, and a couple of big toolboxes. There were shelves stocked with cases of motor oil, filters, and all the other fixings needed for car maintenance.

There were stacks of wooden weapons crates up against the outside of the kitchen area. They were the kinds of crates used to ship small arms like rifles and handguns. There were polyethylene ammo and rifle cases next to the wooden crates.

Two of the polyethylene cases were much longer and wider than the others. They were the kind of cases used to transport specialized weapons or support items, meaning they could hold anything from Javelin rocket launchers to modular footbridges.

It was clear that these people had just about everything they needed when it came to weapons and equipment. This place was a full-blown base of operations any criminal enterprise would love to have.

Two of the wooden crates were open. One was filled with blue metal oxygen cannisters. The kind used for medical purposes. The other crate had similar cannisters, but they were red. Carver couldn't see the markings on them, but he figured they might have acetylene in them. They could be used with the oxygen cannisters to fuel a welding torch.

Dimitri went to the television and turned it on. The screen was split into six windows. Each window displayed a different channel on it. Some were twenty-four-hour news stations and others were local. Most of them were showing the protest march.

Two channels had overhead views of the protests and were replaying the moment when the smoke bombs had gone off. The other channels were doing interviews with protestors or running what looked like canned stories.

Everything changed moments later. Someone had finally found the murdered city councilman. Every news station went live with people on the ground. Live video of the dead man played on one of the stations. The others blurred out the body but showed the sign and everything else.

The city was already a tinderbox. Now it was about to burn to the ground.

CHAPTER 28

Carver looked at the man he'd killed.

He'd passed a test by helping the enemy. It wasn't the first time, and it probably wouldn't be the last he'd had to kill or injure someone to prove himself.

"Hell yeah!" Dex went to the kitchen and grabbed a six-pack of beer from the fridge. He passed them out to everyone except Braden, leaving the last beer bottle in the box.

Braden scowled and reached for the beer.

Dex slapped his hand away. "Hey, you're underage."

"I'm twenty-five, asshole!"

"You look sixteen." Dex turned to Manny. "What do you think?"

Manny smirked. "Have your balls dropped yet, kid?"

Dex snorted. "What balls?"

Rashid didn't touch his beer. He went into the kitchen and put a teakettle on the stove.

Braden snatched the last beer and struggled to twist off the lid. The others watched with amused expressions.

Carver watched the news. People were outraged. The mayor and chief of police held a news conference vowing to find the perpetrators of the hate crime. They were blaming a white nationalist organization called the Sons of America.

Not long after the accusations, a dark-skinned Hispanic man held a news conference denouncing the crime and saying his people had nothing to do with it. The caption said he was the leader of the Sons of America.

The news station switched back to their news anchors before the press conference ended. "We're not going to broadcast his message of hate," the male anchor said. "The SOA has been following the protests from city to city. They've tried to organize counterprotests and have failed miserably."

"You're so right, Joe." The female news anchor scowled. "And now they've resorted to extreme tactics. It's obscene and loathsome, but nothing new from a hate group like them."

"Time for the FBI to shut them down and jail them all," Joe said. "In fact, they need to round up all these crazies, throw them in prison, and toss away the key."

"They're taking the bait." Dimitri clapped his hands. "Perfection."

Dex sipped his beer. "Say what you will about Yancy, but his plan is working better than I thought it would."

"He's a pompous ass." Manny pretended to spit on the floor. "You know what I'd like to do to him."

"Yeah, well you'll have the chance to tell him in person this weekend." Dimitri grinned. "He's coming to see us at the finish line."

"Hell yeah."

Dex snapped his fingers and pointed at the TV. "They're linking our FBI scapegoat to the Sons of America. Man, these idiots are buying it hook, line, and sinker."

"Because they want to believe it." Dimitri shrugged. "They almost make it too easy."

Several news organizations were running stories about Phillip Morgan, a rogue FBI agent who helped the SOA capture councilman Kaden Roberts and brutally murder him to send a message to the protestors.

Only one newsfeed was showing the destruction left in the wake of the rioting and looting. They were interviewing store owners and people who lived nearby. The Kaden Roberts murder was on the runner at the bottom of the screen.

Dimitri pulled one window into focus so the audio would play.

A news anchor with a wide face and thick glasses was talking. "This is terrorism, plain and simple. Homegrown racial radical terrorism that needs to be stomped out. And there's no better way to make your voices heard than by showing up in Washington DC and forcing the politicians to finally do something about it!"

Dimitri switched to another feed. A woman was giving a similar speech. "We have domestic terrorists rampaging through peaceful protests. Murdering innocent people based on racial hatred." She pressed her lips into a thin line. "And this administration supports it one hundred percent. Give them no peace. When you see them in public, you need to make them feel your presence. Know what I mean?" She smirked. "Yeah, you understand."

"How much do they pay for this propaganda?" Dex said. "It can't come cheap."

"That's the best part." Dimitri chuckled. "They have people in charge of hiring the news anchors these days, so they only hire people loyal to the message."

Carver wondered who 'they' was. Was this related to Enigma, the shadow organization that had a finger in every pie, or was it something else? It really didn't matter. What mattered was that he was on the inside now.

Well, almost. He figured there would be at least one more trial by fire before they trusted him completely. He was certain that he wasn't free to leave. They would make him stay here and then test him by having him kill someone else.

He might be wrong. They might mostly trust him right now, but they'd recently uncovered a spy in their midst when Liana's cover had been blown. They wouldn't trust anyone fast or easily right now. He decided to test that theory.

Carver rubbed his hands together. "I'm gonna go to the motel and get some rest. Are we doing something tomorrow?"

Dimitri gave him a knowing smirk. "No need to go anywhere, my friend. We will provide you lodging and food here."

"Yeah, you're not going anywhere right now." Dex bared his teeth in a grin. "You're not even close to being vetted properly."

"Vetted?" Carver raised an eyebrow. "I didn't exactly apply for a job. I just saw something that pissed me off and had fun beating up some cops. I'm more than happy to do it again tomorrow, but I like my alone time."

"Yeah, we kind of drafted you." Dex shrugged. "That's what you get for being capable and useful."

"Well if I'm being kept here, do I get paid for my services?" Carver spread his hands in a shrug. "I got bills to pay."

"Mouths to feed?" Dex said.

"Only mine. And I like to feed it well."

"Don't worry, man." Dex nodded at Dimitri. "If he likes you, you're going to do just fine."

Dimitri walked a distance away and talked on his phone. He glanced at Carver several times and nodded. He ended the call and walked back over to Carver. "Let's go for a ride."

"The kind of ride where I end up dead?"

Dimitri laughed and slapped him on the back. "I like this guy. He doesn't trust no one."

"He ain't as stupid as he looks," Dex said.

Manny tossed an empty beer bottle in the garbage. He burped loudly as he got another one. "Dimitri's not the kind of guy to be subtle. If he wants you dead, you'll know. And then the next minute you'll be dead. This guy used to eat spetsnaz for breakfast."

"And dinner." Dimitri balled a hand into a fist and punched the palm of the other hand. "Don't worry, Sam. If your times comes, I'll tell you. And once I tell you, it is inevitable."

"Good to know." Carver raised his eyebrows. "Well, where are we going?"

"Background check. We had an unfortunate event recently, so we have to be more careful."

"Unfortunate event?" Carver frowned. "What do you mean by that?"

"It's none of your concern." Dimitri walked to a big boxy SUV that was connected to an electric vehicle charger. He unhooked it and climbed into the driver's seat.

Carver hadn't seen this brand of car before. It had Chinese letters on it which told him it was probably an import. In fact, it was the same brand of vehicle as the one he'd seen in Lash Dalton's garage.

He got into the passenger side.

Dimitri rubbed the steering wheel affectionately and stretched. "Very roomy yeah?"

The vehicle was certainly spacious inside with more legroom than was typical in most SUVs. Carver nodded. "Yeah. Chinese import?"

"Yes. You can't even legally buy these here yet. But you will be able to soon." He pressed a button, and the vehicle rotated on its axis a hundred and eighty degrees.

Carver was genuinely surprised. "Did this thing just do a tank turn?"

Dimitri barked a laugh. "Amazing, isn't it? And this thing is half the price of a normal SUV." He hit the accelerator, and the vehicle smoothly shot forward and out of the garage door.

"I'm not much of a car enthusiast, but it's nice." Carver squeezed the leather seat. "Does it cost a hundred grand?"

"Nope. And if things go well, these and a lot of other Chinese vehicles are going to hit the market."

Carver suspected that Dimitri had an inside angle on that happening. "You sound unusually excited about that."

Dimitri laughed. "Do you like money, Sam?"

"Yeah, of course. Dex said I could get paid for doing whatever it is you want me to do."

"Yes. If all goes well, we might make a lot of money. You could easily clear six figures for two weeks' worth of work." He winked. "You like the sound of that?"

"Hell yeah. Whatever you want me to do, I'll do it."

"You're my kind of guy, Sam. And you're lucky because not long ago there would have been no room in our group. Someone else was working with us. Then they left and we never found anyone who could fill the slot quite like they did."

"Is that the unfortunate incident you mentioned earlier? Some guy quit on you?"

Dimitri shook his head. "It doesn't matter. What does matter is that very powerful people want us to succeed. And if we succeed it will be great for all Americans."

"Well, I don't care about all that. I just want to get paid. I've got debts to pay."

"Don't we all?" Dimitri guided the big SUV to the east. He tuned the radio to a seventies disco streaming station. He hummed along, sometimes singing. He didn't have a bad singing voice despite the accent.

Carver was thinking. He was thinking hard. He didn't know what kind of background check these guys were going to do. Were they going to take fingerprints, social security number, and the whole nine yards? Or was it going to be something involving facial recognition?

He took out his wireless earphones and put them in, then made a show of choosing music to listen to.

"Don't like disco?" Dimitri said.

"Nope." Carver picked a rap artist he'd never heard of from the music app Jessica had installed on his phone. She'd also logged his phone into a music streaming app just in case he needed to prove he was listening to music.

"We've been listening over comms," Alicia said. "Beck's drone tracked your phone to an old factory. He's running on overtime now, by the way. Do you want to authorize more time?"

Carver hummed and pretended to sing with the rap. "Yeah, I got the money if the gangster's got the time."

Alicia chuckled. "Affirmative. I'll authorize overtime. But it won't be cheap."

"Ain't nothing cheap for a brother on the streets."

"Maybe you should start a rapping career," Jessica said. "I heard about the background check, so I started working on a fake profile right away. I'm checking to see if what's her face can make it look official. No response yet."

Carver took out an earphone and turned to Dimitri. "I don't know how you plan to do this background check, but I do have a criminal record. Resisting arrest and assault on an officer."

Dimitri laughed. "I'm not surprised."

"Okay, I'll add that to the profile," Jessica said.

"It's a full background check," Dimitri said. "We have an inside track. You can't hide anything from us."

"Great." Jessica groaned. "Probably fingerprints, social security number, and birthdate. I can't create a fake profile with that much detail. At least not without Rachel's help. And I have no idea how long that takes to set up from her end."

"I have a guy at the FBI," Alicia said. "He wants fifty grand."

"Yeah, that's fine," Carver said as if answering Dimitri. "Whatever it takes, I guess."

"Okay, I'll wire him from my own funds, and you can pay me back," Alicia said. "Stand by."

"How long do you have?" Jessica said.

"Where we going anyway?" Carver said. "I'm hungry."

"Not far," Dimitri said. "We can eat afterward." He gave Carver the side eye. "If you're still alive."

Carver wasn't sure if he could take Dimitri in a fistfight. He damned sure couldn't take him right now since the other man was armed. If things went south, then it was mission over even if he could take Dimitri, because there was no way this guy was going to give him any answers.

Alicia came back on comms. "He's got an existing profile he can modify for you. It will probably take him forty minutes he said. You need to stall."

Carver blew out a breath. "Can you just kill me already? I'm starving!"

"It's only twenty minutes away and it will take only ten minutes to collect your information." Dimitri shook his head. "You can wait."

"You'd better find an extra twenty minutes somewhere, Carver." Alicia hissed. "My guy just texted me back. He can get the information changed in ten minutes, but it might take hours for it to propagate across government systems. You'd better consider aborting."

"Not an option." Carver pointed to a fast-food restaurant. "Just go through the drive through."

Dimitri's jaw tightened. "You're lucky I'm hungry too. But not this restaurant." He pointed to another place ahead. "I want tacos."

"Fine." Carver shrugged. "At this point, I don't really care."

Dimitri patted the knife sheathed on his thigh. "Don't try anything stupid. I can hit someone with a thrown knife from a hundred feet."

"I guess you're just an all-around badass," Carver said. "Who the hell did you work for that had you fighting spetsnaz?"

"Ah, wouldn't you like to know?"

"Yeah, that's why I asked. Is it classified or something?"

"It's simply none of your concern." Dimitri turned into the drive-through. There was one car at the order kiosk. The driver tapped the touchscreen to make an order. It was an older guy, and he seemed unfamiliar with it.

Dimitri honked his horn. "Hurry up, old man!"

The old man flipped him off and went back to tapping the screen. Dimitri grinned. "The old bastard is lucky I'm in a good mood. "What do you want?"

"Four beef tacos and water." Carver pulled out cash.

Dimitri waved it off. "It's on me this time."

The old man finished his order and pulled around the bend. Dimitri pulled forward and ordered ten beef tacos and two bottled waters. He went around the bend to the window. There were four cars waiting.

Carver felt a slight sense of relief. This was going to take fifteen minutes, easy. Between this and the drive to wherever they were going, it might total an hour. He might have a chance at beating the clock. A very slight chance.

There had almost never been a time when he'd needed a last-minute fake identity created in government records. The only time he could recall was when Jericho had to accompany him on an operation and needed a new identity.

That had been in Germany. It was much easier to create a fake federal identity there because they had direct governmental cooperation. The United States was different. There were hundreds or maybe thousands of different computer systems and databases spread across countless agencies, none of which talked to each other.

The individual states had their own systems as well and none of them talked to the federal systems unless someone authorized it. When Alicia's guy said it would take hours to propagate, he was actually being extremely optimistic. It could sometimes take days or weeks.

There was no knowing which system Dimitri's guy had access to. It might be a typical FBI background check in which case Carver wouldn't even show up. That was because Scion purged all his records when he joined. He'd done his best not to show up in any government databases since then.

The lack of records would raise all kinds of red flags because only the government was capable of that kind of erasure, at least in theory. There were other ways to erase yourself from public records, but it wasn't easy or cheap.

A woman came to the window and gave the first car a bag. The car pulled away. The next car pulled up. She gave them a bag almost immediately and they left. Apparently, the first car had just been waiting on something, and the other orders had piled up behind it.

That meant this wasn't going to take fifteen to twenty minutes. It was going to take five minutes. They were going to reach their destination much sooner than anticipated. Carver's false identity wouldn't have time to propagate. He would be found out.

And this was going to end badly.

CHAPTER 29

Carver didn't panic.

Panicking never helped anyone, but it sure got a lot of people killed. Provided he wasn't being taken to a location with a lot of armed guards, he could simply run if things went south. They were probably going to an office building where background checks were done. It seemed doubtful there would be armed guards.

The drive-through line moved quickly. They had to wait a moment for their tacos to be ready, but the total wait was barely ten minutes. Dimitri opened the bag and ripped the paper off a hard-shell taco. He drove with one hand and held the taco with the other.

Carver ate his tacos. They were nothing special but good all the same. He hadn't been lying about being hungry. In fact, he wished he'd ordered a couple more tacos. Dimitri ate all six of his tacos in about two bites each. He balled up the bag when he was done and tossed it out the window.

He turned into an industrial area and stopped in front of a gate with a guardhouse. The guard took one look at him and let him through. There were multiple warehouses on the lot. They looked like they'd been built fifty years ago and hadn't changed much since then.

Dimitri veered around a large box truck and parked in front of a door. He gripped the top of the car and pulled himself up and out. The car rocked like it had been hit by a bull. Carver got out and followed him into the building.

The warehouse was filled with pallets and large heavy-duty steel shelves. The pallets were wrapped with opaque plastic but there was Chinese writing on the sides of most of them, leaving little doubt where they came from.

There were four armed men standing around a forklift a few shelves down from the entrance. They were drinking beer, laughing and talking. There was a fifth man, the forklift driver as well, but he wore gray work coveralls and didn't give off the same vibe as the armed men.

Dimitri took Carver into an office. It looked typical for an office in an industrial building with vinyl flooring, fake wood panel walls, and lots of old metal filing cabinets. The four desks inside were steel monstrosities with laminate tops.

A young guy, probably in his early thirties and of Indian descent peered over the monitor at them. He said something into a headset, took it off and set it on the desk. He looked from Dimitri to Carver. "Who is this?"

"Got a new recruit to vet, Arjun." He motioned toward Carver. "This is Sam."

"Does Sam have a last name?" Arjun said.

Carver realized he didn't know. Alicia hadn't told him anything about the new profile. He coughed once. Cleared his throat. It looked like running might be his best option.

He grunted and looked the man up and down. "An Indian? Are you sure you aren't trying to steal my information?"

Dimitri laughed. "That's racist, you know."

"Not if it's true. Indians run all kinds of scams on Americans."

"True," Arjun said. "But I can assure you this is to make sure you aren't running any scams on us."

"So, I give you my last name, social security number, birthdate, and all that? All the things you need to steal my identity?"

Dimitri touched the knife on his thigh. "Either that, or we steal your life."

"It's Pecker," Alicia said. "Sorry, I just realized that I'd muted my mic."

Carver blinked a couple of times and sighed. "Pecker. Sam Pecker."

"What a horrible last name," Jessica said. "Your FBI guy is an idiot."

Arjun typed it in. "Social security number and birthdate."

Alicia told Carver and he repeated what she said.

"You look young for someone who's almost forty," Arjun said. "I thought you were in your late twenties."

Carver just stared at him. "What else do you need?"

"Fingerprints." Arjun slid a fingerprint reader to the edge of his desk. "Start with the left thumb and wait until I tell you to scan the next finger."

Carver pressed his thumb to the reader. "Like that?"

"Yes." Arjun stared at the screen and nodded a moment later. "Okay, index finger."

It took ten minutes to process all ten fingers. Carver estimated it had been a little over an hour since Alicia's guy put his information into the system. Hopefully it would show up when Arjun ran the search.

"I need to capture your face from all sides." Arjun motioned to a chair.

Carver sat down and faced a camera on the desk. "Like this?"

"Yes." Arjun took a picture. "Okay, now your left profile."

Carver did as instructed and let him scan both sides of his face. This was a lot more in depth than a normal background check. A whole lot more. Most places took fingerprints and basic information. It looked like Arjun was going to be scanning for facial recognition as well.

"I've never seen a background check like this," Carver said. "How does it work?"

"It creates a complete profile of a person and queries multiple governmental databases." Arjun tapped on his keyboard. "Some of those databases aren't open to private companies, but we have limited access."

Carver hoped they didn't have full access, or they'd find out that his false identity was just a few hours old.

Arjun held out a hand. "Let me see your driver's license."

"I didn't bring it with me," Carver said. "Just in case I got into trouble. It's easier not having an ID on you."

Dimitri grinned. "Very smart."

Arjun shrugged. "It doesn't matter. IDs can be faked. This background check can't."

"Must be one hell of a background check," Carver said. "Fingerprints, face scans. You need a stool sample too?"

Dimitri barked a laugh.

"Okay, it's submitted." Arjun leaned back in his chair. "It doesn't take very long. Maybe five to ten minutes, depending on the databases."

"Have a seat." Dimitri motioned toward a vinyl sofa. He sat in a chair in front of Arjun's desk.

Carver sat down and crossed his legs to make it look like he wasn't worried about anything. He wasn't sure what would happen if nothing showed up. He also wondered if other results might appear. Results that put him in Georgia, California, or Oregon. Results that tied him to a lot of death and destruction.

"How do you like the YangWang?" Arjun said.

"I love it." Dimitri smiled. "Best car I've ever driven."

"I love mine. Fast as hell and the ladies love it." Arjun rapped his fingers on the desk and stared at the monitor. "Nothing yet."

"Nothing?" Dimitri frowned. "That's unusual."

"The system has been slow today." Arjun shrugged. "The feds were shutting down several agencies today for auditing. Hopefully that won't affect anything."

"It's affecting everything." Dimitri scowled. "That's why we have to succeed. We may not get another chance."

Arjun nodded. "They could have done this anytime over the past few years. Why now?"

"Because they exhausted all other options. Now we have no choice." Dimitri sighed. "Anything yet?"

"No." Arjun typed on his computer. He frowned. "I'm getting good responses from my pings. Thirty out of thirty-four queries finished with no results. The last four queries are running slow as usual."

"Thirty-four?" Carver raised an eyebrow. "How many databases are there?"

Arjun didn't seem to hear the question. He tilted his head slightly and looked like he was about to say something that wasn't good for Carver's future. Then he blinked. "Oh, here we go. Assault and battery, assaulting a police officer, resisting arrest in Los Angeles."

Dimitri grinned. "There he is."

"Attempted murder, armed robbery, and grand theft auto." Arjun's eyebrows rose. "Wow, you're lucky you did that in Oakland or you'd be in jail right now."

"Why's that?" Carver said.

"They're very soft on crime there," Arjun said.

"Crap, I didn't realize this fake identity had so many felonies attached to it," Alicia said. "Sorry."

"FBI has notes on his criminal history, but no convictions because the Oakland and LA district attorneys didn't press charges." Arjun nodded. "Very, very lucky man."

"So, we're good to go?" Carver said.

Arjun's forehead pinched. He looked from his monitor to Carver and back to the monitor.

Carver got up and walked around the desk. "What?"

"Is this right?" Arjun pointed to a number with a dollar sign next to it.

Apparently Sam Pecker's net worth was just north of two million dollars. Carver shook his head. "I don't know where they got that from."

"You sure about that?"

"Yeah." Carver tsked. "I wish I had that kind of money."

Arjun didn't look convinced, but he minimized the screen.

Carver noticed other open windows on the screen. He saw icons for logistics, scheduling, and operations. He also saw a first name on one of the windows. It was the same name mentioned back at Dimitri's headquarters—Yancy.

There was a good bet that this computer system had information linking HLF to the people behind it. Yancy was almost certainly one of them. Maybe his name was somewhere in that list of people who'd bought the undercover agent list. If it was, Carver didn't remember seeing it. He needed a last name to go with the first.

Arjun locked the computer screen and stood up. He stretched. "He's a criminal if that's what you wanted to know."

"It is." Dimitri walked over and patted Carver on the back. "Looks like you're our guy after all."

"Attempted murder, assault with a deadly weapon, armed robbery." Arjun laughed. "Sounds like a real keeper."

"All right. Go wait in the car." Dimitri jabbed a thumb toward the exit. "I need to talk to Arjun about some things."

"I thought you trusted me." Carver put on a confused expression. "What's he got to say that I can't hear?"

"You're a probationary member, not part of the inner circle." Dimitri gripped him by the arm and escorted him to the door. "Go wait in the car or I'll shove you in the trunk myself."

Carver jerked his arm in an attempt to free it, but Dimitri's grip was like iron.

Dimitri grinned and held on a little longer before letting him go. Carver left the room and went outside. He heard footsteps behind him. Probably Dimitri making sure he was out there. Carver went outside.

"Your guy came through," he said to Alicia. "I'm in."

"It wasn't ideal, but it worked. I also didn't know about the net worth thing." Alicia sighed. "Well, I've had closer calls."

"They really like their violent criminals, don't they?" Jessica said. "You need to be careful. They'll obviously kill you without a second thought."

"Yep." Carver walked along outside the building. He didn't see any armed guards wandering around. There were also no cameras on the side of the building. There were windows, but they were narrow transom windows high on the wall.

They were the kind of windows installed before air conditioning, designed to allow hot air out of a building without also allowing a thief an easy way in. There were stacks of pallets and wooden crates along the side of the building. It looked like they staged them there before they were hauled off for disposal or recycling.

Carver climbed onto a stack of pallets and pulled himself onto a crate near the window. He glanced through and saw the inside of the office. He saw Arjun talking to Dimitri. He also had a clear view of the computer screen, but it was off.

The window wasn't open, but it was old, and the glass was thin. He heard Dimitri laugh. Heard Arjun talking but it was faint, and he couldn't quite make out the words. Arjun sat back down at his computer. Dimitri walked around behind him.

Their bodies blocked the screen. Arjun spoke. Dimitri nodded and pointed at the screen. The men laughed. Arjun tapped the keyboard a few times. He wasn't typing. It was like he was scrolling through something with the arrow keys. His keyboard was loud and clicky like a typewriter. Probably a mechanical keyboard.

One of the other men Carver had seen next to the forklift earlier entered the room and said something. His words were muffled due to the bad acoustics and the glass. Dimitri responded to him. The conversation lasted about five minutes. Dimitri jabbed his thumb to the side. The other man nodded and left.

Arjun went back to showing Dimitri whatever it was on his computer. Carver wondered what Dimitri had pointed at with his thumb. It occurred to him that he hadn't been pointing at something in the room. He'd been pointing in the general direction of Dimitri's car.

He quietly slid off the crate to the pallets. Dropped from the pallets to the ground. Hurried to the car. He walked up to it right when the guy from Arjun's office walked outside.

The man frowned. "Where did you just come from?"

"Taking a leak. Why?"

"There's a bathroom right inside the door you moron." He rolled his eyes. "Come with me."

"Dimitri told me to wait out here. I'm not moving until he says otherwise."

"Good news. He said otherwise."

"Not to me."

"He told me to come get you. We need help unloading a truck."

Carver frowned. "Do I look like a dockworker to you?"

"You look and sound like an idiot to me." He patted a gun at his side. "Come help us or I'll kneecap you like a little bitch."

Carver shrugged. "Lead the way."

The man sneered at him then turned and walked inside. Carver followed him. They walked between towering metal shelves filled with goods. It was hard to tell what they were because they were wrapped with green plastic to secure cargo to the pallets.

The plastic wrap had ripped on one of the pallets and small boxes had spilled out. The words *Made in Mexico* were stamped on the sides. Another pallet was full of items with the stamp *Made in Vietnam* on the sides of the boxes.

Carver figured there had to be something illegal in the boxes. Drugs maybe. The boxes were too small and flimsy for transporting weapons, but maybe they had a liner on the inside made to withstand several pounds of heavy steel.

He didn't really care what the purpose of the warehouse was. They could be shipping nuclear weapons for all he cared. He just wanted to find out who Yancy was and if he was the top dog for this organization or just another lap dog.

They arrived at the docks on the back side of the building. A semitruck trailer was docked at one. The forklift Carver had seen earlier was buried under a mound of boxes.

It looked like the driver had tried to move a high stack of pallets all at once and they'd toppled over.

Some items had spilled out of the boxes. One man was cleaning up the items and putting them back into the boxes that had survived the fall. It was the guy Carver had seen earlier with the four armed men. The other armed men were standing nearby watching him pick up the spilled cargo.

His escort pointed at the mess. "Help them clean that up."

Carver grunted. "Is your guy not forklift certified?"

"Shut the hell up and get to work."

His escort went and stood next to the other armed men. It was obvious they weren't going to lift a finger to help.

One of the armed men, a short, burly guy with a bald head clapped his hands. "Hey Jerry, you missed a box!"

The forklift driver looked up at him. "I told you it was going to collapse. Why do I have to do all the cleanup?"

"We brought you a helper, Jerry." Carver's escort patted his gun and gave Carver a meaningful look again. "Didn't I tell you to get to work?"

Carver shrugged and got to it. He picked up toppled boxes that hadn't broken open and moved them to the side, stacking them neatly. He picked up the boxes that had broken open and set them upright.

There were countless plastic bottles littering the floor. Intermingled with them were other random odds and ends from other boxes like office fans, charger cables, and more. Every pallet was loaded with boxes of the same items in most cases, so he started picking up things and sorting them into piles.

Jerry was huffing and puffing from exertion. "Come on guys. Many hands make light work."

The men ignored him.

Carver picked up a box near Jerry. "What happened?"

Jerry spoke in a hushed tone. "Kevin got angry I was only moving one pallet at a time. He said I could stack them five high, so he made me get off the forklift."

"Turns out he couldn't stack them five high?"

"These things aren't designed to be stacked at all." Jerry sighed. "Now I've got to clean up his mess."

Carver picked up another box. It was much heavier than the others. He walked it over to the side. Jerry carried a lighter box alongside him.

"Who are those guys anyway?" Carver said. "Why are they packing heat?"

"You don't want to mess with them." Jerry shook his head. "They're trained killers."

Carver had little doubt about that. He also had little doubt that he'd eventually have to kill each and every one of them.

CHAPTER 30

Carver looked at the group of men.

He turned to Jerry. "What are their names?"

"Their names?" Jerry scratched his head. "Why do you want to know that?"

"I just like to put faces with names."

"Uh, sure." Jerry bent down to pick up plastic bottles and put them in a box. "The short guy is Kevin. He's the boss."

Kevin was the one who'd escorted Carver here. He was five feet and maybe eight inches tall. He was built wide and low like a bulldog. Short but probably strong.

"The bald guy is Patel, the tall skinny guy is Jorge, and the short skinny guy is Craig."

"Kevin, Patel, Jorge, and Craig." Carver gave them a onceover as he set the heavy box down. The cardboard on this box was thicker and heavier than most. It made him curious about what might be inside.

He went back to the big mess around the forklift and picked up a box filled with smaller boxes of nail files. He set them down next to the heavy box and took one of the nail files out. He glanced back at the armed men. They weren't paying attention to him or Jerry.

Carver used the sharp tip of the nail file to rip open the tape on the heavy box. He opened the flap. There were smaller boxes inside. He opened the top one and found heavy-duty caster wheels with nuts and bolts inside.

He closed the box.

"They got a little bit of everything in these boxes, don't they?" Jerry said with a chuckle. "Nothing but Chinese junk as far as the eye can see."

"Some of the boxes are from Mexico and Vietnam."

"Yeah, that's what they say." Jerry winked. "It's all Chinese, believe me."

Carver stacked several light boxes on top of each other and hefted them. "Why do you say that?"

"I mean, it's obvious." Jerry lifted a couple of small boxes and walked with Carver to the sorted piles. "They think I'm stupid. That I don't notice things, but I do."

"Like what?"

"The box of caster wheels is stamped from Mexico." Jerry set down his boxes. He opened the box of caster wheels and took one out. "You see this design? See how it says made in Mexico on the box?"

Carver looked it over. "Sure."

Jerry went to pallets that were stacked against the wall. He looked at the shipping documents on the side and stopped at one with Chinese writing on it. He took out a utility knife and sliced open the plastic wrap, then slit open the side of a box.

He pulled out a smaller box that looked identical to the ones holding the caster wheels. He opened it and showed Carver more caster wheels. They looked identical in every way.

"Notice these creases in the bends?" Jerry pointed to the places where the metal frame was bent down to hold the wheel in the middle. "You can see the stamp where the machine presses on the metal too hard." There were tiny lines imprinted in the metal almost like an asterisk.

Jerry put the box back and they went to the other caster wheels. He pointed out identical marks on them.

"What the hell are you two doing?" Kevin said.

"Figuring out where to put some of the items," Jerry said.

"Well, figure it out fast!"

"Yes, sir!" Jerry went back to the mess around the forklift and got down on his knees to pick up a bunch of smaller boxes and put them into a larger one.

Carver helped him. "So, what does it mean? That the wheels are all made in the same place?"

"Yeah, exactly. They're made in China, shipped to Mexico or another country, and shipped to the US in boxes that say they were made in those countries."

"What's the point?"

"To avoid tariffs, of course." Jerry frowned. "You do know there's been a big trade war with China over the past few months, right?"

"No. Doesn't really affect me."

"How does it not affect you? Everything is made in China."

"I don't buy much."

Jerry tugged Carver's shirt sleeve. "I guarantee you that was made in China."

"I got it from a thrift store."

"Oh." Jerry shrugged. "Well, it was probably made in China."

"Guess you can't blame China for doing what it can to avoid tariffs." Carver finished loading a box and carried it to the sorted stacks. "Is it a crime or something?"

"Yeah, if you knowingly facilitate shipping or selling mislabeled items." Jerry shook his head. "The caster wheels labeled from China cost double what the ones from Mexico cost because of the tariffs but they sell them for only ten percent less."

"So, they sell them cheaper but for a lot more profit."

"Exactly." Jerry dragged a large box from the pile and began organizing the items inside. "They're taking advantage of the tariffs big time. None of the small sellers can compete because they're still buying items marked from China."

"So, it's specifically this place that's doing it?"

"Nah." Jerry looked around on the floor and picked up small boxes with pictures of deodorizers on them. "There's a whole network of these people. I've seen the shipping logs."

"Do they know that you know this?"

"I asked them about it once and they told me to keep my mouth shut or else." He laughed. "Who am I gonna tell anyway?"

"But you're not exactly free to quit this job, are you?"

Jerry paused what he was doing. "I never gave it much thought." He gulped. "But I'll bet you're right."

"Well, I hope the pay is good."

Jerry's face paled. "Damn, why'd you have to say that? Now I can't stop thinking about it."

Carver kept working while he thought about what this meant for his investigation. He imagined a blank spot at the top of a chart with the name Yancy next to it. Below that was HLF and the other affiliated organizations like HOI and others he hadn't heard of. Under that he put Dimitri and his gang.

How did this warehouse and others like it fit in? How were they all tied together? What did this warehouse have to do with their protest psyops? Was the warehouse fraud funding the protests or was there more to it?

Carver realized he hadn't heard from Alicia or Jessica in a while because his earphone batteries had died. He put them in the charging case and tucked it into his pocket. He kept working while Kevin and gang stood and watched.

He carried another box to the sorted stack where Jerry was stacking more boxes. "Do Kevin and his buddies just work at the warehouse?"

"As far as I know."

"What about Dimitri?"

"He's their boss, or at least they act like he is." Jerry shrugged. "They might just be afraid of him." He paused. "How did you end up here?"

"I met Dimitri at a protest. He's forcing me to work for him."

Jerry grimaced. "Kind of reminds me of that girl he brought here once. She looked like she didn't like working for him either."

"Girl?" Carver's interest was piqued. "Like a prostitute?"

Jerry laughed. "No, she was definitely one of his crew. But she asked me some questions about the warehouse. I basically told her what I told you."

"What did she look like?"

"Latina. Real pretty."

Carver grinned. "I haven't seen her yet, but now I want to."

"Oh, yeah, she's smoking hot." Jerry sighed. "I haven't seen her since then."

"Damn, maybe she doesn't work for him anymore." Carver blew out a breath. "The only people I've met are men."

Jerry tapped a finger on his chin. "That was a few months ago, so maybe she left." He frowned. "Or maybe she wanted to leave, and Dimitri did something to her."

"Does Dimitri come here often?"

Jerry waggled a hand. "Not too much. He made a special trip over here because they were gearing up for some big shipments or something."

"What big shipments?"

Jerry shrugged. "They never even told me what it was. If it came through here, I didn't see it."

"Are there other forklift drivers?"

"Over in the other buildings, yeah. This is where they put the small stuff, so anything else would end up in the big warehouses."

"Dimitri drives a Chinese car. Maybe that's what it was."

"Could be." Jerry tugged on a pallet to free it from a tangle of boxes and plastic wrap. "They talk about those Chinese cars a lot. I think they're figuring out how to get them into the country wholesale. That would be real big money."

Kevin walked over toward them. "Less talking and more working."

"It'd speed things up if you all chipped in," Jerry said.

Kevin grabbed him by the collar and jerked him closer. "It'd speed things up if you kept your mouth shut." He shoved Jerry roughly away and stared down Carver. "Both of you."

Carver walked over to him. "Maybe you should stop complaining. I'm not getting paid to do this."

"Yeah?" Kevin yanked out his gun and put it in Carver's face. "How about not getting shot? Does that work for you?"

It looked like Kevin was a real hothead. The other men were watching with amused expressions on their faces. Like they'd seen something like this a hundred times but it never got old.

Kevin didn't have his finger on the trigger. It was flat against the trigger guard like it was supposed to be. Carver ducked sideways. He swung his left hand to the right at the same time. Gripped Kevin's wrist. Gripped it hard.

Kevin cried out and released the gun. Carver caught it in his other hand. He twisted Kevin's arm behind his back. Jammed the pistol into the back of Kevin's head.

"Not getting shot works fine for me," Carver said.

The other men went for their guns, but Carver shoved Kevin away, hard enough for the other man to tip and fall face first on the floor. Carver ejected the bullet from the gun's chamber. He popped out the magazine and tossed it away. He dismantled the gun and threw the parts in different directions.

Carver stood over Kevin. "Don't threaten me unless you want to die. If you doubt that I'm capable, go ask Arjun about my background check."

The other men laughed.

"I told you that you'd piss of the wrong guy one day," Patel said.

Kevin pushed himself up with a groan. He rubbed the back of his head and looked at Carver with a scowl. "You're lucky you work for Dimitri, or I'd finish you right here on the spot."

"Yeah?" Carver backed up a step. "Let's go then."

Kevin's face went red with anger, but he held it in. He shook his head. "Get back to work and I won't tell Dimitri about this incident. You can be damned sure he can clean your clock."

Carver considered his options and decided a man like Sam Pecker would spit on the floor at Kevin's feet and then get back to work. So, that's what he did. He spat at Kevin's feet, gave him a dirty look, and then got back to helping Jerry.

"Hot damn, you put on a show," Jerry whispered as they carried boxes to their sorted pile. "I'm surprised he didn't try to shoot you after that."

It had been a calculated risk. One to gauge how the men would react. Were they a team or just some thugs who didn't form a cohesive unit? It looked like they were mostly the latter. That was good. Real good.

Kevin collected the parts of his gun and reassembled it slowly. He clearly wasn't the kind of guy who maintained his weapons, or he would have been able to put the pieces together in under a minute.

Carver didn't know if these men had anything to do with Liana's disappearance, but he was going to find out. If he could get out of the factory tonight, then he'd come here for a look around. There was a slim chance Liana was alive and being held somewhere. This would be a perfect place to hold her.

But getting out of the factory might not be possible. He wouldn't know until later. Kevin and his men had wandered off once it was clear Carver and Jerry were almost done. That left him free and unsupervised for the moment.

Jerry put a hand on his back and winced. "I think I pulled a few muscles. Thanks for the help even if it wasn't your choice."

"Sure." Carver left him and headed toward the offices until he was out of Jerry's sight. He didn't see Kevin or the others around, so he took a detour outside. It was dark and there weren't many streetlamps lighting roads between the warehouses.

He went to the neighboring warehouse. It was about the same size as the one he'd just been in. A side door was unlocked so he went inside. There was metal shelving inside filled with pallets just like in the warehouse he'd left.

Carver took a quick tour of the building, jogging past aisles and looking down them. Most of the boxes were stamped as being from Mexico and Vietnam just like in the other warehouse. Apparently, it was cheaper to import items from those two countries.

There were no separate rooms where a prisoner might be kept. He wasn't even sure why he was wasting his time looking for Liana. The odds of her being alive were very slim. But apparently, a part of him still held out hope despite those odds.

He exited the building by another door that was just across the road from the last warehouse in the complex. It was about the same size as the other buildings but not quite as tall. He hustled across the street and looked through a window on the front.

There was a small office on the other side but no view of the interior of the warehouse. He tested the handle on the door. It was locked. He walked around the side of the building and saw light emanating from the transom windows along the top.

There were no pallets or crates outside the building so he couldn't climb up for a look. The gutters were lightweight aluminum so they wouldn't hold his weight if he tried to climb them. He went to the other side to the cargo docks. One of the rollup doors was open. He climbed onto the dock and looked through the door.

There were rows upon rows of cars inside. There were various makes and models, but they were all the same brand, BYD. He wasn't familiar with the brand, but he recognized the large SUVs on the back row. They were the same as the one Dimitri had.

There was a row of exotic looking sports cars. They resemble McLarens with their large rear spoilers and curved front ends, but they were definitely not McLarens. They had the same strange symbol on the front that Dimitri's SUV had.

Most of the vehicles didn't have exhausts, because they were electric. Some of the vehicles were covered in dust as if they'd been sitting there a while. Others were clean, either newly arrived or someone had dusted them off.

Unlike the items in the other warehouses, these weren't being sold. They were arriving and ending up in this warehouse because as Dimitr had told him early, it wasn't legal to sell these cars in the United States.

For something that couldn't be sold, there sure were a lot of them. There had to be some reason for that, but Carver wasn't really concerned about it. He was more concerned with finding Liana.

This warehouse had a front office. He went there and looked through all the rooms but found no signs that Liana had ever been there. He stopped in what appeared to be the main office and thought about the possibilities.

The slim hope he'd been holding onto was slipping away fast. If she was here, Arjun would probably know where. If she was dead, maybe he knew where she was buried. Maybe he didn't know a thing because Dimitri handled it himself.

He walked past a desk piled high with shipping papers. He looked at the one on top. It was for a YangWang U9. Point of origin was Puebla, Mexico. There was a lot of other shipping information, but he skimmed through it until he found what he wanted. *Imported by Precise Imports LLC. Broker: Yancy Bancroft.*

There was a local address and another address in California. That was probably the port they arrived in if they were sent by ship. The customs broker would arrange to have the containers with the cars unloaded and pay the customs fees including excise taxes and tariffs. At least, that was Carver's basic understanding of how it worked.

This was good. It gave him a full name and an address that might lead him to Yancy. This was the man who apparently masterminded the plan Dimitri and his men were following. He might be the guy who bought the undercover agent list. He might be the high man on the totem pole. He might be the last person in a chain of people responsible for Liana's fate.

Carver folded the shipping document and tucked it into his pocket. Then he left the vehicle warehouse and made his way back to the first warehouse. He'd been gone about twenty minutes. Hopefully no one had gone looking for him.

He entered a side door and went back to the offices in the front. Dimitri wasn't there, but Arjun was. Apparently, no one had told him that the cleanup job was finished because he didn't seem concerned that Carver had been off the radar for twenty minutes.

Carver stopped just inside the door. "We're done. Where's Dimitri?"

"Dimitri had to go take care of something." Arjun stood and stretched. "He asked me to give you a ride."

"Give me a spare car and I'll go myself."

Arjun shook his head. "He wouldn't like that. Besides, we need to have a talk."

"About what?"

"Let me show you." Arjun motioned him over and sat back down.

Carver walked behind him and saw his background report on the screen. "Didn't we go over all of this already?"

"Most of it. But a couple of things caught my eye." He pointed to the net worth. "I confirmed that you have assets worth just over two million dollars. More importantly, you have liquid assets worth five hundred grand."

"Okay. What does that have to do with anything?"

"I also found this in the facial recognition images." He pulled up a picture of Carver.

Carver recognized the location. He was walking down a street in Asheville, North Carolina on his way to a craft brewery. The image would have been perfectly harmless if not for one thing. If not for one person walking alongside him.

That person was Liana.

CHAPTER 31

Carver knew exactly where this was going.

Arjun grinned. "Houston, we've got a problem."

"What problem?" Carver said.

"Don't bother playing innocent." Arjun tapped Liana. "You're connected to Wendy."

"Who?"

"Wendy." Arjun pulled something from under his desk and rotated his office chair to face Carver. He had a snub-nosed revolver on his lap. "I already know all about her. And if you're connected to her, then I know about you too."

If that was the case, Carver was still breathing because Arjun wanted something from him. He wanted that five hundred grand. "What do you think you know about her and me?"

"You're really going to play innocent?" Arjun blew out a breath. "Look, Dimitri told me she was spying on us for a competitor and that they were close to yanking the rug out from underneath us. He took care of her and he's going to take care of you if you don't make it worth my while."

"Is that all you got?" Carver said. "One picture?"

"It's all I need." Arjun waved the revolver at him. "I could kill you now and tell him later, or I could just let him torture you to death. On the other hand, we could be best friends for the low price of five hundred grand."

Carver wondered if Dimitri had lied to Arjun about Liana's real identity or if he really thought she worked for a competitor. Maybe the agent list hadn't burned her. Maybe something else had happened.

He was just a few feet from Arjun, but even an untrained ape could pull the trigger and put him down before he got close enough to disarm him.

"Fine, you got me." Carver sighed. "My boss wondered what happened to her and sent me to find out. How in the hell did you find out she was working for us?"

"Amazingly, I didn't figure it out. Dimitri found out from somewhere else." Arjun shrugged. "Look, I think competition is good. It keeps us on our toes."

"What's to keep you from turning me in or killing me after I give you the money?"

"Once I get the money, your secret is safe with me." Arjun picked up the gun. "Really, you have no choice."

"I get that. How am I supposed to get you that money?"

"We'll log into your bank account from here. You will transfer it to my account."

"My bank is going to have all kinds of questions about me transferring that much money." Carver shrugged. "I can't do anything about that."

"We'll do it with a wire transfer. When they call you to confirm, you'll confirm." Arjun stood. "You can use my computer."

There was a big problem with that. The money didn't exist and even if it did, he didn't know what bank it was in. This situation was going to end in one of two ways and neither way was particularly good.

"Okay." Carver sighed. "You're really cleaning me out, you know? That's my entire life savings."

"It's for a good cause." Arjun grinned, revealing dark stained crooked teeth.

"Your kid's education?"

Arjun laughed. "I'm not married, and I don't have kids. But I do love blondes and they're expensive."

Carver wasn't sure if he meant expensive to spoil or expensive to buy as a sex slave. He didn't really care to know. All he cared about was that Arjun was just two feet away now. The other man's finger was still on the trigger, but he looked relaxed and confident.

He looked like a man who wasn't worried because he didn't know two things. One, he didn't know how important it was to keep a proper distance between himself and a target, and two, he didn't know the capabilities of his current target.

If Carver was just some guy, then Arjun wouldn't have much to worry about. But even just some guy might try to lunge for the gun or try to escape. Arjun didn't seem concerned about that, probably because he'd been in situations like this before and they always worked out.

He didn't realize that while he might be five and zero in situations like this, it only took one loss to put you out of the game for good. And that was good. Real good.

There was always the possibility that Carver was underestimating Arjun. After all, Carver didn't know much about the man. But it was clear from his physical health and posture that he wasn't a trained killer like Kevin and the other men. It was highly likely that he was just some guy thinking he could make some easy money.

Carver yawned and worked his arms back and forth like he was stretching. Arjun didn't move or adjust his stance. He seemed unconcerned. He had absolute faith in the threat of a gun. That was why he was caught completely off guard when Carver lashed out with his elbow.

It was a lightning quick strike made easier because of the fake stretching routine. Carver's elbow was already head height to the shorter man. All it had required was a fast backswing. There was a loud crunch. Arjun went down in a heap without even making a sound.

The gun was still in his grip when he hit the floor. Carver pried the gun out of his hands. It looked like Arjun had taken his hand off the trigger the instant before being struck. Otherwise, his finger might have tensed and fired a shot.

Kevin and gang probably would have heard the shot and come running. It would have turned the situation into a firefight Carver couldn't win. At least not with Arjun's revolver.

Carver realized why Arjun's finger hadn't tensed. Arjun wasn't breathing. He was slack jawed, drooling, and very dead. Carver's elbow had caught him right on the temple. It most cases that resulted in a concussion. In this case, it probably resulted in a brain hemorrhage.

Now there was a body to clean up. First, he needed to clean up the data on Arjun's computer. He stared at the image of him and Liana in Asheville. That had been a good day. They'd walked around town, eaten good food, and had good beer.

That was one of the few occasions they'd left the lake cabin and risked going out before they went stir crazy. This image was the primary reason why going out hadn't been a good idea. But Carver didn't regret doing it. Not even a little bit. Not even if it almost got him killed.

He deleted the image and cleared the search cache. Then he logged off the computer. Arjun probably wasn't the kind of guy to write his passwords down, so unless someone else knew it, they weren't getting into the computer.

Carver heard loud talking. He heard men laughing and joking around. The sounds were getting closer. He went to the door and looked down the aisles nearest the office. He didn't see Kevin and his men but they were definitely coming this way.

Carver pocketed Arjun's revolver. He slung the man over his shoulder and hurried out of the office. He hooked right and jogged to the door. He ducked outside just as Kevin and gang rounded the shelves.

He glimpsed them but didn't think they saw him. He went down the side of the building near the stacked pallets and dumped Arjun on top of a crate behind them. Keys rattled in the dead man's pocket.

Carver fished them out. There was a key fob for a car. It had the same strange logo Carver had seen on the Chinese vehicles in the other warehouse. The logo looked like two lower-case Ys, one upside down, the other right side up, and both joined at the tip.

He pressed the unlock button on the fob. Lights flashed in the parking lot but the vehicle was hidden behind two pickup trucks. Carver tossed Arjun over his shoulder like a sack of potatoes and hustled out to the trucks. He ducked behind them and found Arjun's vehicle.

It was one of the supercar EVs. Cars like this didn't usually have trunks. Then again, this was an EV so there was no engine. The motors were probably right between the wheels. Judging from the buttons on the fob, this thing had two trunks, a front and a back.

He opened the rear trunk and was surprised to see it was decent sized. Big enough for two carryon suitcases and just barely big enough for a short Indian man. He shoved Arjun's body in headfirst and bent him into the fetal position. He heard tendons snap and bones crunch, but figured Arjun wouldn't mind.

Carver took Arjun's phone from his pocket and used the dead man's thumb to unlock it. The man had countless texts on his phone. Almost all of them were about logistics and warehousing. None were from Dimitri.

He found the icon for an encrypted texting app and opened it. Only a couple of texts hadn't automatically deleted. One was from Dimitri asking when Arjun was bringing Carver back. Arjun replied saying Carver was still helping with the cleanup. Dimitri responded with a curt thumbs up.

The only other texts had arrived just moments ago. They were both from Yancy Bancroft.

The Koreans hit us again. I don't know how they're finding out about our shipments. I instructed Kevin to look into it. If you know anything, this is your one chance to come clean.

Arjun had been holding a gun on Carver when the texts arrived. He wouldn't be answering the texts. Carver closed the trunk and opened the driver's door. It didn't open out like a normal door, but upward like a scissor.

The car was low to the ground. Real low. Carver dropped into the car and got situated. He opened a video app on Arjun's phone and let it play so the screen wouldn't close and lock. He set it on the wireless charging station. An elastic strap held it in place so it wouldn't shift around when he drove.

Carver pressed the brake pedal and the car turned on. The headlights came on automatically. He turned them off and got a warning in Chinese on the screen. He ignored the warning and backed up. The reverse lights lit up the parking lot. He didn't have a way to turn them off, so he put the car into drive and accelerated for the gate.

More messages popped up on Arjun's screen. Carver pulled onto the road and glanced at them. They were from Kevin.

We need to talk about something. Where are you?

Carver reached the main road and turned left to head back into town toward the factory. He didn't remember exactly how to get there, but it wasn't hard. He just had to figure out how to hide Arjun's body and reach the factory without raising too many questions.

Arjun's phone was probably being tracked. His car might even have a tracker on it. There was really no telling. Carver could toss the phone, but he couldn't hide the car with the body in it. There might be another option, though.

The car had a large screen on the center console. The screen currently displayed an image of the car and the map next to it. He used Arjun's phone to search for the vehicle make and model and whether it was self-driving like a Tesla.

There were several results. He played a video about it while he drove. The man in the video was Chinese but spoke in English. He was very enthusiastic about the features of the car and claimed it was far superior to anything made by any other car company.

He explained how the self-driving feature worked and said it didn't come with a nag system that required the driver to keep his hands on the steering wheel. He also claimed it was far safer than any other autonomous system and would soon be used in taxis all over the world.

That sounded amazing. Carver pulled to the side of the road. There was another text from Kevin. *Are you taking that guy back to the factory?*

Carver replied. *Yeah. Just saw your text. What do you want to talk about?*

The Koreans. Yancy is putting everyone through the wringer.

Carver opened the settings for the self-driving mode. He set the max speed to twenty above the speed limit. That was as high as it would go. The car apparently automatically read the speed limit signs and adjusted accordingly.

He put the address for Navy Pier into the GPS. He unpacked Arjun from the trunk and put him in the driver's seat without a seatbelt on. He typed back another response to Kevin.

Yancy can go to hell. I'm not answering any questions.

Kevin didn't take long to reply. *You will if you want to keep breathing. Get your ass back here right now.*

Carver replied with a few choice expletives and put the phone on the center console. He tapped the *GO* icon on the GPS and closed the car door. The car took off down the road, nearly taking off Carver's fingers before he could get out of the way.

He wasn't sure his plan would work. It relied heavily on a lack of safety features in a Chinese car. He figured the odds were good that the vehicle wouldn't make it safely to Navy Pier. Even if it did, there was a good chance it would drive into the river.

If his plan didn't work, it meant he'd have to kill a lot of people a lot sooner than planned. It would be a pain in the ass, but he'd do what he had to do. He started walking down the side of the road while searching for other videos on the self-driving feature in the YangWang U9.

He found one from a social media influencer who imported the car just to test it. He skipped to the section about the self-driving feature. The man warned that the car didn't always see traffic lights and it didn't always read signs in English because it had been programmed for Chinese roadways.

That was promising.

He hadn't been walking long when approaching headlights painted the road ahead of him. He turned around and heard the roar of big engines being pushed to the max. He walked to the outer edge of the shoulder just to be safe and saw the headlights of two pickups approaching.

Carver poked out his thumb and walked backwards. Tires screeched and the two trucks skidded to a stop. The passenger side door opened, and Craig hopped out, a handgun pointed at Carver.

"What the hell are you doing walking?"

Carver shrugged. "Arjun was supposed to give me a ride to the factory. He suddenly got real agitated and pulled a gun on me. He forced me to get out and then took off."

"Son of a bitch." Craig pointed to the truck. "Get in the back."

"What's going on?" Carver said.

"Get in the damned truck, moron!" Craig climbed into the front.

Carver got into the back and buckled in.

Kevin looked back from the driver's seat. "What happened?"

Carver told him the same thing he told Craig.

Craig looked up from an app on his phone. "That's why he stopped a few minutes ago. Now that crazy asshole is going ninety miles an hour toward the city."

"Toward the city?" Kevin gunned the truck forward and got back on the road. "I'll bet he's running to the Koreans for protection."

"Yep." Craig spoke into his phone. "Jorge, he's headed to the city. He forced Sam out of his car first. We think he's running to the Koreans for help."

"He's in that damned supercar," Jorge said. "Can we catch him?"

"Doubtful, but we can track him," Craig said.

The truck hit a hundred miles per hour. Traffic was light so they made good time, but they weren't closing the gap between them and Arjun.

Kevin glanced at the tracker on Craig's phone. "Looks like he's headed straight for the construction zone past the airport. That should slow him down."

"He's an idiot." Craig shook his head. "All the other highways are open at this hour, but he chooses the one route with a construction zone?"

"Yeah, our resident computer genius has no common sense or survival instinct."

Carver agreed with the latter, but he just leaned back and enjoyed the ride.

Craig's mouth dropped open. "What the hell? Look!" He showed the screen to Kevin. The blue blip indicating Arjun's car was driving down a road with red dotted lines. "He's driving on a closed section of road."

"No way." Kevin looked back and forth from the road to the screen. "That's the unfinished bypass ramp, right?"

"Yeah." Craig whistled. "He just came to a complete stop."

Carver looked up the road in question and found pictures of the bypass ramp. True to its name, it was a section of highway that ramped up about a hundred feet into the air and abruptly ended because construction wasn't complete.

The self-driving software hadn't recognized the construction zone and had just blown through it at ninety miles per hour. It went up the ramp and launched into the air before probably dropping like a brick due to the weight of the car battery.

The construction zone came into sight. There was no work being done tonight but traffic was still heavy at the bottleneck where two lanes were cut off. There was a new lane to the right of the closed lanes and multiple barricades preventing cars from driving on the new lane.

Those barricades were smashed to pieces in the center. Arjun's car hadn't detected the barricades and had avoided traffic by driving through them and along the new lane. It had continued up the ramp and driven off.

Kevin looked around. "No cops. No construction workers. They must have the night off."

Craig nodded. "Yeah."

Kevin drove up the ramp. The surface was new and finished for about a quarter of a mile where it ended in a wide gap between this section and another finished section. He parked the pickup and got out. He looked over the side and whistled. "I see the car."

Craig stood beside him. "It's on fire."

The other pickup pulled up behind them. Patel and Jorge spilled out and ran to the edge.

"What happened?" Jorge said. "He drove off the edge?"

"Yeah, the idiot tried to jump the gap or something." Kevin scratched his head. "This makes no sense. Why would he go this way?"

"What an idiot!" Patel looked over the side and laughed. "Wow, that thing is burning like crazy. Those electrical fires are no joke."

Carver didn't go close to the edge. He didn't trust these men as far as he could throw them. But he felt relieved. His cover was still safe.

For now.

Chapter 32

Carver remembered he still had Arjun's revolver in his pocket.

He wiped it down with his shirt while the others were preoccupied with the fire and dropped it over the side. A gun would be nice to have, but the snub-nosed revolver wouldn't be all that useful in a firefight.

He looked around for cameras. Didn't see any. He saw another interstate on-ramp about fifty yards away. It wasn't as tall as this one, but it offered a direct line of sight to the wreck. There was a stopped car on the on-ramp shoulder. A man stood next to it. His phone was out, and he was recording the flaming wreckage below.

Kevin turned to Carver. He frowned. "Did Arjun say anything to you before the car ride?"

Carver nodded. "He said I was lucky I passed my background check. He said they caught a woman working for a competitor not long ago."

"Yeah." Kevin nodded. "I remember that bitch. She passed the background check with flying colors. The Koreans probably paid a lot to get her a complete fake government profile."

"How did you find out she was working for the Koreans?" Carver said.

Kevin grunted. "I don't know. Dimitri found out and told Yancy. Yancy was pissed. He ordered new background checks on everyone, but we all came back clean. He's been paranoid ever since."

Carver relaxed to keep his fists from clenching. "How did Dimitri find out?"

"You ask a lot of damned questions," Kevin said.

"Dimitri has connections all over the place," Jorge said. "He's Yancy's right hand man. If you want to keep breathing, you'll stop asking questions."

The others laughed.

Kevin bared his teeth. "Yeah, if you think we're scary, we ain't nothing compared to Dimitri."

Carver didn't find them all that scary. But now he felt fairly certain of a few things.

One, Yancy hadn't been the one to get the undercover agent list.

Two, none of these bozos had anything to do with Liana's fate.

Three, Dimitri was his primary target.

That was unfortunate, because if someone else gave Dimitri the command to end Liana, he wasn't the kind of guy to volunteer that information freely or easily. Torture probably wouldn't even work. In fact, Carver wasn't sure he could capture the man alive. It would require a lot of fentanyl or a sledgehammer to the skull to knock him out.

"So, what now?" Jorge said.

Kevin shrugged. "We found the traitor, didn't we? No way Arjun would have run if he wasn't working for the Koreans."

"True." Craig nodded. "We can just let the body burn and leave before the cops show up."

"Yeah. Speaking of which, let's get the hell out of here." Kevin hurried to the pickup truck and climbed in.

Carver got into the back. Kevin spun the truck around and gunned it down the ramp. They made a U-turn at the bottom to merge back into traffic. Several other cars had pulled to the side of the road, probably because the drivers had seen the accident. Most had their phones out and were recording.

Kevin jabbed a thumb at Carver. "Let's drop this guy off at the factory. I'm sure Dimitri will want to talk to us anyway."

Craig nodded. "Yeah. Want me to text him in advance?"

"Might as well. He'll be pissed if we don't."

"On it." Craig typed on his phone.

It took fifteen minutes to reach the factory. Dimitri was watching the big TV with all the screens when they walked in. They were showing footage from someone's smartphone. Judging from the angle, it was the man Carver had seen on the other on-ramp.

Apparently, the motorist had a flat tire and was waiting on a tow truck when they saw the car busting through the barricades on the new on-ramp. Like most people these days, their first instinct was to pull out their phone and start recording.

The footage showed exactly what had happened. Arjun's car jetted up the ramp and flew through the air. It smashed into the next completed section and plummeted into the trees below. Moments later, the battery caught fire and the flames spread rapidly.

Thankfully, the same person hadn't recorded Kevin and the others when their pickups drove up there. Probably because he was too excited about the recording he'd just made or uploading it to social media for internet fame.

Dimitri turned to face them, his face taut with anger. "What the hell happened?"

"The Koreans hit a shipment again. Arjun and a couple of others are the only ones who knew the details, so Yancy wanted us to talk to him." Kevin shrugged. "Arjun ran for the hills."

Jorge chuckled. "Or the ramps."

Dimitri didn't look amused. "Arjun is a crooked son of a bitch, but he's no traitor. He makes good money."

"Then why did he run?" Kevin said.

Dimitri regarded Carver with narrow eyes. "He was supposed to bring you back here. Did you notice anything strange?"

"He started driving me back here like normal. He looked at his phone and got agitated." Carver shrugged. "Next thing I knew he was aiming a gun at me and telling me to get out of the car."

"Nothing else?"

"He kept talking about some woman who was working for the Koreans."

Dimitri clenched a fist and looked around the room at the others. "Did he mention this woman to any of you?"

Kevin nodded. "Yeah, right after you told Yancy. He said she was too attractive to kill and wanted to know if he could buy her for cheap."

Dimitri nodded. "I discussed that with him. She was too dangerous for an idiot like him to buy."

Craig chuckled. "He has a thing for blondes anyway."

Carver watched Dimitri closely but didn't ask questions. He didn't want to arouse any suspicions by being too curious about Liana. He was hoping Dimitri would talk about what he did to her, but the big man turned and stared at the news again.

"Anything else?" Kevin said. "We've got to make a run up the Gold Coast tonight."

"No." Dimitri didn't look back at them.

"You got it, boss." Kevin and the others left.

Carver looked around. "Where am I staying?"

Dimitri didn't answer for a while. He stared at the repeating video of Arjun's car driving off the ramp. He turned around. "Follow me."

Carver followed him to the back corner of the warehouse. Several cargo containers were lined up along the back wall. The doors hung open, offering a look inside. They were furnished as living quarters, complete with electrical and plumbing.

"In here." Dimitri pulled open the last container at the end.

Carver looked inside. It was much simpler than the other containers. There was a stainless-steel toilet and sink, a small bed, and a refrigerator. He looked at Dimitri. "You're going to lock me in here, aren't you?"

"Yes, now go inside."

"Is there food in the refrigerator?"

"Probably." Dimitri shrugged. "Go inside now before I throw you inside."

Carver went inside. The door clanged shut and latched from the outside. He went to the fridge and opened it. There was a bottle of ketchup and a bottle of mustard inside. There was a loaf of moldy bread there too.

He went to the bed. The mattress was sunken in but it looked decently clean. He looked around the room. The walls were painted steel like the outside. They were corrugated and strong. No way to cut through them without a welder.

There were no cameras, so that was a plus. There was no television, computer, or any other electronic device inside except for a lamp, microwave, and refrigerator. His cell phone also had no signal.

A section of the wall in the back corner wasn't the same as the rest. A panel had been fastened to the wall, presumably where a section had been previously cut out. Whoever did it had used sheet metal screws and not bolts.

He opened the cabinet drawer next to the fridge and found a table knife inside. He went to the screws and tested one with the knife. They were Phillips head screws, so the knife tip didn't fit into the slots.

Carver looked in the cabinet drawer and found another table knife, some forks, and spoons. Nothing useful for a Phillips head screw. He worked the rounded tip of the knife against the top of a screw. It turned more easily than anticipated. Almost as if someone had loosened it already.

He used his fingertips to loosen it even more. The other seven screws were also a little loose. Someone had done this before. They'd probably removed the screws and put them back using a table knife.

He removed four of the eight screws and pulled the panel out a fraction. There was a narrow gap between the outer warehouse wall and the container on the other side. He could probably fit through the gap if he went sideways.

Escape wasn't part of the plan. He had to stick around and get information from Dimitri. Find out if he was the guy who ordered Liana's death or if there was someone else above him. He seemed more like someone's attack dog than a boss.

Finding out for sure was the next step. There might be something useful on the computers in this place. It didn't seem likely, but it was worth checking out. He just wished he had that leech he'd taken from Plum and Associates.

Maybe he could get Alicia to bring it to him.

He held his phone up and walked around the container. There was no phone signal to be found. He removed the rest of the screws from the panel and pulled it off. He held the phone outside the container and got one bar. That was good enough.

Carver put his earbud in and spoke in a low voice. "Anyone there?"

"Carver!" Jessica's shout nearly deafened his right ear. "I was worried."

"I'm good. They locked me in a shipping container with no cell signal." He climbed through the hole and into the narrow gap. It was tight. Real tight. There was a good chance he'd get stuck on a screw or any deviation in the metal surface.

"How did you get a signal then?"

"I found a crack." Carver slid back into the container. "I need one of my tools. A leech."

"You want me to get it to you?"

"I want Alicia to bring it to me. I think I can get out of this container and meet her outside."

"Um, let me get her."

Alicia spoke a moment later. "What's your sitrep?"

Carver told her. He told her what he needed and why.

"My advice? Kill Dimitri and be done with it. He's the man who pulled the trigger, guaranteed."

"I want to be sure he's the end of it. That he's not just some thug following orders."

Alicia sighed. "Fine. I'll meet you outside at zero three hundred."

"Thanks."

"I'll wait fifteen minutes and then I'm leaving. So don't be late."

"I won't. Over and out." Carver put the panel back in place using two screws to hold it up. He didn't think anyone would pay him a visit tonight, but better to be safe than sorry. He turned off his phone to conserve the battery and put his earphones back in the holder.

Carver went to the bed. The center was sunken in, so he flipped it. When he was flipping it, he noticed two things. Something had been scratched onto the metal floor beneath the bed and the other side of the mattress had blood on it.

It was a narrow streak of blood ending in a round spot where it had soaked in. It had probably been caused by a shallow wound like a scratch. The blood was about where someone's shoulder would be on the mattress.

The bed's metal frame was bolted to the floor and to the container wall. It wasn't going anywhere, so he got on his knees and looked underneath it. There was a date and the initials LC. The date was from two days ago.

Carver stared at it long and hard. He backed out from under the bed and moved the mattress to get more light. There were other symbols scratched into the metal. It looked like shorthand or code.

This couldn't be what he thought it was. It couldn't possibly be Liana's initials, could it? Had she been locked in this same room just two days ago? Was she still alive or had they kept her here while deciding what to do with her?

If they'd brought her here, it meant they'd taken her alive in Minneapolis and brought her here with them. But what had they done with her since then? Was her body buried somewhere on the premises?

Carver took a picture of the code inscribed beneath the bed. It looked like a mix of Latin symbols and special characters. He typed what he could into a search window on his phone. He went to the panel and removed it. He held the phone outside of the container and sent the picture to Jessica.

Find out what this means.

He ran his own search for the symbols and came up dry. It was probably an NSA code. But why would she go through the trouble of writing all of that? Maybe it was like a trail of breadcrumbs in case anyone ever came looking for her.

Maybe she'd left similar writings wherever they took her, provided she had the tools for writing. Maybe she was the person who'd loosened the screws on the panel.

Carver looked around the metal edges of the opening and found a small spot of blood. She must have cut her shoulder getting out. But if she'd escaped the container, why had she come back and bled on the mattress?

Maybe she'd tried to escape and they'd caught her and put her back. That seemed the most likely scenario. But if that was the case, why had the panel screws been put in but not firmly tightened?

Maybe she'd removed the panel and scouted the narrow space, but since everyone was up and about, she decided it would be safer to attempt her escape in the dead of night. She'd returned inside, reattached the panel loosely, then waited for her chance.

But before she could do that, they'd taken her. Maybe they'd moved her to another location. Maybe they hadn't.

Maybe they'd finally decided to kill her.

CHAPTER 33

Carver was ready to risk it all.

But he didn't. He took deep breaths and kept calm. Liana might be alive. She might be somewhere else in this facility. Or she might be dead and buried already. He planned to find out tonight. But he had to be patient and wait for the right moment.

She definitely wasn't in the other containers. Carver had seen inside them all. The other containers looked cozy and comfortable. None of them looked like a jail cell. This was the only one that did.

If Liana was alive, she'd still be alive in a few hours. If she was dead, same thing. Escaping now while Dimitri and the others were still awake wouldn't do him any good. It was likely they were staying in the neighboring containers, and he'd be spotted the moment he exited the narrow gap.

He put the mattress back on the bed. The middle was sunken in from both sides, so it didn't matter which way he put it. He kept the side with the blood on it. Maybe it was Liana's. Maybe it was the blood of a stranger. He didn't care.

It was cold inside the container. There was no HVAC system, but there was a small space heater. He plugged it in and turned it on, leaving it next to the bed. It probably wouldn't do much but it was better than nothing.

He closed his eyes and listened. He could faintly hear a television droning. He could hear someone laughing and talking. He could hear metal shifting and creaking as someone moved around in a neighboring container.

Carver turned off the lights and lay down on his back. He had to go through his relaxation routine a couple of times because thoughts of Liana kept intruding. He closed his eyes and woke up a little after zero two thirty.

He took a moment to listen. All he heard now was dead silence. Everyone was asleep. He got out of bed. It was warm near the space heater, but freezing cold everywhere else. The metal floor creaked softly under his feet.

Carver walked as softly as he could to the panel. He removed the screws with his fingers and set the panel aside. The corrugated metal was thick, but it still wobbled and made noise when he put his weight on it.

He tried to avoid touching the edges, but he needed to brace himself against something. He made it through the hole with a minimum of sound and shined his phone flashlight around the narrow space to see what he was working with.

It was possible to climb up the side of the container and crawl across the top, but that would make a lot of noise. He shuffled sideways instead and reached the end of the gap. There was a small protrusion on the wall that made the exit even tighter.

Carver blew out his breath to deflate as much as possible and pushed into the gap. His right shoulder didn't quite fit. He pushed harder and finally forced it through. His chest scraped through only because he'd blown all the air from his lungs.

This was almost like his little spelunking adventure in North Carolina, except getting stuck here was far preferrable to being trapped in a tight space underground. His other shoulder squeezed through the tight space, and he was out.

It wasn't completely dark in the building. Every third overhead lamp was on, casting some areas in bright light and the rest in shadows. He crouched and listened for several seconds before moving. The first thing he did was check the lock on the outside of his container.

There was no padlock, just a barrel bolt. There was no way to unlatch it from the inside, and it was too thick for brute force. He considered unlatching it so if he got caught, he could pretend it wasn't locked in the first place.

All it would take was a cursory inspection of the inside to find the open panel and then they'd know that wasn't true. Hopefully it wouldn't come down to that. If he ran into anyone out here, he'd probably just have to kill them.

Carver checked the time. He had fifteen minutes until the rendezvous with Alicia. He skirted the circle of light from the nearest overhead lamp and stalked through the darkness to the area with the walled off kitchen and television.

The big television was off. LED lights flashed on the desktop computer, but the screen was off. They were probably in sleep mode. He'd have to wake one of them to use the leech on it. That would be fine as long as no one came to the kitchen for a late-night snack.

He turned on his phone. It vibrated with several messages. There were several from Jessica asking him what the picture was about and then one more saying she'd look into it. Alicia had sent a single message. She was already outside waiting. He picked up the pace and exited the building. A streetlamp lit the area just outside, so he quickly ducked into the shadows.

No one was outside patrolling or guarding the area. Apparently, Dimitri was supremely confident that they were completely off the radar from any governmental agencies. Either that or they were actively being ignored by said agencies.

There were three other large buildings on the property, and a few smaller outbuildings that probably housed utilities. Carver was itching to check them all out, but first he needed his equipment.

He went to the front fence and texted Alicia his location. She and Jessica hurried across the road and crouched outside the chain link fence.

"Enjoying your accommodations?" Alicia passed the leech through the hole in the fence. "Or do you need an exfil?"

"Yeah, a real five-star experience." Carver took the leech. "I'm following this to the end."

Jessica stared at him. "What if that means you're going to die?"

"I don't think it does, but no promises." Carver pocketed the leech. "I found something in the container they locked me in."

Alicia raised an eyebrow. "A toothbrush?"

Jessica showed him the picture he'd texted to her. "That strange message you texted me?"

Carver nodded. "Any luck?"

"These initials." Jessica circled them with her finger. "Are those Liana's?"

"I think so."

Alicia took Jessica's phone and looked at the picture. "Her initials and the date from two days ago."

"Yeah." Carver looked back at the factory. "She was apparently locked inside the same container. Either they killed her here, or they moved her somewhere else."

"That's good news, Carver." Alicia blew out a breath. "Very good news."

"I'm not getting my hopes up," he said.

"I think it's okay to have hope." Jessica tapped her phone screen. "I ran the picture through an AI translator, and it said the code is Portuguese shorthand."

"Smart," Alicia said.

"It says capitol march not me." She circled the last portion of the image. "The rest wasn't legible."

"What does that even mean?" Alicia said.

"There will be another protest march in DC one day from now," Carver said. "It must have something to do with that."

"Well, whatever it means, it's really vague." Jessica zoomed in on the illegible code. "Her hands must have been really tired by the time she got to the second line. Not even AI enhancement could make anything of it."

"Something is obviously going down in Washington," Alicia said. "But none of that matters if Liana is alive here somewhere."

"I'm going to search this place tonight." Carver looked around at the facility. "I guess we'll find out soon enough."

"We can help." Jessica gripped the fence. "We can cover a lot of ground together."

"Not if you get caught." Carver shook his head. "Not a good idea."

"Look, your friend might be alive, and you can't possibly cover this entire place alone." Alicia pulled a pair of small wire cutters from her backpack. "I think it's worth the risk."

Carver nodded. "Fine, but be careful."

Alicia grinned. "Aw, so you do care." She snipped a slit in the fence and slipped through. Jessica came through after her.

Carver regarded her for a moment. "You'd better stick close to Alicia. I don't want you wandering around on your own."

Jessica frowned. "But we can cover more space if we split up."

"We can cover the same buildings faster together." Alicia gripped her arm. "No splitting up, okay?"

"Whatever you say, boss." Jessica nodded at the nearest outbuilding. "Start there?"

Carver nodded. "Let's go."

The nearest outbuilding was an old brick storage shed. The door hung open and the inside had nothing but spiderwebs and rusting shelves. Carver looked inside anyway. He checked the floor for trap doors, but it was an unbroken slab of concrete.

They went to the next building. This one was a little smaller than the building where Dimitri and his men stayed. There was a dump truck parked inside. It was rusty but looked functional. There was a bulldozer and a midsized excavator as well.

Jessica looked up at the excavator bucket. "Maybe they bury people with this."

The floor was concrete, and the walls were cinderblock and brick. Besides the construction vehicles there wasn't much else inside the large open space except for some offices. Carver and the others methodically searched the building but found nothing.

It was already past zero five hundred by the time they finished searching that building. They hurried over to the other small outbuildings, but they were empty as well. That left the main building.

"I'm not going to risk searching it," Carver said. "We don't have much time before people start waking up."

"Agreed." Alicia turned toward the fence. "What's happening tomorrow?"

"Another march through Chicago," Carver said. "I don't know what we'll be doing, but I'm sure I'll find out soon enough."

"Be careful." Jessica took his hand and squeezed it. "We'll find your friend, okay?"

"Thanks." Carver watched them go to the fence and squeeze through the slit. Once he was sure they were out, he returned inside the main factory building. No one was up yet, but it was almost zero six hundred and some of them were bound to be early risers.

He put the leech next to the desktop computer and tapped the keyboard to wake it. A login screen appeared. The leech connected wirelessly and began working. It bypassed the login, probably using a backdoor or hardware level access and started downloading the hard drive.

There wasn't much on the computer so it only took a few minutes to download the contents. That probably wasn't a good sign for it having what Carver needed. He pocketed the leech and hurried back to his container room.

He squeezed back into the gap between the container and wall and made his way back through the hole in the wall. He put the screws in and looked at his shirt. It had rust and dirt on it from the side of the container.

Carver took it off and beat it on the wall to get it a little cleaner. Then he took off his boots and laid down in bed. He'd already gotten a few hours of sleep early so he wasn't too tired, but it was best to get whatever shuteye he could.

The sound of the barrel bolt screeching against the metal woke him about thirty minutes later. Dimitri, Rashid, and Dex burst inside, guns drawn, faces furious. Carver sat up as they came in. It didn't take a genius to figure out that he was in trouble.

Dex and Rashid grabbed him. Carver was already thinking about how he was going to kill them. He sure as hell couldn't make a move with all these guns in his face. It would be easier when they got closer.

Dex put his gun in Carver's face. "Who do you work for?" he shouted. "Tell us who you work for or you're going to die right here right now."

Carver stared at him calmly. "Is that a trick question?"

"Answer him!" Rashid pressed the muzzle of his gun against Carver's temple.

Had they seen him escape? Were there cameras that recorded everything he'd been up to all night? Or was this about something else? He turned his gaze to Dimitri. "I work for you."

Dimitri's anger morphed to a grin. "I told you."

"Well damn." Dex backed away laughing. "Cool as a cucumber."

"Yes." Rashid holstered his gun. "We have no choice anyway."

Carver stood. "What the hell was that about?"

"Making sure you're the kind of guy we need." Dex popped out his magazine to show it was empty. "Yesterday we poured fuel on the fire. We need to make sure the heat stays on high."

"I don't know what more I have to do to prove myself." Carver waved a hand around at the room. "You lock me in here like a prisoner and then wake me up with guns to my head. Hell, I didn't even want to come with you yesterday. You made me."

"We've only known you for a day, Sam." Dimitri shrugged. "We can't trust someone blindly."

"You can't trust a guy who beats up and shoots cops to save your sorry asses?" Carver laughed. "Look, I've been in since before I met you people. I've got scores to settle, and the odds of success are a lot higher if I'm with you."

"True." Dimitri nodded. "You will be free to move around, but you will follow my orders precisely."

"Whatever you say, boss." Carver patted his stomach. "Can we eat first?"

Dex laughed. "Damn, I wish we'd found this guy sooner."

"Come." Dimitri left the container and headed for the kitchen. He stopped to turn on the television. The local news was still playing Arjun's death leap. A couple of national news channels had picked it up too. The Chinese supercar rocketed off the elevated ramp on a playback loop.

Carver went to the refrigerator. There were several cartons of eggs inside, some ground pork sausage, and bacon. He put a pan on the stove and turned on the gas.

"Cook me up some eggs over easy and bacon," Dex said.

"I'm not your personal chef." Carver cracked eggs into a pan. "Make it yourself."

Rashid chuckled. "He's not as easy to command as Gage or Kaden."

Dex spread his hands in a shrug. "I had to try."

Carver kept an eye on the TVs and Dimitri while he cooked. The big man wasn't interested in watching Arjun die on repeat. He was interested in something else. He seemed to find what he was looking for on one channel and opened it in a larger window with the sound turned up.

There was an image of an elderly man over the left shoulder of a news anchor. "Trade talks have stalled due to cold feet in the Senate," the anchor said. "Majority leader Mitch Neuman says he won't schedule the trade measure for a vote because it would be detrimental to the economy of the United States."

The image switched to that of an old Chinese man. "Chinese President Chi has said if the US President can't control his own party, then further negotiations are a waste of time and effort."

Dimitri muted the television and scowled. He took out his phone and called someone. Carver couldn't hear what he was saying over Dex and Rashid arguing about whether eating pork was unholy or not.

Carver scrambled his eggs and dumped them into a bowl with the already cooked ground pork sausage. He left the kitchen to sit at the table near the television. Dimitri had walked away from the area already and was no longer in earshot.

Carver picked up the television remote and unmuted the news. The news anchor was still talking about a trade deal between China and the US. Apparently, the previous administration had been nearing a deal that would have allowed more Chinese goods into the US market, including their vehicles.

The new administration had modified the deal, saying that many of China's technological advances came from stealing ideas from companies they manufactured high-tech goods for. Any import of certain things like vehicles and electronic devices would require licensing fees to compensate the patent holders.

The House had passed the trade bill, but the Senate majority leader said allowing the import of Chinese vehicles would destroy the US car industry unless they also imposed tariffs on them.

"The war of words between the President and the Senate majority leader is escalating and there's no sign of a deal in sight." The image of the President next to the news anchor switched to that of Arjun's car in midair. "Speaking of Chinese vehicles, it's not every day you see a sight like this."

Carver muted the news and started eating. It was obvious now. All of it. He knew exactly what all of this was about.

Chapter 34

Carver had it mostly figured out.

He looked up the Chinese trade deal and familiarized himself with its recent history. It was nothing new. In fact, it had been working its way through the political machinery for nearly two years. It had been modified in committees and finally made it into the House for a full vote.

It had bipartisan support. It had the support of the previous President and the new one. It was supposed to finally fix the trade deficit with China while also opening massive new markets for the US and Chinese tech and auto manufacturers.

The warehouses full of Chinese cars made sense now. Yancy's company had been importing these vehicles to gear up for the passing of the Chinese trade deal. They'd been poised to make a mint.

But the Senate majority leader had put the brakes on the bill after the House passed it. The former President couldn't convince him to put it to a vote despite overwhelming support in the Senate. Then the former President got voted out and a new one got voted in. The new President also couldn't convince him to schedule it for a vote.

One person was holding up everything.

If the bill had passed, the floodgates on trade would have opened wide and Yancy's company would have been more than prepared to answer the onslaught of demand for cheap Chinese vehicles. The warehouse in Chicago was probably just one of many housing those cars.

There had also been shelves full of Chinese smartphones, tablets, and other high-tech devices that weren't normally sold in the US due to patent issues. Instead of making hundreds of millions of dollars in days from selling these goods, Yancy and company were stuck holding the bill.

The new President seemed eager to go forward with his version of the bill. He'd expected the full support of the Senate majority leader, but like the last President, he was being stonewalled by the same man.

Carver saw what needed to happen. The majority leader, Mitch Neuman, needed to be replaced. He was an elderly man but didn't plan on retiring until his term was up in a little over a year. That was too long to wait for Yancy and Dimitri. They'd probably bet the bank on the original deal and were so deep in debt their eyeballs were floating.

Taking out Neuman was their only play.

Given that, how did the protests play into all of this? How would the protests allow them to get rid of the roadblock? Neuman wasn't going to be anywhere near the protests at any point. He was too old and frail to be outside, and besides, the protestors represented the opposition.

It didn't seem terribly efficient to spend millions of dollars marching protestors across the country to Washington when you were already bleeding millions because of unsold merchandise. It would be worlds easier to just spend far less money and effort on a trained assassin.

Carver could see Dimitri's objective, but there was a big gap in his understanding of how Dimitri wanted to achieve it. One thing was certain. It would involve violence. It would almost certainly involve killing.

The problem was, Carver wasn't a political animal. He understood human nature and how to use it, but politics was more than that. Politics involved understanding procedures and laws that Carver typically circumvented with a gun, a knife, or a fist.

There had to be more to this. A whole lot more. It wasn't for him to understand or solve. He'd leave that to the professionals. All he wanted was to find out if Liana was alive or not and unleash his own special brand of justice on the people responsible for her condition.

Dex and Rashid sat next to Carver and ate. Dex switched to a news station discussing the trade deal and watched it with interest.

"Is that trade agreement a big deal or something?" Carver said.

"A real big deal." Dex buttered his toast. "Yancy's shitting bricks about it, that's for sure."

"Who's this Yancy guy?"

"Nobody you have to worry about." Dex bit into his toast. "If you're lucky and Dimitri keeps you on for the long term, then you'll get to know all about everything. Until then, just do what he says and don't ask questions."

"Curiosity is very dangerous," Rashid said. "Especially for the uninitiated."

"How exactly am I uninitiated?" Carver said. "You people threw the damned kitchen sink at me to make sure I could be trusted to do a job I didn't even want in the first place."

"Just keep a positive mental attitude and you'll be good." Dex smirked. "Look, all I'll say about it is that Dimitri and Yancy are partners from way back. They make good money, and they pay people like us very good money to protect their interests. If everything goes down as planned, then the good times keep rolling. If it doesn't go down as planned, then we have very dark days ahead."

"Dark as in dead," Rashid said solemnly. "Yancy did something without consulting Dimitri, and now we may all have to pay for it."

Carver pursed his lips. "Is Yancy a big guy? Bigger than Dimitri? Because it doesn't seem smart to cross someone like Dimitri."

Dex and Rashid laughed like it was the funniest thing they'd ever heard.

"No, Yancy is not a big guy." Dex wiped tears of mirth from his eyes. "It's his family that you have to be worried about even though he's not all that close to them."

"He went out on his own to make his own fortune." Rashid sipped his tea. "He has done very well, even going so far as to take territory from his own family. Despite that, they have not acted against him. They are even somewhat protective of him."

Carver shrugged. "Okay, so even if this deal Yancy made gets screwed up, his family will protect him, right?"

"I don't think anyone can protect him from these people." Rashid leaned back in his chair. "That's all I will say for now."

Dimitri stormed into the area. He looked like a man holding a great deal of anger and frustration just under the surface. "It appears our efforts from yesterday are working as expected. We will just monitor events today to ensure the momentum is stable."

"Sounds good, boss." Dex nodded at the kitchen. "I made a big pot of coffee if you want any."

Dimitri nodded curtly and went to the kitchen. He found a large travel mug and filled it. "Where is everyone else?"

"Manny is scouting the venue." Dex unlocked his phone screen and showed him something. "Gage got picked up by the cops for vandalism and resisting arrest."

Dimitri scowled. "He's still in holding?"

"Yeah. He said we need to come get him."

Dimitri's face shaded red. "We need to come get him? We need to come get him?"

Dex nodded. "Yeah."

Dimitri clenched his fists so hard the knuckles cracked. "Rashid, go get our boy. Bring him back."

"Yes, sir." Rashid set down his tea and left.

"What's the point of having Gage and Cutler?" Carver said. "They have money?"

"They're fanatics," Dex said. "They'll do anything for the cause. Gage helped a lot in the beginning by bringing his rabidly fanatic friends into the cause. They helped us go from hundreds to over a hundred thousand because they're so connected to people like them."

"But now he seems to think he's more important than he is." Dimitri gripped his travel mug tight enough to partially crush it. He set it down. "We're almost to the finish line."

It looked like he was going to say something else, but he seemed to stop himself. He sat down at the table and watched the news, occasionally checking his phone for messages.

Carver got up and poured himself another mug of coffee. He walked around the kitchen and went back to his container. He didn't go inside. He walked down the row of containers. The doors hung open on all of them except one. That was probably Braden's room.

He walked around the inside of the building as if out for a casual stroll, but he was looking for anywhere else they might house prisoners. He found some administrative offices tucked into the back, but they were dusty and empty.

Once he finished his circuit of the building, he went outside and jogged the entire perimeter. His lungs burned pleasantly in the freezing cold. He didn't really feel like jogging, but he did it to put on a show in case Dimitri or someone saw him.

Skeletons of old cranes stood next to the river. They were positively ancient, using manual cranks to load and unload ships. This had once been a cargo warehousing facility. Ships would pull up to the docks, men would unload them and pile everything into the warehouses.

For whatever reason, the infrastructure had never been upgraded. The place had closed down and fallen into disuse. Maybe it had been mostly for local trade or trade with Canada. Now it was just a rotting piece of history.

The only history Carver was interested in was very recent history. Was Liana's body buried on this land? Was she at the bottom of the river? Or was she alive and being held somewhere else?

If she was alive and a prisoner, it wasn't at this facility. All he knew for certain was that she'd been here just two days ago. She'd been alive and she'd left a message. A message about Washington DC.

Capitol march not me.

What did that mean? Clearly it had something to do with the protests that would start tomorrow. Maybe the AI translator had made a mistake. Just one wrong word could change everything.

Carver saw Rashid pulling into the warehouse. He headed back to the main building and found everyone near the large TV. Gage was arguing with Dimitri. A girl with orange hair stood next to him.

"I'm here to make a difference in the world. What I do is my business." Gage flipped off Dimitri with both hands. "You're not my dad."

"You people disgust me," the girl said. "You're not part of the revolution. You're closet capitalists who want to profit off the backs of the people."

Dex snorted in an effort to repress laughter.

"Laugh if you want," the girl screeched, "but the people's revolution is going to bury people like you!"

"Yeah, we're done with you." Gage spat on the floor. "My connections with my people started these protests. Our organizations funded it. The only reason I let you in was because you promised to help burn the capitalist system to the ground. It's obvious that you're in it for some other reason."

Dimitri stared at them without expression. "Your funding was coming from a billionaire. Did you know that? Your organizations would not exist if not for a capitalist."

"That's a lie." Gage shook his head. "What matters is that you aren't who you said you are. This Yancy guy you kept talking about isn't a revolutionary. He's a rich industrialist trying to make money off our labor and I'm not going to stand for it!"

Carver was starting to see the bigger picture. Dimitri saw an opportunity with the protests. He piggybacked on Gage's organization and helped inflame the protests to make them bigger and bigger.

Yancy wasn't the one funding bus rides for thousands of people. He wasn't funding the paid protestors or their logistical needs. They were simply leeches along for the ride.

"Words are power, and we will use our power to bring you down," Gage shouted. "You are done using us!"

"How dare you!" the girl screamed. "How dare—" her words abruptly cut off as Dimitri backhanded her. Her head twisted violently, and she flopped onto the floor.

Gage's eyes went wide. His mouth dropped open. He looked down at the girl as if realizing that his words weren't really power after all. He tried to run, but Dimitri grabbed his arm and bared his teeth in a grin.

"Words are power, little man?" Dimitri laughed. "Perhaps to little men like you who rely on the system to protect them." He shook his head. "Little men like you are only alive because the systems coddles the weak and punishes the brave. So, tell me, little man, where is your system now?"

Gage shivered. "Let me go or I'll call the cops."

Dimitri, Dex, and Rashid burst into laughter. Dex was laughing so hard he was crying.

"Call the cops?" Dex said between bouts of laughter. "I thought you wanted to burn the system to the ground, Gage."

"Let me go!" Gage screamed. "Let me go!" He pounded Dimitri's huge arm with the flat of his fist.

Dimitri watched him with great amusement. Then he cocked back his other arm and punched Gage in the face. Gage's head rocked back violently. There was a loud crack and he went limp.

Dimitri dropped him. Spat on him. He took off his jacket. He wore a short-sleeved T-shirt underneath. His huge arms and chest barely fit in it. He flexed his fists and looked down at Gage. He spat on him again.

Carver noticed a tattoo on Dimitri's bicep. One that looked very familiar to him. He'd seen it on a man in Crimea Ukraine years ago. He'd seen it many times during his unsuccessful mission to infiltrate Ukrainian rebel groups.

The tattoo was a black heart with a knife through it. It was a symbol adopted by Ukrainians who supported Russia but felt betrayed when Crimea was invaded. Some of those supporters were also part of the Russian army.

Some Russian soldiers with Ukrainian heritage had taken it a step farther. They'd created an insurgent group called Motherland's Exiles and spent their time killing Russian invaders. More specifically, they hunted Russian special forces, or spetsnaz.

Most members of that group were former spetsnaz themselves. It made sense why Manny said Dimitri ate spetsnaz for breakfast. Dimitri was big. He was in shape. And he was well trained in fighting and warfare.

He was not the sort of guy you wanted to face in a fair fight. You wanted as big of an advantage as possible when taking on a man like Dimitri. When push came to shove, Carver would just have to make sure he killed Dimitri from a distance.

The girl moaned. Her eyelids fluttered. She looked up and around as if she had no idea where she was.

Dex snorted. "Damn, I thought she was dead."

Dimitri smirked. "She's stronger than she looks."

"Well, might as well put her to good use," Dex said. "Do you mind?"

Dimitri shook his head. "She's all yours."

Dex gripped her by her hair and dragged her across the floor. She kicked and screamed and flailed. He slapped her hard in the face and grinned. "I'm going to enjoy this."

"You have disgusting tastes, friend." Rashid grimaced. "She's so ugly, I don't know how you can bear it."

"Not all of us have your exquisite tastes." Dex shrugged. "Besides, I like ugly girls." He pulled her away, her screams slowly fading in the direction of the containers.

Rashid knelt and touched Gage's neck. "He's dead."

"Dump him in the pit." Dimitri nodded at Carver. "Carry the body for him."

Carver hefted Gage over a shoulder. His body was thin and light. "Where to?"

Rashid motioned him to follow. They walked toward the back of the building passing the containers along the way. Carver could hear the girl screaming from inside one of the closed containers.

They walked out of the building and continued toward the docks. A large metal pylon protruded from the ground not far from the water. Carver had seen it earlier and figured it had been the support for one of the old cranes.

Rashid pushed aside a wooden pallet to reveal a closed hatch. He tugged it open on squeaky hinges. There was darkness behind it. "Toss him in."

The scent of decay wafted out of the open door. This pit had been used before and somewhat recently. His stomach sank as he realized what this meant.

Liana's body might be down there.

CHAPTER 35

Carver made a face.

"Damn, that stinks. How many bodies do you have down there?"

"Only one that I know of," Rashid said. "Supposedly this place was run by the Chicago mafia in the nineteen hundreds so there may be dozens more.

Carver tossed Gage's body inside. There was a metallic scrape as it bumped the side and a distant thud when it hit bottom. "How deep is this thing?" He turned on his phone flashlight and looked down. The light didn't reach the bottom, but the putrid scent of death certainly reached the top.

"Perhaps a hundred feet."

"So, who else is down there?"

"A Korean that our people caught trying to break into our warehouse." Rashid closed the hatch. "He's no longer a problem."

Carver hated to admit how relieved he felt that it wasn't Liana. It didn't mean she was alive, but it made the odds much better. He brushed off his hands. "Now what?"

"Now, we go to the protest." Rashid headed back for the building.

Carver followed him. They were almost to the door when Dex came out carrying a bloody form over his shoulder.

He grinned. "She didn't hold up as long as I expected."

Rashid wrinkled his nose. "She smells."

"Yeah, she shit the bed when I punched her in the face." Dex laughed. "Well, it was fun while it lasted."

The girl's naked body was bloody and bruised. There was no question what Dex had done to her. There was no question that he'd done the same thing many times before.

Carver watched as Dex took the body toward the same pylon where they'd dumped Gage. "You like your women the same way, Rashid?"

Rashid went inside without answering. Carver followed him. Dimitri stood in front of the television next to Manny. He turned around and motioned them over.

"Where's Dex?"

"Disposing of the girl," Rashid said. "What's happening?"

"The protest organizer is moving to Washington later today," Manny said. "Apparently there are large crowds forming already and they want to get there while the iron is hot."

Dimitri pursed his lips. "Let's pack up and leave. We need to be there well in advance of them."

Manny nodded. "You got it."

Dimitri motioned toward Carver. "Do whatever they need. I want to be out of here by mid-morning."

Carver helped the others pack two vans with suitcases, crates, and other equipment. They were ready to move out in a couple of hours. Braden emerged from his container room when they were nearly done.

He wiped the sleep from his eyes and looked confused. "Are we leaving already?"

"Aw, it's the sleepyhead." Dex walked over and slapped Braden on the back of the head. "Get your shit together, dumbass. We're leaving in twenty."

Braden took a swing at Dex and missed. "Leave me alone, asshole!"

Dex and Manny laughed. They circled him, slapping his face and the back of his head and dancing away from his clumsy attacks. They reminded Carver of schoolyard bullies. He didn't much care for bullies, but he wasn't about to protect Braden. That kid had gotten himself into this mess and could get himself out of it.

He left them and put his earphones in. "Anyone there?"

There was a fumbling sound and Jessica spoke. "Carver!"

"The protests are moving out earlier than expected. We're leaving for Washington shortly."

"What? Really?"

"Yeah." Carver blew out a breath. "Just stay put and I'll pay you when this is over."

"Stay put?" She scoffed. "I'm emotionally invested in your success, you big dummy."

"Are you talking to Carver?" Alicia said, her voice distant.

"Yes. They're leaving for DC already."

Alicia's voice grew closer. "I'd like to get paid before you leave."

Carver figured that was coming. "My money bag is in my room. Take what I owe you. I'll come back for the rest later."

"You're just done with him?" Jessica said. "Like some common mercenary?"

"We had a business arrangement, nothing more." Alicia sighed. "My advice to you is to not get emotionally involved. Take your money and go home."

"He's trying to help someone," Jessica said. "Liana might still be alive."

"I'm not driving to Washington DC, okay?" Alicia blew out a breath. "Good luck, Carver. If you die, can I keep your money?"

"No," Carver said. "Give it to Jessica."

"Aw, that's sweet."

"Shut up, Alicia!" Jessica growled. "I'll pack up and leave. I'll bring your stuff with me and take it to the hideout."

"Okay," Carver said. "Just remember that you don't have to."

"I know, but I'm doing it anyway."

"I know you didn't ask me to do it," Alicia said, "but I asked a friend of mine about this trade deal. I asked them what it would take for it to go through."

"Besides killing the majority leader?"

"The majority leader controls the schedule. He can schedule a vote for a bill or just never schedule it," Alicia said. "It kills the bill by default. Only a discharge petition can bypass the majority leader, but it requires a majority of signatures."

"Sounds simple enough," Jessica said. "Why don't they do that if the bill has enough votes to pass?"

"I don't know. Politicians are a bunch of self-serving idiots." Alicia took a breath. "Anyway, he said removing the majority leader would work because most of the other members of the party are eager to pass the bill."

Carver shook his head. "I think if Dimitri planned to assassinate Mitch Neuman, he would have already done it."

"Maybe he's going to use the protests to cover it up," Jessica said. "Maybe they'll storm his house."

"Where does he live while Congress is in session?" Alicia said. "Find that out and compare it to the protest march route."

"I'm looking right now," Jessica said. "Found it."

"That fast?" Carver said.

"Super easy," Jessica said. "His house got doxed ages ago. Looks like there have been tons of protests at his house over the past few years."

"So, where is it?" Carver said.

A keyboard clicked. "His DC house is just a mile from the Capitol building. It's near the protest route but not directly in its path."

Alicia chimed in. "The most likely scenario is that Dimitri's people redirect the protest, so it passes by his place. With that many people, they could swarm it and kill him no problem."

Suddenly everything made sense. Carver knew exactly what Liana's message meant. And he knew for certain that she was alive. At least for now.

"You got real quiet," Jessica said. "What's wrong?"

"I thought about Liana's message," Carver said. "Capitol march not me."

Jessica made a confused grunt. "It's nonsensical."

Alicia jumped in. "They're using her to kill the senate majority leader. They can blame it on a rogue NSA agent and create a huge scandal just like they did with the FBI agent in the Chicago march."

"Which means she's still alive," Jessica said. "At least up until the point where they kill her to make it look like she died killing Neuman."

"Yep." Carver thought it over. "They must have taken her to DC already."

"Why take her so early?"

"Probably for mission prep," Alicia said. "Maybe dress her up and walk her around the neighborhood to make it look like she's scoping out the target. Neuman's house probably has cameras all over the place. Security too."

"They're priming the event." Alicia blew out a breath. "Okay, fine. I'll come along for support."

"I knew you weren't a heartless monster," Jessica said. "Just mostly heartless."

Alicia laughed. "I'll take that as a compliment."

"Thanks," Carver said. "Signing off."

"Be careful," Jessica said.

He put the earphones in the charger and went to the bathroom. He took a shower but didn't have anything clean to change into, so he put his dirty clothes back on.

Dex came into the communal bathroom when he was leaving and looked him up and down. He laughed. "I guess we forgot to get you more clothes." He opened a door to reveal piles of clothing inside. "Find something that fits."

Most of the clothing still had tags on it. The socks and underwear were still in the bags. He put on fresh underwear, a T-shirt, and black cargo pants. He grabbed extra pairs of everything because he'd probably need it.

He met the others at the vehicles. There were two high-top vans and a box truck.

"Help them load the truck," Dimitri said.

"Start with these." Dex went to the stacks of crates near the television.

Carver hefted a wooden crate with oxygen cannisters inside. He carried it to the box truck and slid it inside. Manny stood inside and carried the crate to the front of the cargo space. Rashid and Dex lifted one of the large polyethylene cases by the ends and carried it to the truck.

Dex's grip slipped and he almost dropped it. Carver grabbed the side and helped him steady it.

"Careful!" Dimitri said.

The case was heavy as hell. "What's in this thing?" Carver said. "A rocket launcher?"

Manny grinned. "You might say that."

Carver wondered if it was a bomb. Maybe they planned to blow up Neuman's house to make sure he was dead.

They loaded all the crates into the box truck and filled the back of one of the high top vans with suitcases. They put cases of bottled water and canned foods into the second van. It took them about thirty minutes from start to finish.

Then it was time to go. Dex opened the driver's door on one of the vans. Manny locked up the rear of the box truck and looked around as if making sure they didn't miss anything else. Braden climbed into the passenger side of the truck.

"You drive that one." Dimitri directed Carver to the other van. "The coordinates are already in the GPS."

"Okay." Carver walked toward it. "Can I leave now?"

Dimitri nodded.

"You're not worried I'll take a detour?"

Dimitri grinned. "Detour if you want. Just be at the destination by morning."

Carver figured the van had a tracker on it. There was no way Dimitri would just let him do whatever he wanted. Despite everything they'd put him through, Dimitri wasn't the kind of guy who trusted anyone without a long track record of loyalty to him.

There were plenty of ways around a tracker on the van. He got in and noticed the fuel level was down to an eighth of a tank. He rolled down the window. "Am I paying for gas?"

Dex came up to the window and handed him a thick roll of cash. "Don't worry, daddy's got you covered."

Carver couldn't help but notice the blood on the other man's knuckles and the spots of it on his face. "You still have that girl's blood all over you."

"Yeah, I do, don't I?" Dex grinned. He made a show of counting on his fingers. "I've had eight of these protestor chicks since all this started. Nothing turns me on more than a fat chick with tattoos."

"Because you're a sicko." Manny punched him in the shoulder. "Try a skinny girl sometime."

"Nah, they don't put up nearly the same amount of fight." Dex wrinkled his nose. "And these fat chicks squeal like stuck pigs." His eyelids narrowed with pleasure. He drew in a slow breath. "Makes me hard just thinking about it."

"You need therapy." Manny laughed.

"What did you do with all the bodies?" Carver said.

"I didn't beat them all to death." Dex shook his head. "I like to beat them within an inch of their life. I made an exception this time since we had to get rid of her anyway."

"Aw, you're such a softie." Manny bellowed with laughter.

Carver started the van and shifted into drive. "See you tomorrow morning."

Dex mocked a salute. "Yes, sir. You drive safe now, you hear?" He opened the rollup door.

Carver headed for the main road. The gate was already open. He texted Jessica and Alicia to let them know what was happening. *Headed to DC now in one of Dimitri's vans. Van is probably bugged or tracked.*

Alicia replied with an address. *Meet at this gas station. We'll be there in ten.*

It took Carver fifteen minutes to reach the gas station. Alicia's BMW was already there. She approached the van, a finger to her lips and a device in her hand. She walked around the van with the wireless signal scanner and held it over the engine compartment.

Carver went inside the gas station and gave the attendant some cash. "Filling up on number three." He went back outside and started fueling the van.

Alicia tapped the van's hood. "There's a GPS tracker here." She waved a hand at the rest of the van. "No dash cam or other cameras. No audio bugs. Just the tracker."

Jessica stood next to the BMW. "Can I come over now?"

Alicia nodded.

Jessica hugged Carver. "I'm glad you're okay."

Alicia rolled her eyes. "It's a mistake getting sentimental with this guy."

"I know, but I kind of like the big brute." Jessica backed away. "I did some more digging. If Neuman is taken out, then the governor of his home state will appoint someone to replace him until a special election is held."

"So, they're back to square one?" Carver said.

"No, not at all." Jessica turned her phone to him. There was a picture of a pink-faced man with gray hair. "The governor can appoint anyone he wants in the interim and he's in the opposing party."

"Which means the balance in the Senate changes," Alicia said. "It goes from fifty-one to forty-nine to fifty-fifty."

"Since the Vice President casts the tie-breaking vote, Neuman's party still technically controls the majority, but all of that is moot when it comes to the China trade bill." Jessica tucked her phone into a pocket. "The Senate will hold a vote for the next majority leader. Todd Gruman is the most likely pick, and he's eager to schedule the China bill for a vote."

"Which means it'll pass." Carver heard the clunk of the fuel pump turning off. He put it back on the hook. "All I care about is finding where Liana is and getting her out of there."

Jessica frowned. "Okay, but what about stopping the assassination of a US Senator?"

"Not my problem." Carver closed the gas tank lid. "Maybe they won't do it if they can't pin it on Liana."

Alicia pshawed. "After everything they've done to get to this point, I don't think that will stop them."

Carver opened the van door. "Are you volunteering to stop them?"

She shook her head. "Hell no. Jericho would probably want me to help them. He hates politicians with a passion."

"Good God you two are so jaded." Jessica sighed. "But in this case, I just don't care. Mitch Neuman wrote the Social Media Privacy Protection Act at the request of the social media executives who wanted to kill my startup company."

Alicia smiled. "Ah, so you have personal beef with him."

"Hell yeah, I do." Jessica scrunched her face angrily. "I shouldn't want people to die, but this guy crushed my hopes and dreams for money. He's evil."

Alicia put a hand on her shoulder. "Politicians are trash human beings. They only care about money and power. They betray people like you and me all day long and laugh about it behind closed doors. They deserve to die."

"Neuman's death won't change a thing," Jessica said. "Even if he died before writing the bill that killed my company, another head of the snake would have taken his place and done the job. I just wish I could be there to tell him what a piece of shit he is before he goes to meet his maker."

"That's the spirit!" Alicia grinned. "The sooner you realize that it's us versus them, the better."

Jessica looked at Carver. "What do you think?"

"What I think doesn't matter." Carver climbed into the driver's seat. "I'm going to park the van at the rendezvous in DC, then I'll meet you all somewhere else and figure out our next steps. I just want to get to DC as soon as possible. We need to be way ahead of Dimitri."

"Maybe Liana will be at the rendezvous," Jessica said.

"Doubtful." Carver held out his hand. "Give me your phone." She unlocked it and gave it to him. He typed in the rendezvous address. "It's just an empty concrete lot. Nothing else of interest nearby. If they have a place like the factory in DC, this ain't it."

"It might be nearby," Alicia said. "We'll check all the nearby buildings on the map during the trip." She checked her watch. "Speaking of which, we need to hit the road. I'll take point and scan for cops."

"You have a radar detector?" Jessica said.

"I have a military grade laser and radar detector," Alicia said. "That's why I can drive like a demon anywhere I go."

"Military grade?" Jessica looked confused. "I didn't even know something like that existed."

Alicia went back to her BMW and started it. Jessica stepped up on the doorsill and kissed Carver on the cheek. "I really am glad you're okay. Can I ride with you?"

"Might not be a good idea. Dimitri or his people might catch up to me, or he might have people watching me along the way. I don't want to risk it."

"Yeah, you're probably right." She dropped down off the doorsill, gave him a look, then hurried over to Alicia's car and got in.

Alicia's BMW screeched out of the parking lot and hit the road running. Carver pulled out after her. The van had a decent engine, but nothing that was going to help it go zero to sixty as fast as Alicia's car.

She was far ahead of him by the time he got up to speed. They turned onto the interstate and headed toward Washington DC.

This was it. The next few hours would determine if Liana lived or if she died.

CHAPTER 36

Carver reached Washington DC in nine hours.

Alicia hadn't been joking about the military grade scanner getting him to DC faster. They'd maintained nearly a hundred miles per hour for large stretches of the trip, slowing whenever the scanner notified her about speed traps or police. They'd also minimized bathroom and food stops.

The rendezvous point was just what it looked like on the map, a large slab of concrete that had once been the foundation for a building. Now there was nothing left except a few broken walls and lots of knee-high weeds.

Carver parked the van and looked around. It was late in the afternoon, nearly sixteen hundred hours, and the light was fading fast. The lot was in Brentwood right behind a neighborhood full of red brick public housing. There was a cul-de-sac next to the lot, and a fenced in area full of sanitation vehicles. He caught a whiff of garbage when the breeze blew from the south.

Liana might be somewhere nearby. There were industrial buildings and residences all close by. If Carver had to guess, he'd check the industrial places first. But he wasn't in the business of guessing just yet.

He locked the van and started walking. The rear of a small warehouse was on his right. There were several trucks parked at the loading docks. Hispanic men were loading them with what looked like boxes of food.

On the left was a fenced in area and a large building with a rollup door on the side. A sign on the side of the building advertised a warehouse and flex space for rent. Carver stopped and looked through the chain link fence. It was a big place. Maybe not as big as Arjun's warehouse, but still plenty big.

Did Dimitri and Yancy own this place? Could this be where they were holding Liana? He wasn't ready to climb the fence and go looking just yet. He needed to narrow down the options first.

He reached Brentwood Rd and crossed it. Alicia was parked in a lot on the other side. He climbed into the front seat.

"Where to?" Alicia said.

Carver opened the maps app and found a ratty motel nearby. "This is good."

Alicia pulled out of the parking lot and followed the GPS.

Jessica leaned forward from the back seat. "I ran some searches during the ride, but my laptop battery died."

Carver glanced back at her. "I thought you had an inverter for charging on the road."

"I forgot it back at Hope House." She rubbed her eyes. "I slept for most of the trip, but it feels like I haven't slept at all."

Carver knew the feeling. He was dead tired. He had a little more than twelve hours before Dimitri and the others were expecting him and he needed to use most of that time to find Liana. He could go without sleep, but it was best not to. Not when he might have to fight Dimitri and his goons tomorrow.

They reached the motel in a few minutes. Carver paid cash for a couple of rooms and gave Alicia the key to one of them. "I'm going to get some shuteye. Two hours at most."

"Me too." Alicia yawned and stretched. "That was a long drive."

She went into her room. Jessica followed Carver into his and set up her computer. She plugged it in and watched him strip down.

"I'll keep searching while you sleep."

Carver nodded. "Thanks." He closed his eyes and had hardly started his relaxation routine when he fell asleep.

He woke up with Jessica snoozing next to him. He'd slept for three hours despite setting his internal alarm clock for just two. That was fine. It was probably his body's way of telling him he needed that extra hour.

Jessica's laptop screen was on. A notification window was blinking red with the words, *Matches Found* in the middle. He slipped his arm from beneath her and stood. She moaned and blinked her eyes open.

She sat up and looked from him to the laptop then jolted out of bed and went to the computer. She clicked her mouse, and the notification vanished.

Carver stood behind her. "What did it find?"

"Looks like your buddy Dimitri is already ginning up the protestors." She pulled up the image of a large group of people posing for a picture. There was a red square around the face of one individual, Braden Cutler.

Dimitri stood behind the crowd with his inner circle, Dex, Rashid, and Manny. They appeared to be discussing something, unaware that Braden's pals had just snapped a picture with them in it.

Jessica dragged the image to another folder. "Now that I have their faces, I can add them to the search."

Carver jabbed a finger at the screen. "Where and when was the picture taken?"

"An hour ago at a nightclub in Brentwood." She switched to the maps app and put in the club name, Angel Dust. The address was close to the place where he'd left the van. In fact, it was inside the large warehouse building with the lease sign on the side.

Angel Dust was located at the back of the large building. The Amtrak maintenance yard bordered the backside of the lot. The sanitation truck parking lot was on the left and a construction company was on the right.

Judging from Braden's picture, there were hundreds of people inside the building. The place was big enough to house thousands. It was probably being used as a staging point for buses of protestors. From there it was a straight shot south to Stanton Park where the protest march would begin.

Carver wondered if Angel Dust belonged to Dimitri or Yancy, or if it belonged to the people funding the protests. If it belonged to the former, then it was possible Liana was there somewhere. In fact, the odds were so good that he had to go look for himself.

Jessica looked up at him with big eyes. "What are you thinking, Carver?"

"I need to go check it out."

"I'll come with you."

He shook his head. "No. I can explain things if they catch me snooping around. I wouldn't be able to explain you."

She bit her lower lip. "At least let me and Alicia come along for backup."

Carver gave it some thought and nodded. He needed Alicia to drive him there anyway. He threw on his clothes and knocked on Alicia's door. She answered a moment later looking like she'd just woken up.

"Damn, I overslept." Alicia looked him up and down. "Going out?"

"Yeah." Carver told her what Jessica had found. "You can back me up or leave."

She sighed. "Let me take a quick shower then we'll go." She closed the door.

Carver went back to his room. "She's showering and then we'll go." He stripped down and took a shower since he had a moment. Jessica took one when he was done.

Twenty minutes later, they met Alicia outside and departed for Angel Dust. The gate that had been closed earlier was now open. The rollup door on the building was open and the interior was visible.

Two men in suits were posted at the gate. They looked more like bouncers or doormen than guards. A large sign on the gate confirmed his suspicion.

Party tonight! Protest tomorrow!

Free entry and drinks for all freedom fighters!

"They're shameless," Jessica said. "I'll bet most of the protestors don't even know or care about why they're protesting."

"Ah, the unemployed youth. A propogandist's greatest tool." Alicia looked down at her black jeans and combat boots. "I think I'll fit in okay."

Carver could see the empty lot where he'd parked the van earlier. The van was gone. Someone had probably parked it behind the warehouse.

Alicia drove up to the entrance. One of the men came up to the BMW and looked inside the window.

"Party time!" Alicia squealed. She smiled drunkenly at the man. "You're a big boy, aren't you?"

The man grinned. "Come find me later and I'll show you just how big."

"Ooh, nice." Alicia blew him a kiss. "Where do we park?"

"Out back," the man said. He winked. "Don't forget to find me later."

"I won't." She rolled up the window and drove down the side of the building to a rear parking lot. There were rows upon rows of buses parked on the west side and mostly cars parked everywhere else.

She found a spot and parked. "Now what?"

There was another open rollup door on the back. Lights flashed inside the club. A huge crowd was bouncing up and down in time with the music, fists raised. A techno beat thundered from giant speakers.

Most of the crowd was dressed in black. Many wore hats and masks and had backpacks on. None of it was for functionality. It was just style. The same kind of style that dominated at the protests.

Carver put on a beanie and a cloth mask. He slid on a slim backpack with a few choice tools inside, including his Sig. "Let's go party."

Alicia and Jessica masked up and got out. Alicia wore a concealed holster with a compact Glock on her back. Carver could see the outline of a knife beneath her pants. What looked like a pocket was probably a concealed knife sheath.

They walked through the rollup door and squeezed into the crowd. The space was massive. Only the last third of the building next to the DJ stage was full. The rest of it had a smattering of people here and there.

The building roof rose about three stories high, probably to accommodate warehouse shelves, but there was none of that here. The place was opened up and empty except for offices in the northwest corner of the building.

That area was blocked off with heavy duty temporary fencing. The same kind typically used for crowd control around buildings. The steel panels were eight feet tall and there were no visible gaps between them. The only way inside that section was probably through the office door on the front of the building.

The office windows were covered with venetian blinds. Light bled through the cracks, but there was no way to tell what was on the other side.

"If she's here, she'll be in there." Alicia nodded toward the offices. "Unless the crowd gets bigger, that area is isolated. No way to sneak in from this side."

"Agreed." Carver had already thought it over. "I'm going around the outside for a look."

Jessica tapped on her phone screen. "I ran a search for this club and the building. It's owned by Emerald Entertainment. They're owned by Leisure Holdings, Inc., which is owned by another company and another and another." She blew out a breath. "Long story short, the top company belongs to Nathaniel Ceallach III. I have no idea if that means it's tied to Dimitri or Yancy."

"What kind of name is that?" Alicia stared at the name on the screen. She pronounced it phonetically. "I've never heard that surname before."

Jessica shrugged. "Me neither. Anyway, that's who ultimately owns the club. I don't know if that helps or not."

"It's neither here nor there," Carver said. "I'm going in." He looked around for cameras and saw none on the offices or anywhere in the nightclub. They probably didn't want a recording of what went on in this place.

He went outside and didn't see any cameras out there either. Then he took a right and walked to the opposite corner. Alicia and Jessica followed close behind, neither one saying anything.

He looked down the side of the building. There was an emergency exit a few feet away from the corner, another one halfway down, and another about three quarters of the way down. The one near the far end would lead inside the offices.

Carver hustled down the side of the building until he reached the last emergency exit. The steel door was locked and there was a latch protection plate. He twisted the doorknob to make sure it wasn't already unlocked.

It wasn't.

He pulled on the door handle to test for slack and found a little. He pulled his slim jim from his backpack and worked the latch until the door opened. He eased it open and looked inside. The short hallway inside was well lit.

Carver followed it to the corner and looked down the next hallway. There were eight offices, four on either side of the hallway, and a main office at the far end. He eased up to the window of the first office on the left.

The blinds were closed so he couldn't see inside. The same was true for all the windows in the hallway. The thud of the techno music made it hard to hear if anyone was talking inside the office.

Carver decided to play it straightforward. It might work. He went back to the women. "I'm just going to walk right into the rooms. If Dimitri or someone is inside, I just play it off like I found the place myself.

Alicia nodded. "Just scream if you need rescuing."

Jessica grabbed his wrist. "Be careful."

"Okay." Carver went back around the corner to the first door on the left. He tried the doorknob. It was unlocked. He opened the door and found suitcases and rolled up sleeping bags on the floor.

He closed it and tried the opposite door. There were cases of bottled water and canned foods stacked in the middle of the floor, but nothing else. It looked like they'd unloaded his van and carried everything in here.

The next rooms on the left and right were empty. Four down. Four to go. He was starting to lose hope that Liana was here. The third room on the left was locked. The third room on the right wasn't. It had a small bed and a suitcase inside.

There were also two rifle cases, boxes of ammunition, a stun gun, and more in the corner. The suitcase conveniently had a name on it, Rashid. Apparently, he didn't want his stuff being mixed up with anyone else's.

Carver closed the door and went to the fourth door on the right. It was also unlocked. There was a bed, a large duffel bag with some wear and tear on it, and weapons cases in the room. No names on the bag or anything else. It didn't matter.

The fourth door on the left was locked. The door leading to the main office at the end of the hallway wasn't. He eased open the door. The main office was open and mostly empty with little to no furniture except a table, some chairs, and a big screen television on a rollaway stand. It was probably the same TV from the factory in Chicago.

Dimitri sat at the table with his back to Carver. He was eating pizza and drinking beer. All his attention was on the television. Rashid sat on his right. He was sipping on tea and reading a newspaper. They were the only two in the room.

They were here. That meant Liana had to be here. He shut the door. He didn't have to be too quiet because the music in the warehouse was even louder than before. That was good because of what he had to do next.

He went to the nearest locked door and worked the slim jim into the jamb. He sprung the latch and eased open the door. There was nothing inside except weapons crates. They were the same wooden and polyethylene crates he'd seen at the factory.

Carver tried to open the lid on a wooden crate. He was curious what kind of rifles they were transporting. Then he heard thudding coming from the room next door. He heard a man laughing. Heard more thuds.

Then a woman's muffled scream.

CHAPTER 37

Carver hurried into the hallway.

He knew who was on the other side of the last locked door in the hallway. It was a simple matter of deduction. Dimitri and Rashid were in the front office. That left Braden, Manny, and Dex.

Out of those three he knew for certain one of them loved beating women—Dex. And he was having fun with a woman who was scheduled to die tomorrow—Liana. Carver could see it in his head clear as day.

In a perfect world, he'd use the slim jim to quietly open the door. But his anger got the better of him and he rammed the door open with his shoulder. It was right in time with the techno beat outside, and Dex was focused on a bloody figure huddled in the corner of the room when Carver burst in.

He seemed to sense something was off and spun around. He saw Carver and grinned. "Don't you know it's polite to knock?"

"I just wanted to join in on the fun." Carver looked past him. The woman was face-down. She had tanned skin and long black hair. She was curled into the fetal position. She also wasn't moving.

Dex lunged for his duffel bag and drew a knife. He pointed it at Carver and his grin widened. "By the way, we received a real interesting picture of you today." He picked up his phone with his other hand and turned it toward Carver.

It was the same image of Carver and Liana that Arjun had shown him.

Dex laughed. "Apparently, Arjun had it scheduled to send from his email, because he was long dead by the time it went out."

The time for words and excuses was over. Liana was bleeding on the floor and he had to kill this asshole to save her. Carver grinned back. "You should have pulled a gun on me."

Dex lunged, knife thrusting out toward Carver's chest. It was a skilled thrust. Right on target. It should have gone right into his heart. But Carver had seen it coming from a mile away. He twisted sideways and the blade grazed his shirt instead of puncturing his heart.

Dex must have expected the blade to hit home because his arm was still extended. Carver grabbed his wrist with his left hand and swung down his right elbow onto Dex's forearm. The point of his elbow drove right down through soft tissue and hit the bone. Dex screamed in pain.

His hand opened and the knife fell. Carver caught it midfall. He thrust it three times into Dex's side before the other man even knew what hit him. He booted Dex hard, slamming him against the wall.

Dex collapsed, groaning and bleeding. His lung was punctured, judging from the harsh rasping emanating from his throat. Carver knelt next to the woman. He gently turned her over and moved her hair out of her face.

She wasn't Liana. Aside from the hair and skin color, she didn't even look remotely like her. There were cuts and bruises all over her face and chest. Her breasts were bleeding. But she was breathing, and her pulse was strong.

Alicia and Jessica came into the room and saw the woman. They must have heard the fight through comms.

"Oh my God!" Jessica dropped to her knees and touched the woman's face. "She's alive."

Carver went to Dex and put his boot on the man's chest. "Where the hell is she? Where is Liana, the woman from the picture?"

Dex sucked in a wet breath. "Help...me." He reached up. "I-I'll tell you if—" He drew in a gurgling breath. "Call ambulance."

"I can stop the bleeding right now," Carver said. "I just wounded you because I want answers. Tell me where she is and I'll stop the bleeding."

Dex gritted his teeth. They were stained with blood. He looked at Jessica. "Please, help me."

"Tell me where she is," Carver said. "Or I'll finish the job."

Dex stared at him, eyes bright with fear. "I don't know. But save me and I'll find out."

"You seriously don't know where she is?" Jessica stared at him in disbelief. "How could you not know where she is?"

Carver believed him. He might be part of Dimitri's inner circle, but the only person Dimitri really trusted was himself. He alone knew where Liana was. Carver put his boot on Dex's chest and put all his weight on it.

Dex gasped in pain. "Save...me..." Blood bubbled from his mouth. He tried to raise his hands, but he'd lost way too much blood. Carver had been lying. There was no saving the man, not even if the emergency room was next door. His left lung had been punctured three times by his own knife and now it was full of blood.

It was agonizing to die this way. Carver's only regret was that the man didn't get to suffer for hours before he shuffled off his mortal coil.

"What now?" Alicia said.

Carver showed her the picture on Dex's phone. "My cover was blown earlier, and I didn't even know it. Dimitri was probably waiting for me to come in before springing the surprise on me."

"Great." Jessica stared at the bloody knife on the floor. "So, do we just go in shooting?"

"No." Carver shook his head. "Dimitri won't tell me anything under duress."

"What makes you think that?" Alicia said.

Carver told her what he'd found out about Dimitri. "There's a tattoo on his bicep. A black heart with a knife through it. It looked familiar but I didn't think much of it until I remembered what it was from."

"Is he a member of Motherland's Exiles?" Alicia said.

Carver raised an eyebrow. "How do you know about them?"

"Jericho was interested in hiring them for a job." She shrugged. "It wouldn't have worked out. They're insane."

"Motherland's Exiles?" Jessica looked confused. "What are you talking about?"

"A group of Russian special forces, aka Spetsnaz, didn't agree with the annexation of Crimea, Ukraine and fought back against the motherland." Carver went to the door and looked into the hallway to make sure no one was coming. "They killed a lot of Russians but didn't make a dent in the cause. So they turned to profiteering off of the war."

Jessica's forehead pinched. "What made them betray their country in the first place?"

"Who knows?" Alicia said. "But Carver is right. If Dimitri is a former spetsnaz, then he won't give up information under torture. He'd probably rather die."

"What about Rashid?" Jessica said.

"I don't think he'll talk either," Carver said. "He and Dimitri will assume that I'll kill them after I get what I want, and torture won't work."

"Agreed," Alicia said. "Maybe planting bugs is the answer."

"We don't have time for that. I'm going to try something else." Carver looked himself over. There was blood on his hands, but the black clothing hid any of Dex's blood that might have gotten on him. There was bottled water on the table. He poured it on his hands and wiped them off on a shirt from Dex's suitcase.

Jessica glared at him. "Well, what is this something else you're going to try?"

"Simple," Carver said. "I'm going to see if he'll give up the information willingly."

Alicia laughed. "You're just going to waltz in there and ask him?"

"Sort of." Carver kept watching the hallway. It seemed that no one in the front had heard the ruckus between him and Dex. He could thank the booming techno music outside for that. He took out his phone and wasn't surprised to see a text from Dimitri.

We're having a party. Come to this address tonight. The address was right where he was standing.

Carver showed her the text. "He has that picture of me and Liana. He wanted to see me so he could spring the surprise on me tonight. He probably thinks I'm NSA or working with her."

"I fail to see how this is going to help you."

"He might see this as an opportunity," Carver said. "An opportunity to make it look like two NSA agents went rogue and killed Mitch Neuman. Which means he might put me in the same place Liana is being held."

Alicia's gaze softened. "You're an idiot, Carver. You know that?"

"I need you to back me up. Once they take me to her, you come rescue me."

She pressed her lips together. "I really didn't sign up for this."

"I'll pay you."

Alicia shook her head. "This isn't about money. This is about not getting myself killed. Jericho depends on me to do work for him. Not take random missions from a guy he wants to kill."

Jessica threw up her hands. "You two have the most complicated history I've ever heard of. Can we just stop worrying about dying and worry more about saving a life?"

Alicia chuckled softly. "Ah to be blissfully ignorant again."

"Will you help me or not?" Carver said. "They'll lock me up with or near Liana and then it'll be easy to swoop in and rescue me."

Alicia gritted her teeth and sighed. "Okay, I'll back you up."

"Um, what happens when they find out you killed Dex?" Jessica said. "You can't exactly hide that."

Carver looked at the woman on the floor. "Maybe they'll think she did it and escaped."

"Oh, I highly doubt that." Alicia went to the woman and patted her cheek. "I'll get her out of here. You should go around to the front door. That's where they're expecting you to come from. I'll listen in on the earbud and track your location."

Carver nodded. "Thanks."

Jessica took his hand. "Good luck. Please don't die."

"I'll do my best." Carver went to the woman on the floor and cradled her. He carried her down the hallway and outside. She moaned and her head lolled. She was still completely out of it, but it looked like she'd be fine.

"Set her down and we'll take her into the club," Alicia said. "Someone in there can help her."

"I don't trust the people here to do anything," Jessica said. "And it's too cold to leave her outside."

"We'll put her in the van then." Alicia turned to Carver. "Sound good?"

Carver nodded. "I'm going to walk around the side of the building and walk in the front door."

Alicia put an earbud in. "I'll be listening."

Carver held his earbud in the palm of his hand. "Knowing what he knows now, Dimitri will probably assume this isn't an ordinary earphone if he sees it in my ear." He tucked it into his sock. "Can you hear anything?"

"Faintly. But the important thing is I can track its location."

Carver set the woman down. Alicia and Jessica supported her and took her to the van. He walked back around the building. He went to the north side and found the front door to the office.

He steeled himself. Put on a friendly face. Opened the door and went inside.

Dimitri looked up from his phone. He saw Carver and stood, a big grin on his face. The kind of grin a person gets when they know something the other person doesn't.

In this case Carver knew what he knew. He was probably going to take a beating, but hopefully it would get him locked up in the same place Liana was.

"Ah, Sam, you came." Dimitri laughed with barely repressed glee. "You have no idea how happy I am to see you could come to the party."

"I got bored," Carver said. "I figured I could find a girl here or something and have some fun."

"Yes, yes, of course." Dimitri looked at Manny and smirked. "We can help you find a girl."

Carver looked around. Manny and Dimitri seemed to be the only people there. Rashid must have left by the front door. "Where's Dex and Rashid?"

"Rashid went to see an old friend. Dex already has a girl." Dimitri walked toward Carver. "Let's find you someone suitable."

Manny took out his phone and tapped on it. "How about this girl?"

Here it comes, Carver thought.

Manny turned the phone toward him to reveal the image of Carver and Liana in Asheville. "Will this girl do?"

Carver played dumb. "She's hot. Yeah, I'd love to see her."

Manny looked confused. "Look closer, asshole." He tapped the figure standing next to Liana.

Carver frowned and squinted. "Hey, that kind of looks like me."

"Yes, it's you." Dimitri walked up to him. "Don't play stupid, Sam." He snatched Manny's phone and shoved the screen up in Carver's face. "That's you and a government agent."

"A Korean asset," Manny said. "A competitor who costs us a lot of money."

Carver remained calm. "She doesn't look Korean to me."

Dimitri laughed. "Well, you know who she really is, don't you?"

Manny looked confused. "Is she not with the Koreans?"

"No." Dimitri walked around Carver and put himself in front of the door, probably thinking Carver would try to run. "She's with the National Security Agency. The NSA."

Manny's eyes flared. "The NSA? Why didn't you tell us that before?"

"Because it's none of your concern."

Carver backed up a step. "Okay, look, I can explain." He held up his hands defensively. "I didn't know she was NSA."

"Don't lie, Sam." Dimitri shoved him.

Carver was bracing for a push or punch but he hadn't expected the amount of force Dimitri could exert and stumbled back, slamming into the wall. He wasn't sure any amount of bracing could have prepared him for that much power.

Most of the big people he'd encountered weren't any stronger than him. Most were weaker. Being too big was a detriment. It made bones longer and weaker and there was more surface area for a bullet or knife.

But Dimitri was a mutant. He was one of those rare types who was as strong as he was big. And he was fast and well trained. Carver would probably lose to him in a fair fight. That was no big deal, because Carver didn't believe in fighting fair.

Fighting Dimitri didn't come into play here. He had to let Dimitri have his fun and make him believe that he'd beaten Carver. Otherwise, he might not survive to be locked up with Liana.

Carver grunted in genuine pain when he slammed into the wall. He bared his teeth and charged Dimitri. He swung his fist at the other man's face. Dimitri blocked the swing with his forearm. His other fist connected with Carver's face.

Carver staggered back, stunned. He'd intentionally left himself open for a counterattack and immediately regretted it. He wasn't sure that would be enough to satisfy Dimitri, so he shook it off, roared, and charged again.

Dimitri grinned like a maniac and held his arms wide as if welcoming Carver to do his worst. Carver punched him in the stomach three times and nailed him in the face with a haymaker that would have leveled most men. Dimitri laughed it off.

Then he slammed Carver in the gut. Carver doubled over. The big man lunged forward off his back foot and shoved Carver. It was like being blocked by a professional football lineman. The force sent Carver flying backward again.

He crashed into the wall, leaving a Carver-sized dent in the drywall. He went down on one knee. Spat blood. He stood on wobbly legs, bracing himself on the wall. He wasn't faking the wobble. The punches and body slams had done some real damage.

He just hoped it was enough. Because if it wasn't, one thing was certain.

Dimitri was going to kill him.

CHAPTER 38

Carver held up a hand in surrender.

"Stop, please." He leaned against the wall. "She's my former partner. I came looking for her."

"I knew it!" Dimitri raised a fist in victory.

Manny looked confused but he laughed along. "Man, you caught two NSA agents?"

Carver wiped blood from his face. "Is she alive?"

Dimitri clenched a fist and beat his chest. "You pathetic Americans think you're special. But nothing beats Slavic power. Nothing."

"I'll pay you anything. Just let me take her home." Carver put his hands together as if pleading. "I'll do whatever you want."

"Yes, yes you will." Dimitri grinned. "Yes, she's alive and she's going to help me with something. Now that I have you, both of you can help me. Once we're done, you can go."

Carver didn't believe him for a second, but he put on a hopeful look. "Really? Just tell me what you need, and I'll do it."

"Sam, my friend." Dimitri laughed as if he'd just made a clever joke. "I just want you to rest well and recover. Tomorrow you will do the job and be finished. You and your friend will be free."

Carver nodded. "Can I see her?"

"You can see her tomorrow." He motioned Manny toward Carver. "Frisk him and lock him up."

Manny frisked Carver. He found the Sig and Carver's concealed knife. He set them down. "Where am I locking him up?"

"Tie him up in the truck." Dimitri flexed his hands. "I'll make sure you do it right."

"Can I please see her?" Carver said. "I just need to know she's all right."

"I don't want to disturb her," Dimitri said. "I promise you'll get to see her tomorrow."

Manny laughed. "Yeah, I ain't unboxing her for you. It's a pain in the ass." He put the Sig against Carver's back. "Now, let's go outside."

They went through the back hall. Manny stopped and stared at a trickle of blood coming from under Dex's door. "Damn, he really went to town on that girl he took in there."

Dimitri sighed. "It's his mess. He can clean it up. Keep going."

They went out the back door and to a large box truck. Dimitri rolled up the back door. There were four wooden crates inside. They looked like the ones he'd seen at the factory. The markings on the outside told him that these were the ones with oxygen and nitrous oxide cannisters inside.

Dimitri opened one of the boxes and pulled out ratchet straps. He went to a large crate. "Sit here."

Carver sat in front of the crate. He pushed his back against it. Whatever was inside was heavy because he couldn't budge it. Manny wrapped the wide nylon strap around Carver's stomach and arms where they bent at the elbow. He wrapped it around the big crate and then ratcheted it tight.

He put another strap around Carver's neck and ratcheted it uncomfortably tight, but not so much that Carver couldn't breathe. He put another strap around his chest and strapped his arms to his legs. He finished up with straps around Carver's thighs and ankles.

He did a thorough job. A real thorough job. Carver could bend his knees, but he couldn't move anything else. Even if he had a knife in his hand, there was no way he could position it to cut the heavy duty straps.

Dimitri took a red bottle from a crate. He attached a mask and strapped it to Carver's face. He grinned. "Go to sleep. You have a big day tomorrow." He twisted the valve open. Gas flooded into the mask.

Carver took a breath. The last thing he saw was Dimitri leering down at him and then it was lights out.

"Wake up!"

Carver felt paralyzed. His eyelids were lead weights. It took a moment for his brain to reboot. Then he remembered what happened. A lungful of NO2. Not pure nitrous, but enough to keep him unconscious indefinitely without causing brain damage.

Thankfully, it didn't take too long to flush the symptoms from his body. He felt someone tugging at his bonds. Heard someone talking as if in the distance. It was probably Manny or Dimitri who'd come to get him up.

He played dead. Let feeling return to his body. It took the body about five to ten minutes to flush NO2 out of the system. He was in good shape so it would take less time.

Someone gently slapped his face. "Carver, wake up."

He opened his eyes and saw Alicia kneeling next to him. The nylon straps had been sliced off. "Hi."

She raised an eyebrow. "Your brilliant plan didn't work?"

Carver pushed slowly to his feet. He rubbed his wrists and arms to get the blood flowing again. "Not in the way I intended. They didn't take me to Liana, but they didn't need to. I was right next to her already."

Alicia frowned. "I think you're still high from the NO2."

"Maybe a little, but I'm not wrong." He looked at the box truck's rollup door. It was closed. "Is anyone out there?"

She shook her head. "No. I watched them put you inside. They put a padlock on it and went back in. I figured Liana might be in here with you, but I wasn't sure."

"Nope. Just me."

"Explain what you meant by Liana being next to you already."

"How long have I been in here?"

"An hour. I wanted to go sooner but we had to run to the hardware store for bolt cutters for the padlock."

"Okay." Carver raised the door a little and looked outside. The music was still thumping, and it would probably keep thumping all night. He got out of the truck.

Jessica appeared from behind one of the nearby buses. "She's not in there?"

Alicia shook her head. "Nope. Dead end."

"Well, it wasn't the dumbest plan I've ever heard." Jessica looked closely at Carver's face. "Man, you took a beating for nothing."

"Not for nothing." Carver walked back toward the rear office door. "I know where Liana is."

Alicia grabbed his arm. "Where the hell is she? And are you really going back in there unarmed?"

Carver took a breath to clear his head. "Good point." He jogged over to the car. Alicia opened the trunk and he pulled his MP5SD from his duffel bag. He locked in a magazine and strapped on his ammo belt with four more magazines.

He turned to Jessica. "Wait here."

"I know I'm not trained, but I can still pull a trigger if you give me a gun."

He gave her a Glock 19 and slid in a magazine. "Have you shot a gun before?"

"Yes, at a shooting range."

"Well, that's something. I want you to wait outside. Tell us if anyone's coming." He removed the earbud from his sock and put it in his ear. "Copy that?"

She took the gun and nodded. "Copy that." She looked it over. "Where's the safety?"

"Doesn't have one."

"Your finger is the safety," Alicia said.

"Okay." She nodded. "Let's go."

Alicia held her MP5SD at the low and ready and closed the BMW trunk. "Are you taking point?"

"Yes." Carver weaved through parked cars to avoid anyone at the party from seeing him. They reached the corner of the building. Carver pointed to a nearby bus. "Jessica, be the lookout."

"Roger that." She hustled over to the bus and crouched behind it. "In position Blue leader."

Alicia rolled her eyes. "Let's go."

The back door wasn't locked. Apparently, they hadn't relocked it after taking Carver out. They went into the hallway. Carver peeked around the corner. There was more blood in the hallway and Dex's door was open.

Carver eased up to the door and looked inside. Manny had a bucket and was mopping up blood. He cursed under his breath and kicked Dex's body. He flinched as if seeing movement and drew his gun. He saw Carver and his eyes went wide.

Carver put a round in his forehead before he could raise the gun. Manny's mouth dropped open and he went down. Carver went to the last door on the left. It was locked again. He looked into the other rooms and found his backpack in the first room where the suitcases were.

He opened it and took out his slim jim. He went back to the locked door and jimmied it open then ducked inside.

Alicia came behind him. She looked at the crates and frowned. "Why are we in here?"

"Motherland's Exiles is known for human trafficking," Carver said in a low voice. "And they're known for how they transport high-value cargo."

Alicia frowned. "I'm not that familiar with them."

Carver opened one of the crates with the oxygen cannisters. The next one had nitrous oxide in it. "When I saw this at the factory, I didn't know what to think of it. Then Manny made a comment that told me exactly what I needed to know."

"Just get to the point already."

"He said he wasn't going to unbox Liana." Carver crouched next to the long polyethylene crate. The one he thought might have a Javelin rocket launcher or other equipment inside. Now he knew why they had cannisters of nitrous oxide and oxygen at the factory. Why they had these long crates.

The crate wasn't locked, but it had three heavy latches. He undid them and opened it. There was foam padding inside the bottom. There was a cannister of oxygen and nitrous inside. And most importantly, there was an unconscious woman slumbering peacefully inside.

He'd found Liana.

She was bruised and cut and wearing nothing but underwear and a tank top, but she was alive and breathing.

Carver turned off the NO2 cannister. He put an arm under her head and raised her into a sitting position. He put the oxygen in front of her nose and let her breathe it in.

"Holy shit." Alicia looked at the other identical crate. "You think someone is in that one too?"

Carver shrugged.

She unlatched it and opened it. It was empty.

Liana groaned. She opened her eyes slowly and looked at Carver. She gasped. Tried to speak, but her throat sounded dry as dust. He grabbed one of Dex's bottled waters and trickled it into her mouth.

She gulped greedily.

"You found her?" Jessica said over comms.

"Yeah. Coming out." Carver cradled Liana. Her muscles didn't look too atrophied. Probably because she hadn't been in the crate for that long. They'd kept her in that container in the factory then moved her into the crate two days before Carver went there.

Three days was a long time to be knocked out in a crate, but it was nothing special in the world of human trafficking.

Alicia took point and they hurried to the back door. They ducked behind buses and cars and got back to the BMW.

Carver thought of something. "Where's the other girl?"

"We dropped her at a hospital on the way to the hardware store." Alicia shrugged. "I figured you weren't going anywhere."

"Carver." Liana's voice was a harsh whisper. She gripped him in a fierce hug. "Guess I should have listened to you."

He smoothed her hair back and set her gently into the back seat of the BMW. "Nah, don't be stupid."

She laughed softly then looked around. "Where the hell are we?"

"Washington DC. Your boy Dimitri is about to assassinate the Senate majority leader."

"That bastard almost broke my ribs." She winced. "I think he was going to kill me but then decided he could use me for his little plan."

"Did you know his plan?"

She nodded. "He didn't tell me, but I overheard him planning it with Rashid, Dex, and Manny. Those were the only people he trusted with the full plan."

"Who told him you were with the NSA?"

"He said he had an insider who told him. Apparently, someone with ties to the old administration gave him a list of undercover agents."

"Did he name anyone specific?"

She shook her head. "No. He put a bag over my head and locked me up somewhere for days. They moved me somewhere else and locked me in a cargo container."

"I was in the same container," Carver said. "I saw your message."

"You what?" She looked confused. "How in the hell did you end up there?"

"Why didn't you escape through that panel? I assume you're the one who loosened the screws."

"Yeah, I did. But they were still up and about, so I decided to escape when they were asleep." She sighed. "Then Dimitri came and told me he hadn't killed me because he had a use for me. He said I was going to help him shift power in the Senate. Until then, he said he'd put me on ice."

"Meaning the crate," Alicia said.

Liana nodded. She frowned and looked at Alicia and Jessica. "Who are your friends, Carver?"

"We'll discuss that later." Carver swung his strapped MP5SD back across his chest. "I'm going to put Dimitri on ice."

"As much as I'd love to see you do that, I'm just going sit right here," Liana said.

Carver turned to Jessica. "You stay with her. Alicia, can you watch my six?"

Alicia nodded. "Might as well finish this. Save the day and all that."

"This isn't about saving the day," Carver said. "I just don't like Dimitri or his friends. And I want them dead for what they did to Liana."

She grinned. "I can get behind that."

They made their way to the back door and entered cautiously. In the ten minutes they'd been gone, no one had come into the hallway. They cleared the rooms to make sure no one was inside any of them and then came to the main office door.

Carver opened it.

Rashid and Dimitri were sitting at the table watching the news on television. As usual it was about the China trade deal. Their backs were both to Carver.

Dimitri turned his head slightly as the door clicked shut. "Did you clean up the mess and find the girl, Manny?"

"Not exactly," Carver said.

Rashid jumped up, hand drawing his sidearm. Alicia put a bullet in his forehead and he dropped.

Dimitri raised his hands and turned slowly. He grinned. "Did this girl save you? Another NSA agent?"

"I'm an independent," Alicia said. "And yes, I saved his sorry ass."

Dimitri grunted. "So, what now? You shoot me? If you do, you'll never find your partner."

"I already found her," Carver said. "I took her out of her crate and took her somewhere safe."

Dimitri deflated slightly, like a poker player realizing that his winning hand had just been trumped.

"Did Plum and Associates sell you the undercover agent list?" Carver said. "Is that how you found out who she is?"

"I will tell you nothing." Dimitri shrugged. "Shoot me and be done with it."

"Your entire plan is done for," Carver said. "There's no harm in telling me."

"You want to know who to go after next, don't you?" A smile spread over Dimitri's lips. "I will not satisfy your curiosity. I will not help you. You will never know who else is responsible."

"You won't even give me a fake name, so I'll go kill someone who's not even involved?"

"What's the point?" Dimitri said. "I will be dead. There is no satisfaction to be gained."

"Yeah, I guess not." Carver aimed. A part of him hoped Dimitri would try to strike a deal. Even the toughest guys often pleaded for their lives when they knew for certain they were about to die.

Not Dimitri. He lifted his chin as if prepared to die. And then he kicked his chair and dove to the side. The chair whistled past Carver's head and clipped Alicia's gun, knocking it to the side.

Carver fired. Dimitri dove toward the front door. A bullet caught him in the leg. He went down to one knee, then roared and pushed outside. Carver shot him again and chased after him. Dimitri dodged around the corner.

He was trying to run but his leg wasn't cooperating. Carver caught up to him. He put two bullets in the man's back. Dimitri clenched his fists and roared defiance. He spun on Carver, swinging wildly but was too far away to hit him.

"Fight me like a man!" Dimitri shouted. "Coward!"

"Did you fight Liana like a man?" Carver said. "Or that girl Dex killed?"

Dimitri tried to run at him, but his leg failed. He fell to his knees and howled in fury. Carver put two bullets in his forehead and Dimitri finally went down.

"Guess we should have brought the elephant gun," Alicia said from behind him.

"Yeah." Carver put another bullet in the back of Dimitri' head to make sure he was dead. He looked around. There was a black SUV parked near the office. Dimitri's body was behind it and it was dark in the area, so no one would find him for a while.

It was finally over.

CHAPTER 39

Carver took Dimitri's phone.

He unlocked it with Dimitri's thumb and looked through it. Dimitri used the same encrypted messaging app Arjun had so there was nothing useful in the regular texts. There were almost no pictures and no social media on the phone either.

He had, however, manually saved several conversation threads between him and Yancy. They were mostly about shipments from China and who they were supposed to go to. One conversation was about the China trade deal.

It was the date that got Carver's attention. It was the same day that Liana's cover had been blown. The same day Dimitri put a bag over her head and imprisoned her. There was a third person in the conversation. A person listed only by their initials, CP.

The third person had sent a picture and two texts. *FYI you have a rat. Liana Cardoso, NSA.* A picture of Liana followed the text.

Dimitri had simply replied, *I'll take care of it.*

Yancy replied moments later. *How did you get this information?* The sender hadn't responded. Yancy had sent another message later. *We're partners. I expect you to be forthcoming about where you got this information.* The sender had either never replied, or the messaging app had deleted the replies.

It was interesting that Dimitri had saved this message thread. Maybe it was because of the picture of Liana and her information. Carver would probably never know. What he did know was that this anonymous sender had burned Liana.

There was nothing else of interest, so he wiped down the phone and left it on the ground next to Dimitri's body. He and Alicia went back through the building. She stopped at the room with the crates.

"We touched a lot of stuff. Probably too much to wipe down."

"What do you suggest?" Carver looked at the wooden crates. "Should we burn them?"

"I think so." She went into Dex's room and picked up a lighter from the table. She went back to the crate room and pulled the lids off several of them.

One crate was filled with old handguns, most of which were missing serial numbers. Another had boxes of ammunition. There were teargas grenades, smoke grenades, gasmasks, and crates filled with empty glass bottles and rags. The same kind of bottles Dimitri and gang had used to make Molotov cocktails.

There were four crates of oxygen cannisters and four more of nitrous oxide. Another crate had little packets filled with pills and other drugs. The contents were labeled on each package. They were probably handed out as party favors for events like the big rave happening right outside in the warehouse.

The last crate was packed with stacks of hundred-dollar bills.

Alicia whistled. "Maybe we should just take this crate."

Carver picked up a stack of hundred-dollar bills and rifled through them. "Do we really have time to load up your car?"

She left the room and returned a moment later with a suitcase from the room down the hall. She emptied the clothing from the suitcase and then packed it with the money and zipped it up.

Carver smashed a wooden crate with his foot. He put some of the loose clothing under the wood and set it on fire with the lighter. It started burning hot enough to catch the wood on fire, so they hurried out of the building and went around the side.

Carver saw Jessica waiting at the BMW. She wasn't alone. A familiar person was standing in front of her, and he didn't look happy. That person was Braden Cutler.

Braden lunged at Jessica and grabbed her hair. "I'm taking you to Dimitri. I'll let him handle you."

Jessica kneed him in the crotch. He went down squealing. She towered over him. "I told you to leave me alone."

Carver and Alicia reached the BMW.

Braden saw Carver and his eyes widened. "What the hell? Are all of you with the Koreans?"

"Koreans?" Liana was leaning out the window. "We're NSA agents!"

Braden paled. "NSA?" He staggered to his feet and backed away. "I've got to tell Dimitri!" He bolted for the warehouse.

Jessica started after him, but Carver stopped her. "Let him go. There's no one left for him to tell."

"Let's get the hell out of here." Alicia put the suitcase full of cash into the trunk. Jessica hopped in the back and Carver got into the front. Alicia started the car and casually drove toward the exit. She waved goodbye to the doormen at the fence. "See you later big guy!"

The man who'd flirted with her on the way in tried to wave her down. "Hey, what about me showing you my big—" Whatever he said next faded into the distance.

"What's in the suitcase?" Jessica said. "Did you steal someone's clothing for Liana?"

"We're not that thoughtful," Alicia said. "We found some things we wanted to take, so we took them."

Carver looked back and saw smoke pouring from the building. "Looks like the office will burn nicely."

There was a thunderous explosion. The roof of the warehouse shot into the air and a mushroom cloud of smoke formed above it.

"Doesn't NO2 help combustion?" Alicia said. "Or am I thinking of something else?"

"That was more than the oxygen and nitrous cannisters exploding," Carver said. "I think they had ammunition stored somewhere nearby too. Maybe kerosene for the Molotov cocktails too."

Jessica put her head out of the window. "Did you two just blow up the entire warehouse? Holy crap that was loud!"

Liana laughed weakly. "Now that's what I call a rescue."

Carver hadn't planned on an explosion, but at least there would be no traces of anything left behind.

"Where to?" Alicia said.

"Here." Carver gave her the coordinates for the carriage house.

"I might get out of here tonight," Alicia said. "Things are about to get real hot around here."

"I understand." Carver massaged his jaw. It was sore where Dimitri had punched him. "Split the money fifty-fifty?"

"Sure. But keep my share to pay everything I owe you."

"Fair." She grinned. "Jericho should really reconsider killing you. You're walking vengeance, Carver, and that's what he's all about."

"It would be great if you could convince him to forget about me," Carver said. "But I'm not interested in working with anyone. I just want to get back to the beach."

"You soft, sappy son of a bitch." Liana leaned forward from the back and put her hand on his shoulder. "You came after me. You might as well stop acting all tough and admit that you're just a big fluffy rabbit."

Alicia and the others burst into laughter.

Carver didn't think it was all that funny, but he gave her a smile all the same. "That's me. Mr. Fluffy."

Liana leaned further forward with a groan and kissed his cheek. "Thank you, Carver. I don't know why you came for me, but I'm glad you did."

Jessica snorted. "He's not really walking vengeance as much as he is a walking contradiction."

"He's mostly selfish, but he does right by people he considers his brothers in arms." Alicia glanced at Carver. "You got mixed up with us by trying to help Rich because he served with you in the SEALS."

Carver didn't answer. He just patted Liana's hand and thought about the message from the anonymous sender. The message that burned Liana's cover. "Jessica, is there any way you can find out who this Yancy guy is and who his partners are?"

"I already ran searches about him, so there's probably something in the indexes." She nodded. "I just need to get back to my laptop."

They stopped by the motel to get their things and then went to the carriage house. Liana was pale and shaking with hunger, so he made some eggs for her and got her water. She ate greedily and gulped the water.

"I thought that was it for me," she said. "My great return to the NSA failed in one mission."

Carver thought about the texts between Dimitri, Yancy, and the anonymous sender. He couldn't think of anyone with the initials CP. They probably meant nothing. Just some random letters by Dimitri for the contact.

Jessica sat at her laptop staring at the screen. She tapped on the keyboard a few times and sat back waiting for results. Then she stopped moving and leaned forward. "I think I have something."

Carver sat next to her. There was a picture of Yancy, a tall, pale Caucasian man with light hair. He was thin with a little girth in the waistline and a mouthful of big teeth. "Is he British?"

Jessica laughed. "It was the teeth that gave it away, right?"

"What are we looking at here?"

"It's a picture of him with some politicians." She pointed to the caption under the picture. "No mention of partners, though." She scrolled through several more images. Yancy had a lot of friends in Washington, it seemed. He was pictured with senators and representatives from both sides of the aisle.

Jessica sighed. "Nothing."

Carver remembered something. He pulled the leech from his backpack and handed it to her. "I copied the contents of a computer when I was in the factory. Didn't seem to be much on it, though."

She plugged it into her laptop and browsed through the folders. "The leech must be really fancy. It decrypted the documents."

"How do you know?"

"There's a documents folder labeled decrypted."

"Ah." Carver watched as she went through the folders. She stopped at one labeled contracts and opened it. There were lots of folders inside, each one labeled with names like Broad Enterprise Ltd., Consolidated Enterprises LLC, and so forth.

Jessica's eyes brightened. "Now we're onto something." She opened a folder called *Master Chart* and found a single image file inside. The image was large and filled the screen. She clapped her hands. "It's an organizational chart for shell companies." She tapped the screen. "This is the whole shebang."

Alicia walked over and looked at the image. "Does it really matter?"

"Yes. This thing is hyperlinked to the contract files." Jessica clicked a name and it took her to the incorporation letter for that corporation.

Carver scanned the first few lines for the list of officers and owners. Yancy Bancroft and Dimitri Sokolov were the executive officers.

Jessica clicked several more links below that one. The officers listed were different for each one. "James Smith? John Brown?" She shook her head. "These names are so common that they could be anyone."

"That's the point," Alicia said. "The top-level corporation owns the ones below it so as long as Dimitri and Yancy are the executive officers for the primary one, it doesn't matter who's listed for the others. That's how they hide themselves."

"Okay, so if they have a third partner, would they be in one of the subsidiaries or the primary?" Jessica stared at the chart. "I just realized these are organized by country and region."

"You're right." Alicia pointed to the other side of the chart. "That branch is for China."

"There are top level corporations for each region." Jessica pointed to the top line of the chart. "Eastern Industries International is the top level for their Chinese companies." She clicked on it.

Like the other top-level corporations, this one listed Dimitri and Yancy. But it also listed five other people. One of the names caught Carver's eye. He pointed to it. "Look up that name and cross reference it with Yancy Bancroft."

Jessica typed in the names and brought up two images. It was from seven years prior, and the caption read, *New trade deal will remove China trade restrictions.* She frowned. "Does this mean anything to you?"

Carver nodded grimly. "Yeah. This trade deal was almost done seven years ago, but it failed due to Neuman back then. Then it languished for all these years until now." He tapped the man in the picture. "That's the third partner. The one who burned Liana's cover."

Alicia looked closer. "You think he bought the undercover agent list and told Dimitri?"

"Maybe. Or someone gave it to him." Carver typed in another name and pulled up an image. "That person being his son."

Jessica read the caption under the photo. "Newly sworn in senator Paul Callahan promises to open free trade at any cost."

Alicia put a hand on Carver's shoulder. "As much as I'd like to pay him a visit, we can't kill a sitting senator. The heat would be insane."

"Yeah you'd get five stars for sure," Jessica said.

Alicia frowned. "Five stars?"

"Sorry. Videogame reference."

Liana walked over on shaky feet. Carver got up and let her take his seat.

She smiled. "What a gentleman." Her smile faded when she looked at the person who'd betrayed her. "You're certain he did it?"

"Ninety percent," Carver said. "He's sleeping with Rachel Evans, the deputy director of the NSA."

She whipped around to face him. "Are you saying she gave him the list?"

Carver shook his head. "No. Two high-level staffers from the previous administration sold it. Callahan probably got it for free from the seller. He found out there was an agent in one of his operations and burned your cover."

Liana's fists clenched. "Maybe it is a really bad idea to kill a sitting senator, but I'm willing to take that chance."

"A sitting US senator is way too powerful for us to mess with." Jessica shook her head. "I agree with Alicia. It's suicidal."

"I have a better idea," Carver said. "Let's burn him."

Alicia's eyebrows arched. "Literally or figuratively?"

He turned to Liana. "What do you know of Rachel Evans?"

"Almost nothing. But if she's cheating on her husband with a senator, then I don't think she's all that trustworthy."

"If you ask her to help us burn Callahan, then she'll be burning herself too." Alicia shook her head. "That's not the right angle."

Jessica sighed. "We also don't have definitive proof that he's the one who gave Dimitri the list."

Carver figured they were right. "Yeah. I guess we could release the evidence to the media and let them handle it. That's about all we can do."

Liana took his hand. "Carver, I can never repay you for this. I'm just glad to be back even if that snake is still walking free."

He nodded. "Are you going back again?"

"Yeah. Maybe that's stupid, but I feel like I can do some real good from the inside."

"Not as much good as you could do from the outside." Alicia put her hands on her shoulders. "We have openings for skilled people."

Liana frowned. "Who are you, exactly?"

"Careful," Carver said. "Do you really want to invite an active NSA agent into the fold?"

Alicia shrugged. "Having someone on the inside could be very useful."

"That's not how I operate." Liana shook her head. "Let me just enjoy being alive for a little while. Then we can talk business."

"Sounds good." Alicia walked over to the refrigerator and pulled out a beer. "I say we relax tonight and go our separate ways tomorrow."

Carver nodded. "Sounds good." He went downstairs into the garage and outside. He sent a text and received a fast but concerned response. He replied. They went back and forth a few times, but an agreement was reached.

He went back inside. He took a shower and changed. He came out to the den and found Liana looking at him suspiciously.

"I'm going to get more food and beer." He walked toward the stairs. "I'll be back soon."

"We all know that's not what you're going to do." Liana walked over to him and took his hands. She stared into his eyes. "You're an idiot, but you have my blessing."

"I don't know what you're talking about."

Alicia groaned. "Do you need backup? Not that I want to help, but I'm curious to see how you pull this off."

"Pull what off?" Jessica looked confused. "What's going on?"

Carver worked his jaw back and forth. He came to a decision. "Fine. Everyone put on ballcaps and masks and get into the car."

"Into the car?" Jessica looked around wildly. "Where are we going?"

Liana rubbed her hands together. "I'm not sure, but I know it'll be interesting."

Carver thought of something else. Something that would be icing on the cake. "There's one thing you can help me with before we leave."

Jessica raised an eyebrow. "What's that?"

"I want to write a letter."

Alicia, Liana, and Jessica looked confused until he explained the letter. Then they were all for it.

Once they were done, Carver drove them to the destination. They got out and walked through the pedestrian entrance. He led them into the building and into his condo unit.

"Nice place." Alicia looked around. "Very nice."

Carver turned on the laptop and the camera. Now all he had to do was wait. It didn't take long. The prey appeared on camera moments later.

He'd texted Rachel Evans. Told her if she didn't help him lure Callahan to the condo that he was going to release evidence that would burn Callahan and by extension, her. He showed her some of the evidence and she quickly agreed because she was fearful that if Callahan went down, he'd take her down with him.

Paul Callahan's career was going to end tonight.

CHAPTER 40

Carver had told Rachel Evans what he planned to do.

He told her that he deserved it for what he'd done to one of her own agents. Evans had reluctantly agreed. Not so much because she cared about Liana, but because she had a career and reputation to protect. If word of her affair became public, she would be fired and disgraced.

Things would be even worse for her when it was revealed Callahan had burned one of her agents and nearly gotten her killed.

When Callahan appeared on the screen, Liana shook her head in disbelief. "Carver, how in the hell did you get him to come here?"

"I told Rachel Evans to arrange a meetup with him."

"And he came running?" Jessica whistled. "Wow, she must have some fire kitty."

Alicia snorted. "That's one way of putting it."

Liana watched Callahan as he poured himself a glass of wine. "So, he comes without any security, nothing?"

"Yep. Nobody knows he's here." Carver handed out nitrile gloves to everyone. "Put your hair under your ballcaps and keep your masks on for now."

They followed his instructions.

"Okay, let's go talk to him." Carver exited the condo. He used the keycard for Callahan's condo. The door lock beeped, the lock disengaged, and he walked in.

"Hey there, sexy." Callahan walked around the corner, an expectant grin on his face. The grin turned to a look of absolute confusion when he saw the man with the gun pointed at him. He looked even more confused when he saw the people flanking Carver.

"Hi," Carver said. "We need to talk." He gestured with the gun toward the bar stools. "Have a seat."

Callahan threw up his hands. "Who the hell are you? Do you know who I am?"

"I'm very well aware of who you are." Carver gestured with the gun again. "Take a seat, or I'll make you."

Callahan sat on the stool. "What's this about? Money? Are you going to ransom me?"

"No."

Callahan looked at the women. "Who are they?"

"Concerned citizens." Carver walked to the counter. "Kyle Svensk. Hector Jiminez."

Callahan flinched. His eyes flared. "What?"

It was the reaction Carver had been hoping for. "I see you're aware of the people you sentenced to death."

"I don't know what you're talking about."

"The interns you put on a hit list. Abby Smith, Tarah Hernandez, and Sharon Reese are the ones who survived." Carver stared at him for a moment as if daring him to contradict it. "All because you thought they found out about the undercover agent list."

His eyes widened. "Who the hell are you?"

"I'm with the NSA. We know what you did, and we're here to have a conversation."

"Shit." Callahan looked panicked. "I accidentally printed the list when I got it. Tarah brought it to me, thinking it was something I needed, but I could tell she was concerned by all the names and organizations listed on it. I saw her talking to her friends and couldn't risk her telling anyone about it."

"So, you decided to kill her and all of her friends just to be safe."

"Yes." He sucked in a breath. "Rachel lured me here, that stupid bitch!"

"We know about your affair with her and told her she had to do this, or it would become public knowledge."

Callahan shivered. "Look, that China trade bill has to pass. You don't understand how long we've waited. And that idiot Neuman has been in the way for too long. But we have a plan to fix that. A plan that will tie everything up nicely and you only need to sacrifice one agent. Is that too much to ask?"

"Just one agent?" Carver pretended to think it over. "That's a reasonable ask." He turned to the others. "What do you think?"

Liana nodded. "Yeah, it's just one life. No big deal."

"And the country will make billions." Callahan looked moderately relieved. "I'm willing to make sure all of you profit as well. How's a million each sound?"

Carver whistled. "I like the sound of that."

"I'm in," Jessica said.

Liana nodded. "Me too. Definitely worth trading a life for."

"Great, then it's settled." Callahan rubbed his hands together. "How do you want to do this?"

"A contract," Carver said. "That's the best way to secure this deal."

Jessica nodded. "Yeah, because it don't mean nothing until you sign it on the dotted line."

"Yes, I can have my lawyers draw up a contract. I'll make you full partners in my China Ventures LLC so it looks legitimate." He breathed a sigh of relief. "This will work out just fine."

"We already have a contract," Carver said. "We figured the conversation might go this way and none of us were going to turn down a big payday."

"Oh, really?" Callahan looked confused. "So that was the plan from the beginning? Scare me and then ask for a bribe?"

"Wouldn't you do the same in our place?" Alicia said. "This is business."

Liana nodded. "And we have all the blackmail material we need."

Carver pulled out a sheet of paper. There was no signature line at the bottom. "Just sign here."

"But—but there's no contract." Callahan looked confused. "What is this?"

Carver put a hand on Callahan's shoulder and squeezed hard. "Just sign it, or the deal is off."

Callahan winced in pain. "Fine, I'll sign it!" He scrawled his signature.

"Thanks." Carver moved the top sheet of paper to reveal the text. "Read that over and let me know how it sounds."

Callahan stared at it and paled. He gasped. "What the hell—"

Liana came up from behind him and put a medical mask over his face. Callahan sucked in a lungful of nitrous oxide and slumped. She strapped the mask on his face. "Okay, let's do this."

They took him to the master bathroom upstairs. There was a huge clawfoot tub next to a large window. They kept the lights off and filled the tub. Once it was three quarters of the way full, they took off Callahan's shirt and eased him into the water.

Alicia pulled out a scalpel and handed it to Liana. "Do you want the honors?"

"I would, but my hands are still shaking."

"It'll look more realistic that way," Alicia said.

"I can't watch this." Jessica shuddered. "I'm waiting outside. Otherwise, I'll puke."

"Yes, please don't puke," Alicia said.

Liana took the scalpel with a trembling hand. She stood behind Callahan and put the scalpel in his right hand. She squeezed his fingers together and drew the scalpel from his wrist almost to his elbow. The cut was crooked but as Alicia had said, it would make it look more realistic, as if Callahan was scared.

She put the scalpel in his left hand and did the same to his right arm, cutting from the wrist up to the crook of the elbow. That was the surefire way to cut all the veins in the arm rather than cutting across the wrist as was commonly portrayed in movies.

They put Callahan's arms in the tub and let the blood drain for a moment. Then they removed the mask. He slowly came to, his system clearing out the effects of the gas. The blood loss caused him to regain consciousness much more slowly.

His eyes fluttered open. He saw the bloody water. He screamed, he thrashed, he tried to get out. But it was too late. Way too late. He flung an arm over the side of the tub. Blood poured on the tiles.

"Please," he rasped. "Please."

Liana removed her mask. "I'm the agent you burned, asshole. I hope you burn in hell."

His eyes widened. He drew in a shuddering breath.

And then, Paul Callahan died.

Liana smiled and turned to Alicia. "Thanks for letting me do that. It was cathartic."

"Yeah, usually Carver kills everyone before anyone has a chance to get in a one-liner." Alicia shook her head. "He's such a death hog."

Liana snorted. "That is a word combination I never want to hear again."

Alicia grinned. "I don't know, it sounds kind of metal."

"Why are you talking about hogs in there?" Jessica called out from the hallway. "My god those screams were horrible."

"Music to my ears." Liana turned to Carver. "Shall we go celebrate?"

"Sure." Carver left the bathroom and found Jessica standing halfway down the stairs. She looked pale and rattled. "You okay?"

She nodded fervently. "Yeah. I'm just ready to go back to being normal. If that's even possible now."

"Of course it is," Alicia said. "The question is, do you really want to go back to being normal?"

"I'm not ready to answer that right now." Jessica hurried downstairs. "Let's just get the hell out of here."

Carver stopped in the kitchen. He put the glass of wine Callahan had been drinking next to the paper he'd signed. Carver put the wine bottle near it too. That would make it more convincing.

He looked over the paper one more time. It was a letter. More specifically, it was a suicide note. Seemingly in his own words, Callahan detailed how he'd paid hitmen to kill his intern and her associates to cover up another crime.

That crime was receiving a list that named undercover agents from several federal agencies. He'd been given the list by a high-ranking member from the previous administration and realized that there was an undercover agent threatening one of his businesses.

That business imported goods from China for sale in the US. More importantly the business was entirely focused on removing tariffs from those goods and allowing the import of high-tech Chinese goods like smartphones and electric vehicles into the country.

It detailed how he and his partners, Dimitri Sokolov and Yancy Bancroft were losing millions because Neuman had blocked the trade deal despite bipartisan support. It detailed how they planned to assassinate Neuman so he could be replaced by someone willing to schedule the bill for a vote.

Lastly, it explained how they planned to use the undercover agent that had infiltrated their organization to pin the assassination on the NSA. Then everything had gone wrong, and the plan had fallen apart. He couldn't take the scandal and decided to end his life rather than face the legal consequences.

It wasn't the best letter in the world. Carver and the others had crafted it quickly before leaving the carriage house. They'd only spent fifteen minutes on it but decided that it was good enough to pass muster, especially since Rachel Evans would run interference on any investigations.

Paul Callahan had died in disgrace. Yancy Bancroft would probably be arrested and questioned as well. Mitch Neuman would get to keep on breathing by default. That would come as a great disappointment to many people since he apparently wasn't well liked by anyone.

But it was what it was.

They masked up and went into the hallway. Carver went to his condo and removed the laptop. The camera footage was stored in the cloud, so he'd wipe the hard drive. The authorities might find the hidden cameras in Callahan's condo, but since it technically wasn't his condo, they'd rightly conclude the cameras had been installed by the owner.

They left the building, left the condominium grounds through the pedestrian gate, and got into Carver's Chevy Suburban. If anyone saw it on the cameras, they'd assume it was government issue. The windows were darkly tinted so cameras couldn't see inside.

They returned to the carriage house to clean up and change clothes, then they went to a restaurant for pizza and drinks. Liana was recovering quickly. Spending two days under the effects of nitrous and not being properly fed had weakened her, but she was going to be fine.

Jessica didn't seem permanently scarred by everything she'd been through. Alicia talked to her about possibly joining their cause. Liana pointedly ignored them because she wanted to return to her day job at the NSA.

Carver sat back and quietly enjoyed the evening. He'd started out thinking Liana was certainly dead, so finding her alive had been a big plus. Bringing someone home alive was always the goal when he was in the SEALs. Scion had almost been the opposite.

He liked this feeling. He wanted to hold onto it a little longer. But once everyone went their separate ways, he had just one place he wanted to be. At the beach with a beer. Enjoying the sun, enjoying the surf.

And most importantly, living another day.

EPILOGUE

Carver had one more loose end to tie up.

Well, technically two. Those loose ends weren't really threats, but it was the principle of the matter. They'd played major roles in this fiasco. In fact, they'd been the origin of the entire thing. But killing them wasn't the plan. At least not right away.

Jessica had come up with another idea. An idea that Liana and Alicia agreed was the proper way to put a knot on things. Carver preferred to kill them and be done with it. But he figured Jessica's idea wouldn't be too hard to implement.

They visited Peter Harris first. After leaving Washington DC, he'd gone home to live with his parents just outside Portland, Oregon, despite having fifteen million dollars. The money was stored in an offshore account because dumping it directly into his domestic bank account would have raised all kinds of questions.

Carver and Alicia infiltrated the Harris family home in the dead of night. They took Peter Harris without incident from what looked like his childhood bedroom. The man still had a racing car bed and posters of kid's movies on the walls.

Peter never woke up during his extraction thanks to the nitrous oxide mask over his face. They put him in a polyethylene crate in the back of their windowless van and let him keep sleeping.

Then they headed east to pick up his partner in crime, Kim Robinson. She was living in Breckenridge, Colorado, and she was living high on the hog. Kim hadn't been shy about withdrawing large sums of money from her offshore account.

She had a new car, a new house, two Great Danes, and five cats. The house was nice. Real nice. It had a craftsman design and was located not far from the local ski resort. According to a realty website, she'd bought it for two million dollars.

There were two new Subaru Outbacks parked in the driveway and a decked-out Ford Raptor in the garage. The Raptor belonged to Kim's live-in girlfriend. One of the Outbacks belonged to Kim's son from her previous marriage. The other one was hers.

Kim liked to day drink, so nabbing her wasn't difficult. She went drinking at a local Mexican restaurant. Carver parked the van next to her Subaru, so it blocked the view of anyone inside the restaurant.

When Kim staggered out a couple of hours later, Carver opened the sliding door on the van and yanked her inside before she knew what happened. He gave her a lungful of NO2 and laid her down in a matching polyethylene crate next to Peter's.

Carver drove the van to Denver to an industrial-sized building owned by Hope House, the charity Jericho set up as a front for his operations. They tied Kim and Peter to chairs and took off the NO2 masks.

Carver turned off the lights in the room and turned on bright LED lamps, shining them directly into the faces of their prisoners. It took Kim and Peter a few minutes to regain consciousness.

Peter blinked blearily and winced at the bright light shining into his eyes. "What the hell? Where am I?"

Carver didn't answer.

The man struggled but his chair was bolted to the floor and he was strapped to the chair. "Help!" he shouted. "Help!" He wriggled vainly. "Who are you? Why are you doing this?"

Kim groaned and woke up a moment later. She also panicked. She also screamed. She also begged.

Liana sighed. "Music to my ears."

"Who said that?" Peter squinted and looked around. "Answer me!"

Carver stepped into the light. He wore all black. He wore a ski mask and gloves. He also wore several stainless steel knives on a belt around his waist. Just for show. He figured that was all he'd need.

He stood in front of the prisoners.

"Who are you?" Kim said. "What the hell are you doing? You're violating my First Amendment rights by keeping me here! Did you know that?"

Carver heard Liana laughing behind him. He heard Jessica saying something to Alicia about the Constitution.

"I have money," Peter said. "We both do. We can pay you to let us go."

The light bulb in Kim's head seemed to come on. Her eyes widened. "Wait. You have me and Peter here. That must mean—"

"Yeah," Carver said. "It's about exactly what you think it is."

"Hey, we signed a contract." She shook her head. "We haven't violated any clauses of the contract with you people. So what in the hell are you doing?"

"You mean the contract you signed with Lash Dalton?" Carver said.

"Yeah, that one."

"Lash Dalton and his employer are dead."

Peter gulped. Kim's mouth dropped open.

"The information you sold them got a lot of undercover agents burned. It got a lot of them killed." Carver shook his head slowly. "You messed with the wrong people."

Kim stiffened and raised her chin. "I was a staffer for the President of the United States. Do you really think you can do this without repercussions?"

"Yeah, we do." Liana stepped next to Carver. She also wore a ski mask. "You almost got me killed. You got a lot of other people killed."

"Are you going to kill us?" Peter said.

"That depends." Carver drew one of the knives from his belt and held it to Peter's cheek. "We're going to take back the money Dalton paid you. We're going to login to your accounts and transfer it all to us."

"No way," Kim said. "That's my money! I earned it!"

"You earned nothing." Liana gripped the other woman by her throat and squeezed. "But you will earn a lot of pain if you don't do what we said."

Kim gurgled and choked as she tried to reply.

Liana released her throat. "Well, what's it going to be?"

"You can have it!" Peter said. "I haven't even touched it yet."

"I already spent three million," Kim said. "I bought a house, some cars, and another house up on the mountain."

"We'll just take what's left then," Carver said.

"Really?" Peter's eyes widened. "You're just going to let her keep what she bought? That's not fair!"

Kim worked her jaw back and forth. "This is why I hate you military people. You think you're better than everyone else, but you're trash. You're idiots who think they're being all heroic by signing away your lives so you can kill innocent people in other countries."

"How about if we kill a criminal like you in this country?" Liana put a knife against Kim's neck. "Just say the word, and I can make you go away forever."

Kim froze. "Fine. You can have it. You can have everything."

"There, was that so hard?" Liana pulled away the knife and then slapped Kim hard on the cheek. "You get to keep on breathing."

"You promise you won't kill us?" Peter said.

"Yes." Liana nodded. "I promise that we won't kill you."

Jessica, also masked, brought in a computer. She logged into Kim and Peter's bank accounts with the information they gave her. She transferred it all to an account held by Hope House. Once that was done, she closed the laptop and left.

"Okay, so let us go," Kim said. "And just so you know, I have friends in high places. Don't think you can hide from us."

"I'm not worried about that." Liana took out the NO2 mask. "Sweet dreams, you evil bitch." She put it over Kim's mouth and the woman fell asleep.

"What are you doing?" Peter's eyes widened with panic. "I thought you were going to free us."

"We are," Carver said. "Just not here." He put the mask over Peter's face and put him to sleep.

They put the pair back into their polyethylene cases, turned on the oxygen supplies for each case, and then loaded the cases onto the van.

"My contacts with Motherland's Exiles will pick them up this evening," Alicia said. "I normally abhor human trafficking, but in this case, it just seems right."

"They'll wake up in Ukraine tomorrow?" Liana said.

Alicia waggled a hand. "Well, within the next day or so. They'll be conscripted into the army and sent to the front line to fight Russia."

Jessica blew out a breath. "This is the craziest way of getting revenge that I've ever heard of."

"Yeah, it's brutal." Alicia shivered with delight. "And these garbage humans deserve it."

Jessica sat down at a table. "Looks like the other wire transfers I started have gone through. We emptied Martin Plum's emergency accounts."

Carver looked at the sum total for the Hope House account. It was at nearly seventy million dollars. Martin Plum had set up dozens of offshore accounts in case of emergencies. He'd stored that information in one of the files on their servers where they archived all the information they bought and sold.

Jessica had transferred all that money to the same Hope House bank account where she'd put Kim's and Peter's money.

She logged into a foreign crypto exchange using a VPN and began purchasing Tether, a crypto with a value that always equaled one US dollar. She set it to slowly purchase the crypto over the next few days so it didn't upset the market.

"Okay, phase two is complete." Jessica frowned. "Or is this phase three? I lost track."

"No idea." Alicia turned to Carver. "Are you coming along for the next part?"

Carver had decided it was still winter and too cold to go to the beach, so he might as well go along for the ride. "Yeah. Let's see things through."

The contacts for Motherland's Exiles picked up Kim and Peter that evening, keeping them in their packing crates for the long journey ahead. No money was exchanged. They were happy to get two people for free who would fight for their cause in Ukraine.

After they left, Carver and the others got into the van and started the next phase of the operation. They drove to Minneapolis first. Once there, they cashed out some of the crypto and put the cash into duffel bags.

Each bag had a million dollars in it. It was just a nice round amount in hundred-dollar denominations, weighing in at about 22 pounds. Jessica had already done the online legwork, finding names and addresses.

They stopped at a small house not far from downtown Minneapolis. The house was just down the road from a shopping center that had been burned to the ground during the protests and riots that Dimitri and gang had inflamed.

Jessica went to the front door and knocked. A middle-aged Asian man answered. He looked confused and concerned at first, then curious.

"Does he speak English?" Liana asked Carver.

Carver shrugged. "No idea."

Jessica took out her phone and pointed at something. She unzipped the bag and showed it to the man. His eyes widened. He turned and shouted something. A middle-aged Asian woman hurried to the door, presumably the wife.

They spoke. Her mouth dropped open and she burst into tears. She gripped Jessica in a tight hug and sobbed on her shoulder. The Asian man hugged his wife and cried too.

Jessica smiled and backed away. She showed them something else on her phone. They nodded in understanding. They hugged her again. Jessica waved goodbye and hurried to the van. Tears filled her eyes.

She got inside and wiped her eyes. "Wow, that was emotional."

"Did they speak English?" Liana said.

"Not very well, but I used a translator on my phone. I told them not to go crazy with the money to avoid problems with the IRS. They understood." She took deep breaths. "Wow, I'm a mess. I'm so glad we could help them."

"They'll use the money to rebuild?" Liana asked.

Jessica shrugged. "If I were them, I'd use it to get the hell out of this place. Maybe buy a house with some land in a part of the country that doesn't freeze your ass off in the winter."

Liana laughed. "True."

They went to the next address, a worn down duplex not far from the first couple. An old black man answered. He'd owned the liquor store next to the first couple. He'd lost everything in the riots like all the small business owners in the burned down shopping center, and the city was ignoring their pleas for help.

Carver took the bag this time. The man looked Carver up and down and got a worried look on his face. "I told Carlo that I'd pay him back when I could. But my store is gone." His lips trembled. "I ain't got nothing, man."

"Who's Carlo?" Carver said.

The man blinked. "I'm sorry, I thought you were someone else."

"How much money do you owe Carlo?" Carver said.

The old man blinked. "A little over a hundred grand. But I owe the bank too. And all my suppliers. Insurance refused to pay for my store. They said it wasn't covered. And the city council don't care at all about me or the others. They left us hanging out to dry like we're nothing to them."

Carver nodded. "I'm part of a charity that's here to help business owners like you."

"Help me? How?" The man looked down. "I can hardly feed myself these days."

"Would a million dollars cash help?"

The man blinked rapidly. "I'm sorry, what?"

"A million bucks. What would you do with it?"

He gave it serious though. "I'd pay off Carlo, the bank, my suppliers, and then I'd move to Florida and get a house on the beach."

"A man after my own heart." Carver unzipped the bag and showed him the money inside. "A million bucks, no strings attached. Just be real careful when you pay back Carlo. People like that will take more if they think you have it."

The man's mouth dropped open. "Am I dreaming? Is this a trick?"

"No trick." Carver pursed his lips. "Tell you what. Tell me where Carlo is and I'll pay him. I'll tell him insurance paid up and your debt is erased. You take what's left in the bag and go to Florida. Get that beach house."

The old man started crying. He hugged Carver. "You're my guardian angel, aren't you? God finally heard my prayers?"

Carver patted the other man on the back. "Nope. Just a man with a bag of money." He took out a hundred grand. "Will this cover your debt to Carlo?"

"It's a hundred and twenty grand." He wiped his eyes and told him Carlo's address. "God bless you, young man. God bless you!"

Carver took out twenty grand. He gave the bag to the man. "Do what I said and get out of town now."

"Oh, I will. By tomorrow evening, me and my sweetheart Cordelia are going to be sitting on the beach in the warm sun even though it's the middle of winter."

"Good." Carver went back to the van.

Jessica wiped tears from her eyes. "How can you not cry, Carver?"

Liana laughed. "The only time he ever cried was when he talked about missing the beach." She tutted and shook her head. "Saddest thing I ever saw."

Alicia laughed. "I think Carver's tear ducts were surgically removed at birth."

Liana laughed harder. "I think you're right."

Carver started the van. "We need to pay a visit to a man named Carlo."

"Is he on the list?" Jessica said.

"No. But the old man owes him money. I figured it was safer for us to deliver it."

"Man, you're getting soft." Liana kissed Carver on the cheek. "Better be careful or you might develop a heart."

"And tear ducts," Jessica said with a grin.

The others laughed. Carver offered them a smile then shifted into drive and headed toward Carlo's. This wasn't the beach. It wasn't even close. But he had to admit one thing. It made him feel nice and warm.

And that was fine. Just fine.

BOOKS BY JOHN CORWIN-

Books by John Corwin
Want more? Never miss an update by joining my email list and following me on social media!
Join my Facebook group at https://www.facebook.com/groups/overworldconclave
Join my email list: www.johncorwin.net
Fan page: https://www.facebook.com/johncorwinauthor

PSYCHOLOGICAL THRILLERS
The Family Business
AMOS CARVER THRILLERS
Dead Before Dawn
Dead List
Dead and Buried
Dead Man Walking
Dead by the Dozen
Dead Run
Dead Weather Days
Dead to Rights
Dead But Not Forgotten
CHRONICLES OF CAIN
To Kill a Unicorn
Enter Oblivion
Throne of Lies
At The Forest of Madness
The Dead Never Die
Shadow of Cthulhu
Cabal of Chaos
Monster Squad

Gates of Yog-Sothoth
Shadow Over Tokyo
Into the Multiverse
THE OVERWORLD CHRONICLES
Sweet Blood of Mine
Dark Light of Mine
Fallen Angel of Mine
Dread Nemesis of Mine
Twisted Sister of Mine
Dearest Mother of Mine
Infernal Father of Mine
Sinister Seraphim of Mine
Wicked War of Mine
Dire Destiny of Ours
Aetherial Annihilation
Baleful Betrayal
Ominous Odyssey
Insidious Insurrection
Utopia Undone
Overworld Apocalypse
Apocryphan Rising
Soul Storm
Devil's Due
Overworld Ascension
Assignment Zero (An Elyssa Short Story)
OVERWORLD UNDERGROUND
Soul Seer
Demonicus
Infernal Blade
OVERWORLD ARCANUM
Conrad Edison and the Living Curse
Conrad Edison and the Anchored World
Conrad Edison and the Broken Relic
Conrad Edison and the Infernal Design
Conrad Edison and the First Power
STAND ALONE NOVELS
Mars Rising

ABOUT THE AUTHOR

John Corwin is the bestselling author of the Amos Carver Thrillers, Overworld Chronicles, and Chronicles of Cain. He enjoys long walks on the beach and is a firm believer in puppies and kittens.

After years of getting into trouble thanks to his overactive imagination, John abandoned his male modeling career to write books.

He resides in Atlanta.

https://www.facebook.com/groups/overworldconclave

Join the Overworld Conclave for all the news, memes and tentacles you could ever desire!

https://www.facebook.com/groups/overworldconclave

Or get your fix via email: www.johncorwin.net

Fan page: https://www.facebook.com/johncorwinauthor

Printed in Dunstable, United Kingdom